Praise for Rochelle Distelheim's
Jerusalem as a Second Language

* * *

"*Jerusalem as a Second Language* tells a necessary story that I'm surprised hasn't been told for American readers before. With wit and complexity, Rochelle Distelheim takes on two cultures whose differences are daunting and she manages to represent both with convincing detail and, most importantly, with sympathy. Her book builds a bridge over a deep chasm that her characters walk across with dignity and just enough mordant humor to convince us they're real."

—Rosellen Brown, author of *The Lake on Fire*, *Before and After*, *Tender Mercies*, and *Civil Wars*

"Meet Manya, who grudgingly trades Russia for Israel. Shimmering with wit and bittersweet insights, Rochelle Distelheim's *Jerusalem as a Second Language* is an emotional travelogue that begs the question, how does a secular Jew find her place in the world?"

—Sally Koslow, author of *Another Side of Paradise* and the international bestseller, *The Late, Lamented Molly Marx*

"Quick on the heels of her smart, charming, and deeply humane novel *Sadie in Love* (2018), Rochelle Distelheim's *Jerusalem as a Second Language* introduces her devoted readers to a whole new cast of displaced characters. As secular Jews who have fled to Jerusalem from an increasingly corrupt and dangerous Russia, the Zalinikov family struggles against displacement, loneliness, and danger in a country that is as strange to them as it is compelling. Simultaneously tender and steely-eyed, often funny, and occasionally sorrowful, Distelheim's elegant prose plucks at the heart of what it means to be a family at odds with their new country, and with each other."

—Elizabeth Wetmore, author of *Valentine*

Also by Rochelle Distelheim

Sadie in Love

JERUSALEM
AS A
SECOND
LANGUAGE

Rochelle Distelheim

Aubade Publishing
Ashburn, VA

This story is a work of historical fiction. As the story is set primarily in the cities of St. Petersburg, Russia, and Jerusalem, Israel in 1998, some of the persons, events, and locales are actual as of that time; however, their use in the novel is the product of the author's imagination and they are used fictitiously. Any resemblance to other actual persons, living or dead, is entirely coincidental.

Edited by Joe Puckett

Cover design and book layout by Cosette Puckett

Library of Congress Control Number: 2020931797

ISBN: 978-1-951547-06-6

Published by Aubade Publishing, Ashburn, VA

Printed in the United States of America

This book is now, always,

for I.H.D.

My *Beshert*.

Foreword

In Loving Memory of Rochelle Distelheim
(December 16, 1927 – June 12, 2020)

"Being a writer," my mother once said to me, "is the closest I can come to living more than one life." It was an idea that had probably occurred to her on all the childhood Saturdays that she'd spent walking back and forth between the public library and her family's apartment on Chicago's West Side, reading the one book she was allowed to check out, finishing it by the time she reached her front door and then turning right back around to go check out another, again and again, so that, by the time the day ended, she would have spent it walking back and forth along the sidewalk, devouring stories the way other children might have been devouring lollipops or ice cream cones.

For as long as I can remember, I have understood that, for my mother, the world shimmered with stories waiting to be told. Stories that she seemed to be able to pluck with ease from the air around her. Give her an overheard conversation, a glimpse of an encounter, a happened upon tidbit of drama or the sudden rise of a memory, and there she'd be, reaching for her pen. Or send her into a room full of strangers and, because she was so warm and magnetic, and because she was so able to empathize with others, no matter what their situation, she'd inevitably emerge not too much later with an address book filled with the names of new friends and a notepad stocked with new ideas. They were everywhere for her, these seeds of stories, waiting for her voice to make them bloom.

It was that voice, which she channeled—throwing it, like a ventriloquist—into her characters' souls, that helped her realize her dream of living all those other lives. Follow my mother's voice to where it takes you in her stories and you'll come to know what it is to walk through this world inside someone else's skin. What it is to be a corporate lawyer accustomed to gliding through a life that has now skidded out of your control. To be a seven-year-old girl sweating through the steamy somnolence and scarcity of an inner-city summer in 1935. To be a homesick immigrant in Israel, hoping to finally get a taste of belonging by accompanying a timid neighbor on her quest for a marriage wig.

You'll come to know what it is to be a barely-making-it single mother, waiting on a crowded subway platform in the blurry hours of a just-begun workday, when sudden disaster comes barreling through. To be the wife of a dying man, frantic to convince yourself that you can stop time by dancing the tango with your husband across the refuge of your porch. To be an undocumented immigrant, looking for hope. An expert in Byzantine archeology, looking for love. An octogenarian widower, looking for relevance. To be a lonely pregnant teenager, standing at the edge of your hometown in California's high desert, watching the waning light erase the Joshua trees from the horizon as a summer dusk purples toward night.

My mother lived all those lives, and many others, too, in her short stories. And in her debut novel, *Sadie in Love*, published when she was ninety, she inhabited the skin of Sadie Schuster—Polish immigrant, matchmaker, suffragette, and lover of ballroom dance—who was living on New York's Lower East Side in 1913. When I watch Sadie poof up her hair, spritz toilet water behind her ears, slip on her white kid boots, and—after informing her reflection in the mirror that "I smell success about to happen"—set out into her world, jangling with hope and determination and desire, I can hear my mother's voice.

I will never stop missing hearing the music of my mother's actual voice in my ear. But I will be forever grateful that, during her time on this earth, she lent that voice as freely as she did, so that I can always find that music's echo within the written words she left behind. And now here it is, that voice again, in her final work, coming out through the mouth of Manya Zalinikova as she struggles to find a home for herself in a confusing new land. Here it is, that voice again, breathing life into the soul and the spirit of Manya Zalinikova—striver, questioner, yearner, dreamer—who will go on singing the song of my mother for as long as there is even one person left in this world to reach for this book and turn to its opening lines.

—LAURA S. DISTELHEIM
Chicago, Illinois
July 16, 2020

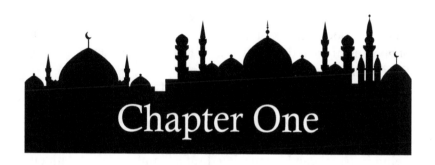

Chapter One

Jerusalem, 1998

The Russian authorities smashed the keyboard of my piano. Someone was enraged that a Jew would own such an instrument, that we would have such solace in our possession.

I speak of the early 1990s, when the Soviet Union divided into a collection of smaller countries. I speak of the man in charge: brave, but naïve, Mikhail Gorbachev, his dream of a Western-leaning Russia bringing a dollop of sanity into our lives. Gorbachev was the one who said to the Jews what had never before been said: *Go, find happiness, find love, good luck,* sending us off to other countries in a blizzard of applications and visas and papers stamped in gold leaf.

Allow me to introduce myself: Manya Zalinikov. Zalinikova, if I choose the feminine ending. Russian *émigré,* now living in Jerusalem.

"Manya, *please,* do not call us *émigrés.*"

This is my husband, Yuri, an atheist like myself—or so I thought—burning with a sudden fever to "live like a Jew."

"Speak up, Manya, say where we have arrived. *Olim,* new Israelis, this is who we are."

Yuri is correct. Our family is now, since eight months, Israeli. But *olim* does not evoke the sensation of caviar crushed against one's tongue, of sour cream sprinkled over cinnamon-scented *blintzes* the size of a thumb, steaming Black Crimean tea, sipped while seated by the stained glass windows of St. Petersburg's Café Novotny, looking out at the lights edging the Neva River embankment. Nor does it speak of the sting of dry, fresh snow on the skin, of opening night at the Kirov Ballet, Katarina Chedlenko dancing the *Firebird.*

On the day this atrocity was enacted on my piano, we had already left Russia; Yuri, I, and, with profound resistance, our daughter Galina—twenty, beautiful, complicated, mourning Gregor, the young man we found unsuitable—and were safe, if being in Israel can be considered safe. Trunks packed with our books, family photographs, a few silver serving pieces, the brass samovar and cut-velvet shawls left to me by my mother, and my piano, were to follow. The piano: a Kesselstein-Beinberg concert grand. Rosewood. Hand-carved and gilt-edged. One hundred twenty-five years old. Impossible to replace.

Someone in Federal Migration Service, someone squat and muscular, with a primitive haircut, wearing a suit of undistinguished cut, white shirt, stiff collar, vulgar tie, committed this criminal act. How do I know? This man, *these men,* followed me—as they followed most Jews—through the streets of St. Petersburg when I was at university, scribbling in black leather notebooks: *Zhid! Zhid! Medium height, midsized, dark-haired young woman, possibly—probably—guilty of something. Jews always are. Carrying black market money, subversive pamphlets. Western literature?* Matzos, *perhaps?* A ridiculous suspicion, in my case. Until coming to Israel, I had not known the taste of *matzos.*

He entered the warehouse where our possessions awaited transfer to a ship, lifted the keyboard cover and, seeing the exquisite symmetry of black and white, said, *Nyet,* then swung an axe at the keys, cracking all but six in a clean line across the center, severing each one into precise, equal pieces.

In that moment between evil impulse and evil act, he surely wished it were my family he was about to maim. But the random luck of living in the era of *perestroika*—openness—had placed

2

us beyond this criminal's grasp, yet not beyond his fierce wish to humiliate.

Where was I at that moment? In the absorption center/hotel in Jerusalem, perhaps, stumbling through instruction in beginning Hebrew. Or, perhaps, wandering Jerusalem's Old City, a labyrinth of pale, ancient stone walls within walls, willing myself to feel, as Yuri did, that I had come home. Feeling, instead, that I had lost one home and not yet found another.

Why my yearning for Russia, where, until now, one's Jewishness was treated as a birth defect? Unreasoned longing. Or, perhaps, a sad knowing that I cannot slip out of my St. Petersburg life as easily as a snake slips out of its skin.

༄

When Yuri first spoke of leaving Russia, I said, "Why now? The old Soviet Union is dead. No one—well, *almost* no one—asks, who is, who is not a Jew."

"That is not enough," he said. "I want to live as a Jew."

A stunning confession. How does one do that? You must have precedence, instruction. More important, you must have feeling. Always, we had agreed, the less Jewish a Jew was in the Soviet Union, the safer he was. *Deny, deny!* My father, Stefan Gamerov, a Christian name. My mother, the same: Tatiana. Hair the color of winter wheat, Galina's exactly; sliding green eyes, Tartar eyes. Few people guessed. If anyone spoke Yiddish to us in a public place, we blinked ignorance. If guests spoke Yiddish in our home, we raised the volume on the radio.

Then, one year ago, our cleverness failed. A commissar in charge of causing difficulties for Jews idly flipped through personnel records at the St. Petersburg University, where Yuri conducted mathematical research, and read: *Zalinikov?* An unfortunate name; foolishly, carelessly, passed down from father to son. The commissar stamped "State Suspect" in red on the appropriate papers, attached gold seals, punched a single key on his computer. Yuri's job no longer existed. Yuri no longer existed. Our cards for purchasing luxuries—strawberries, chocolate, silk underwear—for gasoline, for telephone privileges outside the country, were withdrawn. Permission to travel outside of St. Petersburg, to own a tiny *dacha*, to send our child to the Academy for Gifted Children, was withdrawn.

We Jews, however, are survival artists. Through sympathetic allies, we bought the required licenses, the essential gold seals, and located for Yuri another way of earning money as a merchant, a way that served our purposes for a short time, but in the end, was responsible for our leaving Russia.

༄

One month after we reached Israel, the piano was delivered to our flat in Jerusalem. I lifted the lid, wild to run my fingers across each key, to play for my family a Strauss waltz, a Liszt mazurka, a Chopin *ballade*, with Yuri and Galina dancing, welcoming music once more into our lives. I saw the devastation and screamed, "Yuri, help, please, *please!*" My fisted hands beat at the air, at the damaged keys, imploring him to undo the crime. I wanted him to send up a cry of obscenities. I wanted him to wish for our new enemies a roasting in hell. He found comfort in a quickly murmured prayer and a small sip of vodka.

Later, sitting in our small Jerusalem garden, watching the lowering sun strike fire on the onion-shaped domes of the Church of Mary Magdalene on the Mount of Olives to the west, he suggested we practice our Hebrew and, as though in an earlier life he had spoken this language, his harsh, guttural sounds mingled with the fragrant night air in a series of confusing sentences.

"I am filled to my upper extremities with happiness," he said. Smiling, he waved his glass as though it were a baton, trying to thaw my grief with the heat of his enthusiasm, while I huddled inert, sour. Lifting his face to the azure sky, he said, "This night is beautiful, like a healthy woman."

Galina, her skin already showing signs of sun and wind, despite my warnings—"Cover yourself! Do you want to age early, like Israeli women?"—caressed her honey-blonde hair, settled back and giggled. "Bravo for you, Papa." Turning to me: "Eh, *mamochka*, always so brilliant, say something."

At that moment, I hated these sudden strangers attempting to lure me to the other side of a divide I could not negotiate.

"Now you, Manya." The vodka and his eagerness to please slurred Yuri's words.

My mouth, my voice, my *being,* refused to make peace with the severe demands of spoken Hebrew. A hot surge of spite pickled my tongue. "How about this," I said, lapsing into the security of Russian, "I am filled up to here"—running a finger across my forehead, I added "with" and then dove into my small store of English words—"the farm animal excrement!"

Shocked silence. Then: "Bravo *mamochka!*" from Galina, who rarely flattered me, slapping her sandal against the stone floor. Turning to Yuri, she said, "She means bullshit, Mama means bullshit."

ゆ

Not an easy assignment, learning to be Jewish. When asked, am I from Moscow, from St. Petersburg, Kiev, Odessa—Israelis ask many questions, even when they barely know you—I say: *yes.* I say: *I am from all these cities.* I say: *I am Russian, still Russian.* I don't say: *Please, I cannot help it, I feel Russian.* This would be taken to mean I do not feel Israeli. My new countrymen are many things, and proud is among these. They want everyone who comes here to love it.

After Yuri was dismissed by the Academy, we leased a stall in the central district of St. Petersburg, where street stalls attract shoppers on weekends. People with money, *new* money, so much money they carry it in shopping bags rather than trust it to the banks, eager to find places to spend it, as well as those without money, who are simply crazy for a way in which to divert themselves from thinking about the anarchy—almost lawlessness—that had infected Russia like a virus.

Yuri sold tape recorders, cell telephones, compact disc players, radios; imported, not always legally, from Warsaw, from Prague, Budapest and Munich. This pursuit was not satisfying work for a brilliant mathematician who, at twenty-three, had earned his *Kandidat nauk* studying calculus of variations, but it was profitable and, we mistakenly thought, allowed us to remain anonymous.

One unseasonably warm Saturday in September of last year, when the sky was an assertive royal blue, even as inconsequential ice bits floated in the Neva, and Galina and I were present to help, a pugnacious looking man in his forties, wearing a belted leather coat, sunglasses, in the style of the new wealthy class, visited the stall.

He had an expensive haircut, possibly Italian, and square gold cuff links, and a cell telephone in each of two coat pockets. I want to say he was a stranger, but Yuri later told me he recognized the man from photographs in the newspapers.

In this way we met Mikhail Dushkin. In the old days, he was an *apparatchik,* a petty bureaucrat in an obscure ministry, undoubt-edly poring over papers in a dusty basement cubicle in one of the dreary gray cement government buildings near the Admiralty. In the new Russia, he was a *biznesmeni,* a member of the new oligarchy, clever enough to connect himself to politicians who had amassed many millions in dollars, pounds, deutsche marks, yen; politicians with business interests everywhere: real estate, aluminum, gas, highway construction, the television stations, making it possible for them to influence who was, and who was not, among the democratically elected officials ruining our country.

He introduced himself, and half bowed. Along with the money, he had assumed a thin patina of elegance. Slender for a Russian, but muscular, he used his shoulders as dramatic props, like a dancer or juggler, turning slowly, to better survey the scene before speaking. His eyes were hooded, darting from Yuri to me, back to Yuri. Nothing escaped this man. Some, not I, would have found him attractive—compelling, certainly.

Speaking to Yuri, he said, "I understand your business is going well." I shivered, as though an alarm had sounded. Focusing his attention upon me, he went on to say that, while he was not himself Jewish, our success made him happy. "Now your husband is in an enviable position." He paused, closing, then opening his eyes, timing it for dramatic effect as an actor or public speaker would, before continuing: "Now he can afford certain fees."

"Fees?" Yuri asked. "What fees, to cover what services? I need nothing from anyone."

Galina gestured toward the jewelry stall opposite, where there were gaudy, but tantalizing, brooches, earrings, bracelets: imitations of famous designs, stolen, no doubt, from Paris, Madrid, London, and then she left. I saw Dushkin watch the sway of her too-tight, short skirt, her black silk legs, as she moved away.

"Your daughter?"

"Yes."

"Lovely." He continued to look in the direction in which she had gone.

Yuri cleared his throat and rubbed his hands together, nervous mannerisms with which I was familiar. Dushkin smiled, one gold front tooth winking at us, and glanced toward a black limousine parked across the street, in which sat three men wearing sunglasses. "My bodyguards," he said, and laughed. "A foolish expense, but my colleagues insist. One cannot be too careful."

"A Mercedes," I said, an inanity meant to delay what I knew would not be good for us.

He nodded. "One must give those clever Germans their respect, despite all we have suffered at their hands." He reached into an inner pocket of his jacket and removed a slim silver case, holding it up for a moment so that we might assess its value. Here was a man of importance. Of power.

Looking directly at us, he maneuvered his fingers and wrists, opening the case with an almost musical click, then removing a sizable cigar, the tip of which he clipped with tiny golden scissors that had been cleverly secreted in the cover of the case. "Do you have a light?" he asked, as casually as though the three of us had met over lunch, or at a wedding reception.

Yuri said nothing. I shook my head. "We do not smoke," I said. In my case, a lie.

"Ah," Dushkin said, "a health enthusiast," and took a silver lighter from another pocket. "My own doctor recommends I do the same, but, sadly"—now smoking, he browsed among the stacks of merchandise, dialing the telephones, clicking the radios on, off, on—"I have an appetite for pleasure."

Yuri seemed about to speak, but just then both of Dushkin's cell phones rang, and he answered both, talking first into one, then the other, finally putting the mouthpiece of one telephone next to the ear piece of the other, so that his callers might speak to each other. Then he rocked back and forth, looking amused.

One of the bodyguards rolled down the car window and beckoned. Dushkin slipped the telephone into his coat and thrust his hand into an inner pocket. I thought he was merely rearranging his things before leaving, but no. When he pulled his hand out, it held a small, flat gun, which he offered to Yuri as casually as if it were a newspaper or cup of coffee. Yuri stepped back, then seemed unable to stand, and I put my arm around his waist.

At this point Galina returned, wearing vulgar, silver-mesh earrings. Noting the gun, she stepped at once around Dushkin and to my side, linking her arm through mine, as she had in her childhood, on those days when she felt the need not for talk, but for physical contact, the two of us walking, hips brushing, laughing together over some inconsequential nonsense, as we no longer do.

Again, the smile from Dushkin, the flashing gold-tooth. "Oh, my mistake," he said, in a soft, please-do-not-think-ill-of-me voice, and returned the gun to his pocket. "I am so busy, I confuse details." He was, he said, leaving for Kiev, but would return in one week to conclude what he called "negotiations." Turning, he pressed a business card into Galina's hand. "I always have room in my business for intelligent, beautiful women."

"*Krisha*," I whispered to Yuri, as we watched Dushkin maneuver toward the curb, signal with one raised finger to the driver, then gracefully, for such a tall man, slide into the passenger seat.

"You called him *what*?" Galina said.

"*Krisha*. 'Roof' in Russian. Its meaning in the new society: the person one pays for protection, the person one counts upon to make certain he is not killed. Say something," I prodded Yuri, as the car pulled away from the curb.

"I heard what you said."

"Then answer what I said."

Galina glanced at the card. "This man is rich?"

"Do not speak of him," I said, knowing, even as I uttered the words, they were a match set to dry tinder. "Do not consider him a human being."

What followed was a Galina-gesture, a perfect collaboration of chin and shoulder, as graceful as it was irritating. "I am no longer a child," she said, and slipped the card into her purse.

"Keep your head in your books. There is time for these things."

Lately, she had been scrutinizing herself in the mirror; putting on, taking off, earrings and lipstick; brushing and teasing her hair; pressing black-penciled beauty spots into her chin, her coquettish look splashing like perfume over her words. I was acutely aware of how much she was no longer a child. We had not spoken of this before. I was waiting for—what? Possibly for the wisdom my mother, Tatiana, had when I was Galina's age; possibly, improbably, for Galina to lose interest in her face and hair.

A family's forward motion into its future can change in minutes, swerving from the expected to the unexpected in the time required for a stranger to stand in an open-air marketplace and ask that you do not think ill of him. In ordinary circumstances, Dushkin's visit would have incited my fierce capacity to protect those whom I love. What ensued the day following Dushkin's visit, however, was anything but ordinary.

Yuri remained in bed in a state of sorrow, a Chekhovian melancholy, a condition rampant among many Russian men, but never before Yuri. They imbibe it with their mothers' milk, it causes their lips to curve downward, permanently creases their forehead, paralyzes their will. A difficult malady to invite to your dinner table, difficult to take into one's bedroom, one's bed. Soon, a condition even more troubling, also Russian, invaded our home.

Yuri, I soon noticed, was drinking: expensive, crystalline vodka purchased in the rear salon of the French pastry shop on Casimir Square, the bottles hidden in our bedroom armoire behind a nest of carved, painted cedar boxes my father had given to me on my sixteenth birthday.

When Dushkin returned to the market stall two weeks later, we were still too shaken to attend to business. He found our surrogate in charge, Rudolph Brunovich, an old friend who was eager to step in while we pursued the necessary travel documents.

"Zalinikovs go away," he told Dushkin. "Leave Russia." Dushkin, he reported, was annoyed. He made exaggerated, dismissive gestures with his shoulders, turning, turning again, to assess everything in the stall, sniffing at the empty air, jutting his chin, saying, without speaking, that he was a man who was forced to suffer undeserved losses. "Go where?" Dushkin asked, finally, "Did they leave a message for me?"

Brunovich reported that he stared into the distance, offering no information.

Dushkin said, "Tell them, please, we will meet another time," signifying anything but a desire to wish us well.

ﭼﭙﺢﺃ

Five months later, February, the sky a sullen patchwork of gray, clouds clotted with new snow, I purchased labels and attached them to our luggage: Denmark, Czechoslovakia, Italy and, at the last moment, India; countries where we had never been, but an announcement to the world: *Here are not ordinary Russian Jews, here are world travelers.* We left our country with rolls of rubber-banded American dollars sewn into the lining of my hand luggage.

That week, life expectancy for Russian adults had been lowered from sixty-two to fifty-seven.

ﭼﭙﺢﺃ

My task, on a daily basis, was now this: *Learn to feel Jewish.* Learn the constancy of street noise: cars, trucks, building cranes, vendors in open-air markets, diners in sidewalk cafés, street peddlers. Learn to tolerate the demonstrations every half block, hordes of people carrying placards, shouting demands *for* something, *against* something, sometimes both; boom boxes as large as accordions swinging from young shoulders, balanced on their hips. Democracy in action, Yuri called it. *Turmoil* was a better word.

"I didn't expect quiet," I said. "Quiet is for the cemetery. But I hoped for—"

"Israel *is* a little eccentric."

"Eccentric I can live with, but I hoped for an orderly eccentric."

"If this country seems . . . messy, that is because being Jewish is not a simple thing. Try to relax yourself into it."

"Relax? Yuri, the word *relax* and the word *Israel* should not appear in the same sentence."

Learn the First Rule of Survival: The Pushing Principle. In Israel, fighting your way to the lead of any line is an Olympic sport; to stand in the path of that pursuit is to risk serious injury. Adjust to a climate of hot winds and unrelieved sunshine, certain to prove ruinous to delicate skin.

Transfer your life to a city that closes on Friday at noon, births and deaths the sole exceptions. Learn to speak a language that—to the *olim*—sounds like every syllable is urgent, is reporting a crisis. Learn to listen to everybody talking at once, because, in this place of thousands of outsiders, talking means the power of choosing. Talking means you count for something.

Learn to live with the background of whirring helicopter propellers, screeching trucks filled with soldiers racing to investigate the possibility of still another street bomb, loudspeakers warning: *Stop your automobiles. Stand back. Leave the area, Danger, Danger, Danger.* And this, perhaps the most astonishing, almost everyone a Jew: the police, truck drivers, garbage collectors, the bankers, opera divas, generals, the oily-faced adolescents behind the counter at McDonald's. The waiters, whose rapid talk—all sparks and jagged edges—sounds like bulletins announcing disaster; the overworked clerks at the post office; the street musicians, most of them Russians, performing Mozart, Beethoven, Rachmaninov, for coins dropped into a hat; the self-important, chatty taxi drivers, who, hoping for higher fares, say, "Meter? Lady, lady, much better without." The miniskirted girls and muscled boys rollerblading on the walkways in Independence Park. The prostitutes—sad-eyed, plumaged women in lacquered hairdos, vivid-colored pantsuits, stiletto heels—lingering around the Central Bus Station.

And last, learn to pause, if only for a few moments, in the center of this wholly new, unfamiliar city—along the Ben Yehuda Mall, or on Jaffa Road—and practice saying: *Where I am today is where I will be for the rest of my life.*

Chapter Two

W e arrived in our new country by way of Warsaw, dazed
from lack of sleep. Israel, as seen through the small
square of the plane's window, was royal blue and sunny.
Fourteen hours earlier we had left the gray and white Russian
winter. Have I said I prefer snow in February?

The three of us, burdened with our many small pieces of
luggage, struggled through the plane's exit ramp and into the
terminal, confused about where to deliver ourselves. A sudden,
hysterical keening from behind us. A group of our fellow passengers staggered down the ramp, stumbling forward a few steps,
before falling to their knees, eyes fixed on the ceiling. Distraught,
some sobbing, they shrieked words I could not understand, but later
came to recognize as Hebrew: "*Eretz Israel*," they wailed—the
land of Israel.

Yuri stepped back, moving among them, his face luminous with
wonder, here and there patting a shoulder, urging me to *look, look*,
as though my eyes were closed.

Galina moved toward a row of empty seats in the passenger
lounge, stepping over a terrified-looking woman and a crawling
infant, before sitting down and extracting brush, mirror, hair spray
from her purse. I needed a bathroom, cold water splashed across
my face, a cigarette.

Oblivious to the blare of loudspeaker announcements, or the
crush of people surging down the corridor, aware of only those

weeping, sorrowing persons, many of whom were now kissing the terminal floor, Yuri continued to rotate among them, looking at each one as though he longed to join them. I looked for a sign announcing a bathroom. "These people are filled with ecstasy," he said.

"As I would be if I could find a toilet," I replied. I looked around for someone whom I might ask, but everyone was moving too rapidly; everyone except the young soldiers, who weren't moving at all. In their official, muscled way, they commanded the corridor, eyeing us with suspicion layered over boredom. Could anyone doubt that they would have preferred being on a beach with a bottle of wine, a radio, a dark-eyed girl? But life is random and often unfair, and their lives had tossed them into the midst of this collection of nearly hysterical *olim*.

I had to make a decision: sit, stand, find a toilet? Absolutely, a toilet. However, that was not to be, as two worried-looking, middle-aged men in dark-blue suits and knitted blue skullcaps arrived, "Jewish Agency," in Hebrew and Russian inked on tags pinned to their lapels. They waded into the sea of praying passengers, clapping their hands, tugging at elbows, shoulders, legs. When this failed, they pleaded in Russian: "Up, up, please—*up.*"

Slowly, the passengers looked up, dazed, as though emerging from a trance. The men counted us, wrote on their clipboards, then herded us, like lost, cranky children, down a staircase, along an endless corridor, into a small auditorium, and said to take a seat. At the front of the hall three not-young, not-old women, one holding a microphone, sat on a platform smiling. On both sidewalls, open cubicles; in each, a young man or woman in uniform behind a desk.

Galina scrutinized the women. "Uniforms, bureaucrats, clipboards. I feel at home."

Three o'clock. No bathroom in sight. The crowd was rapidly filling every seat.

Yuri said, "Please, sit."

"Sit," I said, "as one directs a dog?"

"Speaking of dogs"—Galina pointed to a white-haired woman in a flowering blue jacket at the back of the auditorium, holding a wire cage containing a small, brown dog—"do you think the dog is Jewish?"

"Only if his mother was," I said. "The question is, is the dog religious?"

"Or circumcised?"

At that moment, the microphone-woman rapped for attention. "Welcome," she said, in Russian, "to my country, and now yours." Yuri beamed. She pointed to a bulletin board. Here were instructions in Russian, directing us to Hebrew language classes, government offices, social service agencies. Those who had no friends or family in Israel would be housed temporarily in Absorption Centers; hotels, really, with language classes nearby. Her smooth voice rolled into the news that army service would be deferred for two years for both young men and women.

Army service! My head snapped up. I pulled at Yuri's sleeve. "You said the army would not take new Russian girls. Ever." He shrugged. "She will not go for *two years*—is she crazy? Not for two hundred years, if I'm alive."

The woman was still talking. Now she tipped her microphone toward the cubicles. Only the head of the family was to bring papers for registration, and would receive a portion of the government cash intended for each family. Yuri stood; I stood with him. "Both of us," I said.

Galina stood up. "All of us."

Our bureaucrat was no older than Galina, and remarkably handsome: wavy black hair, eyes the royal blue of the St. Petersburg sky at Easter. He was kind, but crisp, asking, in Russian, did we have relatives in Israel, what work would we seek, where would we live after learning the language, taking note of Galina, as he spoke to Yuri and myself, her reconstituted face and hair, now pulled back with a purple satin ribbon. Her perfume, Volga, wafted from her in scented waves.

I liked him. No Russian official, were he meeting you at the airport, or even in your home—especially in your home—would be so reassuring. And yet, *yet*—through my fatigue and hunger, through my need for a clean bathroom, through every bodily function, and lack of function, the word, *armyarmyarmyarmy*, banged against the inside of my head. "You have been a soldier?" I said.

"Yes, of course."

Galina moved closer to me. "Your sister, as well?"

"Three sisters. Two already out of the army, one soon to go in."

"I am sorry for your mother," I said.

"Not our business," Yuri said.

The young man laughed. "Already, your wife is behaving Israeli. You meet someone in the market, she asks, why aren't you married, why is your sister going out with that terrible such-and-such, does your brother have a job yet?"

"I want to go home," Galina said.

"You *are* home," Yuri said.

"*Home,* home."

Yuri's nose and mouth bunched up in disapproval: his radish look. "I cannot believe—"

"Believe," I said. "This is a dangerous country."

"Being Jewish is dangerous," the young man said. Now came a barrage of rapid stamping on our documents, the top sheet marked *Absorption Center: Hotel Diplomat.* "It gets better, easier, give it a month. Any questions?"

"Yes. Where exactly is the women's toilet?" I said. "Please."

～

Twenty minutes later, much relieved, I found the benches near the exit where we were to wait for the bus to our hotel. I hadn't bothered to inspect my face in the bathroom mirror; it felt hot and was probably flushed, my eyes shot through with red threads.

Through that door—I looked to my right towards the exit, perhaps five meters, where a young soldier stood patting his machine gun—across the parking lot, onto a bus, and, so, into our new lives. We were dependent now on the willingness of people we had never met to be interested in us, most of them Jews who were more Jewish than I could ever be: dark-skinned Jews, blond Jews, Jews in turbans, marriage wigs, side curls.

I sucked on my lemon drop, and closed my eyes, conjuring up the Satsarian Tea Room on the movie screen inside my head—a place of satin drapes and string quartets, just behind the Metropole Hotel, near the shops my mother frequented on Saturday after-noons—while I rehearsed chamber music with three friends from the Conservatory.

Tatiana and I often met there at four o'clock for strong Crimean tea and cream wafers, blinis and rum biscuits, the musicians playing Schubert, Beethoven, Brahms. My mother always had a funny story, a fresh bit of gossip about someone's poorly concealed love affair, or disastrous attempt to invest secret household funds in foolish get-rich schemes.

The unfortunate heroines in these narratives were not the wives of the party hierarchy; *those* women were rarely seen in public. They were Tatiana's friends, married to doctors, diplomats, painters, actors, professors. She'd use her tapered fingers, her strong, expressive shoulders, to depict a husband scolding, a wife weeping—exquisite performances that made me giggle into my napkin.

On a day empty of gossip, we'd amuse ourselves by guessing the cost of the clothes worn by the other tea drinkers. Summers, they wore ruffled silk, or flowered challis, pale matelassé, smuggled into St. Petersburg by husbands returning from conferences in London or Paris; in winter, jewel-toned velvets, velour, clever knits.

Now Tatiana leaned forward and whispered something I couldn't hear, as someone tapped my shoulder and I sat up, startled. I was not in the Satsarian, but in the Ben-Gurion Airport, and a white-haired woman with a dog was standing over me, asking if the empty seat next to me was available, or was I saving it for my husband?

Yuri was on the opposite bench, lost in his Hebrew dictionary; Galina had wandered off in search of the airport shops. I shook my head and slid over to make room for her. She smelled of lavender cologne and toothpaste. "I am Nadia, from Belorussia. Minsk."

"Manya, from St. Petersburg."

"Last names come later," she said, "when we see each other a second time. *If* we see one another a second time."

"If?"

"Strangers come and strangers go. How many have you met since leaving Russia?" Without waiting for my answer, she poked her hand through an opening in the dog's wire cage, and patted its thick, curly coat. "Ben-Gurion," she said, "his new name, since last week, for the first prime minister of Israel. He isn't fully acquainted with it; at home his name was Khruschev, then Yeltsin."

Opening her makeup case, she began applying thick, blood-red lipstick, looking up suddenly to say, "People give all the credit to Gorbachev. It was Khruschev who dug the first hole, and whoosh"—she dropped her lipstick; we watched it roll under the next bench—"communism began to fall into it. Never mind the lipstick, we're in Israel. Anything I need I can buy."

"Ben-Gurion is the name of an airport, and also a man?" This seemed safer than an argument about which Communist was the best Communist.

"I picked Khruschev for his name because I was executive secretary to the administrator of the local council for years." She used her lace handkerchief to blot her lips. "Executive secretary, not stenographer. Later, I worked for city council people who hated Communists." She was watching me closely to see how this information was being received.

"A good idea," I said, not sure what the idea was, exactly. I regretted not napping on the plane.

"Not easy, a Jew working for the Communists." Nadia kept her narrowed eyes on me, as though making sure I understood the danger she'd handled so successfully. I didn't urge her to go on, but it was clear she couldn't be stopped. "We, I mean the other Jews and myself, we were not considered to be *real* Russians." Wrapping her coat around her shoulders, she leaned closer, lowering her voice. "You undoubtedly know all this, or why would you be here? You appear to be a woman of high intelligence."

Fatigue had fogged my brain, concentrating was a problem. She, however, was determined. "I spread a few rubles in the right places, and—a big *and*—my boss liked women. Days I worked with my brain, nights and weekends I worked with my hips. Twelve years." Why was she telling me these things, where was Galina?

"Surprised I should tell you such things?" Nadia said.

I shook my head, then nodded. This was not the place for social lies, the kind that pasted people together at parties, or over a cup of tea; not here, in a place with bombs blowing up in the streets, and Galina about to be pulled into the army—*all that beautiful hair, cut off!*—a gun in her hands, people telling her: *shootshoot!* "You are a brave woman," I said. "I was not political, only musical."

Suddenly somber, she trailed her fingers between the cage

wires; the dog licked them in a frenzy of affection. "Nothing for me is as it was, nothing. Three husbands, all dead, no children. Who knows what my life will be in this place?" She turned once more to me, as though asking my opinion. When I offered none, she went on: "I've decided not to hide anything, I'm tired of hiding—the hell." She tapped her handkerchief against her lips and laughed, a fast, hard sound that slid into a sputtering cough.

I looked at her more closely. My first assessment, that she was a pleasant-looking older woman, was mistaken. She was not much older than I, in her early fifties, perhaps, her hair a thick, smooth spill of silver white. Her eyes were almond shaped: Tartar ancestors, a Cossack who had raped his way into the family years earlier. *Let us stop here and pull down the pants of every Jewish girl, leave behind our mark for the next generation to wear as green eyes, red hair, muscled shoulders.*

The jacket Galina and I had noticed was even more attractive up close: pale-blue leather embroidered in an intricate floral pattern, with a variety of fanciful buttons sewn into the center of each flower. "I like your jacket," I said, hoping to change the subject.

She patted the collar. "I wore it this first day to show these people"—she waved her hand in a gesture that said, *everybody here is included*—"I may come as an immigrant, but I am a woman with important possessions."

Her jacket, then, was for her like our travel stickers from the GUM department store. Affection for this stranger flooded me. I opened my cosmetics case. "This." I held up a pair of long, cream-colored leather gloves worn thin at the fingertips, Tatiana's for the opera. "When will I need these in this country? Yet"—I shrugged—"it is important they know I *can* wear them if I want to." I folded the gloves into the case. "I also brought four fuchsia satin dressing gowns and a lavender rabbit fur scarf, ten-feet long."

"Save them for Purim, you can dress as Queen Esther." I shook my head. "You don't know Purim?" She leaned closer. "For you, this, *this*"—the hand gesture again—"is terrible, or wonderful? Or both?"

"For me, terrible. For my husband"—I nodded toward Yuri, now smiling down at the dictionary—"wonderful."

Nadia scrutinized me. "You are Jewish?"

"Would I be here if I were not?"

"On both sides?"

"On every side."

"You'll be fine, it takes time."

"You know this because you have been here before?"

"I am playing soothsayer, an oracle. I learned, working for the Communists, the difference between a lie and the truth is saying something often enough, and sounding convinced yourself. Soon everyone believes you. *You* believe you."

"So"—I felt a sting of satisfaction. This Nadia was as frightened as I, but she better disguised it—"you are here also not from choice."

⌇

Galina appeared as we boarded the buses, carrying three shopping bags, and took the seat behind Yuri and myself, brought out earphones, tape player, magazines, stationery, cosmetic case; planning, I guessed, to sink into the comfort of the music to which she was addicted, sad stories about women complaining of abuse, then begging the abusive men to return.

"Put those away," Yuri said. "Look around, this is your new home."

"Exactly, Papa. This is why Russian music is so beautiful." She rearranged herself in an elaborate layering of coat and magazines, earphones in place and, studying the ceiling of the bus, tapped her foot against the back of his seat.

The highway between Tel Aviv and Jerusalem was, at that hour, endless cars, trucks, buses, taxis, hurtling forward at great speed, everyone changing lanes, everyone honking, and waving fisted hands. Galina poked my shoulder. "I read somewhere that more Israelis are killed in traffic accidents than in wars."

Yuri said, "Concentrate on the landscape."

"Where are the date trees," Galina said, "the olive trees, the milk and honey?"

"The milk and honey comes later."

Galina leaned forward and talked into the back of my neck. "The milk and honey is an advertising slogan Russians made up to get the Jews to leave."

I looked past Yuri to where the sun was beginning to lower behind the pale, bony hills ahead, and closed my eyes against what I felt.

⟡

The bus entered Jerusalem one hour later. Looking out the window, I strained to find *something*—something that would fulfill the description, holy—among the gray and tan stucco buildings and vacant lots and billboards and throngs of pedestrians, but saw only jewelry shops, supermarkets, hotels, sidewalk vendors, women pushing strollers, lovers holding hands on the benches at bus stops. Ordinary, ordinary, ordinary. I wanted extraordinary. I wanted divine. I'd come all this way because my husband needed the divine, and I wouldn't accept anything less. A thin, high-pitched wail filled the spaces between the city noises, a man's voice. "A *muezzin*," Nadia said, from across the aisle. "Muslim, calling the men to evening prayers in a mosque."

"Like a rabbi," Yuri said, "only theirs?"

"You read about this?" I asked.

"I saw, on television," she said. "Some evenings the city seems full of *muezzin*s, voices coming from loudspeakers everywhere, all at once. You feel surrounded."

"What about our side?" Galina said. "I don't hear anyone singing in Hebrew."

"Do they come when they hear him calling?" Yuri said. "Where?" He stood to get a fuller view. The wail was repeated, ending on a long and, even to me, thrilling falling away, a slow descent into what seemed almost a sob.

"How do you know he isn't," Galina said, "you know, sending out a coded message: *Kill the Jews*! It's Arabic, after all."

⟡

We turned finally into a series of narrow streets, then into the gravel parking lot of an official-looking, gray stucco building. A sign in orange neon letters spelled something in Hebrew; next to that, atop a tall metal pole, the blue and white Israeli flag.

"Hotel Diplomat," the driver called. "Home."

Once off the bus, we stood around awkwardly, attempting to look friendly without staring at one another. A babble of Russian, Hebrew, Polish floated over our ragtag group. Nadia set her suitcase upright on the gravel and sat on one end, placed Ben-Gurion's cage at her feet, and invited me to occupy the other end. I sat and looked at the sky. A brief curve of moon, no stars. I was safe with the sky. I wouldn't cry if I looked up.

Here and there in the crowd I saw cheap Russian plastic shoes, several scruffy Russian fur jackets, the familiar, unflattering cut of a man's poorly fitting wool suit. A sheet from a Russian-language newspaper blew past and came to rest against my legs. Lights blazed inside the hotel, but no one came out to greet us.

"A good time to be a smoker," I said.

Nadia rummaged through her purse, bringing out a pack of Gauloises; strong, French, forbidden. My yearning for nicotine sprang instantly to life, a crouching monster sleeping inside me, always waiting to be revived. I had smoked heavily until three years earlier, when Yuri, an un-smoker, pinned to my pillow a report from a British medical journal on the rising rate of lung cancer among women. "More prevalent than among men," he'd said, "female hormones." I repeated the incident to Nadia.

"Female hormones, good to blame everything on them. We have too many, we have not enough. We have them too early, or too late." She laughed her raspy, barking laugh, ending in a choking sound that caught Yuri's attention.

"Manya." He eyed the cigarette pack in Nadia's hand. "You are not about to smoke?" He looked directly at me—so directly, I was certain he would see inside my head to where I was already lighting up.

"Me, smoke? *Again*? After almost dying of deprivation those first weeks when I quit?"

Nadia lit her cigarette. "A terrible habit." Yuri's eyes glittered with annoyance.

"That is not something to say to Nadia," I whispered, but not softly enough.

She shrugged. "Not a problem," and blew a smoke ring, laughing an uneasy, hollow laugh. "Addiction," she said to Yuri,

"I have an addiction. A habit is more easily broken. But that is the nice thing about no longer being married." She tapped ashes into the palm of her hand. "One does not have to abandon guilty pleasures."

Coaxing Ben-Gurion out of his cage, she snapped his leash onto his collar and—still smoking, the three of us watching as though viewing a play—she walked off with the dog toward the metal fence surrounding the parking lot.

For a moment, we both stared at her retreating figure. Then Yuri shook his head, as though trying to clear it, before stepping toward me, pulling me closer. We stood this way: holding on to one another, or holding one another up, I couldn't say which. I looked across the parking lot to the building. "This is not pretty, like the hotel in Odessa. Our honeymoon."

"The Caspia. It had flowers everywhere."

"I never wanted to come here in the first place," Galina said, pulling her coat tighter, two lace handkerchiefs clutched in one hand; just in case, I guessed. In case this country turned out to be dirtier than St. Petersburg, hardly possible; or, more crumbling, also not possible. A second bus arrived, and another, until all six buses in our caravan had parked in the lot, the passengers emerging in stunned silence. Two youngish women in sweaters and trousers called out, "*Shalom, shalom*," and then blue-suited men with clipboards were everywhere, urging us to line up, directing us, finally, to the far end of the building.

We push-pulled our suitcases across the parking lot, entered a dimly lit corridor, then two sparsely furnished rooms, the first with a large double bed and sink, the one beyond, with a twin bed. A small alcove with a desk and bookcase connected these sleeping areas. The single light bulb in the ceiling was too small, there was no bathroom, the air was heavy with the scent of unfinished wood, layered over the smell of barely dried paint.

Yuri stood in the doorway and looked around with a look I would call peaceful acceptance and, dropping his suitcases, held his arms out, cupping the empty air, as though thanking whomever he thought of as being in heaven for bringing us here—or, perhaps, reading my mind, asking this someone to add a bathroom to our small area.

Galina dropped her suitcases in the smaller room and punched the mattress. "I cannot close my eyes on this army cot," she called out, coming back to our room in search, I guessed, of comfort. I was too exhausted to speak. Yuri sighed annoyance. "Worse than an army cot," she continued. No responses from us. Sighing, noisily kicking off her shoes, she retreated, and, fully clothed, threw herself onto the bed, falling instantly asleep.

I laid down on the other bed in time to tell the El Al flight attendant what I wanted for lunch: *Blintzes, please, with heavy sour cream and sliced strawberries, toasted whole grain bread.* She tugged at my foot. When I protested, Yuri was removing my shoes and covering me with a blanket. He laid down beside me, murmuring something, turning on his side to face me, and then fell silent.

Breathing Israel into my lungs, breathing out fatigue and sorrow, I pushed myself against him, until he cupped my head in one hand, as though offering solace.

Chapter Three

This is the man who brought me to Jerusalem.

Allow me to transport you to St. Petersburg—once called Leningrad in the fifties, sixties, seventies. Yuri's family and my family were coconspirators, with powerful friends who cared not at all about punishing us for being Jewish. Our role in this bargain was never to speak of religion. Why would we, when we moved through life as easily as minnows through the Caspian Sea, immersed in privilege, allowed to shop in government stores where chocolates and winter strawberries, fresh vegetables, perfumes, and scented soaps were plentiful; allowed to live in spacious, sunny, high-ceilinged apartments in the neighborhood of the Neva River; encouraged to own small, wooden *dachas* in the nearby pine and cedar forests; allowed to send children to private academies.

Yuri's father and his grandfather were professors at the St. Petersburg University. Mine were physicians, and high-level bureaucrats, who corresponded with colleagues in the West, published in professional journals, and attended conferences in Paris, Berlin, London—too well-known by foreigners to be in danger of suddenly vanishing.

Yuri was, from the moment we met—I was ten, he, one year older—my dearest friend, the bright moon illuminating the darkness of Communism, always asking the right questions, always interested in my answers.

His nanny, mine, Yuri and I, in the Catherine Garden on spring afternoons, sitting on the grass, facing one another. We talked as children talk, both at once, in noisy spurts punctuated by shy silences, feeling the joy of being understood. I told him of my love of music, hoping to infect him with it. He spoke of mathematics as though it were his private discovery, and the key to the universe. We dissected my fear of sleeping without a night light, and he described the shadows hovering on the ceiling of his bedroom, encouraging me to refuse to allow the unknown to terrify.

In my eyes, he seemed enormously beautiful. Later, his looks were idiosyncratic: mouth too wide, dark hair tumbling into unruly curls, oversized ears and wire-rimmed glasses. I loved his hands, his long, tapering fingers looking both competent and graceful. His hands were what told me first that we would be lovers. At fifteen, sixteen, seventeen, I dreamed of them: tender, graceful, urgent.

September 1961. Seventeen, I was leaving for Moscow to study in the Tchaikovsky Music Conservatory. We would not see one another until Christmas. My qualifying work was Chopin's *Ballade* No. 2; radiant, but restrained in its lyrical opening, building to chaotic passion, the full wildness resolved only in the closing moments. Studying that work, living inside it for months, performing it for the panel of admitting professors, I yearned for something, someone, to match that rush of feeling, someone to help me seize this wildness, someone who would then calm me.

We were to meet in the park one last time, late on a Saturday afternoon. Madame Sophia Garbasova, my piano professor, lived just across the park, but was at her *dacha* for the weekend. I had the key to her flat. I also had, tucked into my music case, a perfumed French prophylactic object, stolen from the small pile secreted in my father's bottom drawer, under his folded underwear.

Yuri wore the green loden student's cape I loved, and looked as he had at twelve: sweetly serious, distracted, yet arresting; or, should I say, arousing? Certainly arousing to me, in my fevered state of mind, in the way he moved his lean, strong body, lowering himself onto the grass where I sat. He carried a cluster of small yellow flowers and, blushing, held them out, looking into the distance, rather than at me.

My blood singing, I took the flowers, brushing my hand along his arm. Perhaps I was too bold, but we had no time for asking,

Can we? Should we? And, *then what?*

I can see him, I can see myself, as vividly today as at that moment. His hands were in his lap and, still holding the flowers, I pressed forward, placing his hand against my breast. He seemed caught unaware, startled, almost frightened; then slow understanding flooded his eyes, and he said, "Manya," as though it were a question.

"Yes."

Once inside Madame Garbasova's flat—three tiny rooms, the allotted nine meters; bedroom, parlor, kitchen, furnished in splendid Victorian style: a Louis XIV wedding chest, a carved desk of Hungarian oak, lovely things she'd inherited from a French grandmother—we were shy. Yuri stood in the foyer, hesitant, then switched the lights on. I switched them off.

"We mustn't waste electricity," I whispered, and went into the kitchen, where I filled two glasses with water. This somehow established our right to be in that place.

He was still standing in the foyer when I came back with the water, looking frightened, taking his loden jacket off, allowing it to slip from his hands onto the floor. The shafts of light falling through the frosted-glass door panels behind him made him look almost ghostly. I put my hand out. He took the glass of water, then my hand, and I followed him into the bedroom.

What followed that day were years of study, long separations, and Tatiana's questions: "You—and *Yuri?*" But how could we, why would I, we were too young. And the matter of money. We had none: marriage required more than love.

The first time, the only time, I said *yes* when she said *no*. There were tears, wild pleadings, promises. I swore, if she supported us in this, we would make her happy into her old age. I completed my degree in music as Yuri took his doctorate in mathematics. We were married in my parents' parlor, my mother splendid in royal-blue satin, her mother's diamond and pearl brooch at her throat. She played Handel's *Water Music* on her piano, and wept.

Yuri was splendid in a gray morning suit, his thick, unruly

hair tamed for the occasion, but he looked so solemn, my breath caught in a ragged stitch as I walked with my father to where he waited. *He doesn't want to be here,* I thought. He stood in front of the Minister of Justice, who would perform the ceremony and, when he stepped forward to take my hand, I saw the surprise of tears welling in his eyes. Then he reached for me and, leaving my father's arm, grasping Yuri's, I felt such clarity, such joy—stunned by the sheer good luck of being delivered to this moment.

On our first morning in Israel, we waited in line to be interviewed by a small, blonde hurricane of efficiency, leather-bound notebooks in neat piles on her desk, a cup filled with sharpened pencils, a saucer of paper clips. Her name tag read Rosemary Califano. A blonde Jew with an Italian name. Nothing about this place was completely normal.

She asked in Russian if we knew any Hebrew, emphasizing *any,* as though less than any would offend; asked Yuri if he had attended *cheder,* religious school, or had a *bar mitzvah*—terms he needed repeated, proving he had done neither.

No, and *no,* and *no.* In that case—she gazed at us with both regret and disappointment—we'd be placed in the Aleph class. Beginners; the dunces' class, to judge from her expression of remorse. Galina's face remained blank, as though she was already in another room. Yuri was, as always, patiently courteous. I feigned complete lack of comprehension, managing not to look wounded or hostile.

That day, and the next, six weeks of days, we lived in Hebrew. Every conversation with a teacher, a helper in the cafeteria, with the small, dark-skinned, perpetually smiling woman who doled out clean towels and sheets, with the muscular, auburn-haired woman who vacuumed and mopped the bathrooms—and who, in any other country in the world, I would have suspected of being anti-Semitic because of her sour, closed-off face, the cold cast to her eyes when I nodded—every question asked of the bus driver who took us on get-acquainted-with-Israel excursions, had to be in Hebrew.

Please speak Hebrew. These signs, written in Russian, French,

Spanish, were posted everywhere. The bathtub was one of the few venues available for speaking Russian. I considered asking Yuri to bathe with me, but the only tub on our floor accommodated ten bedrooms, and we would have been accused of antisocial, if not lewd, behavior. "As punishment, would we be sent home?" I asked him.

"Not at all. We would be forbidden to bathe."

"But that is the central idea of an *ulpan*." Yuri, our fourth day. His patience made me impatient. We were in our rooms following lunch, an oasis in the desert of Hebrew-language classes. We had learned to say *hello, goodbye, thank you, yes, no, how much*. My mouth was filled with longing for words like *Tatiana, dacha, blintz, Baryshnikov, Crimean, borscht*.

Standing at the bureau mirror, brushing my hair, I was trying to identify the unrecognizable meat I had just eaten. In the mirror I saw Yuri behind me, pantomiming the dipping of an invisible object into a pan. "Immersion," he said. "Total."

I turned. "Is it a major sin to request butter for a roll?" One of the attendants behind the cafeteria steam table had shaken her finger at me, *tsk-tsking*, when I held up my roll and patted it with an invisible knife, hoping she would understand butter. And deliver it.

"*Kashruth*, the dietary laws, no dairy can be eaten with meat," Yuri said.

"How did you grow such a vocabulary on that subject in four days?" I suspected, but did not say, that the woman behind the cafeteria counter spoke Russian. Her cheekbones, Slavic, absolutely. She pretended not to understand.

"Kiev," Galina called from the next room, where she was paging through one of the dozens of Russian fashion magazines she'd brought from home. "I noticed her, *mamochka*, definitely Ukranian. Those people are spiteful. Remember that dressmaker we had, what was her name? Cecelia? Natalia?"

"Don't call people *those people*," Yuri said. "It sounds unfriendly, even angry."

"I *was* angry," I said, "I wanted butter."

"Nobody dies of not having butter. I am explaining something more important, the idea behind an ulpan; total immersion. How else can it be done in six weeks?"

"It cannot be done at all," Galina said. "A Russian mouth cannot speak Hebrew."

"*Will* not," Yuri called back. "Anything that can be done for survival must be done."

If I had not known my husband well, I would have, at that moment, called him smug, the worst social sin in our family's lexicon. I wanted him to be desolate, as I was. Pessimistic would do, or wary. Warily pessimistic would have been perfect. I looked at him more closely; his usually pale skin looked slightly golden, as though he and the Israeli sun were already close friends.

"Ha!" Galina dropped something metallic. "We were surviving in Russia."

"There is surviving, and there is *surviving*," Yuri said.

"I am not finished with my butter story. Today I learned a new word. *Treif.* Yiddish."

When I said butter in Russian, the woman shook her head, someone behind me laughed, a marvelous belly laugh, and sang out, "*treif.*"

"Nadia," Galina called. "Did she have Ben-Gurion with her?"

No beginner classes for Nadia. She'd studied Hebrew in Russia, and had been placed in an advanced class, so we hadn't seen much of her since arriving. Once, I'd come upon her chattering—the rate at which the words spilled from her mouth sounded to me like chattering—in the social hall with several other *olim,* and hurried past, unwilling to bring my few butchered Hebrew words to the conversation, unwilling to listen, nod, shake my head, grimace, in all the wrong places, while my uncomprehending face looked as blank as a doll's.

That day in the cafeteria, I'd spun around to see who had laughed, and was delighted to find her. She wore a bright, ruffled silk blouse and graceful, long flowered skirt—unlike my functional woolen trousers and cotton sweaters—giving the impression she was attending a garden party, or a gala lunch, rather than tedious language classes.

I repeated, "*Treif,*" as closely as I could.

"Yiddish," Nadia said, in Russian. "Not kosher."

"You speak Yiddish?"

She held up her baby finger. "This little bit. You don't?"

"My mother warned me not to." She looked puzzled. I told her about my grandmother, Sophie, who spoke Yiddish to me, singing folk songs when she rocked me, that she'd died when I was five or six, and Tatiana, when asked if she knew Yiddish, said, "Why would I want to?"—pulling me to her, adding softly, "For a Russian Jew to speak Yiddish is an act of folly."

Nadia said, "I've always been attracted to folly." I asked after Ben-Gurion. "Learning to wag his tail in Hebrew, eating kosher hamburgers, chewing on bagels, having a flirtation with the poodle living two doors away. She's French, however, and has the basic French contempt for Eastern European Jews, unless they're royalty from the Czar's family."

Now Yuri moved toward the door. "Time to go."

Galina appeared in the doorway. "Please, not yet. Talk to me in Russian one more minute, or I'll perish." She sagged against the wall.

Yuri smiled, but opened the hall door. He was fastidious about not being late, one of the afflictions of being a mathematician. I gathered my books. "I'll speak Russian with you, Galina. Chekhov"—I stepped toward the door—"Dostoevsky—"

"Czar Nicholas, vodka, Rachmaninoff," she said, her dimple coming and going, a sign she was, for this moment, anyway, happy.

"Please." Yuri rattled the doorknob.

"Prokofiev," I said, and, grasping her hand, followed him down the hall. The surprise of finding myself my daughter's accomplice evoked a rush of delight, like a too-rapid swallow of champagne, like dancing the last waltz with my father at the Reserve Officer's New Year's Eve Ball when I was a child.

"Diaghilev," Galina said, head back, arm waving. "Deeaaahh-gaahil-evvevev!"

Yuri turned. A smile, yes, the tip of a smile. "Manya, Galina, *please.*"

"Gorbachev," I said, "Yeltsin," and Galina and I exploded into laughter.

༄

The next few weeks were a thick forest to lurch through, one word at a time, bringing me, rarely, to a clearing of sudden understanding. Despite my efforts, my tongue, teeth, lips, could not sufficiently form themselves around the sounds of Hebrew; the taste of this language in my mouth was bitter. Even when the sounds turned soft—as in the name Sheva, the shy young woman who sat next to me in class, or *yom shenee*, Monday—the lovely *shush* sounds fell from my lips more hiss than song.

I most succeeded at clipped, assertive sounds: *cain,* yes; *lo*, no; *bo*, come; *sa,* drive; *rutz,* run; *kar,* cold. However, to string such unconnected words into a sensible conversation was difficult. How often does one have occasion to say, *Yes I will come, I will run; no, I will drive cold?*

༄

The last week in March, our fifth in the *ulpan,* an early spring arrived in Jerusalem. In the small park a block from our hotel, enormous beds of flowers and stretches of lawn decorating the otherwise barren space appeared, seemingly proof that a band of magicians had visited while we were sleeping. On several afternoons, lured outdoors by the surprising warmth, Yuri, Galina and I walked there when we should have been studying or speaking in Hebrew, making those dreadful, hilarious faces that helped produce the strange sounds.

༄

One afternoon I invited Nadia to join us for a picnic lunch. I brought goat cheese, hard-boiled eggs, olives, pickles, fruit, a dark whole grain loaf of bread, and wine, purchased in a small shop—a *makolet,* a word I enjoyed sounding out—on nearby Meir Feinstein Street, from an amused, but patient young woman, who put up with my pointing and facial expressions, shoulders up, shoulders down: *This and this, no, no—that! Toda raba*—thank you, thank you.

Galina, always the dedicated student of the irrelevant, was

fascinated by Nadia's clothes, especially so when she learned that she'd worked briefly as a stylist in a Moscow boutique. That day my daughter imitated Nadia's flair for fashion with her own black-and-silver-flowered silk skirt, a crocheted black T-shirt, red-and-fuchsia-flowered shawl, her rebellious hair caught and tamed by a marquisette and ebony clip.

At lunch, Nadia, unusually relaxed, looked up from peeling an orange. "I am not in Israel because I am a Jew." The molecules of air, which had, until that moment, caressed my bare skin, shifted slightly and coarsened, like the sudden rearrangement of clouds before a storm.

Yuri, lying on his back, his head pillowed by his cupped hands, sat up abruptly. "Why then are you in Israel?"

Well, I thought, *so much for this friendship.*

"I wanted a new life, and I wasn't welcomed by the United States. Australia said, *come.* I thought, Australia—where is that? South Africa, Germany, said yes." Her laugh was more bitter than amused. "Can you imagine Jews, however lapsed, choosing Germany?"

"Can you imagine Russian Jews choosing Israel?" Galina said.

"Well, Galina"—Yuri pivoted to face her—"so you say, but what this country urgently needs is Jews."

But I *am* a Jew," Nadia said. "Grandparents, great-grandparents, both sides." She smiled a surely-you-understand-me smile. "Russia reminded me of this fact often."

"I mean Jews who are happy to be Jewish," Yuri said. The telltale tic visited the corner of his eye. I offered him a glass of wine, hoping to defuse this conversation, to perhaps introduce levity, a joke; but we were not a family of jokesters. He accepted the wine, holding it without drinking. Galina had the good sense to lie back, be silent. Or had she retreated to the fantasy world of rock music inside her head?

"Oh, I am perfectly happy to be Jewish," Nadia said, her eyes alive with delight. She was enjoying the controversy. "As long as I am free to do nothing about it."

"Such as?" Yuri's voice had an unpleasant edge. Perhaps I was overly sensitive to the subtle inflection, the manner in which one half closes one's eyes, then pauses for a beat too long. Perhaps I was unwilling to admit that I agreed with Nadia, rather than with my husband.

"Such as"—Nadia frowned—"synagogues."

"Synagogues?" Now Yuri looked hostile: darting eyes, a sniff, a sharp intake of air that marked, for him, low-level outrage. No danger of an outburst, not from my impeccably polite husband, but absolutely his face was a pantomine of disapproval.

"All those rules about eating." Nadia half closed her eyes, as though trying to recall a list she'd heard decades ago. "No meat with milk," she said, finally. "No pork, or those marvelous shellfish"—her hand described the miniscule, delicate arc of a single shrimp. "The kind I brought home from a small shop in the central market in Minsk."

"Or retreating to a semi-stuporous state, supposedly for the purpose of talking to God"—she uttered *God* as though describing a foreign object—"who does not wish to speak to me. I live my spiritual life in private."

Yuri looked stunned. I surveyed my fingernails. No one spoke for a moment and, encouraged, I looked up to see Nadia brush a crumb from her cheek. She was at peace with her view of the universe which, for me, made our situation, Yuri's and mine, feel messy, disordered.

We had discussed it often, his doctoral dissertation on the calculus of variations, the holy blueprint for his work at the university. Though my understanding was limited by my terror of numbers, Yuri pointed out that variations meant— and why should this intimidate me?—the process, state or fact of being varied. One thing different from another, both coexisting, the differences measurable through mathematical formulae. Plotted, predictable. Yuri, the scientist, approaching the world through unyielding numbers. Until now.

"And so . . ." Yuri, now sitting up, frowned at the yellow blaze of jonquils clustered at his feet. Galina had pulled a Russian style magazine from her purse and was deep into its seductions.

"And so . . ." I stood up. ". . . and so . . . so many different ways to live a life," I said. Everyone stared at me. Galina's astonished mouth told me more about how I sounded than I wanted to know. Snapping the paper cups, dishes, plastic forks into a garbage sack, I shrugged. "Further, it is unimportant."

"Unimportant? *It*?" Yuri said. "What is this *it* that is unimportant?" I shook my head. Nadia watched Yuri. Galina watched everyone. The silence was dense; even the bird had abandoned its serenade to beauty. Finally, he stood up and, with exaggerated but graceful strokes, brushed the grass from his trousers. "Well, then," he said to no one, to everyone. His voice was once again normal.

"Yes, exactly," I said, "well, then." I looked around at the others. "That expresses the situation perfectly."

Chapter Four

On the day we left the *ulpan,* dust, gritty winds off the Judean hills. This climate was aging. I took out my hand mirror. Dark circles under my eyes, new wrinkles, mottled skin. I appeared closer to fifty, to fifty-five, than forty-seven.

Our plan to locate housing was very simple, very Israeli. Phone calls, faxes and emails were sent and received under the direction of several Israelis we'd met at the *ulpan*; people who whispered of their connections, people who would contact other people who contacted other people, nobody asking the wrong questions, everybody certain of what the right answers were. Lawyers would do their lawyer work, fees would be charged, and paid, thanks to our black-market dollars. No receipts exchanged.

The apartment was on the street level of a two-story, brown brick building, a half mile from the Jaffa Gate into the Jewish Quarter of the Old City. The previous owner, an American rabbi who summered in Jerusalem, had recently died, leaving heirs who were more interested in owning a second home in the United States of Florida than in Israel.

We arrived by taxi in a neighborhood of clipped, velvety lawns and extravagant flower beds. The street was quiet, though dense with people—most in sweat suits walking their dogs, chatting, sipping from bottles of water—no abandoned newspapers or empty cans. I had not anticipated this sense of prosperous, peaceful well-being in Jerusalem, and felt the surprise of my grudging approval. Yuri said nothing; his smile spoke for him.

Galina stood at the curb, looking up, then down the street. "Is this a place of only old people and dogs?"

Genevieve, from the Absorption Center, short, squat, dark hair pulled into a humorless bun, answered in Russian that, yes, on many Jerusalem streets, dogs outnumbered people.

Yuri, already at the front door, took a handkerchief from his pocket and wiped his forehead. Eagerness—or was it joy?—made his movements seem graceful, a dancer's movements, a young man's.

We followed him through five light-filled rooms that still held the slightly sour odor of fresh paint and varnished wood; his excitement, as we moved from room to room, breaking over him like a fever. In the kitchen he turned on the sink faucet, cupping his hands under the stream, then turned it off, on. He caressed the pale wooden cabinets, clicked the doors open, peering inside, clicked them closed again with a clean, sharp snap.

"Look, Manya . . . look at this!" He flung the gleaming-white refrigerator door open and rattled ice cube trays, bins and drawers. "Do you see this, *this*—"

"Yes, Yuri, I see. Ice, real ice, inside our house, nothing like this has happened to us, ever." The image of our squat, square, chipped, rattling Russian ice box, wheezing on, sputtering off, sat inside my head. I'd fed my baby out of that machine. I should hate it, hate St. Petersburg. I wanted to. I couldn't.

"Galina," I said, turning toward the doorway, where I'd seen her last, "we have ice, real ice."

She stepped into view. "Oh, yes, ice, wonderful," she'd heard the Israelis had invented it, and vanished.

"And this! Wait, you won't believe"—Yuri beckoned, vanishing into a long, narrow space off the kitchen, and again the white, a washer, dryer, shelves, cabinets—"a laundry inside your house"— he gestured to the machines, a master-of-ceremonies introducing a spectacular circus act, studying my face for signs of ecstasy. "No more washing machine on the balcony, no more clothes lines outside in freezing weather."

Genevieve was right behind us. "*Motarot*," she said, "luxuries. Most Israelis don't have these things in their apartments."

His smile was a very un-Yuri-like grin. I thought I knew this man. Had we not been playmates from our sandbox days in Kretchmeerhoff Park, then friends, then lovers? Until that moment in the laundry room of the townhouse on Ben Lassar Road, in the twenty-third year of our marriage, I would have declared him too serious a mathematician, too depressed a businessperson, to grin. I would have declared him a scientist with few illusions about the makeup of the universe, or his place in it; a man not given to the worship of ice, lacquered wooden cabinets, the play of clear, unambiguous light on white plaster walls.

And yet, following me into the kitchen, he stood in the sunlight splashing across the counters, grinning at me, then at Genevieve. I was astonished, but not too astonished to blow him a kiss, rather than speak, afraid of what I might say. Genevieve looked away, as though she'd witnessed a moment of unbearable intimacy, before glancing at her watch and tapping her pencil on the counter, anxious to finish with us and get on to her next problem clients.

A part of myself wanted to say to my husband: Yes—oh, yes! Instead, my need for Russia flowed unbidden, like desire, from the empty spaces inside me. I stepped through a sliding glass door onto the patio, a small square of pale, crushed rock, shaded by a profusion of rhododendron bushes. *Repeat after me: Israel, Israel, Israel. With Yuri, with Galina.*

Yuri followed, calling my name, his eyes brighter, livelier, happier than I'd seen in a long time. I looked at him, *really* looked, as one rarely scrutinizes a daily companion, and saw, in the way he held his head erect, in the way he moved his arms, as though taking charge of the air through which he moved, the buoyancy that had seeped from him those last months in St. Petersburg. Surely there was no longer any vodka in his life.

"I love it," he said, "don't you?"

"I do," I said, "love it." I did not say I wanted this flat to be situated on Risnikov Parkway opposite the ice skating rink; or on Mansisky Boulevard, where my parents took me on fine summer evenings to listen to string quartets in the Victorian wrought-iron gazebo. I did not say: this flat is beautiful, but it doesn't feel like home. *Home,* home.

"But?" he said.

"I need time. I need to find a place for my piano, the parlor is too small." He was watching me, a deep watching, as though trying to get so far down into my mind, he would *be* me, and I would be him. I stepped toward him. *Hold me, just hold me, don't talk.* But Genevieve coughed in the kitchen, and I knew that, if we stayed too long, or if I cried, or if Yuri argued, and *then* I cried, she'd bustle out, asking us to please hurry, please answer her questions, she had other people to see.

"What are you saying?" he insisted.

"My piano. You forget, we are Russian." Even I heard the idiocy of linking these two facts.

Galina stepped through the patio door. Yuri moved toward her, arms out, as though he wanted to grab her and waltz around the room; body contact, that would innoculate her with his joy. She shrugged, lips clamped, which meant she was thinking about saying a lot, but later. He said, "Not our St. Petersburg flat, eh?"

"What," I said to Galina, "something is wrong?"

"Don't you find this street too quiet, like a—"

Yuri said, "What? Like a what?"

"A cemetery," Galina said. "Perfect flowers, perfect shrubs, no noise, nothing alive."

Genevieve was listening from the doorway. "If you don't like the quiet, Miss Galina, wait. There will be a bomb going off somewhere soon, a siren, ambulances, all the excitement one could desire, enough weeping to fill a small lake."

"The closets," Galina said, "there are none." She pointed. "In the bedrooms."

"Never any closets," Genevieve said. Her smile was heavy with implication: *this fact was known by everyone in Israel, no closets, none. What was wrong with us?*

Galina and I stared at her, then at each other. "Our clothes?" I said.

Genevieve shrugged. "One buys closets from a shop after one buys the house. Not a problem."

"Please." Yuri spoke to her, but looked at me. "Make your telephone call."

"Not a problem for you," Galina murmured, but Genevieve was punching in numbers on her cell phone, identifying us as the

Zalinikovs, yes, *those* Zalinikovs, the *olim* from the Hotel Diplomat *ulpan*, the Russians who paid the fees. In cash. Israeli cash. She asked someone to arrive in fifteen minutes with the necessary documents.

In the meantime, she wanted us to know that most *olim* lived in bleak, temporary shelters, even tent cities. Most *olim* arrived penniless. We were in the kitchen now, Galina somewhere down the street in search of drama. Genevieve sniffed, patting her clipboard, uncapping her pen. There were forms to complete, questions to answer, official papers that must be filled out before one was permitted to take up ordinary, daily living. Did we understand all of this?

I said, "Yes, of course." Hoping she heard my irritation. "Russia is also papered in documents asking for permission."

She seemed to think about that, then said, "Good."

"*Good?*"

She had questions, she said, holding up a clipboard. Yuri cleared his throat, his way of telling me without telling me that I shouldn't try to take charge.

Genevieve turned to him and asked: "Occupation?"

"Mathematician."

"He brings a doctorate degree," I said.

A tip of a smile. "So many of you arrive with those," she replied.

"A Jewish custom," I said.

Her smile soured. "Unhappily, we don't have many jobs for doctorate degrees. Employer?"

Yuri said, "None." Genevieve's head snapped up; she breathed through her mouth. "At this moment," he added.

"I mean, in St. Petersburg."

"Self-employed," I said, "importers. We were entrepreneurs." She looked skeptical. Survivors, I wanted to add, write that word down as our occupation, very Jewish, time-honored.

"You were self-supporting?"

"Also some inheritance," I said, groping for some magic word that might give us a dot of social status, enough to impress her into accepting us as perfectly respectable new Israelis, good enough for her country, good enough to be added to the mix I'd seen on the streets. Mixed-in, mixed-up Israelis, here we come, like it or not, ready or not.

"*Your* family," she said to me, "this inheritance?"

"Ahhh . . ." Yuri blushed. He detested lying, hated liars.

I, on the other hand, felt good about doing what needed doing. "Yes."

"Your parents are living?"

"Sad to say, no."

Genevieve wrote on the clipboard, then looked up and sniffed, her way of stalling for time before placing the knife in the chest. "I have never known *olim* to arrive with inherited money."

"Yes," I said.

"*Yes?*" Her eyes bulged. She resembled an irritated frog with an unraveling bun on the back of its head.

"As you have this moment said so well"—Yuri seemed to be waiting for an opening when he could object. I rushed on—"ours is not a usual situation." Again, the sniff. "But then, Israel is not our usual destination."

⌇⌇⌇

The furniture store was a paradise of abundance unknown in Russia. Occasionally, rarely, a trade show would come through St. Petersburg's municipal display halls, with merchandise from Italy, Germany, from Spain, none of it for sale, not that anybody had the money to buy. We looked, we sat, we touched, we dreamed.

That day in the Jerusalem store, Galina preferred smoky gray mirrors, quilted black suede sofas, white fur rugs, suggestive of Hollywood, USA. I insisted upon simplicity and function: bright colors, white wicker sofas and chairs upholstered in a black-and-gray floral pattern. Hydrangeas, I believe the salesperson called them, very non-Russian. I also purchased a forest of ferns in white pots to feather every corner of our new home.

In those first weeks—when Galina took her sun creams and beauty lotions and tape player and magazines to the patio, and Yuri was lost in Hebrew-language newspapers, or walked the streets seeking *something,* even he did not know what that might be—I devoted mornings to snipping stray leaves, watering, feeding the soil, inhaling this waxy, teeming fertility.

Galina, weary of the patio, now had a new look, one I called her pastoral period: pouty red lips, hair tweaked into fat curls caught up with a ribbon, lace-edged, gingham skirts of various checks and floral themes, balloon-sleeved peasant blouses.

"Your new clothes," I said, one morning at breakfast, "charming. From Russia?"

"From a small shop I found"—she waved toward the window—"out there somewhere. I took a bus."

"Congratulations. Tolstoy peasant discovers Israel. However, while on the subject of *out there,* out there is also Hebrew University."

Nyet and *nyet* and *nyet.* She knew no one in that school, even the bathroom signs were in Hebrew; how would she find one when she needed one? She missed the St. Petersburg coffee houses, the cafés, her girlfriends, Russian perfume, Russian music. Russian *everything.* And the bridges, oh, those beautiful works of art opening and closing like wings over the Neva River through the night. No other city had anything to compare. The loss of the bridges alone made her weep.

"I read in a traveling book that the city of Chicago, in a state of Illinois, in America, also has bridges over its river," I said.

"Chicago," she said. "*Chicago*! It is located in the middle of a prairie, on the moon, America. We will never see America."

"Kokushkin Bridge is beautiful," Yuri said. "I crossed it on bicycle every day I went to university. But what is past is past."

"Papa, how can you say? This bridge is the bridge Raskolnikov crossed on his way to murder the old lady in *Crime and Punishment.*"

"You behave like a child." This, from my husband, from whom criticism was as rare as Russian humidity.

"Would you like my list of objects for which I mourn?" I said. Galina poured coffee into her cup and worshipped her fingernails. Yuri was once again reading his newspaper. "Good. I know an interested audience when it bites me in the face. To begin"—no notice from either that they were listening—"the cinnamon strudel in the Lusnauya Café on Sunday afternoons." Galina yawned. Yuri rattled the paper, but didn't look up. "Hot beet borscht with swirls of beaten sour cream served in white bone china bowls at Dagliahoffs, after the ballet."

"Never did I see white bone china at Dagliahoffs," Galina said.
"White bones, maybe."

"The Viakoff Theatre Players in Pliasetska Square doing
Chekhov," I said.

A sudden sweeping up of Galina's coffee cup into one hand, her
muffin into the other, the click-clack of stiletto heels against tile,
the slam of a door, and silence. Then sobs, between parentheses
of silence.

꒰꒱

She remained in her room for a week, emerging at night for food.
On the eighth day of her seclusion—during which Yuri and I
dealt with an assortment of movers and delivery persons, who
complained that depositing our cartons in the proper rooms was a
bizarre way to handle furniture, followed by allowing us to console
them with generous tipping—I decided, *enough,* and knocked at
her bedroom door. Silence. I knocked once more, opening the door
without waiting for a reply, talking as I advanced. "Today is the
day the collectors of trash visit this street. Any old magazines,
newspapers, paper cups?"

Galina, sitting on her bed, was an island of despair in a sea
of discards, supported by a small mountain of pillows, wearing
nightgown and robe, hair meticulously arranged in a series of
intricate braids, makeup perfectly applied, including the dark
beauty spot on her chin.

The room, as I expected, was the wake of a Russian windstorm:
books, magazines piled everywhere, clothes, photographs,
compact discs on the floor and bed, empty soft drink cans, the
cold, crumbled remains of sandwiches, cosmetic containers flung
across the night stands, the bureau, and the flowered chintz chair.

"You continue in mourning for Russia?" I gathered debris from
the floor into a large, plastic garbage bag. Yuri, his eyes sorrowful,
stood in the doorway, as though ready for flight.

"Israel is a wilderness," Galina said.

"Moses wandered in the wilderness forty years," Yuri said, then
looked around as though wondering who had just said this. I felt a

sudden wish to protect him.

"Moses—ha!" She tore open the half-empty bag of potato chips on the nightstand.

"You do not approve of Moses?" I asked.

"Approve? He was stupid. Forty years in the desert, and his reward was a box of *matzos*." She crushed a handful of potato chips, the shreds filtering onto the bedspread. At that moment, in the shaft of sun falling across the carpet, our daughter looked like splintered light: dazzling, yet fragile.

"You miss Russia, because we are not yet Israelis," I said, bringing out Yuri's argument with me.

"Say something I don't know." Galina brushed her hands and, jumping up from the bed, snatched a pair of shoes from the floor, then a jacket, a magazine. We were being asked to leave.

"Neither are we any longer Russian," I said, not believing this. From the corner of my eye I saw Yuri start to go, then turn back. I shook the bedspread clear of crumbs and continued gathering trash.

Galina stopped, chin jutting: her I-dare-you-face. "I miss Gregor."

"So—we come to Gregor. He was not nearly good enough for you."

"And who is? Nobody . . . nobody yet born."

"Gregor is not the point."

"This country has made you hard." She gathered more books, a glove, two candy wrappers, flinging them across the bed.

"A difficult country, difficult solutions." I watched Yuri's eye again for the tell-tale twitch.

"You sound like an advertisement on the television," she said, "or a writing across one of those T-shirts they sell in Ben Yehuda Street."

"Here then, is one further motto," I said. "Learn to laugh in Hebrew, a beautiful girl like you. Pretend to be sweet, act friendly, you'll find everything you need."

She'd heard enough. Turning her back to us, she clicked the radio on to mournful, throaty strains of Israeli music, a mix of Mediterranean harmonics and Portugese fado. "To return to our immediate problem," I said, "you would perhaps prefer a job as a waitress to classes at the university?" I snatched a newspaper from the pile on the bed, turned to a page of *Help Wanted* ads, and held it up. "In that way, you can get exercise while learning the language."

"Classes, the university—ha!" Galina snapped the radio off. Anger rouged her creamy skin, an altogether charming look, even as it annoyed. "Soon the army comes to get me."

"Army. What army?" I dropped my newspapers onto the bed. "There is no army, not for you. You say this to torture me."

She kneeled in front of her bureau, stuffing clothes into drawers. "The girls said."

"What girls?"

Yuri said something. I wagged my hand behind me in a gesture of *not now, please*!

"At the *ulpan*. They said Israeli girls and boys go into the army before they go into university. You know about this, you must know, you know everything!" She fell onto the bed.

"But it's as you just said, as the woman told us when we arrived, *Israeli* girls. They don't mean you, you're not Israeli. Yuri"—I turned around—"tell Galina she's not Israeli."

"She's Israeli." He sat down on the bed. "We all are. You arrive in this country, they ask, were you born Jewish, you answer, yes . . . you're Israeli."

"The woman at the airport said the army's put off for two years, but I didn't think . . ." Galina looked up at me, hugging a lumpy collection of scarves, sweaters, shoes. "She said *army*, I stopped listening, I never thought *girls* in the army, so much was coming at us." I didn't say, I never thought we'd stay in this country long enough for the army to strike. The three of us looked at one another. "Only we could come to a place worse than the place we left."

"What's worse, " Yuri said, "*what*? To pay back something to your country?"

"Pay back, for what? Where's the debt? Tell me. We haven't taken anything."

He stood up, looking around the room with the air of someone who'd lost a valuable object. "I'd say we have. So far, if we add up the pluses and the minuses—"

"Did you know before we came here that this is the way this country works?"

"Everybody knows."

"You knew, and you came to this place anyway?" Inside my head, the Palestinian boys were throwing stones, the rabbis in white gloves, on hands and knees, scraping bits of flesh and bone from the street. A sudden thought struck. "Yuri"—I grasped his arm—"there must be people of influence, a bureau in charge of these things, someone who can stamp *Exempt* on a certificate." I mimed someone wielding a stamp. "Finished, next person!"

"For what reason, exempt?"

"For a generous consideration, of course, these things are not cheap. For the proper fees everything can be fixed."

"Not this," Galina said, "this isn't Russia. Everyone goes."

"Yuri"—he was in the doorway. Every movement of his shoulders, his arms, said to me: *stop*. I pressed on—"the procedures for buying this flat; someone knew somebody who had a cousin whose father-in-law lived down the street from a rabbi who died." I snapped my fingers. "He died, we bought, everyone got what everyone wanted."

"Not the rabbi," Galina said.

"Galina said something important," Yuri said. "We are not in Russia. Israel is not Russia."

"Not Russia," I said, "no, indeed not. Russia doesn't send our daughters to war." I turned away. When I turned back, the doorway was empty. Galina looked at me. Wavering ally, or enemy? Then, without speaking, she stomped around the room, snatching at the scraps of refuse still splayed across the floor and furniture. "We'll think of something, some way," I said.

Two weeks later, carrying a phone programmed to ring our number, she boarded the Number Sixty bus to Hebrew University, eyes, face, body announcing her Galina style of indignation, ready to assure anyone she met that she was present in body, but her mind was in Russia. A noisier, more vivid version of me on my worst days.

Chapter Five

The morning following our army discussion, breakfast was a cold, silent business. Neither Yuri or I were willing to stumble through the Hebrew words for coffee, toast, milk, marmalade, pointing at each object, giggling at our clumsy pronunciations. One cannot poke fun at oneself and hold on to anger. I was irritable. *Prickly*, Yuri called this mood. At that moment, prickly was called for.

We moved around the kitchen, circling one another, helping ourselves to food, crunching our cereal with as much dignity as we could summon. Afterward, I took my coffee cup to the window. Yuri still sat at the table with a Russian-language newspaper, turning pages without pausing to read. I recognized his signal. He wasn't happy. This was one of my husband's dearest qualities, which, in the past, I'd cherished: his refusal to be happy if I was unhappy.

I toyed with my coffee cup, looking out onto the patio, seeing St. Petersburg. A Saturday in September, one hour before we knew there was a Dushkin in this world. I was sponging a stain from my black silk tunic. Tatiana's tunic; mine, after she died, as were her sapphire-blue Japanese silk robe, the ruby and fuchsia cut-velvet scarves, the black alligator-skin handbag.

We would be at the theater that night, Dmitri Dimunetzski in *Uncle Vanya,* later meet friends at the Café Jablonska, eat rum cakes and whipped cream petit fours, drink steaming black tea, and talk about Gorbachev and Raisa, a woman whom I greatly admired, the Raisa part of her, not the Mrs. Gorbachev part.

Yuri had stopped paging through his newspaper. I heard, "Let me tell you a story." St. Petersburg vanished.

I didn't turn. "What kind of story?"

"An adventure story, a love story, as well. A man and a woman, specifically, a husband and wife, they moved from their home of many years across the world to a new country where they would make a new life."

My back still to him, I said, "Why?"

"For many reasons; principally, for one important reason, to be free to make choices."

"They were not free persons before?"

"Only within severe limits."

"The man and woman, the husband and wife, did this move make them happy?"

"The husband, yes; the wife, less so." A soft pull of his breath. "Much less so."

"What then do you see as the solution to this, this . . . I won't call it a triangle, unless we speak of their new country as the third element." Pale shafts of morning sun burnished the pale stones of the patio. Beneath the window, a thicket of broad-leafed rhododendron bushes showed signs of early budding, swollen ovals of pink poking through the leaves. Israeli seductions: sunshine, grass, birds, flowering bushes. St. Petersburg streets would still be white, deep wells of slush to be negotiated at every corner. Much healthier for the heart, cold weather in March.

"A triangle, yes," Yuri said, "possibly an isosceles trapezoid: two sides equal, the third side the variable." I tapped my coffee spoon against the cup. "Then, again, possibly not." This was Yuri being lovably, maddeningly reasonable, using mathematics, tricking me into conceding: *yes, yes, a logical solution was possible.* I heard a chair scrape against tile, then footsteps, and he was standing behind me.

"Unfair," I said, turning around.

"Unfair—how?" He frowned, drawing together of his eyebrows, eyebrows I'd always said were too beautiful to be wasted on a man.

"You're the Doctor of the Calculus of Variations. I'm no match for that."

"Good," he said, and gently pulled me to him. "At least in this one thing I have a small advantage. But—"

"But?"

"Patience, please. We cannot know so quickly what our lives will become here."

"But I do know."

"What do you know?"

I pushed away from him. "I see it: Galina in the army, you off with your God, and me"—I raised my shoulders—"nothing."

"A victim?" he said. "Not you. Anyone acquainted with Manya Zalinikova"—he reached for me—"knows she is no victim."

༄

Nadia telephoned. We hadn't heard from her since she'd left the *ulpan* with her cousin—the Reb Turrowtaub, a man who knew everybody, and had helped her find a flat.

After the shrieks of joy on both sides, and the how-are-you's, she said, "This is a wonderful country, with a marvelous invention, telephone information services that work. Absolutely unknown in Russia, as unknown as rolls of toilet tissue in public bathrooms. Remember what happened when we dared to ask for a telephone number? We put a man on the moon, but information from a telephone operator—nothing. If the rest of Israel is this forward thinking, I'm staying forever."

She didn't wait for my answer, but rushed on to say she'd found a flat, enormous by Russian standards, twenty meters, with a private bathroom that worked, and a radiator and a lock on the door, no cockroaches—none she'd seen, anyway—near a park and a bus stop, and only one mile from her cousins, the Turrowtaubs. She was searching for work, not certain what kind of work she wanted, but absolutely not secretarial. She hadn't come to this country to type.

"You know so perfectly what you want, what is good, what is less than good," I said. I felt a pinch of envy.

"Exactly what my cousin Schlomo says. He's absolutely unlike anyone I knew in Minsk. A perfect *sabra*, which means someone who was born here, which he was not. Soft on the inside, prickly on the outside. You must meet him. And his wife, Ahuva, I love; a strong sense of humor, which she needs to live with my cousin."

⌇⌇⌇

The following week Nadia arrived after dinner, unannounced, carrying a basket: two bottles of French wine, a pâté she swore was made only by a Turkish woman she'd met while shopping for herbs at the Damascus Gate, who had stolen the recipe in Ankara from her ex-husband's mistress; and two jars of queen bee honey, a gift from an Armenian rug dealer who imported it from his brother in Kuwait. She held the jars to the light. "These cost a fortune, but you're worth it."

Following her, pulling two small rolling suitcases, was a very tall, very wide man, her cousin, the Reb, I guessed, in dark trousers and white shirt with *tzitzit* tassels trailing from under his vest, and a beardier beard—salt and pepper in color, meticulously shaped to a V, as though trimmed with a ruler in his hand: a Czar Nicholas beard—than I'd yet seen in Israel. His thick, dark hair was too much for one small, blue, knit skullcap to restrain, and it flowed in waves over his ears so that, if he had side curls, which he did not, they'd have been smothered. His deep-set eyes blinked annoyance and curiosity at the same time. Before introducing him, Nadia pointed to the suitcases. "My Russian trinkets. I brought to give to you."

Galina, standing in the doorway, looked suddenly alert at the word *trinkets*.

"Nests of dolls," Nadia continued, "flowered shawls"—she transferred the suitcases from her cousin to Galina—"painted boxes, painted spoons, what my mother called in Yiddish *chochkas*. Take what you like. I'm shedding my Russian personality, I am one hundred percent Israeli from this day forward."

"Good exchange pieces," Galina said, "souvenirs from Russia for an Israeli something-or-other."

"Something or other—*what*?" Yuri said.

"Don't ask," Nadia said. "She understands her new country perfectly. Take, go." Nadia waved our daughter and her prizes out of the room. Turning to us, she said, "And now, my cousin, the Reb Turrowtaub"—he began, then abandoned, an awkward bow—"to whom I am indebted for my foothold in this country. These people are my dearest and first friends in Israel, Manya and Yuri Zalinikov, formerly of St. Petersburg." She looked at the empty doorway. "And their daughter, Galina, who is by now deep into my suitcases."

The Reb sniffed and shook Yuri's hand, examining us—a side glance, a serious taking in of details, without seeming to examine.

Nadia planted a goodbye kiss on her cousin's cheek. "Now everyone I love knows everyone else I love. Except Ahuva. She comes later."

The Reb turned toward the street. "I'll be here in one hour."

"Please," Yuri said, "come in, share Nadia's banquet." I saw on his face curiosity about this man, who, Nadia had told us, was a brilliant professor at the Seminary, the author of numerous articles on theology, a successful public speaker, bird watcher, gardener. Enough remarkable occupations for him to be triplets.

"Thank you, another time," the Reb said. "My wife is waiting for me to drive her to her sister, always a matter of life and death."

⌁

Yuri and I agreed, the dollars from our market stall would buy us time to breathe in the strange scents of our new country, to extract meaning from confusion, to find suitable work.

Perhaps—this I did not say to him—I would also find a solution to what I had come to think of as my army problem. That first week of April was devoted to walking through the city, deciphering street signs and route numbers on the enormous yellow buses, sorting out the sirens on ambulances and fire trucks from those on police cars escorting the Prime Minister to and from the airport. The ambulances shrieked, the police cars wailed.

On Jaffa Road, a half mile away, we mingled with shoppers, mothers with babies, schoolchildren, beggars, underdressed lovers. The clock on the tower atop the indoor shopping mall where King George Street meets Jaffa Road, chimed a song every noon, a song Galina said was the American spiritual, "When the Saints Go Marching In."

Passing one day as the song began, I said to Yuri, "Why this music?"

"Why not this music?"

"Galina tells me this music is Christian, saints and marching."

He huffed impatience. "Manya, Manya"—looking at me with not a friendly face. "Don't make a fuss for everything."

"Saints, Yuri." A young, intense-looking man in a black coat and hat, the fringe of his *tzitzit* flapping from under his shirt, walked past us carrying a load of books, and a live-or-die commitment to crossing the street without dropping them. "Even I know saints and Israel do not match up."

Yuri stopped and took my hand. "What would make you happy this minute—*what*?" He looked miserable.

"What I want . . . ," I said, looking around at the crowds brushing past us. A teenaged boy tossed an empty soda can into a litter basket, a girl no older than Galina sat on a cement stoop outside of a record shop swaying to music pouring from her boom box. "I want to holler something Russian, something like . . . *kak dela, kak dela* at the first person who will listen."

"Do it," he said, "holler," and then he did: "*Kak dela?*"—how are you?—at a young woman in sunglasses and a shaggy, brown fur cape, coming up the sidewalk just behind us, pushing a buggy.

She startled, then looked up and, seeing us watching her, pulled at a whistle hanging from a chain around her neck, and blew, shouting, "*Mishtarah,*" which later we learned was Hebrew for *police*—pointing at us. Rather, pointing at us for only a second, and then pointing at empty air, because we ran, Yuri in front, and me close behind, and didn't stop until we were back on Ben Lassar Street.

Chapter Six

What had begun as Yuri's wish "to live as a Jew" was now black serge, bleached linen, starched white cotton, the front door closing behind him at six o'clock each morning. The nights: we lay alone together, if one can be both together and alone; a philosophical question, not a mathematical one. One plus one made one. Just as well. His attention—the great white heat generated by his oversized intellect when he was concentrating fully on a particular subject—was otherwise engaged. First, on his new religion; second, on the question of why I was not following him into bliss.

"Faith doesn't come with the clothes." This startled Yuri, who repeated what I had just said, forcing me to say: "If I wear a marriage wig and long skirt and long sleeves, if I keep a kosher kitchen, do I automatically *believe*? Shouldn't it be the reverse?"

Study the texts, was his answer, devote yourself to learning, the Torah, the Talmud, talk to other women who believe, listen, ask questions. You're a smart woman.

My attention was focused on missing our habit of sleeping with his hand brushing my hip, or my hand across his shoulder, one body curving to fit spoon-fashion behind the other. The scent of his skin, when I had rested my head against his chest, was slightly minty.

"Try, Manya," he said, "for me."

"Not for me?"

"For us."

⟋⟍

Early mornings: barely breathing, not wanting Yuri to know I was awake, I peered from under the quilt and watched him dress in the far corner of our bedroom. Undershirt first, then bleached white *tzitzit,* the fringed, vest-like garment Orthodox Jews wear to assure that they always approach their God in a state of impeccable cleanliness. White shirt, black trousers, black jacket, black hat.

⟋⟍

He'd discovered a dim, ancient, and, to me, sour-smelling synagogue in the Jewish Quarter of the Old City, a warren of tiny, windowless rooms, connected by a series of intricate, winding stairways. The building dated from the second, or was it the fourth century? This country speaks of "BC" as though it happened twenty years ago.

Each sunrise, after a twenty-minute walk to the synagogue, he wound the black leather river of his phylacteries around his left arm, fixed the tiny box containing the miniaturized Ten Commandments written in script on white parchment paper to his forehead, and joined a group of men dressed similarly for morning prayers, then study, then a lively discussion of what had been studied, ending, usually before lunch, in an ecstasy of hand-clapping and singing.

I sometimes observed him approaching our front walk shortly after noon. Religious fervor had made his walk prematurely stolid, measured, as though he had been given so many steps to last his lifetime, and didn't want to squander them.

His face, however, was usually a bright moon radiating joy. "Since coming to Israel," he said, after the first month, "my soul has been seated at a perpetual feast." Here was not the man who took to his bed after the visit from Dushkin. Here was not the man who hid bottles of vodka in our bedroom armoire.

"I'm glad," I said, feeling a mix of glad and otherwise.

What does he say to them, Galina wanted to know, what could he possibly say? They frightened her, these men in black, their stern, closed faces with women. They were, she said, so . . . so primitive.

"He speaks to God."

"To *God*? About what?"

☙

Dawn doesn't happen in Jerusalem as it did in St. Petersburg, where the dark yields to sudden gray light, and the day had begun. In my new city, the night faded gradually, a faint shimmer of orange and golden rays suffusing the sky behind the sculpted mosques, churches and synagogues on the Mount of Olives, followed by arcing light and clouds of translucent radiance, so stunning a process that, even lacking faith, one was forced, if only momentarily, to believe in the power of redemption.

I had begun to also leave the house early to walk through the Old City, feeling, despite my resistance to this bewildering place, a strong surge of curiosity. Perhaps, if I memorized its shapes and sounds, the silent spaces between buildings, the slant of sunlight on its surfaces; if I could imprint one image, then another, upon my memory, then, when I closed my eyes, rather than calling up the majestic Church of the Savior on Spilled Blood, or the ornate wooden gazebo in Kempinski Park, out of the darkness would float the Tower of David, the Western Wall, the Great Synagogue on King George Street.

The Jewish Quarter in the Old City was like no other place on earth: a maze of pale stone walls within stone walls, each one catching constantly shifting light wholly different from the flat, hard, unyielding Russian light. A rich, damp smell rose from the craggy surfaces, as though earth and air and water had been transformed into building blocks.

I entered the Quarter through the narrow street just inside the Jaffa Gate: a Muslim street teeming with peddlers, with guides grasping anyone who might be a tourist and, behind them, shopkeepers in white turbans and shabby dark coats, sucking the stems of water pipes, seated on low stools, waiting, beckoning, hissing: *Come in, lady, change dollars, lady, you like almond nut, coconut, raisins?*

Skirting the newspaper kiosks, the donkeys, the Palestinian boys wheeling enormous platforms loaded with bricks or breads or shoes, I would pause at the medieval parapets of the Tower of David just inside the gate, looking up, *up,* in dazed awe.

St. Petersburg had its grandeur: Catherine's Palace, Peter and Paul's Fortress, the Admiralty. But those buildings, Yuri said, were architecture, nothing more; architecture made deadly or holy or useful. Those buildings were *theirs.* These buildings—these Jerusalem buildings—were *ours*; Jewish stone, Jewish mortar. A narrow dirt moat surrounded the Tower, preventing me from pressing my face against its corrugated surfaces, from feeling on my skin their terrible, disorienting roughness.

The ancient lanes of the Quarter itself were passageways, each one no wider than a donkey trail. I often passed a young boy of eight or nine in *payos*—earlocks—and a skullcap, the fringed edges of his *tzitzit* fluttering into sight as he yawned, lifting his shirt to scratch his belly. In his basket, fragrant loaves of twisted *challah*—egg bread—still warm from his mother's oven.

That day, early April, I followed the boy with the breads out of the Jewish Quarter, into the Christian Quarter, a narrow street heavy with sharp stones that cut into my sandals, stopping, when he did, to admire the fragrant purple oleander crowding the wrought iron fence surrounding Saint Christosos' Sanctuary. Sensing that he was about to turn away, I called out to him and, offering several coins, pointing to his breads.

His sunburned, freckled boy face delighted me, made me want to speak to him, to practice my terrible Hebrew, ask him to correct my pronunciation of bread, *lekhem*—that middle gargle I couldn't speak without spitting—of money, *kesef,* of thank you, *todah-ot,* the final *ot* changed by my mischievous, wholly independent tongue to *oat.* But he moved on quickly after our transaction, down the hill toward St. Stephen's Gate, the Lion's Gate, in the Muslim Quarter, where, I guessed, he would sell his breads at the outdoor market.

I followed, hoping to catch up with him, until he turned a corner and I lost sight of his bright, bobbing head with the crocheted, blue skullcap. I was almost at St. Stephens' Gate, unfamiliar territory. I peered into a row of ramshackle shops, dusty shelves stacked with jugs of oils and vinegars, spices, herbs, woven packets of thyme, basil, marjoram, shops perfumed with strange, seductive scents.

In the last shop, a short, stout man, a sorrowful look on his pocked face, wearing a long white tunic and embroidered red vest, called out to me, "Please come in, buy, cheap. Everything cheap." Inside my head, Yuri warned: *mesukan*, dangerous. I followed Wadie inside—his name tag was pinned to his tunic—sniffing the heady smells, telling myself I'd stay only long enough to buy a few woven packets of herbs.

Poking through a basket of tarnished copper coins, I felt a gentle tug at my skirt and turned to find a toddler with black curls, black eyes, a runny nose, his diaper sagging, smiling up at me.

"*Nekhed.*" Grandson. Wadie scooped up the child.

"And he is—"

Wadie understood my timid Hebrew. "Yassar," he said, "for our leader. An honorable name." He kissed the child's neck. "Do you agree?"

"Yassar who?" But there was no time for Wadie to answer. The child pointed to the *challah* in my string bag. Breaking off one end, using hand gestures, I asked Wadie if I could give it to the boy, then stood next to him as he took deep, satisfying pulls on his water pipe; a man who might as well have fallen to earth from the moon, for all I could know of his life. There we stood, two strangers nodding and smiling affectionately at a baby with spittle running down his chin.

This, too, was Israel: this man, this child, these smells, the ancient, tarnished coins. Wadie and Yassar were at home in this country, they felt a blood-pull I couldn't feel. A rusty fan churned up the dusty yellow air, a parrot in a white wicker cage squawked its complaint in a language that might have been Arabic, the slap of sandals against the cobblestone street floated through the open door. If I closed my eyes, I could have been in a dream country. St. Petersburg, at that moment, was a vague rumor.

The parrot squawked, "*Merde, merde, merde*," a familiar word from my schoolgirl French, and Wadie shook the cage, threatening death, or worse, in Arabic, which he translated into Hebrew. Accepting my packets of herbs, I pretended to understand. He executed several bows, and, not knowing what else to do, I hurried out of the shop, and into the sun-soaked street, before I could make a fool of myself by crying.

A stranger in the neighborhood, I cannot remember if I walked left or right as I exited the shop, only that I looked down, studying the cobblestones, intent on not showing passersby my stirred up responses to sounds and smells and people so outside of what had been my familiar life, I couldn't yet swallow them down. Nor could I break up the man, the baby, the parrot, the shop, into bite-sized pieces. The whole experience with Wadie stayed stuck in my throat, blocking off the air.

At the first corner, thinking, where is the Jaffa Gate, I bumped up against someone, a tall, wide someone; a man, but not just any man. I looked up and up into the face of the Reb Turrowtaub, Nadia's cousin, in full, formal Reb clothes: long black silk coat, black wide-brim hat, white vest, silky fringe fluttering from under his jacket.

He carried an armful of books, one of which he dropped, and was chewing something; seeds, I guessed, sunflower seeds, an Israeli habit, a way of surviving national nervousness: the traffic, the street noises, so many soldiers, so many guns, the bombs. Gum, as a response to nervousness, was for school children; seeds for adults.

"Reb Turrowtaub." Thanks God I remembered the name.

"Mrs. . . . something"—he snapped his fingers—"something with a Z, Nadia's friend from Russia." He dropped a book. Then, a confusion of bending down, both of us, a bumping of our heads, and, finally, his capturing of the book, and my embarrassed laugh, a false, silly giggle.

We exchanged polite how-are-you's, he suggested a cup of tea, coffee, seltzer water, and, not waiting for my answer, steered me by the elbow to a tiny café just opposite. We sat outside. "I like sunshine," he said, although the early hour had not yet delivered enough sun to mention. Settling back, he looked at me as though he had called a meeting to order, and I had promised to deliver important news.

"And so . . .," I said, desperate to say something.

"Exactly." His finger pointing at me. "You are my cousin's dear friend." He paused, as though waiting for confirmation or denial. I nodded. "Therefore, I think it a good idea that I come to know you." His face arranged itself into a friendly crinkle. The knot in my stomach untied itself. The Reb's Hebrew was too fast for me, I lost every other word, but he released each word as though it were a pearl, and his voice was loud. Elbows on the table, chin resting in his palms; so close, I heard his breathing, he said, "You, and your husband, of course."

"Yuri." This seemed the safest reply.

"Yuri, yes." Now he hunched forward over the table. I slid back in my chair. "I have questions." Had we lived near Nadia in Russia, had we attended the same schools, and this one—after he'd taken a small, black leather notebook from his pocket—were we practicing Jews? These were the words he used. Or were we, like many Russians he'd met, nonbelievers?

Nonbelievers? I suspected strings, long enough to trip me, hanging out of that question. I thought, *yes, Mr. Reb, and no. About your nonbeliever question: I am now, I have always been, what you said, not a believer. My husband was also, but is not now. Now—he believes. Do not ask me what he believes; my understanding of that area is slight.*

"Please, I hope I do not offend." He shrugged, spreading his hands out, palms up. "Ahuva, my wife, says I am too direct, blunt. She says many people dislike such an approach." He laughed, but not because anything he'd said was funny.

"Well"—was it better to stay strictly with the truth, or with an easy answer he could write down in his book, and then I could stand up, shake his hand, and go? He couldn't prove my condition with God and, even if he could, this much I knew: not believing was not breaking the law, even in Israel—"if I may also be blunt," I said, "some people ask, what is there to believe?" Questions were spilling all over his face. "Some say, if you ask this question, what is there to believe, you would not understand the answer."

"What do *you* say?"

Spit-spat, no beating around bushes. I had an admiration for the way his mind worked. I liked it so much, I would give some of it back. "What *I* say is"—breathing now from deep into my shoes—"if one does or does not believe"—I had his undivided attention; his eyes were two floodlights aimed directly on my face—"is not anybody's business."

"Business?" Just then the waiter came up to ask for our order.

"Coffee," I said, wanting to say, "I'll have nothing," followed by standing up, followed by leaving.

The Reb ordered tea—very hot, with three slices of lemon—and turned back to me.

"Religious faith is not a business, believing in God is not a business. It's a matter of accepting the truth of your heritage, the covenant Abraham made with God, all the Jews who came before you, thousands of years of our history."

He was throwing more at me than I could catch, but what did I have to lose here? This man already thought me a monster. I said, "Whose truth?" His eyes, which to now had seemed friendly, even kind, turned into a dark, wild look. "Is that not a question here?"

"I see." He sat back and drummed his fingers on the metal table, a kind of rat-tat-tat attack. "Have you had a Jewish education, Mrs. Zalinikov?"

So, he did remember my name. Now he could please forget it. "None," I said.

"And that is a satisfactory state of things?"

I had never thought of it as satisfactory or unsatisfactory; I thought of it as my life. Before he attacked my education, he should tell me: had he ever learned to play the piano, or any musical instrument? Music—*that* was my truth. My faith was Mozart, Tchaikovsky, Mahler.

We sat for a few moments, staring into each other's eyes, each of us convinced of being right. Finally, I stood up. "Well—"

"Stay, please. I speak to you from my soul." His look was now half anguish, half irritation. "Your coffee?"

From somewhere far away: a high-pitched wail drenched in sadness, so faint I wouldn't notice if I hadn't been at that moment on a silent street, unusual for Jerusalem, but not for the Old City, where most streets were too narrow to fit the passing of automobiles. The sadness of the sound only pushed deeper my own unhappiness at that moment.

"A *meuzzin* from the mosque"—he pointed up the street—"in the next quarter. Morning prayers. We must all have something to believe."

I breathed in donkey dust and donkey droppings. This street was a pathway for Palestinian vendors carrying oranges and lettuce and pomegranates to the open market near St. Stephens Gate. "Well," I said, eager to go, reluctant to offend. "I am sorry to go, I thank you for the invitation to sit, for coffee, but"—I glanced at my watch—"my husband waits for me."

"Yes, your husband." His eyes were still an aggressive dark brown, like tar, or coffee without cream. He stood, offering his hand, which I shook, barely.

Playing our conversation over in my mind as I walked, I regretted what I hadn't said: some wise, clever thing to put the Reb on notice that I was not a needy *olim,* waiting to be instructed, eager to follow anyone with a fancy tongue. I had come to Israel fully baked; a nonbelieving piano player.

I wasn't sure of my location, or the location of the Dung or Jaffa Gates, which were near the little spice and leather and photography shops I liked to inhabit. Further up, a street sign in Hebrew and English read: *St. Stephens Gate,* with an arrow pointing. My shaky geography told me to go out of the Old City through that gate, and not turn back into the twisting alleyways, then follow the stone wall to the Dung Gate in the Jewish Quarter, about ten minutes away, where I could once more enter the Old City.

Not yet nine o'clock, the traffic triangle straight ahead already clogged with vehicles. A cement truck and two school buses screeched to a stop at the traffic light, startling an elderly man in an embroidered cape and flowered turban who had been slapping the donkey pulling his wooden cart.

The bus driver closest to the man thrust his head through the open bus window and, waving his fist, hollered something menacing in Hebrew. The old man turned his head to the driver, delivering a long, smoky stare, then shouted in Arabic at his donkey. The donkey urinated, marking this street as his territory, yanked his head back and howled, then sat down in the center lane, blocking traffic. A police officer just emerging from the Old City watched the drama for a moment, shrugged, and walked off.

A good response, the shrug: emotion without language. Tonight I would practice before my mirror, urge Yuri to do the same. We might devise a series of shrugs, an entire vocabulary of shrugs. I could shrug my thoughts in Russian and they would be interpreted in Hebrew, in English.

Ladies and Gentlemen, meet Manya Zalinikova, master shrugger, her amazing eloquence with shoulder, chin, eyelids, unequaled anywhere in the Western World! I closed my eyes, lost in my reverie; someone snickered. I realized I had been shrugging, amusing the turbaned donkey driver, whose animal was seated on his haunches, uninterested in clearing the traffic lane.

I shook my head, as though that explained everything, and followed the police officer, waiting until I had gone a dozen or so yards, before beginning aloud my practice of my secret Hebrew, words I loved, not for their meaning, but for their sounds: ice, *kerach*; organic, *organee*; fringe benefits, *hatavot*; words chosen because I enjoyed the caress of the soft *k*, the breathy *h*, the positive *o-r-g* beginning, the sensuous taste of the *ha* sound in my mouth. Words I thought of as a sweetening to the bitterness of learning this difficult language.

Within minutes, I was walking behind a small group of female soldiers in olive-green trousers and shirts, sleeves rolled to the elbows, vests, berets. They were chattering among themselves, more like schoolgirls on an outing than like warriors. One—tall, slim, her hair a collection of burnished curls—seemed to be shepherding them, walking slightly ahead, half turning from time to time to say something over her shoulder.

I imagined Galina in uniform, imagined her carrying a gun, although these young women carried sunglasses, water canteens, books. "Girls," I called out in Hebrew, "you, soldiers" But they were too engrossed in their own bantering. *"Khayelet-alot!"* I called: female soldier. Two of the words we'd learned in the *ulpan*, along with rifle, hand grenade, terrorist, war, victory. An Israeli lexicon of everyday life.

The three young women closest to me turned and, walking backwards, looked at me with patient skepticism, waiting for me to continue.

"Cain," I said. Yes. I loved that word. It came out so easily, making me feel, for that moment, anyway, in charge of the language I was garbling. Their faces registered nothing. I said it

again, and nodded. Enthusiasm, spontaneity, our ulpan instructor had suggested; when speaking to Israelis, be lively, keen, acute.

"Yes?" This soldier—a head of bright-yellow curls, light-filled eyes—didn't look old enough to drive a car. Surely her mother must have been, at that moment, paralyzed with grief.

The soldier next to her—short, bulky, brown eyes the color of good cognac—called out "*chaki!*" Wait! The others stopped walking, and we were suddenly standing in a circle, nine pairs of curious, intelligent eyes focused upon me.

I longed to say: *Tell me everything. Is the army safe? Do you work hard? Where are your guns? Where do you live, how is the food? How often do you see your mothers?*

"*Bat,*" I said: daughter, "*anee.*" Me. The young women next to me—dark hair in a thick, silky braid down her back—tried valiantly to determine where my daughter was stationed. I gestured in response to her gestures, until a sudden spark of understanding leaped into her eyes, and she explained to her companions that my daughter was about to go into the army.

Everyone nodded and smiled at me. Not ready to let them go, I asked, "*Baal?*" Husbands?

This brought giggles all around, a few blushes, a scrunched-up face from the soldier with the yellow hair. The leader, whose name was Shira, shook her head, placing her hands in front of herself, side by side, palms down, then flung them apart.

"Married women . . . army . . . no?" A wild guess in my best Hebrew.

Two of the soldiers said, "*Lo.*" No.

Relief, like a benediction, fell upon my shoulders. "*Le'olam lo?*" Never?

"Never."

I am certain neither Shira nor the others could guess why I embraced her, kissing her on both cheeks, then insisted upon shaking everyone's hand. Another crazy Russian, they probably reasoned, you meet them everywhere these days; we'll get used to them eventually.

They walked on, leaving me squinting in the sun, watching them disappear, biting off chunks of my bread, slowly taking into my body the elusive, yeasty taste of this city.

At the Dung Gate, I dropped my *challah* into my string bag before joining the line of people waiting to enter the Jewish Quarter. Going into the Quarter through this gate was complicated by both geography and history. Straight ahead, the Western Wall, Judaism's holiest place of worship. Above, reached by ramps and a ribbon of narrow steps, the Temple Mount, with its sacred Al Aksa Mosque: the third holiest Muslim shrine, with its stunning gold dome, and mosaic-tiled courtyard, where worshipers had to bathe their feet before entering.

The soldiers at this checkpoint scrutinized everyone's everything, whatever the hour, pulling suspicious looking parcels apart, poking into baskets of fruit, knapsacks, baby carriages; especially baby carriages, which could carry hand grenades or small pistols, along with the baby.

Three months in this city, I had learned to respect the Israeli calculus: Should I walk to the right, rather than to the left? Should I take this bus or a *sherut*, group taxi? Should I walk down these stairs or wait for the elevator? Ordinary decisions, except that, in Israel, the ordinary often glides into being extraordinary.

At any moment the invisible line separating a peaceful day from one of unspeakable horror can be blown away by the sudden swerve of a dynamite-packed automobile into a gathering of young people at a sidewalk café, or the *ssshhewww* of a gasoline canister tossed into a crowd of shoppers.

That day, as the line of people ahead of me moved past the security booth, I saw the two soldiers on duty bantering back and forth. A good sign. Tense soldiers can deny entry. As I came closer, however, I saw the younger soldier—a squat, muscular blond, sleeves rolled to his elbows—stopping every third or fourth person, asking them to open purses, packages, briefcases.

A heavyset, middle-aged man using a cell phone called out from behind me, "Say, listen, I'm trying to get to work." The soldier ignored him. The young couple in blue jeans and sandals preceding me passed through quickly, but the soldier held his hand up to signal me to stop, pointing to my shopping bag. "What's in there?"

Every part of me shook at once: the hand that held the bag, my leg, my chin; an outbreak of the Russian-Jewish syndrome—fear of discovery. My shreds of Hebrew deserted me. I opened my mouth to speak, but managed no more than, "*Arrumph.*"

"What do you *think* she has in there?" said the young man immediately behind me, appearing religious in a long brown tunic and straw hat, clutching a sack of oranges. "This is idiotic." Several others in line grumbled agreement.

The soldier looked at the man. "Friar?" he said. The man nodded. "Sir, who's in charge here, you, or me?" Someone hooted. The friar shifted the bag of oranges to his hip and cleared his throat, but said nothing. The man with the cell phone asked if he could have the phone number of the district military supervisor, adding, to anyone interested, that he'd lived in Israel long enough to know there had to be a district military supervisor. He'd make a call to that office; something had to be done, someone had to do it.

The soldier turned back to me. "Empty, please." I pulled my *challah* from the bag; someone laughed, several others applauded. The soldier struggled against smiling, holding up the remains of the bread. "A good place to hide a hand grenade."

A woman called out, "Be sensible."

A second woman said, "What kind of crazy recipe, a hand grenade in a *challah*? Raisins, maybe, but a hand grenade? Never."

The second soldier, slicked dark hair, dimpled chin—Galina would love that face—stepped forward. He did not look amused. "Our job is to protect you."

"From a *challah*?" the friar asked.

Before I could speak, the two not young, not old men behind the friar, dressed like the Reb—long black silk coats, wide-brimmed black hats, carrying briefcases—exhaled impatience. The shorter one, his pale, gaunt face showing signs of early ruin, said, to no one in particular, "My class begins in two minutes."

"Okay, okay, rabbi," the first soldier said, putting his hand up, as though warding off an assault.

The man's face darkened. He seemed about to respond, but his companion, annoyed because his cigarette wouldn't light, flicked the match onto the pavement and pressed forward, his face inches from mine. "These Russians are troublemakers," he said, "everyone knows that."

"Russian?" I repeated, unable to say anything else.

The cell phone man asked how he knew I was Russian. My tormenter pointed to my string bag, purchased in the Warsaw airport, *St. Petersburg* printed in large, white letters down one side. The silence that followed seemed an abyss, interrupted by a high, thin, squawking: the soldiers' radio. Several people hissed; one woman called out, "Nazi!"

"Our students," the first black-suited man shouted and, pushing me aside, he and his companion ran out of line, veered to the left, and up a narrow stone stairway.

Several people applauded; an old man in a long, white silk robe, seated on a stone stoop reading, looked up and shouted after them, "Good riddance! May the angels close the gates of paradise on your fingers."

The soldier dropped the bread into my bag, mumbling a few words I took to be an apology, and told me to please pass through, "Before we have a riot."

ↄﺟﻭ

How could this be, I asked myself afterward, even before I asked myself what to do about the news from the young women soldiers. Jews shaming Jews? If I told Yuri, would he pat my arm and dismiss it? *But Manya, you didn't understand; your Hebrew is still not good, nobody wishes to hurt your feelings, nobody wants you to be unhappy here.* Nobody.

Chapter Seven

*M**arried women do not serve in the army.* Words more beautiful than any found in the Torah, more poetic than the Song of Songs; at least, those bits and pieces read aloud to me by Yuri. If not divine, then certainly heavenly. Good luck was as undeserved as bad, but I recognized it when I saw it.

I needed a plan. In this way Israel resembled Russia: both places were about who you know more so than what you know; about the heavy use of contacts, people who owned thick file folders of hard-to-locate, important names, people who knew the answers even before the questions had been asked.

Nadia? Could Nadia be my ally? She was the smartest woman I knew, but she was job searching, and—a big *and*—she was not a mother. Also, she was in love with adventure. In her view, eighteen months in the army could be the best next step for Galina.

I thought of the pharmacist in the shop on King David Street: a Hungarian with Yugoslavian ancestry, a lively man in his sixties with the build of a boxer. Something, or someone, had squashed his ample nose, giving him the look of a sorrowful Russian troll.

The following morning after breakfast, Yuri and Galina gone, I walked down King George Street in the direction of Independence Park, stopping for the first time to drop half a shekel into the cap of the beggar who'd claimed the sidewalk at the corner of Agron Street as his property. A bent ruin of a man, his book propped up on his lap, he was able to read and insult pedestrians at the same time. My coin clinked into his cap. He looked at the money, then looked up at me. "What's the matter," he said, "no more '*nyet, nyet, nyet*' today? You sick?"

The pharmacist, alone in his shop, was happy to see me, beckoning with his meaty arms to come, come, here at the rear. In my shaky Hebrew, I tried to talk about aspirin and cough syrup, before moving into the serious conversation. He answered in Yiddish, a language as foreign to me as Arabic, calling me *sheyna punim,* pretty face, telling me not to *schlep* so many heavy packages. "Call me Sol," he said, "Solly, for short. Don't be afraid. I could be your father, how old are you?"

I managed to get the words army and daughter and frightened into the same sentence. He switched to Hebrew. "*Ha.* Of course, frightened, but only at the beginning. How wonderful, sending a daughter into uniform. This country needs all its young people. This is your chance to repay Israel for taking you Russians in."

The dry cleaner from Turkey, with the missing teeth and head wrapped in a series of embroidered turbans, next came to mind, a man who chewed sunflower seeds and smoked a water pipe. "Cigarettes will kill you," he'd said, when I'd delivered our first package of dirty clothes, with ash residue on a skirt. "Chew gum instead, here." He offered a handful of peppermint, golden honey, anise. Then, jiggling a palmful of pistachio nuts, he dropped them into my cupped hand, holding on to it with sweaty fingers for a beat too long.

Now he greeted me with a gap-toothed smile. "No clothes today?"

"Today I have a problem."

"*Aahh.*" He poked his forefinger under the front of his turban and scratched his head. "I am good for problems, especially ladies' problems. Maybe your problem is with your husband. He beats you?"

Simon, the man behind the counter in Nussy's New Age Delicatessen, at the top of the winding steps on Beit Habad Street in the Old City, was from Shanghai. "Not a lot of Chinese Jews around here," he'd said the first time I stopped in his shop. "Not a lot anywhere." He laughed, and his enormous belly shook. He seemed kind and wise enough, someone who had studied his country's rules and knew which would bend, which would bend him.

"Before coming to Israel," he'd said that day, "I never saw a dill pickle or bagel or *blintz*. Here." He thrust something gray and oily, wrapped in a paper napkin, into my hand and whispered, "Smoked snake, a great delicacy where I come from. Try."

I bit into something rubbery and gray, chewing, but not swallowing. "*Meanyen*," I said. Interesting.

Delight dimpled his cheeks. "Tai chi," he said, "it makes a difference. Try it sometime. The Middle East Institute for Meditation and Higher Truth, near the Damascus Gate. You have a family?" He turned away to serve another customer, in time for me to spit bits of chewed-up snake into my handkerchief.

That day, when I arrived at the delicatessen, Simon was in the rear, reading the newspaper. I asked for an expresso coffee.

"Plain seltzer is healthier. I'll throw in a slice of lime, no charge."

"Thanks. I like expresso."

"You're from Russia?" he said, handing me the coffee, "Kiev, St. Petersburg?"

"Russian and homesick." I sipped. The coffee was bitter.

Surprise split his leathery face. "No one misses Russia. Shanghai, perhaps, but Russia . . . never."

I took Galina's photograph from my purse. "My daughter, at university, soon to be twenty-one."

"Lovely girl, soon to go into the army?" He returned the photograph.

"That is why I have come."

He beckoned. I followed him to the back of the shop. He poured cold, sweet, apricot tea for both of us, adding two drops of an amber-colored liquor to his, three to mine. "Mediterranean ambrosia," he said, "my wife bottles and sells. Drink up."

His tea was much better than his coffee. "The army," I prompted, "my daughter."

He winked. I was right; this man enjoyed conspiracy as much as I. "Are you a patriot?"

"This depends upon who is asking."

"*I'm* asking."

"I'm a worried mother."

"Find her a husband. Married women don't go. Or, find her a

rabbi to write a letter. The ultraorthodox don't go, either; which, to some people, not me, mind you . . ."

He leaned forward and lowered his voice. "Everyone is absolutely entitled to his own opinion. If you want to be a fanatic, be a fanatic, that's what I believe. We live in a democracy, thank God." He peered at me. "Are you a fanatic? Most Russians are not."

"I pick the husband solution, not the rabbi."

He disappeared into the kitchen, returning with a newspaper page filled with small advertisements under the heading, "Personals." "Boys looking for girls, girls looking for boys. Everyone looking for someone." He winked. "A real business, romance. If I get tired of running a delicatessen, I'll open up a matchmaking store."

I scanned the ads, understanding every third word, picking out *wonderful cook*, *dreamy dancer*, *intellectual*. This was not the way for Galina. "Something less, less . . . public," I said.

He closed one eye, hummed, tapping his fingers on the metal table. "You want a Russian husband for your daughter?"

"A good place to begin."

"Then go where the Russians are."

☙

Where the Russians are. A place like The Municipal Center for Immigrants, maybe? I had the name, even the address, on a card from the *ulpan.* *Yael* something, the woman sitting in the lobby the day we moved out, from the city of Boston; the one who left America and turned into an Israeli. She gave me a brochure and her card. "Come to my office," she said, "if you have any problems." Galina said, "Oh, we'll have problems," and everyone laughed.

I dug the card out from a pile of papers in my desk. If, like she said, *olim* came there for jobs, cash loans, places to live, bus passes, information on how to vote, find a doctor, why not husbands?

Simon had advised: "Post a notice, they've got a bulletin board. Give them *schmaltz*; go heavy on your daughter's plus points."

He made Galina sound like a listing of a house for sale. I felt disloyal to my child, but not as strongly as I felt afraid the army would get her and teach her to kill. They'd cut her hair and put her into a cheap, khaki uniform rough against her skin. Galina didn't like rough against her skin. She liked silks and satins, chiffons and taffetas. No army hair dryers, no makeup cabinet, cell phone, CD player.

She could stun me, say she's too young for marriage. If we were living in Russia—our normal life—of course, too young, but we left normal behind when we left Russia. Still, she could say the army was acceptable. *Why not the army? Living with you*, mamochka, *is a little like living with an army sergeant. Now, isn't it—admit.* Then she'd turn her beautiful head just enough to look at me sideways, with her green Tatiana eyes. A mysterious person, my daughter; part woman, part little girl, neither half fully knowable. Most children are mysteries to their parents, however tight the bond.

⟡

The following morning, I sat at my kitchen desk and began listing her virtues to impress upon this American, this Yael Wurtman, who might prove a valuable ally. Or, she could stare me down with her unblinking American eyes, say I was mad to try to arrange a grown daughter's life.

I wrote: *Beautiful, educated, talented, sensitive young lady, keen sense of humor, interested in music, literature, dance. Loves fine food. To eat, not to cook. Family background: cultured Russians.* Should I make it, *cultured, secular Russians*, to screen out replies from orthodox young men? This was true of only two-thirds of our family, and winning Yuri over to my plan would be difficult enough without pouring the religious question into the mix.

I added: *Unusual hair, honey in color, an extravagant abundance, not to be tampered with*, but wasn't entirely satisfied. If Galina married an orthodox, *really* orthodox—no meat eaten with cottage cheese, Friday night candles, a monthly visit to the *mikvah*, the kind of man Simon would call fanatic—could she insist that she be allowed to keep her hair? She would be expected to cut it, shorter than even the army would cut it, then tuck the remnants under a scarf. Or, worse, a *sheitel*, a marriage wig. If the man turned out not to be orthodox, her hair would remain her hair. I erased the *not to be tampered with.*

Like a tongue trying to avoid a sore tooth, my mind skittered away from including Yuri in the fanatic category. He had not yet mentioned hair or Friday night candles, visits to the *mikvah*. But once that faucet was turned on, the flood would drown me. This country was not just a country: it was a dilemma. A manual of dos and don'ts should be handed out at the border.

The front door clattered open. I heard a tap-tap of heels, and something heavy drop onto the floor, and Galina came into the kitchen, holding up a long white envelope, her face flushed.

"You are not at school?"

"School today is closed, a holiday, a name I cannot remember." She held up a long white envelope. "This"—the word sounded like a plea. She slid the envelope toward me.

"What . . . ?"

Sitting down at the table, she squeezed her hands into her eyes, one of her childhood habits whenever she was one inch away from tears.

A fifty-pound weight clicked into place in my chest. I made a wild guess. "The army?"

"The army."

Chapter Eight

For days the letter sat on the kitchen desk, unopened, propped against a jar of pencils, radiating heat, as untouchable as a steaming kettle. Neither Galina nor I was eager to know exactly when the army wanted her, preferring to imagine its contents.

It could say, *come at once, come in a month, never mind the woman at the airport who said olim don't serve for two years.* Gorbachev put on a happy face and said a lot of things when he wanted the people to stand with him.

Or the letter could say, *you are excused for reason of weak eyes,* except that Galina's eyes were perfect. Or this: *you are too short, too heavy.* Galina was five foot six, one hundred twenty pounds; exactly right for her, exactly right for the army.

Or, in my daydreams, the letter said this: *You are brilliant, Miss Galina, stay in university; come see us when you have a PhD. We'll put you to work doing something complicated but fascinating. Something safe.*

We didn't tell Yuri about the letter. He would have embraced the news, no matter how soon the army wanted our daughter, as though it were an unexpected inheritance. The envelope sat in full view: white, gleaming, a magnet for my eyes, but unnoticed by my husband.

By the end of the week, overcome by fear that we were breaking the law—*You, Russian draft evader, step over here*—Galina and

I steamed the envelope open. Yuri was out. One page, filled with words, top to bottom. Our Hebrew-Russian dictionary revealed a few. *We are pleased to inform, fine young woman, military,* and one full sentence: "Welcome to Israel." The other sentences were ice coated, slipping away from us.

The next day the letter and I visited Yael Wurtman in her office on King George Street. She was on the phone when I arrived, dark hair brushed into a graceful French roll; lively, intelligent eyes of a special mahogany color. She smiled and, as though I visited her office every day, waved me into the chair opposite her desk. This gave me time to admire her American smile. No other country grew such admirable teeth.

Galina, not a kind critic, had approved of Yael's clothes on that day at the *ulpan,* which were much like what she wore now: a blue silk blouse; dark tailored jacket—skirt or trousers, I couldn't detect from where I sat—clever gold pin on her lapel; pearl earrings, one removed to make speaking on the phone easier.

"*Cain, cain,*" she said into the phone, expressing herself with shoulders and hands, her whole body talking. "*Shalom.* Goodbye." She smacked a noisy kiss into the mouthpiece; a very Yael-thing to do, I would discover. Deena Mirovich from Kiev, whom I had met at the *ulpan,* told me that morning, when I phoned to ask if she had done any business with Yael, that Yael was a one-woman fountain of charity: blowing kisses to clients, sales clerks, waitresses, beggars, a gentle sun shower in a country heavy with heat waves.

Out of her magic purse, Deena said, as easily as other people dispensed chewing gum, flew tickets to plays and concerts, bus passes, vouchers for medical clinics. What she did best, however, was listen and nod, murmuring, "Yes, yes, that is the way *olim* feel when they arrive. It gets better, easier." *Olim,* by the very act of coming into Israel, had been given a sack of concrete to carry everywhere—Yael's figure of speech, according to Deena—but every day the sack got lighter, until one could throw it out the door.

Yael put the phone down. "An old client, a lovely woman from Turkey, living in Ashdod now"—she paused and looked at me with a cheerful expression I would come to call Yael's happiness face—"with her new husband, an Israeli. But that's not important. You are here, I'm glad, how are you?" Three thoughts, one sentence.

"How I am," I said, "is worried. Lots of trouble in this envelope." I took it out of my purse.

Yael took the envelope, put it down without opening it, then took a thick pad of paper from a bin on her desk. "I have to officially add your name to our list of clients." She wrote, then looked up. "And ask a few questions." Any sisters, brothers, aunts, cousins in Israel? What work had I done in St. Petersburg, what had I hoped to find in Israel?

Hoped? I had hoped to turn around, return to St. Petersburg. This woman with the large, dark eyes—who had grown up in America, and knew how to sit in a way both relaxed and graceful; who talked in a kind, silky voice, even to the boy who brought us cups of tea—turned me mute. One minute we were drinking tea, and the next I was mumbling and weeping, although I'd tried to blink against the tears. Then she stood up and said, "Come, we're going to the zoo. Do you like animals?"

"No . . . yes. Some." Should I lean over, take the envelope from the desk, open it myself?

"I want to show you species that go back to the Old Testament. You have come to a very special place; no other country in the world has this."

Never had this happened to me before, but I was coming to see that most things that had never happened to me before were going to happen to me in Israel. "Another time, perhaps," I said. "Today I need you to read my letter." I fought against retrieving it, handing it to Yael a second time. Too pushy.

She sat down and opened the envelope. When she looked up, she said, "Wonderful."

"What's wonderful, Galina a soldier?"

"Not for two years." She slid the letter across her desk. "Read the third paragraph. New *olim* are exempt for two years."

"I don't believe." I seized the letter and searched for something familiar among the stubborn, opaque, infuriating black squiggles. Yael reached across the desk for the letter but, not wanting to give up control, I twisted away. "Two years, or maybe you mean two months . . . *where,* show me!"

I handed her the letter; she read it again and, giving it back, pointed. "Two years, as I said. Galina can stay in the university for two more years. Feel better?"

I read, *shtaayim shanah,* two years. "In the end, they still get her."

"They *get* everyone," she said, "the boys, the girls, the men for one month every year until they're in their fifties. My Aaron usually goes in July. Aliza's graduating from high school and wants to go into Intelligence, but it's difficult to qualify."

I *tsk-tsked.*

"No, don't sympathize. We understand the need for everyone to serve, it's our country—"

"*Your* country."

"Galina's, yours, your husband's, *ours!*"

This was not her I-love-you voice. I took my handwritten listing of Galina's virtues from my purse. "I have an idea so they will not get Galina." I repeated what Simon had told me.

Yael read. Her dark eyes turned serious. For the first time I noticed frown lines growing between her eyebrows. "I wouldn't do this if I were you."

"You mean if I were you, but I'm not." I felt like a schoolgirl defying a beloved teacher. "You have how many children?"

"Four."

"I have one. Do you think I can step aside and say, 'Take her,' see her shot apart by a bomb?"

"Civilians are also at risk. The buses, the cafés. All it takes is a determined Palestinian and a hand grenade."

"Don't remind me."

"Anyway, you don't have all the facts; I'm surprised, an intelligent woman like you."

"Don't try to flatter, intelligent." Nevertheless, I felt flattered; this young woman whom I admired thought I had a brain, even if it didn't work in Hebrew. "Right now I'm angry at this country, I'm afraid, I'm—"

"Listen!" Yael came around the desk and sat on the edge, right under my nose. "Most female soldiers don't come near the fighting, they don't even stand guard duty at the borders." Welcome news, but I was not ready to shout, "Wonderful!" I looked mildly interested. "They work in offices with curtains and cafeterias and coffee machines. They work in schools; they train soldiers in physical fitness."

"All right," I said.

"All right?" Yael looked suspicious. "Good, settled."

"I believe you." I did—and I didn't. This country was no friend to mothers. "Guarantee me curtains, cafeterias, coffee machines, and I say, fine, it could improve my daughter if she didn't always think about clothes, a new hair style, or film stars, lived with girls her age. An only child, sharing is, for her, not easy. She could laugh a little, learn her Hebrew."

"Two years for the girls," Yael said, "three years for the boys." She turned and reached into a desk drawer for her purse. "Come, I need some lunch."

"Not yet," I said. She snapped her purse shut. "I want your word that my daughter will not be a real soldier, only an office soldier." I snatched a piece of paper from a pad in my purse and tapped my pen against it. "Sign here." She couldn't have looked more astonished if I had broken into a tap dance or yodeled in Russian.

"I can't speak for the Army, no one can." A don't-say-no-to-me voice, a voice that shouted *Principal, Supervisor, Commissar.*

"So"—I reached across the desk to retrieve my list—"tack Galina up on your bulletin board." I heard the sharp tone to my voice, and added, "Please. That is why the board is there, am I correct? To give *olim* important news, help them find what they need?"

Yael glanced down at the paper, but didn't take it. "Like a newspaper advertisement for a used refrigerator, or pots and pans." Her voice was less irritated, but not yet kind.

"Like a mother looking for her daughter's safety."

She sat down at her desk again and scrutinized me, as though weighing whether to ask a question, shrugged, and asked it: "Does Galina know you're doing this, looking for a husband for her?"

I waggled my hand. "Yes, and no."

"Which?"

This was not a woman to fool with half stories. "The answer is mostly no."

"I thought so." She tapped her fingernails on her desk. "Even if you tell her, and even if she agrees, and I don't think she will, why not place an advertisement in *Maariv* or *Haaretz*?"

"Everyone reads those newspapers. Turkish, Moroccans"—I struggled for another name I'd read in Yuri's Russian-language newspaper. It came to me, but in pieces: "Argenthing something. South America. I want only a Russian person."

I saw a small ping of annoyance in her eyes. Too bad for her. There were not many things I liked about my new country, but this I did like: I was free to say, *yes* to this, *no* to that. Yuri said God had his reasons. In His infinite wisdom, He had sent us to Israel. Possibly, He had also sent a young Russian man to Israel to marry Galina and keep her out of the army, to make her happy. To make me happy.

I thought of one more argument. "The newspaper is public, the *Olim* Center has more—dignity. Dignity is important to our family."

"What's the rush? Two years from now is a long time."

"Not if you're Galina's mother. My daughter can be difficult to please about a new necklace, a purse. Imagine a husband."

She shook her head. "Let's talk."

"*Talk*! Everyone in this country talks so much, like talking is a full-time profession." At that moment, the contrast between what my life was now and what I wanted it to be, organized itself into a fireball, a furious roaring in my ears. "Talk won't keep my child out of the army, talk won't get me back to my country, talk didn't keep Tatiana healthy." I blew my nose in a not-so-ladylike manner Tatiana would have hated.

Sparks of sympathy flashed in Yael's eyes; she waited for me to recover from my tantrum. I blew my nose again, more delicately this time. "Whatever you decide, Manya, find a husband for Galina, or wish her good luck in the army, there is risk. You and Yuri were in danger in St. Petersburg; that business with the gun you told me about."

"St. Petersburg danger is not Jerusalem danger. In St. Petersburg, danger is only sometimes. 'Danger' is another name for this country."

She thought, her intelligent eyes hard to read. She tapped a pencil on her desk, she looked at me, then looked away. In the end she decided the following; having no choice, I accepted. She would post my listing on her bulletin board in the section labeled *Social Notes*, but not until Galina and she had discussed my plan and its, what she called "implications," this word spoken in English.

I knew about implications. Everything that had happened to us since that September day in our market stall sprang from implications. The implication behind Dushkin's asking for protection money with a gun in his hand was that violence, possibly murder, had made its way into our lives. The implication of this fact was that Yuri would no longer live in Russia; worse, he would no longer live as a watered-down (his word), secular Jew. The implications of finding oneself face-to-face with a small hand pistol, on what had been an ordinary day, had turned three lives inside out.

Galina and Yael met later that week, without me. As Yael reported the scene, my daughter laughed, amused by what she called my "boldness." "Oh, well, *mamochka,* after all, so much energy, so much imagination. I continue to be her most urgent project." Asked if she was offended by the advertisement—Yael refused to call it a listing—Galina said, "Maybe, not too much. Anyway, nothing will come of this. And perhaps it is not a bad idea if I meet some new boys. I have only girlfriends at the university."

How did she feel about going into the army?

"You wish me to be honest? Not very well."

♫

Nadia, for me an example of rational, grown-up *olim* behavior, had begun a new job that, she said, ran eighteen hours daily. We hadn't seen one another since the evening of the wines, the honey, and the Reb. I phoned; she'd squeeze me into her lunch hour at a café on Ben Reuven Street, where crowds of musicians stood around beating drums and shaking bells for coins.

I arrived early. She arrived in Nadia style: waving, talking, dropping paper parcels as she twisted between the small tables. We'd talked on the phone since her visit, but I had not had time to discuss my meeting with the Reb in the Old City. Nadia said always that I and the Reb were the people she loved most, so how would she feel about the Reb and me in a tangle of disagreement?

Hugging me, then signaling to the waitress, she told me about her job, researcher for a political columnist in a Russian language newspaper: endless hours, too little pay, a staff of brilliant women and not enough men. She looked around. The waitress had disappeared, and she had only forty minutes.

The young woman, red hair twisted into a high bun, dimpled chin, more hips than necessary, who had seated me wasn't anywhere. Then she was, approaching us with glasses of water and her order pad.

Nadia held on to her annoyed look. "A small bowl of borscht," she said.

The waitress said, today, no borscht and, tapping the menu in Nadia's hand, suggested that she look.

"On other days you have borscht?"

"Never borscht. We have vegetable soup, beef barley soup, chicken—"

"You make no plans to please the Russians who dine here?" Nadia said, pinching open a packet of artificial sugar, trailing grains over the table.

The two women at the next table stopped their eating and looked at us, turning away when Nadia sent them a black stare.

"Many of our Russians order the vegetable soup," the waitress said. Her eyes registered boredom.

"Not the same thing like borscht," Nadia said. "Please tell *your* Russians, whoever these are, vegetable soup is not beet borscht." Now she pinched a second sugar packet open. "*My* Russians prefer borscht, preferably with beets, but also with potatoes."

"Come to my house," I said. "I'll make borscht for you."

"Not the point," Nadia said. "This country talks diversity, it talks welcome to Russians, and never can I find a bowl of beet borscht." She looked up at the waitress with a stiff smile. "We need time to go through the no-borscht menu."

"Nadia Elena Stamirova," I said, when the waitress had left. "Bad manners, I am sorry to say. That young girl"—I pointed to the waitress, now taking an order from two men seated nearby—"not her fault there is no borscht. Israel is not a borscht location."

"So, now you're an Israeli patriot." The two women were still listening. Nadia turned toward them, raising her water glass.

"Hello, ladies. Didn't I know you in Moscow? The opera, perhaps?" The wider woman looked flustered and dropped her purse onto the floor. The other woman studied the ceiling.

This was not the time to talk to Nadia about her cousin. The waitress returned; I ordered salads for both of us, slipping into another topic. "Speaking of Galina, I know you want to know how she is." I slid a copy of my Galina notice across the table.

She read, clucking her tongue as she went along, then looked up at me—not with admiration. "Manya, you stop at nothing."

"I stop at the army."

She took her mirror out of her purse, puckered her lips, and applied fresh lipstick. "Israel may not go to war again, now we have the Oslo Accords," she said.

"With Oslo, without Oslo, I want my daughter close to home, outside of a khaki uniform, without a gun."

"I have my own theory I don't tell everyone. Are you ready?"

"If I said not ready, you'd tell me anyway."

"We will never have peace."

I shook my head. "I don't want to hear."

"It's simple. We were here, and we left, then they were here—"

"Who's *they*?"

"The Palestinians. We came back, and now we're both here. So we fight." She slapped one palm across the other. "Bad neighbors don't turn into good neighbors unless the neighborhood is big enough and rich enough and safe enough for everyone to own a nice house with a two-car garage and a barbecue on the patio."

"You talk politics, everything laid out so neat," I said. "I talk people talk. Where does that put the Palestinian mothers? I see the newspaper photos: crying and carrying their dead babies. They love their children the way I love Galina."

"Of course." She shrugged. "Let the men figure it out, they've got the testosterone."

"Whatever that means. What you say is easy to say when you don't have a daughter."

"Wait"—the waitress brought our salads—"I have a wonderful story. I have to tell it before I forget. Three men walked into a restaurant in Tel Aviv: an American, an Israeli, and a Russian."

"Nadia, Nadia"—this woman was a mix of what I loved and what made me crazy—"the story can wait."

"Not with *my* memory. Tomorrow it will be gone, whoosh"—she snapped her fingers. "An American, an Israeli, a Russian—"

"This happened?"

"If you believe it happened, it happened. A sign at the door read, 'Please excuse the shortage of steak today.' The Russian said, 'What is steak?' The American said, 'What is a shortage?' The Israeli said, 'What is this *please excuse*?' " She leaned back and looked at me as though expecting applause.

"Eat your salad, it's getting cold."

"Salads are supposed to be cold. You didn't laugh, everyone laughs."

"I can't laugh and chew my tomatoes at the same time."

"Let us be serious for one minute. You are not going to like this." I prepared myself to be annoyed. "You didn't expect me to be an accomplice in this?" She held up my sheet of paper.

"I expect you to be enthusiastic."

"I'll be honest instead. There are two possible outcomes, both terrible. One"—she sniffed—"you will *lose* Galina; as a friend, I mean. Two, you will push her into a terrible marriage both of you will regret for the rest of your lives." *Pit pat*, she had my whole life and Galina's set out. We had a moment of silence, populated by angry looks between us. "Listen—"

"No, *you* listen." Now I leaned forward, but I don't remember if I lowered my voice. Probably not. "I don't like your cousin."

She looked startled. "Schlomo?"

"The same. We met one morning, on the street, an accident."

"He told me."

"What did he tell you, your friend has a fresh mouth, no respect?"

"He lives with a wife who is full of opinions, and I give him a few pieces of my mind when I have to. Schlomo is a smart man, even a brilliant man, but"—Nadia frowned into the distance, then at me—"he's really two men."

"All right, I don't like either one of him."

"A calm, religious scholar, and an excitable of"—she looked around—"stuff."

"What means *stuff*?"

She rubbed her hand down the front of her black, expensive-seeming jacket. "Suede jackets, French wine. The newest, the best, the biggest television player."

"He has money for these things?"

"Yes . . . and no. He is good with dreaming up ideas. But, in spite, his religion, it's like his skin and his eyes; that's how much a part of him it is." She clapped her fork against her salad plate. "Finished."

I thought about this, but suddenly, very unusually, I had nothing to say.

⟡

The week before Passover, Yael tacked the notice to the bulletin board, bringing me a problem: What to tell Yuri if a young man answered the advertisement; how to explain his coming into our home, sitting on the parlor sofa, trying not to stare at Galina, concentrating instead on Yuri's offer of wine, my cheese and crackers?

I would do the only practical thing: lie. The son of a friend had come to Jerusalem and would be stopping by. Nothing special; a cup of tea, conversation.

In town, Yuri would ask, *from where?*

Anywhere. *Tel Aviv, Beersheba, Eilat.* The point is: don't look guilty. *My friend Katya's son . . . you remember Katya, from the music school? The St Petersburg Conservatory? Short, not thin but not fat, black hair, her Romanian grandmother's side of the family, beautiful singing voice.* Even in imagined conversations, I wandered into irrelevance when nervous. *Mikhail's on holiday from the Tel Aviv University. I invited him to come to the house; he shouldn't be lonely.*

⟡

The next evening, Galina in her room, door closed; a three-part assault of voice, guitar, drums, like thunder filling all the empty spaces in the house. I told Yuri we could expect a visit from a young man, the following week, perhaps, or the next.

Yuri listened, mysteriously quiet, which I mistook for agreement. Until: "Have you forgotten Passover?"

85

"How could I?" In St. Petersburg, Passover came and went, a date circled on the calendar, then ignored. One year a woman telephoned and whispered: "Free *matzos,* the Pastonovich Street entrance to the University Community Hall. Tonight, eight o'clock. Wear black, carry false papers." We didn't go.

We knew from *babushka* stories, whispered only at home, the radio tuned to Russian marching music—who could be sure what neighbor was listening, taking notes, ready to denounce—about the elaborate preparations, eight nights of specially prepared foods. But first, before one bit of festival food could be carried into the house, pots, pans scoured, dishes as well, the house cleansed of all *chometz,* the forbidden wheat.

"April 14 this year," Yuri said. "The Jewish calendar is different each year, depending."

"Of course. Depending." A splendid solution. Why not invite a guest to our small Seder? Even I knew it was considered a blessing to welcome Jewish strangers into one's home on holidays.

"He will travel on the holiday? He has no family obligations, no one expecting him at their table?" Was Katya Jewish, was her husband? Already damned, this young man who did not exist.

જ⁊ઈ

Jedediah Fischl Rachmann. Formerly—meaning six years earlier, when his family lived in Kiev—Rachmannoff. "As in the composer," he said when he arrived, carrying a bouquet of lilacs. "Almost, but not quite. I am myself a flutist." He held up a small black case. "First flutist, Israel Camerata Orchestra Jerusalem."

He had gone to the Municipal Office to inquire about a driver's license, read my advertisement by chance; entirely accidental, he never read that kind of thing. But then he'd met Yael, who said my daughter was unusual: educated, charming, beautiful, from a good family. He was living alone in a nearby suburb, performing most nights and weekends, and had no opportunity to meet other young people.

"He's an interesting young man," Yael had told Galina when she telephoned about their meeting; adding with a small, hard-to-define laugh, "with a number of idiosyncrasies you may find charming."

Galina knew the word for idiosyncrasy in Hebrew: *regeeshoot*. She didn't like the sound, or the meaning.

I liked Jedediah's long, narrow, intent face, his dark-blond hair he combed into a high, theatrical pompadour, somewhat like Anna Karenina's Vronsky, or, like Vronsky's as he lived in my mind. Mostly, I was captured by his pale-blue eyes; the color of the sea in Odessa.

Happily, Yuri was at the library. I was about to offer wine, cheese, a chair, but Jedediah was looking past me into the parlor. "Please, you have here possibly a music room?" He had seen the piano. A soft, delicious sigh fluttered from his lips, as he moved toward the instrument, followed by another sigh, bordering on ecstasy, as he was about to lift the keyboard cover.

Galina—who I had not seen a moment before, pausing at the top of the stairs to assess her caller—hurried into the room, wearing a black silk something, her hair caught in a cat's cradle of scarlet ribbons. Moving toward the young man, perhaps too swiftly, she said, "I am Galina Zalinikova," as though announcing a curfew. "Happy to make your acquaintance," she said as she thrust her hand out.

Jedediah gazed at her with sweet approval and held on to her hand for a long moment. "Jedediah Rachmann," he said, and, gesturing at the piano, again held up his flute case.

"The piano is seriously damaged," Galina said.

"Damaged?" Jedediah looked at me.

Hearing this young man perform would have suited me perfectly, and there was the matter of inquiring about his family, his education, his work. But now Galina's hand was under his elbow. "We can go now," she said, guiding him toward the foyer. Jedediah sent a look of longing at the piano, brushing past me with a faint, "A pleasure, Mrs. Zalinikova," and they were gone.

"Almost Rachmaninov . . . *almost?*" Galina said, when she returned from a concert, a walk through Independence Park, a coffee at Cyrano Café. "Almost is not enough. His name is missing an i-n. In English i-n means *in,* inside. Jedediah is not only not *in,* he is *out.*"

"It was only one evening," I said. I heard Yuri running the water in the bathroom. I had to go upstairs quickly, or he'd come down to ask what was causing the fuss, and Galina would describe Jedediah, and he would say, "*Who?*" And I'd say, and Galina would say, and so on, into one more set of lies.

"For him, for this self-impressed, boring person, I stood in front of the mirror separating my eyelashes, combing, powdering." I moved toward the stairs, but she wasn't finished. "That name, Jedediah."

"Poetic."

"In Hebrew, Jedediah means beloved by God. *This* Jedediah is beloved only by Jedediah. He is in love with his pompadour, fussing with it, pushing it up higher, and his tie, he patted like a man pats a woman. But, worst of all, he kissed like I was his flute." She frowned. "No . . . his harmonica."

I said nothing.

"*Mamochka*—"

I heard Yuri open our bedroom door. I called to him, "One minute—"

"After this, no more strange men," Galina said.

Yuri went back into our bedroom.

"There are no strange men," I said, "only men you have not yet met."

"Not yet met is a good way to keep the situation."

"Of course," I said, moving toward the hallway, "but you will perhaps find the army less happy than Jedediah to accommodate to your moods."

Chapter Nine

The next night, Yuri poured Passover wine into two glasses, and we sat on the patio after what I would call a satisfactory Passover dinner. Not perfect, but, as prepared by me, a heathen, good enough: chicken soup, roasted chickens, and steamed eggplant, prepared with the help of Yael, in her kitchen, and carried home to warm in my oven.

We were alone, Galina in her room studying, listening to music, talking on the telephone, all three at the same time. Yuri had on his mind a man whose name came to him from someone in his synagogue; a man, he said, of enormous wisdom, a scholar of Hebrew history, philosophy, who held intellectual discussions with students, only a select few; a man who could be of enormous importance to us.

"Us?"

"We must meet him."

"*We?*"

"I will begin; later you can join us."

A dangerous proposal. A Hebrew scholar, a man in black, probably six feet tall, with a flaming red beard; he and I in a small room from which there would be no escape, knee to knee. Certainly not mind to mind. He would make shredded beet borscht of me, with my almost nothing knowledge of Torah, Talmud, Genesis, Exodus.

"And so, Mrs. Zalinikova, today we will discuss *Mishna*"—a

word I heard for the first time from Yuri—"and ethics."

Yuri was waiting for my answer. "I cannot say." A lie. I *could* say: *No.* But at that moment, I was too well-fed, and had sipped too much wine, and wanted for the evening to hold on to the peaceful, even romantic view of being Jewish in a world where—these were Yael's words—at that moment, Jews, every kind of Jew, were sitting at dinner telling the same story of Passover.

"His name is Reb Schlomo Turrowtaub, a rabbi who is not practicing as a rabbi. He prefers teaching."

"Impossible. Nadia's cousin is Reb Schlomo Turrowtaub. You met him. I met him. That night, remember, he brought Nadia and her suitcases. Then I bumped into him in the Old City; he bumped into me on the sidewalk, and we had coffee—"

"There must be two Reb Turrowtaubs. Nadia's cousin didn't appear to be . . ." His voice trailed off.

"To be . . . *what?*"

Yuri shrugged. "Not important. Whoever this Reb is, he's brilliant, a scholar. My friend told this man about me, and he's willing to help me learn to live as a Jew."

"For a fee, of course. He'll help you learn for a fee." Was Nadia's Reb *this* Reb? Not impossible, but Israel was filled with Rebs, filled with Turrowtaubs.

"Why not a fee? We paid for the man who fixed our broken washing machine, we paid the man who put stone down on our patio."

"We're in Israel; we *are* living as Jews. Would we live here as Chinese?" This was not what I had intended to say. What I intended to say was much longer, much louder, and wouldn't fit inside my mouth alongside the sadness already there.

"There are Chinese Jews," he said, "did you know that?" A splash of his old mischievousness. The old Yuri, the *before Yuri*, from when we agreed about most things, when the question of how to be Jewish, how much to be Jewish, didn't sit between us like a thousand-pound monster.

I wanted to make the moment last. "Do Chinese Jews eat egg noodles?"

"Kosher egg noodles."

"Oh, Yuri . . ." I could have kidnapped him and taken him to bed.

I could have laughed, or cried, whichever happened first. I stood up, still grasping my glass of wine.

"Come with me to meet the Reb," Yuri said, "he'll help us."

"Ha!" I sat down hard, spilling wine.

"What is this *Ha*?"

"The Reb is Orthodox?" Yuri looked confused. "The Reb is famous, widely published, a scholar of the Old Testament? Yes, or no?"

"Why do you ask?"

"Answer, please."

"Yes."

"He would not take a woman as his pupil." Certainly, the Reb of my coffee shop conversation would not. "That is the first problem. The second problem is this: *if* he said yes to a woman, an *if* as big as the Western Wall, it would certainly not be a woman so ignorant, so illiterate in Hebrew, I wouldn't know what questions to ask."

"He will talk, you will listen."

"No questions?"

Yuri shrugged. "Not immediately."

"That means not ever. When have I sat and listened, like a lump, without asking questions?"

"That, then, is your problem." The old eye twitch surfaced.

"Not my problem, my approach to life. And besides—"

"Always a besides."

"Yes, most definitely, and especially this one. I have a more urgent agenda. Galina."

"What about Galina?"

"You know what, the army. I will not allow it."

He looked at me, incredulous, as though I had said I wanted to run for president of this country, or open a falafel stand in Independence Park. "You will not *allow*?"

"Things can be done."

"What kind of things?"

"As I said—"

"Marriage?" His face, in the muted light of the patio, anyway, seemed etched in sorrow. "A terrible idea; a disastrous idea."

And so on, and so on, without resolution.

Troubles enough to chew on, to take to bed, to wake up to: Yuri swallowed whole by religion; Galina in danger of army duty. My Israel was three people wide, with the addition of Nadia, and now, Yael, to whose office I went the following morning. I found her in one of her cheerful, we-must-get-on-with-it moods: a personality flaw I'd noticed in Americans. Over-optimism, in the face of facts that said otherwise. Yael's up and my down were never a good combination.

She poured coffee for herself—another American addiction—tea for me in a glass, two sugar lumps set out on a napkin, and asked how things were.

"How can things be?"

She smiled. "Wonderful."

"Why wonderful?"

"In spite of yourself, you are becoming Jewish."

I frowned.

"Two Jews meet on the street, and one says to the other, 'Don't you want to know how I am?' So the second Jew says, 'How are you?' To which the first Jew says, 'Don't ask.' " She grinned in an expectant way, as though, if she waited a minute, I would understand. I sipped and said nothing. "Don't you see, Manya? That kind of nay-saying is rooted in our culture. We're afraid of tempting the gods to punish us if we say everything is going well. It's the verbal equivalent of knocking wood against evil spirits when someone says you look healthy, or have beautiful eyes."

"Why should I *say* everything is going well? Nothing is going well."

"Every *olim* says that; you are exactly on target. However"—she looked at me, as though wondering if she should continue—"you didn't come to Israel expecting it to be America, only with more Jews, did you?"

I blinked my annoyance.

"Begin at the beginning."

I began with the disastrous Jedediah Rachmannoff, and continued with Reb Schlomo Turrowtaub, who, I added, I had already insulted. Her face turned from cheerful to borderline sad.

I sat back, pleased to have ended her irrational happiness.

She poured more coffee. "Let me think for a moment. We need a plan, *something*, to jump-start your life."

"What is that, jump-start? It sounds American."

"A sudden surge of energy; something that starts the adrenalin flowing. It means making something good happen." She frowned, then smiled. "Music. Give piano lessons."

"On what? My piano is damaged."

"Have it repaired."

"Tatiana's piano, I couldn't have a stranger just . . . not yet."

She leaned back and regarded the ceiling. I hummed, I sniffed. I read the cover of the magazine on her desk, waiting for her next suggestion, which was equally futile. I should join a chamber music grouping. The city was filled with them, how perfect, most of the musicians were Russian; just look up that little arty club in the German Colony, Dostrovska something or other. I'd love it.

"I'd hate it," I said. "Chamber music groups are run by tyrants, usually the violinist, a man with sensitive nerves and streaming hair. In St. Petersburg I called these people 'Music Nazis.' "

She looked unhappy for a moment, then said: "This *is* perfect. Play the piano at The White Nights Supper Club. Have you been there?"

"The only white nights I know were every summer in St. Petersburg."

"It's new and very sophisticated, everyone is raving. Wildly expensive. Opposite Independence Park, on that quaint little paved street that looks like an alley but isn't, behind the Four Georges Hotel." She practically vibrated with excitement. "It would be a perfect match; you, in a ruby-red chiffon tunic, with gold embroidery down the front"—patting her blouse—"or, one of your mother's hostess gowns. I can just see it: you, music, and elegant Russian dining."

"Is the food kosher?"

Yael's eyebrows shot upward. "*Kosher* . . . you?"

"Not me, Yuri."

She turned stern-looking, almost schoolteacherish; an unbecoming attitude, I thought, for such an attractive young woman. "We're talking about *you*. Yuri has his own agenda, a difficult one for you to accept, but he's entitled to find his own way, and this minute it's absorbing him. You need your own place in Israel. You cannot make a career of finding Galina a husband, or objecting to Yuri's religious fervor." I inspected my fingernails, and, for a moment, said nothing. "Do you agree?" she prodded.

This scenario of what my life had become since arriving in this place was not attractive. Yael was not my friend, or she would not state it in this hurtful way. I sipped my tea, refusing to look at her.

"You can kill the messenger, try to, anyway, but you can't kill the message." She tapped her fingertips on her desk, a habit I disliked. Tatiana had always said ladies of a certain social status didn't use their hands in this way.

"Please don't," I said.

Clasping her hands in her lap: "All right, but do you agree?"

"With some things, not with all."

cʃ̃ɔ

She made a phone call to a man she described as *different*, Dmitri Kanov, from Moscow, chatted with him in Russian, described me, my piano playing—"Enormously talented, the Conservatory in St. Petersburg, an elegant woman, you'll like her"—wrinkling her nose at me as she talked. Finally, she came to my interest in working at The White Nights. "*Cain, cain*," she said. Then, lapsing into Russian: "Tell us when."

"He'll get back to us," she said, when she'd hung up. "Let me tell you about this man." Her good humor had returned, and I must admit that my curiosity had entered the room. "No one knows who he is, exactly," she said, "and apparently he's made a great deal of money in nobody knows what."

Immediately, Dushkin and his bodyguards leaped to mind. "The Russian mafia," I said.

"Don't be so dramatic; people make money legally. About a year ago he appeared, spending bundles of cash at the gambling casinos that float around in unmarked ships in the Red Sea, staying weekends in Eilat at the glitzy hotels with an army of men, who I heard had questionable manners, and beautiful women, most of them Russian, jewels everywhere, their ears, their navels. More important, he flaunted stacks of cash for vodka, caviar, drinks for everyone in the room. Every day was a party, and he picked up the bill."

"How do you know these things?"

She smiled. "There's a Russian underground in Jerusalem, and it talks. One million of you have come over. Very little goes unnoticed in a country the size of a postage stamp. I knew that sooner or later, we'd meet because of my work, he and I. Then, six weeks ago, he opened The White Nights Supper Club. Aaron and I went as somebody's guests; we couldn't afford even the appetizers on our own." They hadn't met that night, he was away; Paris, possibly, or London, Berlin. She left a note and her card. He called, introduced himself, and said she must get in touch if she ever needed a favor.

"What does he look like, this person?"

"Nice enough looking, from what I hear: hair thinning a little, medium height, slender build. Someone said he works out in a gymnasium he's built in the basement of his house. But this is the interesting part." She leaned forward, looking directly at me. "He has enormous style, dresses in only custom-made clothes, wears a cape, a black felt fedora"—she put one hand to her forehead in a mock salute—"in a country where no man wears a tie."

"He is vain, in love with himself."

She laughed. "Probably. Not a crime in this country, unless you hurt somebody along the way. And remember this, Manya. He is also interesting, imaginative, and has enough shekels and rubles to give employment to a lot of people."

"So, Mr. Dimitri Kanov from Moscow, meet Manya Zalinikova from St. Petersburg."

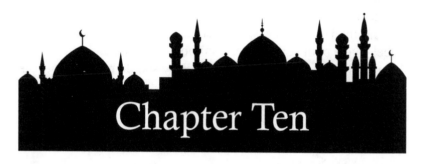

Chapter Ten

Reb Schlomo Turrowtaub—born in Krakow, Poland; the fifth son of Herschl Semke, blacksmith, repairer of horses' reins, and his ambitious, intelligent wife Tsimma, a woman who earned money writing letters to lovers, debtors, relatives who had left for America, and had so many clients the skin on the third finger of her right hand was permanently calloused from grasping the pen—sat in the book-lined study of his house in the Rehavia section of Jerusalem. He was reading from commentaries on Exodus by Rashi, the eleventh century Hebrew scholar. Reading, and glancing at the enormous wall clock his family had brought from Poland when he was a boy, when the country was known as Palestine.

April, already. Soon, heat without relief; another Jerusalem summer, fine yellow-brown dust blowing up from the arid hills in the west, the desert in the south.

The Reb enjoyed escaping the too-hot Jerusalem summers. When the children were children, they went to a rental cottage on the sea, outside Natanya. More recently, they stayed in a borrowed studio apartment in Safed, the holy city in the hills, an artists' colony, giving him and his wife, Ahuva, an opportunity to catch up on who was painting what, whose work was selling, who was buying. He liked to think of himself as a man of the arts, as well as of the Book. But this week Ahuva had said: "Eilat, two weeks in August, a hotel villa."

"You have been speaking to your sister?"

"One is available next to the one Deena and Avram are taking."

"Deena and Avram, as I suspected. Safed is no longer desirable?"

"Eilat is cooler, by the Red Sea."

"Deena did not say that Eilat is where everyone is going this year, all the new millionaires from the chipping business?"

"The internet business, with chips. She said nothing. It's me, I feel like a cool sea breeze, a sailboat ride to watch the sunset. Beautiful. Eilat is a feast of beauty. Why should only the tourists enjoy it?"

The Reb inserted the tip of his small finger in his ear and wiggled it. "I am surprised such an important man as our brother-in-law, with his important real estate business, can leave Jerusalem for two weeks."

"Summers are slow in the real estate business."

"*Slow* is not a word I associate with Avram."

⌘

This morning the Reb was expecting three men. Two, he'd never met. The third, Yuri Zalinikov, he'd met briefly when he'd delivered his cousin Nadia to the Zalinikov home early in March. Delivered was not the correct term for driving Nadia to her friends. Nadia was not a package one delivered. Nadia was a force who delivered herself into every situation, taking over the discourse, directing the conversation.

Interesting, the way coincidence had reintroduced Zalinikov into his life, after his calamitous attempt at coffee with Manya Zalinikova, proving what, for the Reb, required no further proof: most Jews were connected in one way or another. Avram Spikof, a close friend whom he'd run into in the library of Sacred Torah Seminary, where the Reb often lectured on Maimonides, Rashi, and Buber, told him about a newly arrived Russian whose education in Judaism was sparse, but whose interest in living as an observant Jew was sincere. Perhaps the Reb could be of help.

Their conversation in the Old City had told him that Mrs. Zalinikova did not share this interest. Nevertheless, he would be happy to help. Was that not his calling, to assist Jews in becoming

98

better Jews, leaving the world a better place than he had found it? There *was* the matter of his being compensated, in a small way, of course, the term small being subjective, one man's small often another man's large.

He was about to call out to Ahuva to bring another iced tea, and perhaps a slice of her lemon poppy seed cake—thin, and only one slice, remember his weight—when he heard door chimes. Two o'clock exactly. Today's students were punctual, a good sign.

Three men—two younger than the Reb had expected—in black hats, black suits, white fringe floating from beneath their shirts, followed Ahuva into the study, removed their hats and waited for the Reb to invite them to sit.

"To begin," he said, raking his fingers through his gray tweed beard. He pointed to the wooden chairs facing his. The men sat. The Reb asked questions. Ahuva appeared with iced tea and slices of cake.

Yuri Zalinikov spoke first, and often, sometimes interrupting the others to make his point. No, Israel was not especially difficult for Russians. It was important to remember that life in Russia had been so, so—*Godless.* It was change itself that was difficult. The other men considered this, but neither agreed nor disagreed. One reached under his skullcap to scratch his head. The Reb frowned, raked his beard, and wrote in his small leather-bound notebook. The clock ticked.

When his visitors had left, the Reb asked Ahuva, who was gathering dishes, glasses, napkins, her thoughts on the men.

"These are nice people," she said, brushing crumbs into the pocket of her apron. "So nice, they probably do not fully understand yet how hard life here can be."

Her husband tented the fingertips of one hand against the fingertips of the other. "For everyone," he said.

"Compared to living in America, let us say."

The Reb snorted. "*Who* would live in America, among so many thousands of non-Jews? They could swallow us up."

"However—nevertheless, to use one of your favorite words—if you will allow me to complete my sentence."

"Complete, I am all ears."

"According to this country, it is like you always say, Schlomo. In

Russia these people are the Jews; in Israel they are the Russians."

The Reb was delighted. He reached for the final slice of cake, as Ahuva was about to tuck it into a napkin. How blessed he was to have a clever wife, especially a wife who quoted her husband to make her point. He broke off a corner of the cake. "They came to me for help in becoming better Jews."

Ahuva stopped at the door, resting her tray against her hip. "And that depends upon who is saying what does or does not make a better Jew."

The Reb's eyebrows shot up. "*Who* is saying? *I* am saying." Ahuva moved toward the kitchen. The Reb called out: "Little pigeon, you want Eilat for two weeks in August, yes? Eilat is expensive."

⌒⌒

The Reb welcomed students in the mornings. Early afternoons were often devoted to digesting Ahuva's bountiful lunches, and late afternoons to the Reb's own work; or, if the press of publishing or lecture deadlines permitted, to gin rummy with the crowd from the back room behind Yussel's, the delicatessen on Ben Yehuda Street. Today, however, the Reb was not thinking about lunch or gin rummy. He was thinking about mathematics, reading "The Constancy of Variables," by the Russian scholar, Vladimir Fenster.

Zalinikov, whom he had begun to meet on Tuesday mornings, suggested he read it, when the Reb asked him the frequency with which variables appear in quantum physics, say, or astronomic sightings. A fine mind on that one, he told Ahuva at breakfast, the book propped against his cream pitcher.

"That was the first thing you said to me, Schlomo, remember? The very first thing." Ahuva, seated opposite, poured a cup of coffee. "That I had a fine mind."

The Reb squinted above his toast, which he'd layered with pickled herring, cucumber slices, wedges of tomato. He did not remember, but said he did. He loved his wife, loved everything about her, with the sole exception of her sister's husband, who, after many years, remained an irritant, a constant reminder that Schlomo had chosen a life of faith, of scholarship, while Avram chose to be wealthy.

What Ahuva failed to recognize was that, since that long-ago meeting, still so vivid in her mind, so dim in his, he had researched and written eight books, tutored at least three hundred students, held lectureships at both the Hebrew University and the Jewish Theological Seminary. He could not be expected to remember what he said to her when courtship, not scholarship, occupied his mind.

"We were talking about poetry," Ahuva said. Her dark eyes were dreamy with remembered pleasure. "Yehuda Amichai. I was reading him for my class in modern Hebrew literature. You said anything I loved, you would love also."

The Reb nodded, hesitant to say anything that could lead his wife to ask for specifics.

She looked unusually radiant this morning: pink cheeks glowing, curly auburn hair brushed back, gathered in a knot at the top of her head. A special pleasure, given her exceedingly lovely hair, that the Modern Orthodoxy did not require women to wear the marriage wig. Through the years, his wife had become to him even more beautiful than the young college student/poetry reader she was describing. The Reb blessed his good luck and knocked wood, but quietly. No need to flatter. Ahuva was not unaware of her virtues.

"The first time we had an evening out together"—she sipped—"without my mother and father."

Ahuva's parents, dead for more than twenty years—pleasant people, even generous upon occasion—had faded from his mind into the black-and-white photographs hung in the study. Six-by-eight, five-by-seven memories, fixed in frozen, silent images that, with time, demanded nothing more than to be included among the archives decorating the walls, and to be remembered in prayers for the dead. Frightening, the way whole layers of one's life slipped away, leaving behind only images.

"It was Fall, Schlomo, remember, 1969? Israel was young, and so were we."

"I remember as though it were yesterday," he said, quartering a blueberry swirl, another of Ahuva's triumphs. "A piece?" he asked, offering his plate to her.

She looked startled, regarding her husband with a mixture of affection and regret. The Reb knew his wife well; knew she had an appreciation for their dissonance, and the delicate ways in which he reconciled them. She had, after all, with her eyes open, married a man who, like every Orthodox man, puts on his *tefillin* for morning prayers, and thanked God he had not been created a woman. Yet, these words notwithstanding, didn't he over the years show, through gesture and speech, that he had only the highest regard for her?

"Tell me about Yuri Zalinikov," she said, accepting the pastry.

"We met earlier." Ahuva nodded. "He, his wife, are friends of Nadia's."

"Nadia has friends everywhere."

"This man is a genius of a kind, astonishing, recites from memory entire sections of the *Midrash* on *Exodus*. Rarely does this happen, except in academic circles."

"And the wife?"

"A musician, a pianist, a woman with certain"—how should he say this? Ahuva turned testy if she thought he was being patronizing to a woman—"with some, should I say, lapses in matters of religion. We talked once, briefly, too briefly. I felt a slight sensitivity on Zalinikov's part when I inquired about his family. I didn't probe." He was anxious to return to his original point. "However, he is the one who delights: brilliant, yet modest, entirely unexpected among my students."

Ahuva cleared the dishes from the table. "Israel is a country of the unusual and the unexpected."

The Reb thought for a moment. "In fact, my love, if I didn't know Zalinikov is a Russian—*was* a Russian, I mean—except for his dreadful Hebrew accent, I'd say he was descended from Polish scholars, or was born here, an Orthodox *sabra*. That's how genuinely spiritual he is."

"A spiritual Russian, this is always good news. A few months here, maybe he'll do better than a lot of the Russians. Maybe he'll fit right into his place." She considered the sunlight filtering through the window over the sink, then her fingernails, before telling her husband that this wife—the musician, an artist, after all—must be taken slowly, with delicacy, through the soul, not the head. "This approach is not always your specialty." The Reb said nothing. "Ask Nadia about her. Nadia knows everything."

CHAPTER TEN

c)"ㆆ

Yael telephoned to say Dmitri Kanov would be in his office at ten
the next morning. "Dress simply, but distinctively. Mr. Kanov is
fond of beautiful clothes."

"Did you tell him I play the piano, or model for clothing?"

"This man is rich and smart and very sure of himself."

"Then we share two of these things."

"Do you want this job?"

Her voice brimmed over with irritation, and I imagined her face:
the two fine lines between her eyebrows, where annoyance had
worn a groove, the way she raised her chin when she was impatient,
lips pursed into an unhappy curve. "I'm not sure," I said.

"You don't have to be sure this minute." We were silent while I
considered whether working for this man would be more trouble
than pleasure, and what of Yuri? Yael was thinking what she
usually thought, and usually said, when I defied her: *Stubborn
Russian, stubborn! No wonder your country is in such a mess.*

Ha! My reply, always, before saying: *Russia is such a mess,
because being Russian is . . . messy.*

"You'll get the job. There aren't many Russian piano players in
Jerusalem with your . . ."

"My *what?*"

"I don't know the word in Russian. In Hebrew we say *makseema*.
Look in your dictionary."

"How did I acquire this thing you speak of?"

"Mother's milk."

"Tatiana didn't do breast feeding."

"Then Mother Russia's milk. Whatever or whoever put it in place,
you have it."

Makseema. I did look it up in my Hebrew-Russian dictionary.
"Adjective. Describes a person who exudes energy, charm, intelligence; who commands admiration, affection, respect." And so,
my dear, admired Yael, became one of only two Israeli friends—if
I counted Nadia, and nobody failed to count Nadia; but *she* was
still Russian, not yet Israeli, and saw the world through eyes very
much like mine.

103

⌒〕꯭҂ᴐ

To meet Dmitri Kanov, I wore red wool, a dress and jacket with brass buttons I'd bought in St. Petersburg three years earlier at a small, hidden-away boutique behind Nevsky Prospekt, patronized mostly by tourists and diplomats' wives. Yuri loved this outfit because so little in St. Petersburg was bright, except the pink and blue and green concrete apartment buildings near the Neva, and those, like most of the city, suffered from neglect.

I straightened my jacket, turning to catch sight of my rear point of view. What if I were to walk in advance of Mr. Kanov? I bent from the waist, tugging at my skirt. My mirror gave a favorable report: I was still acceptable in red. From the kitchen, Galina noises. I called to her, then called again to say, nothing, nothing. I needed fashion advice, but didn't want to get into the story of Dmitri Kanov, The White Nights.

Now she ignored my do-not-come and, carrying her coffee cup, stood in the doorway, appraising me with mild curiosity.

I told her Yael and I were meeting her friend.

"A friend? Why such a fuss with what you wear?" Her eyes had that *look*; some bit of information was being withheld, something interesting, slightly dangerous. She couldn't be certain of what it was.

I shrugged. "Today nothing looks right."

"Red, it's your color."

"Tatiana's advice," I said.

"We should always listen to Tatiana." She straightened my jacket. "You look good enough to meet a friend"—watching me, her eyes telling me she was ready for a secret.

⌒〕꯭҂ᴐ

"The White Nights Supper Club," the sign over the door read in large, white script letters scrawled across a black background. Underneath, another, smaller sign: "By Dmitri Kanov."

"*By* Dmitri Kanov," I said. "*By.* He is God?"

"Ask him," Yael said, and opened the large glass door. She wore a mauve cotton sweater matched to her skirt, and a strand of pearls. Her "American look," she called it; an altogether calm and in-charge look, I called it, that made her appear to be with authority. That day, she was two heads higher than I. Amazing, the way greater height puts one in charge of a situation, or was it simply that she had nothing at stake and could relax into each moment?

We passed through a dimly lit area with black carpeting, red velvet drapes and starched, white cotton tablecloths, each table with a single red rose in a crystal vase.

The mysterious Mr. Kanov was waiting in his office behind an enormous wooden desk, smoking a long, foul-smelling cigarette, Turkish, undoubtedly. He had a great deal of dark hair, perfectly arranged, longer than Yuri's, thinning at the top; gray eyes that seemed not to blink, and a prominent chin with one of those clefts some women—not I—think attractive. A man after all, I thought, only a man.

He stood and half bowed, a formal European gesture he probably practiced in front of a mirror, then came around the desk and took Yael's hand into his. He held it, rather than shaking it, looking directly into her eyes, an actor fully aware of his graceful movements and their effect upon his audience. Dushkin, I thought—*something* in the way he used his shoulders, his hands. Yael smiled, in her sweet, knowing way, before introducing me.

What a relief," he said, taking my hand in his powerful grip. "We can speak Russian." He smiled a smile of enormous confidence, a smile I read to mean that he forgave in advance any difficulties I experienced with the Hebrew language. A tempting offer.

A spiteful obstinacy, a refusal to allow him to assume control, made me say, "But, no"—glancing at Yael, who was examining the silver water pitcher and tray at one corner of the desk—"we must speak this country's language, after all."

Someone tapped on the door and, without waiting for Kanov to respond, came in; a slight, short man, the build of a jockey, bald, but bearded. He wore dark trousers and a red-striped vest over a crisp-white shirt. He looked from Yael to me, skipping Kanov altogether, with an expression that said, *how nice to find you here.* I liked him at once.

"Ah, Alexsei . . ." Kanov introduced us. "Tell my number one assistant what you would like to drink. Make your requests demanding; Alexsei is a master at doing the impossible."

I requested mineral water, Yael asked for coffee, Kanov, nothing. Alexsei was back within minutes, it seemed, with linen napkins, a small dish of salted cashews, and our drinks. *Who is this man?* I wondered. *Israeli? Russian? Neither?* He hadn't spoken, only nodded.

"Well." Kanov sat down behind the desk, looking first at me, then at Yael. "We three, strangers until now, drawn to this fascinating city." With a self-congratulatory look on his face, he smiled. No, he *beamed*, as though he had revealed a marvelous secret. I felt like Irina, or like Olga, in Chekhov's *Three Sisters*, sitting in front of a fire before dinner, sipping sherry, gossiping.

He continued: "I came to Jerusalem by chance, and could have just as easily settled in Berlin or Paris. Australia was also a possibility."

My turn to smile. A Russian Jew who dressed as he dressed, and knew—if Yael was to be believed—every politician, journalist, and influential businessman in the city, choosing to live in Australia? Not likely.

Yael said, "Chance had nothing to do with our moving here. My family left the States for only one reason: Jerusalem."

"And you?" Kanov said to me. "Also fated to live in Jerusalem?"

"Not at all," I said. "I had never considered it. My husband's idea."

The whole room ticked with a heavy silence while, I guessed, Kanov tried to formulate polite questions, and Yael groaned inwardly, thinking: *foolish foolish foolish.*

Ever the rescuer, she stood up and, smiling her calm, healing Yael smile, said, "Would you like to have Manya play the piano now?"

As though someone had just consulted me, I said, "Yes"— jumping to my feet—"I'd love to."

We went into the café, where a Hammerstein Baby Grand, similar to the instrument of my music teacher Madame Garbasova, stood in a far corner. It was so gloriously sculpted I could have wept as I ran my hand across the polished burled wood, then the pale ivory keys. Their sound was rich and clear, as compelling as a sorceress. I didn't ask permission, but moved immediately into a mélange of Russian folk songs, a Chopin *ballade*, a Liszt waltz.

I forgot Kanov, who was now seated nearby, waiting to be pleased. I forgot Yael. I thought only about the music. It entered my body through my fingers, flowed through my blood, settled in my brain and on the endings of nerves, pulling me back to my lost life, to Tatiana, in her flaming-fuchsia chiffon tunic and pearls, tapping out the measures with her curved, scarlet fingernails, urging me on, making me feel I was a rare treasure, *her* rare treasure.

Pausing, I was startled when Kanov applauded. He came over to the piano and playfully tapping his fist against the music rack, said, "Yes, yes, yes, you're quite wonderful. Hired."

"Didn't I tell you as much?" Yael said. She fussed with her silk scarf, her smile too bright, too fixed in place, like a plea for all of us to get along.

Kanov looked down at me, his eyebrows raised in a show of expectancy, as though he thought it would be a good idea if I jumped up from the piano bench and hugged him.

"So quickly?" I said. My voice was edgy, one millimeter short of being disagreeable. For a moment, he seemed about to sit down next to me. I shifted awkwardly. When I caught the warning in Yael's eyes, I shifted back.

"But why delay? When I see something I like"—Kanov snapped his fingers.

Yael laughed a watery laugh and said, "I like a man who knows his mind."

"And you, Manya," Kanov said, turning to me. "What kind of man do you like?"

A question from a spy movie. All background music and innuendo, a guitar strum, the moan of a cello. We needed the European movie star Paul Henreid to enter, two cigarettes between his lips: one for himself, the other for the female. Kanov's gray eyes were smoky now, but alert, somewhat amused. *He's made me uncomfortable, and he's glad.* "A wholly human kind of man, a Yuri-kind of man," I said finally, probably startling Yael. Kanov looked confused. "Yuri, my husband."

࿇

The only way to tell Yuri I had taken a job playing the piano in a Russian restaurant—*restaurant* being a safer name for The White Nights than *supper club*, which evoked images of interesting-looking men and sensuous women bending toward one another over drinks—was to tell him. Directly, without frills, or what he called my *un-lying lies*, figures of speech that papered over difficult or unpleasant facts. Such as: *habitually talkative*, for the elderly Ukranian woman who came to our flat to alter my clothes and stopped chattering only long enough to drink gallons of my expensive, difficult to procure Crimean herbal tea.

I opened the subject the following morning at breakfast.

"How soon?" Yuri said.

"Saturday."

He blinked. "Saturday . . . the Sabbath?" He set his newspaper aside.

"Saturday evening, after dark, after Sabbath, long after Sabbath." *Don't, please, don't ask about the man who owns the restaurant. Don't ask what he looks like, if he's nice, polite; don't ask if he's one of the good Russians, or a Dushkin kind.*

"Why?" He poured another spoon of sugar into his tea, the third.

I ducked and reached for the cigarettes I kept secreted in my purse for crisis moments; one, just one, to get me through this. Fiddling with the unlit cigarette, not brave enough to take it out of the pack, I watched Yuri stir his tea, and wait for my answer, regretting my decision to take the job, flip-flopping on the question of whether this smooth, overly fashionable person Kanov was to be trusted, or was too much the shallow egotist, and why did it matter? I returned the cigarettes to the purse. "We can use the money," I said. "I can use the music."

"And the Reb?"

"Who?"

"Reb Turrowtaub, Nadia's cousin."

"Oh . . . him."

"*Him*, yes." He spoke softly, but an edge of sarcasm. "Two, three times every week I study with him in his home. I thought you lived with me, aware, interested. I read texts and *Torah*. What do you think is going on in my life? Do you see me anymore?"

His face was tragic. I had no answer, only regret. Could I, even if I tried, even if I studied *Torah,* and advanced Hebrew, and an introduction to kosher cooking, and wore a marriage wig, and learned how to haggle with the vendors at the Agrippa Market, and sat upstairs with the other women at synagogue services, could I ever in my lifetime be what he needed me to be?

"Later," I said, "not now."

"*When*, later?" The tic beat in the corner of his eye. He looked close to tears. *Don't, please don't, not here, not now. Wait—until you're alone, so we won't have to talk about the ruin our marriage has become.*

We sat looking at one another, not speaking. I heard birds calling out from the thick bushes we'd planted at the edge of the patio, then the frantic beating of wings that announced a traffic accident among them, two birds reaching for the same cluster of seeds or worm at the same moment.

Yuri cleared his throat, a call for attention. He wouldn't believe the kind of attention I wanted to give him. I wanted to lick his pale, dry lips with my tongue, slide it into his mouth; play the tricks we played our early married years, grasping one another's face and breathing hard.

"When?" I asked, without energy, knowing I couldn't say when.

A tender sorrow came into his eyes. Pressing forward, he reached for me, his long, gentle fingers smoothing the hair from my forehead.

"I can wait," he said, "I'm good at waiting."

⌇⌇⌇

On that Saturday evening, I arrived at The White Nights Supper Club in a state of anxiety, dressed as I'd seen Tatiana prepare for a wedding or holiday ball: her flaming-red chiffon tunic, black velvet evening skirt, a triple strand of pearls, my hair brushed into an intricate chignon, where I anchored an oyster-white camelia, thinking, as I placed it exactly-so, that I could be a sensation, or I could be home in an hour in tears.

Galina had insisted upon coming with me "to hold your hand while you play." My daughter was herself dressed for a party in a black silk dress, clever rhinestone earrings, hair twisted into a black velvet snood. "Are you excited, nervous? Which?"

"Yes . . . no. Both. I haven't played music in months."

She watched me finish with my cosmetics. "This man, Mr. Kanov, what is he like? Difficult to please? An enormous ego, like most men?"

"Always the cynic. A businessman. He wants the full value for his shekels spent."

"Enough shekels to make you nervous?"

"Who appears nervous?" My voice was sharper than I'd intended.

She fidgeted with my makeup brushes. "His name is everywhere in the newspaper columns. Some of the words to describe him are *mysterious, powerful, brilliant,* and"—she smiled—"*sought-after.*"

"Who is seeking him?"

"Everyone." She touched her earlobes with a drop of my most expensive perfume, Marquis de Sade. "Many times married, many times divorced. The stories make one believe he is something of a . . . a magician, almost."

"More of an iceberg. Ninety percent of him down underneath, and unknowable."

✦

We left the house before Yuri returned from evening prayers, my note taped to our bathroom mirror: "Galina and I will be home before midnight, pray for me." Would he see this last as irreverent? I wavered, in the end erasing it, adding, "I love you, M."

The White Nights was only half filled when we arrived, but something seductive, as palpable as perfume, permeated the room: the combined aroma of beautifully dressed women and attentive men, the roses on the tables, scented candles, the clink of silver against china against soft, murmuring voices. My skin told me I had been in a room like this before. The Dragonfly Club on Rostrosky Parkway, open only to Russians with special identity cards. Open to my parents, with special letters of approval from powerful friends. So. This place was to be the Second Coming, courtesy of that magician Kanov.

The thought brought the man. Kanov stepped into the small cloak area just behind the dining room, in a velvet-collared tuxedo—*velvet*, chosen for impressing, of course— hair arranged exactly-so, gold cuff links. I felt a slight thrum of pleasure when he clasped my hand as I introduced him to Galina; she, staring—no, *gawking*.

He stretched his arms out, embracing empty air, and grinned, as though to exclaim: *What a surprise, the three of us meeting here! How grand it is to be us, how grand to be alive, and what a coincidence that this moment is the best possible moment in which to be together in this very place.*

I caught the contagion of his exuberance, half expecting him to invite me to dance. Suddenly serious, he rubbed his hands together. "But we must speak of music. My clients enjoy anything soothing. Jerusalem is so . . . tense."

"Anxiety," Galina said, "the national Israeli disease."

"Exactly!" He clapped. "You have a brilliant daughter."

Galina's face bloomed with color. "Well, then," I said, not knowing what else to say, and moved toward the dining room, the two of them behind me.

The piano gleamed, even in the dim light. I patted it as one would a loved child, tinkering with the keys; middle C appeared to be in tune.

"Perfect?" Kanov looked childishly eager. "We want it to be perfect for you."

"Nothing is fully perfect." Disappointment clouded his eyes. "But this is close." I went on with my tinkering; pressing, listening, pressing. "Seven o'clock," I said, finally, "a good time to begin."

Galina cleared her throat. Of course. Dinner. We hadn't eaten at home; I never do before performing. "Is it possible for my daughter to have a light supper?"

He stood silent for a moment, not moving. I wondered if he'd heard me. Then he became all motion and energy, snapping his fingers, nodding to a waiter—who hurried over and listened to him whisper something, the young man bobbing his head as though he'd been asked a question—before beckoning Galina to a corner table near the piano. Moments later, Kanov joined her, and a chill of unease swept through me.

I played Viennese waltzes, mazurkas by Chopin, arias from Rimsky-Korsakov and Borodin operas, Saint Saëns's *The Carnival of the Animals*, and that confection *Für Elise*. When the conversations turned the room into a buzzing hive, I turned to a medley of French and Italian operetta tunes remembered from adolescent afternoons spent with Tatiana in small, private music halls.

My relationship with my music was so intimate, of such a long history, I didn't have to think about the notes—they were part of my muscles' memory—but could, at the same time, watch, without watching, Galina's table. Now she and Kanov laughed, in the easy manner of close friends; now he wandered off to tend to business, returning to once again amuse my daughter with a funny story of Russia, a witty observation of Israeli life. Or, so I guessed. Everything he said made her laugh. A sophisticate, at home anywhere in the world, this man. For those moments, Galina—amused, delighted, flirtatious—was his avid student. And I— I watched, hoping my daughter would not fly higher than a height from which she could easily climb down.

✥

What country am I in, I wondered as I played. Whose city? The only certainty was the music. I wrapped it around myself, almost able to *see* the notes as they rose, lifting, then lifting still higher, until the ceiling was coated with music, and why was everyone speaking that strange-sounding, unmusical language?

Several diners sent waiters with wine. I thanked them in my limping Hebrew, but refused, and one man—a diplomat, to judge from the small tri-colored pin in his lapel—came to the piano himself, and attempted to pass several paper shekels to me. "*Todah, todah,*" thank you, he said, spewing scotch fumes, and bowed: a deep, dramatic sweep that almost undid his balance.

"*Boker tov,*" I said, and waved away the knot of paper money he held out, not realizing, until he laughed, then repeated and translated my words, that I had told him, "Good morning."

✥

At eleven o'clock, I gathered my music and, looking to Galina, who, at that moment, sat alone, nodded a we-are-leaving nod. She raised her glass, puffed her cheeks, and blew out; a sweet, silly gesture

112

from her adolescence. So, tonight had made her happy. Good. Or, perhaps, not so good.

I turned toward a burst of noise behind me. Yael. "You were, *are*, sensational," she said, pulling me into a vigorous hug. "I've never heard you play. It isn't fair; beautiful, brilliant, and now a talented musician." Such flattery from Yael tied my tongue, but she needed no response, and went on to say she'd had dinner with friends, then stopped in to listen from the doorway, and now had to run to pick up her husband from a boring business evening. "Is that Galina?" She waved her over to us.

"You have met our Mr. Kanov?" My daughter gave a recitation about Kanov's marvelous everything. Yael sniffed skepticism. "Pure alpha male, that's American for power package, in charge." She ran her hand across her chest. "Silk-screen that on a T-shirt."

⌇⌇⌇

Since that evening, I have asked myself many times why some of us are placed in the vast universe, among all those other places where we might find ourselves, exactly where we don't wish to be, or where, for our own well-being, we shouldn't be? As we waited for a taxi at the curb, a white, un-Russian-looking limousine pulled up, and a chauffeur hopped out and opened the back door for three large men in dark suits. The last man to emerge, the tallest, the slimmest, carried a briefcase.

Something about this man—strong appearing, hair combed into a perfect pompadour, his every movement precise, as though he were a performer—nudged my memory. It had to do with the way he stopped, taking a lighter and cigarette case from the pocket of his jacket, tapped the cigarette on the case, lit it, inhaled, and blew a series of smoke rings. He was aware of being watched, of being worth watching.

Galina grasped my arm, and I *knew*. He glanced at us, glanced away, then looked back. He asked his companions, who were about to open the door to the club, to wait. Stepping toward us, he said, "Ah, Mrs. Zelman . . . Zinkoff . . . I've forgotten." His eyes were alert, excited; his manner radiated calm and control. "You must excuse me, I am not good at remembering names. It is faces I never forget. In any case"—he extended his hand.

"Zalinikova," I said. "Manya," and shook his hand without enthusiasm.

"St. Petersburg," he said.

"I meet so many people."

A flash of irritation in his eyes, then his face relaxed into a smile, and he turned to Galina. "Your daughter, I believe. Not easily forgotten." She pressed against me.

"Are you here on holiday?" he said.

"Very much like a holiday." I looked past him, hoping to see our taxi. "And you?"

He smiled, but his eyes were cold and fixed on me. "I would like to say the same, but I have little time for pleasure these days."

"You've come to a good city," Galina said, "if you are not looking for pleasure." Neither Dushkin nor I said anything. "I mean, Jerusalem is a serious place, and"—she looked suddenly flustered—"no bridges. Can you imagine, a city without bridges?"

I looked again for our taxi. Dushkin flicked ashes, regarding his cigarette as though it were something strange, then crushed it under his boot. "One must pay close attention to business, or one is left behind. Isn't that so, Mrs. Zalinikova?"

"It is so if you say it is so."

"We must have similar tastes; this is my favorite Jerusalem club. Do you know Dmitri Kanov?" When I hesitated, he said, "The proprietor, do you know him?"

He was playing with me now, the way he said *proprietor,* as though it were a royal title. "No," I said. "I mean, yes. Slightly."

"An interesting man, Dmitri. We are old friends, from our school days in Kharkov. But, please"—he raised his chin and half closed his eyes, as though delighted with what he was about to say, a gesture I remembered from his visit to our market stall—"come inside. We'll have a drink together, the four of us."

He stepped toward me as I stepped back, bringing along Galina, whose arm was now wrapped around mine. I glanced at his two companions, who were all muscled attention, waiting at the door to the club. Each man was taller than six feet, and both of them wore sunglasses, although it was almost midnight.

Our taxi pulled up to the curb, and I moved toward it with as much calm as I could manage, pulling Galina along. At the door, now feeling safe, I turned back while Galina clambered into the automobile.

Dushkin took another cigarette from his case. "I meant no pressure." He shrugged. "Fellow travelers from the same country, meeting this way. It is, you must admit . . ."

"It is . . ."

"*Kismet*," he said. "Not a Russian word, *kismet*."

"Turkish."

"Yes." He looked annoyed, that small, stingy upward curve of the lips; but his voice continued in its smooth, flat way: "A kind of destiny, meeting you so many thousands of miles from home." The night air was mild, Jerusalem was much warmer than St. Petersburg, but he turned his collar up and looked at the sky, as though expecting rain.

"*Kismet*," I said, through the open window of the taxi. Terror or not, I wanted to leave him with the sense that I, not he, was fully in charge. "I must learn to speak this word in Hebrew."

"*Goral*."

"It seems you know everything, Mr. Dushkin."

"Only everything I need to know, Mrs Zalinikova."

Chapter Eleven

So. Our friend with the threatening gun was now flying between countries—to do what? Extorting protection money from assorted small businesses was not sufficiently profitable to provide airline tickets, a suite at the Hilton or the King David Hotel, a uniformed chauffeur. Kanov was too shrewd to pay for these amenities if Dushkin were not providing *something* of value: information, drugs, foreign currency, diamonds?

Diamonds. Stones pulled from the earth. One of the many interesting, but obscure, facts I had learned since I had begun reading the Jerusalem Hebrew-language daily newspapers was about diamonds, pulled out of the earth by terrified, poorly paid black persons, working for guerillas in between their fights in African civil wars.

In Africa, always a civil war to be found. The guerillas—feverish with revolutionary zeal, usually rich in facial hair, gaunt, in a bizarre way, surprisingly clever at commerce—then sold these diamonds to dealers, using the money to purchase arms. A grim cycle, full of irony and death.

And so, I guessed, the diamonds would be sold by Kanov to his Israeli contacts, experts in buying and selling precious stones—the profits divided between himself and Dushkin—to be fashioned into jewelry for tourists. So much the better for everyone, retail prices in Israel for this vanity being lower than in Belgium, Amsterdam, New York.

The following morning I telephoned to Yael to tell her of my diamond narrative.

"You jump from zero to one hundred," she said, "in the space of a second." I was certain, judging from the wrinkle of superiority in her voice, that her eyes held that funny little squint, the smart-little-girl look she summoned when saying something intelligent, which was often. "It isn't a crime to show up in Jerusalem with a briefcase and a hired car, or to have a friend who owns a night club. Two Russians, friends in school, what could be more innocent? You have an—"

"To show up? What does this mean, *to show up*?"

"It's English, no, *American* slang for making a sudden or unexpected appearance. *Aglahoh*, slang. In Russian to show up is . . . I don't know."

"We have no such word in Russian, *show up*, and I know nothing of that *aglah* word. I am attempting speaking in Hebrew, I am thinking in Russian, and now I am facing a third language: American."

"Manya." Her scolding voice. "Can we talk about your friend, Dushkin? Be prepared to hear from him. Nothing you've told me makes me think he'll be shy about punishing you and Yuri for skipping out on him."

"Skipping out?"

"Meet me for lunch. With my slippery Russian and your budding Hebrew, face-to-face is much better than the telephone."

She suggested the Veggie Garden, a health-food café on Ben Yehuda Mall, next to the T- shirt shop. I remembered seeing the sign over the window. "Yes, yes, but what is a veggie?"

❦

I arrived first, and walked along the Ben Yehuda pedestrian mall—a mixed-up collection of cafés, clothing, jewelry and music shops, with a few money-changing kiosks thrown in—mingling with the shoppers, tourists, the young people out to inspect, and be inspected. Amazing, these Israelis. Every one of these lively, here-to-enjoy-themselves persons got up this morning, dressed, ate breakfast, and left the house, not thinking that today could be the day they could be blown up. A talent, an art, a gift, learned along with learning how to suck their mother's milk.

The Veggie Garden was anything but a garden. More a cavern, seven or eight cube-sized tables, one up against the other. Diners gave their orders to a girl behind the counter and, on a fine day, carried their trays to the outdoor tables.

That day, the aroma of squash, zucchini, carrots, red peppers, simmering in chicken broth, brought Tatiana's kitchen into my head. I stood in the doorway and stared into the small space, where now only two teenage boys were eating, and dreamed Tatiana onto one of the empty chairs.

This Israel, she would like. She would love the fresh fruit and vegetables stacked in bright pyramids in the Agrippa Market, the street singers in embroidered caftans and head scarves, strumming zithers, shaking tambourines on street corners. She would love the way little children wandered in the parks from picnic to picnic, as though their own little selves were gifts to be appreciated by the grownups; tasting a little tahini here, some pomegranate there, happy this day had no bombs, happy that *ema*—Mama—was happy, today, anyway, in a city where peacetime was also wartime.

Now I ordered two bowls of soup, two salads, pumpernickel bread, grated cheese, carrying my tray outside, and there was Yael under the shade of an umbrella. I waited for her to begin her soup, for the gypsy child who hovered at our table for coins to take several and leave, for the birds chirping in the tree just next to our table to be quiet, and repeated my diamond theory.

"Unbelievable," she said, and continued eating.

"Some people will do anything for money."

"It's the evidence of your theory that's unbelievable: a briefcase, a limousine, a false smile from a man you dislike."

"Dislike? *Loathe.* Dushkin's not here to talk about schooldays with Kanov." Manya blew at her soup. "Where does Kanov get his money? He opens a supper club, buys an enormous house, parties in Eilat?"

"I cannot say," she said, "and anyone who does know won't tell you. What makes you feel entitled to know?"

"I will not work for a criminal."

"So, this is your good citizen conscience speaking?" She started on her salad. Apparently arguing during lunch didn't dull Yael's appetite. "You will telephone the police when you have your answers?"

"Perhaps. I was there for Dushkin's evil smile when he lit his cigarette and played with Yuri. Cruel. I cannot bear cruelty. Yuri had done nothing to him, and still he took pleasure in seeing his naked fear, Yuri caught on the end of his dagger. What angers me is your refusal to understand."

"Manya, Manya, you would be so much happier if you didn't attempt to control the world, putting everyone, everything into categories. You go day to day asking, is this good for me? No?" She looked up. "Out it goes. Is this other thing good for me? Yes? It stays."

Later, lunch over, the memory of Yael's word stung as I walked onto King George Street to the Supersol food market six blocks away. If not diamonds, then something else illegal, and immoral. With or without Yael, I'd discover what.

ᝌᐤ

On many days, shopping in an Israeli supermarket was an exercise in controlling your blood pressure. First, at the entrance, the usually old man sitting on the high stool reading his newspaper, irritated by being interrupted to inspect purses, briefcases, packages, this being the only country in the world where one was searched on the way *into* a shop. That day, my inspector waved me into the store with his usual glum indifference. The only persons comparable to these old men are the plump, dour *babushkas*, old women pension-ers, stationed on chairs in the corners of every gallery in every museum in Russia, eyeing the viewers, waiting to pounce should anyone stand too close to a painting, place a finger on a sculpture, or sneeze on anything other than another viewer.

My least-favorite cashier was a short woman about sixty years of age, built like the letter *I* in the American alphabet, three warts on her chin and always another radiantly colored, sequined bow pinned onto the back of her wiry, bleached blonde hair. That day she stood at her register.

She and I did not agree on anything. Either I was mistaken about the price of the tomatoes I had bagged, or the thin rye crackers I had seen advertised as being on sale were not on sale, and could I please speak to the manager.

I deposited my food on her conveyor belt one second before she posted the "Closed" notice, bringing the sign down on my hand. No and no and *no*. She would not, even if the Prime Minister asked, check me out. I must go to another place. She pointed to a web of lines, each one inhabited by at least ten shoppers.

We shouted at one another; I, louder than she. In Russia, should two people shout as we did, someone would run for the security officer. "Why are you so rude?" I said, finally, in terrible Hebrew, made more terrible by my choked fury.

"Ha," she barked, "we have here a philosopher." She reached behind her head to pull at the bow, which, by now, was wobbling. "Now I will ask you a question. Why am I so late for going home; is that a good enough *why*?"

Customers in line at the next cashier barely looked up. Rage in the supermarket, a common disease. Rage anywhere in Jerusalem is no surprise; it is people's fear turned inside-out. Rage in the Knesset, in the automobiles, at the post office and gas stations and banks. Like the weather, it is hardly noticed.

Mila—her name, written on a badge pinned to her black smock—pushed a button beneath the counter, summoning the manager, who was short and wide and belligerent, whisker hairs in his nose, and black gypsy eyes. His name tag read: Sebastian. Turkish, or Greek. One more prize for Israeli diversity.

Sebastian listened to my woes, then turned and shouted, "Mila," at the woman, who now was at the far end of the counter filing her nails and did not look up. Fierce in the face, he walked to her. "We do not slam down our signs on the fingers of customers."

"I did not slam," Mila said, filing. "I tapped. Her finger got into my path."

I held up my little finger. "Certainly." I loved that word, *betakh;* it gave me the chance to pronounce my terrible *ach* ending, my impolite gargle.

"I will charge your items over there." Sebastian pointed to a nearby cash register. To his credit, his expressive dark eyes were expressing genuine sorrow.

It was not Sebastian's sorrow I wanted. "If you do not mind," I said, "I am owed an apology." Sorry. Mila, no longer filing, patted her hair and looked at me down the length of the counter, sniffed, but said nothing.

A bearded young man in a yellow poncho—a student, to judge from his handbag of books—stood behind me. "I saw," he said. "She put the sign down"—he demonstrated, one hand slicing over the other—"on this lady's hand. Hard." His accent sounded Mideastern, with a splash of European.

"Liar," Mila called out. "Don't believe a Sufi, one of those crazy students hanging out at the Institute, plotting God knows what."

Sebastian, his round face a mask of irritated patience, turned to the young man. "It is now"—he consulted his wristwatch—"six minutes past five o'clock. Since getting out of bed this morning, I have been sorry for dozens, for hundreds of things. If I apologized for all, we would be here until midnight."

He turned back to me. "Please, check out. Let us have no more international incidents." He nodded toward a nearby freezer case. "Do you have children, grandchildren?" I didn't respond. "My apology for this incident. Take yourself popsicles, ice cream, frozen mud pies." Still, no one looked up from their shopping carts, or stopped selecting frozen juices from the freezer cases, or comparing red grapes with green grapes.

I left with my packages, without popsicles, stopping at the old man on the inspector's stool, who was now reading a book on *Mysticism and the Kaballah.* "Would you like to inspect my bag?" I said. Watery gray eyes squinted up at me. I rattled my plastic bag open. "Maybe I stole the bottled water, or the lemons, some tomatoes."

"Lady, lady, what do you say? Carry *out* anything. I am here to stop you from carrying inside a bomb. *Hefetz Hashood.* I look for suspicious packages on their way in. Carry out the whole store, I don't care."

"Thank you, one time I will. That expensive imported Russian caviar, I'll take a dozen cans, you'll promise not to inspect my bag."

"You are welcome." Still seated, he half bowed.

At the corner I stopped at the flower stall for a spring bouquet, reds and oranges, blazing yellows, to sing in a glass vase on my kitchen counter. This flower habit, bringing them home from a flower kiosk—all over Jerusalem, a kiosk on every other corner—is the nicest Israeli custom I've discovered. Especially so on the Sabbath, bouquets going home with some family member to brighten the house, to add their aroma to all the kitchen smells permeating the Sabbath eve. Except in our house, where the kitchen smells were usually burned smells.

I hadn't told this to Yuri, but the lowering the decibel level of this city, the thought of a family at dinner with wine and candlelight; these rituals delighted. If, along with the candles and flowers and dinner, I did not have to affirm my belief in God, I would lower my own decibel level, and bless the Sabbath. Occasionally.

The old lady with the gold hoop earrings the size of small wheels, and the gauzy blouses that exposed her brassiere straps and freckled shoulders, was at her hat kiosk at the next corner. Had I been in a better mood, I would have stopped and tried on one bowl-shaped velvet hat after another, pulling them down, down, over my head, until they swallowed my ears. Pot without handles, I called them, looking, in each one, like a fervent-eyed, bald person of an uncertain age.

Today I hurried past, feeling the hat seller's eyes burning into my head, holding up my bunch of flowers as a greeting, patting my wristwatch.

"*Meookhar*," she called out? "Late?"

I nodded without waving. "*Cain, cain.*" Yes, yes. "*Makhar.*" Tomorrow. Another of my favorite gargling words.

By the time I arrived at my street, I knew I could not remain annoyed with Yael. I would phone, half apologize for my sour mood at lunch, concede that perhaps, only perhaps, Kanov and Dushkin *were* dealing in diamonds. But, considering the ugly nature of most Mafia dealings in Russia, diamonds were a clean choice, better than oil, and think of the beauty these gems bring to the world.

From the kitchen window, I saw Yuri on the patio reading the newspaper, a small, pale, completely round spot the size of a large button beginning to show beneath the thinning hair on the top of his scalp. I could have cried. That bald spot seemed more intimate a sight than if I had seen him sitting outside naked.

I realized, if we were lucky, we would grow old together; me, with my spreading hips, the dark smudges under my eyes, brown spots like raisins sprinkled across the backs of my hands. I watched him slump further into his chair. *Yuri, Yuri, don't die before I do.*

I carried two glasses of soda and lime to the patio, and sat down opposite him. "Hello."

I slid one glass across the table. My smile felt starched, false.

He looked at me as though waiting to be introduced. "I came home for lunch; you were gone."

"You didn't announce coming home for lunch."

"You didn't ask."

"No afternoon studies, no discussion groups?"

"I wanted to hear about your new job."

I felt suddenly shy, as though he'd asked about something too intimate to discuss. "Too soon to say."

I waited. "Good." He didn't look happy. "A good thing to like your work, especially when it occupies your evenings. The owner"—I felt a faint quickening in my chest—"he is nice?"

"Very." I hesitated. "Usually. Sometimes Mr. Kanov is a little temperamental. But who is not?" He smiled. The old Yuri, the St. Petersburg Yuri. I didn't want to say this then, I didn't want to say it ever, but I did. "There's a complication."

"With Mr. Kanov?"

"With his friend, Dushkin." I expected an instant performance of the eye tick, I expected him to tremble, his hands, at least. I expected a pale, anxious face. He said nothing, as though he'd forgotten who Dushkin was. "Dushkin," I said, "the market stall, the gun."

He nodded.

"Well"—I pressed forward, my hand on the table next to his, in case he needed me to soothe him. I told him about our street meeting, about my diamond theory—"Yael thinks I'm wrong, too hysterical."

A small, sad smile. "Yael is correct."

"You don't see Dushkin coming to Jerusalem as terrible news?

He's doing something illegal; if not diamonds, then—"

"He can go straight into hell."

That caught my attention. "You never speak this way."

He sipped, glancing at me over his glass, a glance that, in any other man would have been seen as teasing. But this was Yuri, no mischief, no teasing, straightforward, kind, reasoning Yuri.

"Israel is changing me. The Reb himself says, if one feels the need for a few swear words occasionally, nothing extreme, say them. Better for your health than swallowing down your emotions."

The Reb. I should have known his finger would be somewhere in this mix. "Cheaper than a psychiatrist, your friend. Does he, this scholar of the Torah, swear?"

"Rarely." He blushed. "Sometimes."

"That's the nicest thing you've said about him."

"What harm can Dushkin do to us here? We have no commercial business; he makes no profit from us."

"Nevertheless"—one of the few Hebrew words I loved, *bechol zot*; so commanding—"I don't trust him."

"Is he a friend of Mr. Kanov's?"

"Schoolboys together."

"Nice friends, your Mr. Kanov has."

"He's not *my* Mr. Kanov."

"As I think about it"—I started to say something, but he plunged on—"let us say Mr. Kanov, coming out of Russia, a difficult country, and he of more-than-average intelligence, is a man who knows how to survive."

"*Survive!* This man is very wealthy."

"This is not a criticism. Noah built an ark, Joseph found a coat of many colors"—a grin slipped out, an actual grin, such as I had not seen since before he lost his job—"Abraham wanted a son. Sarah was too old, he consulted with her maid."

"And so . . . *so?*"

"So, Noah, Joseph, and Abraham and Mr. Kanov are survivors. If one of his friends is a Dushkin, so be it."

I felt suddenly exhausted. Too many people, too many opposite ideas. Where did one go in this country to simply *be?* "Is this your Torah portion for this week?"

His cheeks flamed. "I'm preaching?"

"Yes."

He shrugged and picked up the newspaper.

His hand was on the table; I covered it with mine. "I like sitting here with you, talking like grown-up, rational people. No anger or accusations."

He smiled. "Any time."

"*Any time*?"

"Any time sounds too . . . modern? I learned it in the card parlor behind Minkoff's Delicatessen on Ben Yehuda Mall. I went there with the Reb." He saw my look of astonishment. "Once, only once."

"My God!" It slipped out.

"Manya, *please*."

"Sorry, sorry, sorry. Did you win?"

"Nothing. I lost maybe twenty shekels. I didn't play cards in Russia, remember?"

"You didn't do a lot of things in Russia."

"Such as . . ."

"Pray."

His eyes took on their Jerusalem look. "Come with me."

"To Minkoff's?"

"To the synagogue one morning. Any morning."

"What would I do at the synagogue? I'm not counted as part of the *minyan,* women don't count."

"Of course women count; you deliberately distort."

"Let us begin at the beginning. Present in the synagogue are eight Jews, all male—"

"This is a story?"

"A fable. Morning prayers can't begin, two Jews are missing to make up the *minyan.* Prayers are delayed."

"You cannot simply—"

"The door opens and Yuri and Manya Zalinikov appear. We now have ten Jews, but only nine are male. So . . . do we have a *minyan*?"

"Manya, Manya"—he looked sorrowful, but not apologetic—"so good with words, and yet, so . . ."

"Yes—*so*?"

"So afraid of what happens between the words." He stood up. "I am sorry to leave."

"You are going . . . where?"

"The library at the theological seminary."

He slid open the glass door to the house but, before going inside, turned and looked at me. I hoped he would say something: *I miss you, I need you. I—you. Us.* A sentence not with love in it, but a sentence that was loving. He hesitated, his face clouded, no doubt with feelings that, in the same moment, stretched in two opposite directions.

"An important man, the Reb," I said. "Don't keep him waiting."

Chapter Twelve

If any moment could be recognized as the turning point in my struggle against Yuri's plunge into religion, it was *that* moment, a late April day splendid with tender breezes and sunshine, a sky bursting with its royal-blue colorings, the ancient apple tree edging our patio, a family of noisy sparrows serenading, my husband opening the patio door, and me watching him pass through it to his other, his new life.

And, if any action can be seen as pushing me toward uncertainty and, yes, even danger, rather than in the opposite direction, toward what I will call—for lack of a more perfect word—loving passivity, it was my picking up the telephone in our kitchen, calling the Reb, to ask: "Could we meet, please?"

He was silent, then a whoosh of breath into the receiver, and a hearty, too hearty, as though he'd been expecting me, which gave me a butterfly stomach, "With pleasure." He was not busy for the next hour; reading, but he could always read. "Come now."

In the taxi I rehearsed my speech. *You have no right to kidnap my husband's mind for the purpose of reshaping his soul. Yuri has chosen Israel, and un-chosen me.* Is un-chosen an actual word? Not important. I wouldn't have the talents to keep up with this man in the matter of language anyway.

The Reb would likely say that he hadn't known Yuri from the other thousands of Russians arriving in Israel daily, that Yuri came looking for him, that Yuri chose for himself. However, to be less literal, and more subjective, and I *am* subjective, Yuri, being new to this business—a risky word to use here, *business*; the Reb told me at our first face-to-face meeting that religion was not a business—and Yuri being new to Israel and to being Jewish, he was perfect for someone with the Reb's powers of persuasion.

To prepare for our conflict—I had no doubt that conflict described what would happen between us—I tried to guess what he would say next. He could say, in fact, he *did* say, in the Old City when we drank coffee, that Yuri was coming home to his own history, was becoming, in his every day practices, what he'd always been in spirit underneath the layers of unreligious Russian life.

This argument would taunt, being beyond my ability to understand, and certainly beyond my ability to answer. Isn't that what religion often becomes: somebody's personal translation of the meaning of the universe wrapped up in fancy language, glossed over with elaborate and puzzling rituals, repeated numerous times with conviction, until other somebodies, and then still more somebodies, enlarge it, and pass it on?

⌇

The Reb lived on the opposite side of Independence Park, only ten minutes by taxi, on a respectable street of spacious houses, well-tended bushes and lawns, and budding trees; a street, *sabras* liked to say, of Americans temporarily transplanted to Israel, made prosperous by paying lower income taxes to the US government than they would to the Israeli government.

My taxi driver, an old man in an ancient woolen army jacket and squashed army cap, squinted at the address posted on a wooden board nailed onto a tree at the curb, and pulled into the gravel driveway. His name, Boris Oransky, was sewn onto the jacket where his medals might have once been pinned. Throughout the ride, he'd said nothing. Silence in an Israeli taxi driver is unusual; so unusual, it's sometimes seen as ominous. Now he turned his head, holding out his hand.

"Eight shekels." A menacing smile flashed.

"Eight?" A shocking amount for a ten-minute ride.

"Lady, lady." He swung his head around to look at the white stucco house, then back to me. "I don't live in such a nice place. I only drive people who do."

"I don't live in this place either."

With that, the front door swung open, and there was the Reb, smiling, beckoning.

I nodded to him and held my hand up, to signify important business in progress. "But your meter is blank, you didn't turn it on."

"Better without," the driver said.

"Better for who?" I got out of the taxi and stood at the driver's side. "For you, I recognize you're Russian, seven shekels."

"You have trouble?" the Reb called.

"None," I said, giving the driver six shekels.

He counted the coins, and looked up, his mouth sour. "No tip?" A sudden glint of evil understanding came into his eyes. "Oh, now I see, you're from Moscow. Terrible thieves, Muscovites."

"Can I help?" the Reb called, and began moving toward us.

"No, please, I'm fine," I called back. "We're discussing geography."

The driver saluted, taking off, then putting his cap back on his head. "Welcome to Israel, lady. We need lots of people like you." With an abrupt skidding of tires, gravel scattering wildly in all directions, he drove off.

The Reb came down the path and grasped my hand in both of his. "Taxi drivers are an everyday problem in Israel. Come, I'm in the library." He led me through several light-filled rooms, populated by shining wooden floors, glass-topped tables, inviting upholstered chairs, tall, palmy plants. Beautiful objects were everywhere. I wanted to pause, to exclaim over a vase or dish, a painting; but he didn't stop until we reached a large, paneled room with bookshelves to the ceiling, and, at the far end, a fireplace with a carved wooden mantelpiece. The entire back wall of the room was glass, windows and double doors, leading, I guessed, onto a garden.

The Reb watched me scrutinize the very large portrait above the mantel—a woman of middle age, wearing a stiff marriage wig and an overpowering dark dress trimmed in lace. Her eyes were tragic.

"My mother," he said, "just before I left Poland. A saint."

"Did she leave as well?"

He shook his head. "I never saw her again; the Holocaust, everyone in my family"—he snapped his fingers—"poof." Now *his* eyes were tragic. "Our middle child, Emanuela, was named for her. Eva, her name was Eva."

So—he and I had the same sorrow, both of us losing much-loved mothers. I looked at him with new eyes, not expecting a rush of sympathy between us, but hoping for some possibility of agreement. Should I mention how impressed I was with the house, or should I begin at once about Yuri? Fortunately, he took over and invited me to please, sit, sit, *there*, opposite his desk, where he sat down.

Was Ahuva at home? I listened for sounds, and caught the rich, delicious scent of chicken soup, but no noise. My stomach reminded me that I was terrified of this man, my most developed enemy in a place where there was no shortage of enemies.

He opened and closed a series of drawers, looking up at me from time to time with a sweet expression, as though his next sentence could be, "How nice to see you."

I squirmed in my chair, but said nothing. "You wished to speak with me, Mrs. Zalinikova?" That he used *wished*, a more flowery word than *wanted*—which, in contrast, seemed demanding, harsher—was not lost on me. He hoped flattery would take him where disagreement would not. What remained a mystery was why Yuri was such an important prize to him.

His question was the hand that opened up the dam. Out poured my full feelings, an encyclopedia of feelings, about him, about the happiness Yuri and I had shared for more than twenty years, about how being an Orthodox Jew was not a possibility for me or our daughter, ending with, why couldn't my little family be Israeli and Jewish in a—a less serious way? Immediately, I regretted that word, *serious.*

His face was a mask; no anger, no denial—nothing. Dangerous, however, for me to take a peaceful face for agreement. He pressed forward, elbows on the desk, and tented his fingers. "Mrs. Zalinikova"—now his eyes took on what I'd label a superior look, and his voice was a mix of chilly over warm—"if I can speak to the points you raise . . ."

If I can. A trick, asking my permission, a man who didn't

require permission for anything from anyone. He didn't wait for my answer, but spoke with energy, touching upon each of my points, emphasizing certain words, lowering his voice to make a point, when lowering served better than raising.

He included a quote from the Talmud: *Ten measures of beauty were given to the world, nine of them to Jerusalem.* Anyone who had walked as I had through Ben Yehuda Mall after a busy day of commerce, among discarded Styrofoam coffee cups, twisted papers from fast food, cardboard ice cream cups, would not be in agreement. I kept my silence.

"And so," he said, finally, "between you and me, what would serve best is cooperation." What would serve him best would be my disappearance. "How do you want us to arrive at this?" As I observed his variety of nervous tics—the habit of rubbing his thumb along a scar on his forehead, as though making certain it was still there, the heavy breathing in advance of making a point—I began to relax and draw upon techniques I'd developed through years of Madame Garbasova's severe corrections of my musical mannerisms. Utter silence, a blank face, quiet hands. Their effect almost always unnerved the opponent.

"We want the same result, yes?" His eyebrows shot upward, he cracked his knuckles; certain signs that my method was working. If I was expected to nod, or say *yes* at that moment, I disappointed, continuing my silence, my motionless body. His face bloomed with a faint rosy tinge of annoyance, but he smiled in spite of this, as though wishing to assure me that we were, underneath, good friends.

"That result," I said, finally, "is . . . what?"

"For your husband to become as fully himself"—as though suspecting I was about to interrupt, he rushed on—"his most profound self, as possible. He is a deep thinker, a sensitive man." The Reb paused. I waited. "Also a brilliant intellect, a rare combination." Again, my waiting. "Finding peace, spiritual fulfillment, for this kind of man, is not easy. Further, and very important, this . . ." He pressed forward, body language that signaled he was about to say something especially unforgettable. "Your husband, given nurturing circumstances, is destined to make important contributions to the literature and philosophy of his people. *Our* people."

"Nurturing circumstances," I repeated. "Meaning, I am to encourage him to go on with his severe ties to Torah?"

"*Severe* is not a word I would use."

I had no appetite at that moment for dictionaries. "I should encourage, as you say, nurture, his bathing in deep religious waters, up to his neck in praying and chanting and otherwise activities about which I know nothing?"

"But you can learn; you *will* learn." Sparks of certainty shot from his eyes. "You must." So—one more *must* to fit my life around. *Now*, I told myself, and stood up.

"Mrs. Zalinikova, you need something?" A heavy rush of breath, followed by an array of finger tics.

"Nothing, Reb. I need nothing." I moved toward the string of rooms that would, I hoped, lead me to the front door.

He jumped up. "Did I say something to upset you?" He was speaking now to my back.

I stopped and turned, trying to pull up a tip of a smile to make my exit less fiery, so that, when the Reb reported to Yuri, I would get a rating of being pleasant, although difficult. "Nothing, Reb, you did nothing."

I was grasping my purse as though it would keep me from drowning. "You believe, stop me if I am wrong, you believe it is not important that my daughter and I are the victims of my husband's dreams." He stood in the middle of the room staring at me. Now *I* breathed deeply. This was the longest sentence in Hebrew I'd ever spoken to a Hebrew-speaking expert.

He said nothing, but followed me to the door. Moving swiftly from room to room, I didn't acknowledge his presence behind me, thinking wildly: must I walk home, from where will I find a taxi? I would not, in any case, ask to use the telephone. To my surprise, and possibly the Reb's, the front door opened as I reached it, and in came Ahuva. I knew this woman was Ahuva from Nadia's description: soft, but angular face; a hide-and-seek dimple winking where her cheek met her chin; long, curly hair on the auburn side of brown; intelligent eyes; ample, round body.

At first, she was startled, then a look of pleasure came over her face. "Ah, you are Manya, our cousin Nadia's friend. So happy to finally meet you." With that, she grasped my hand and shook it with a force related to her husband's fierce handshake. "You are leaving?" She didn't wait for me to answer, but looked over my shoulder to the Reb, whose eyes announced a full mix of contrary feelings.

"Mrs. Zalinikova and I have finished our conversation," he said. I nodded.

"But *I* want to talk with her." Still clutching my hand, "How could I tell Nadia I didn't give you a cup of tea, a glass of water? I have *mandelbrot*, fresh baked only this morning." Moving with a burst of graceful energy, considering her size, she thrust her shopping bags and packages at the Reb, who didn't cooperate in the transfer until she murmured, "Schlomo, *please*." She smiled at me, her dimple came and went, and I saw a glimpse of what Nadia described as "Ahuva's magnetic personality." She tugged at my hand. "Come." I went.

I'll sum up our talk. We saw eye to eye about most matters: the anxiety soaking into every detail of Israeli lives; the high cost of gasoline and taxes; the scarcity of sturdy plastic bags, or *any* bags, at the supermarkets; the murderous traffic; the more murderous suicide bombings.

And this startling accusation from her: my new country was less a country than a dysfunctional—a word I wrote in my notebook for looking into later—family, everyone hollering at everyone else; until, by the second cup of tea, she said, "That brings us to the matter of religion."

"Why?"

She shrugged. "In this country, sooner or later, everything brings us to the matter of religion." She leaned across the table. "Simple. I take people the way I find them, especially people I like. Schlomo says that includes everyone I meet, but he's . . ." She closed the door to the hall. ". . . he's not always the final word. The way you practice your religion, or don't practice, is nobody's business, only yours, but don't go around robbing banks or stealing away someone's husband."

She'd grown up in a traditional family, with only one way to be Jewish: Orthodox.

Nobody asked questions, nobody had other suggestions. Sliding one palm across the other. "Finished. Today..." A shrug. "A new philosophy, pro-choice." She saw my look of surprise. "You think I don't read? A lot of American books. Cynthia Ozick"—a name I didn't know—"a brilliant Jewish woman, I'll loan you one of hers, I have them all. Time Magazine, we watch CNN."

I was stunned. Nadia had said Ahuva was smart and strong-minded, a treasure to have in her family, but nothing prepared me for this. I said so. She looked pleased, her dimple looked pleased, and then she said, "I have three children, they bring me lots of new thinking. I try to keep up."

"Does the Reb"—I looked toward the door—"does he know?"

She wagged her hand back and forth. "I say yes to two rules that Schlomo makes a life-and-death importance, then skimp on the third. I call it my underdog philosophy." She stopped, hand still in the air. "No . . . *underground*."

I couldn't believe my good luck. My first native-born Israeli friend, a woman of intelligence and wit and, a big surprise, a free thinker. When I left—*No, no, don't drive me, I'll take a taxi*—we promised to meet soon again and, while neither of us said, *but not here*, we both understood. At home, I went straight to the telephone to tell Yael about the Reb and Ahuva, the only two Jews in Jerusalem she hadn't met.

Chapter Thirteen

The Reb had been focusing upon Genesis: the question of Eden, the significance of the snake, upon whether God forgave Eve, or had Adam seduced, then betrayed, then succeeded in fooling the Lord?

But now, in the evening, he was eager to talk about something other than religion. Yuri, his best, his favorite student, was about to gather his notebooks, texts, pens, glasses, and leave, when the Reb asked if he had a moment. Yuri consulted his watch, and nodded. "Wonderful." The Reb closed the hall door. "I am writing a book." He studied Yuri's face, hoping for signs of delight. "A book about sexuality." He crumbled one of Ahuva's cookies into his mouth.

Yuri's mouth was a dark circle of surprise. He cleared his throat. "I am not certain I understand exactly the word you use. My Hebrew—"

"Do not be misled. This word, *sexuality*, is not the central point of my book. I use it for one reason only. Arrest the reader's attention with a title that carries emotional weight."

Yuri looked relieved. "Titles such as those with words like anti-Semitism, Palestinian, terrorist?"

"Close."

"Holocaust?"

"I'll explain. I used the word *sexuality* because, as everyone agrees, no one is without it"—Yuri blushed, and looked into a far corner—"yet, no one wants to dissect, to discuss. The center of my book is sexuality and *kashruth*."

"I apologize, Reb, I don't follow. *Kashruth*, religious ritual?"

"Think about it, Zalinikov. I sweeten the second word by connecting it to the first. If I titled the book, *Kashruth for Young People*, or, *How to Prepare for Marriage Through Kashruth*, who would read it? Would you?"

"Would *I* read a book about . . . ?" The Reb nodded. "Well, I think"—Yuri gulped the remaining tea in his glass—"I am no longer young, and, happily, need not prepare for marriage."

"More to the point, would you read a book on *kashruth* and sexuality?"

A soft croak of dismay dropped from Yuri's lips. *Kashruth and The Seven Mysteries, Kashruth and Maimonides,* perhaps."

"No, no, you miss my point," the Reb said. "My book is not for scholars. I want a wider audience."

"How wide?"

"Wide. My idea is simple: bring together young men and young women, Jewish, of marriageable age." The statistics, he explained, were not easily dismissed, one could not argue with alarming numbers recently published by the Bureau of the Interior. Marriages among secular Jews were declining, divorce was increasing; worse, the number of marriages between Jews and non-Jews was rising.

"Among the Orthodox and non-Jews? Surely not."

"No, no . . . God forbid that catastrophe. I mean those others, the disco dancers and computer chippers in Tel Aviv, the *treif* eaters in Haifa, the body surfers in Eilat. One is tempted to think we are becoming infected with certain social viruses from America."

Yuri looked grieved.

"My book is one solution, but not enough. Young people are not book buyers. Magazines, television, the movies, and the internet, yes, but not books." A better idea, this was where he needed advice, was to speak to them in person; talks advertised on billboards and posters all over the city, perhaps all over the country, the banner above his photograph—or below, a detail he'd leave to the discretion of the poster designer—reading, "How to Be A Kosher Soldier in the Sexual Revolution." If he could believe all he had observed on the television, the word *sexual* would pull in many more enthusiasts than the word *kosher* would put off.

"Coupling is holy, Zalinikov, surely you agree." Yuri's smile was shaky. "Coupling, however, within the boundaries of sacred matrimony. Like should hew unto like; witness the animals on the ark. Did Noah match a giraffe to a hippopotamus?"

"What I am asking is this: would young people listen to advice from an unglamorous, middle-aged Reb? I am not what my young colleagues at the seminary call *high profile*. Remember the short attention span among the young. Remember, also, I do not play the guitar, which is their instrument of choice."

Yuri shrugged. "Reb Turrowtaub, I am a mathematician. You need someone who is wise in these sophisticated projects."

"Wrong. I need someone with strong moral fiber, intellect, vision"—he pounded the desk—"a devotion to the truth."

"Reb!" A single, angry syllable.

The Reb blinked. Perhaps he had been too demanding, insensitive. Perhaps Ahuva was correct, he steamrolled over everyone's resistance.

"Please, forgive me; I meant no disrespect. It is difficult to struggle every moment against what I consider is too much knowledge of the world." Gathering his things, Yuri turned toward the door, pausing before opening to say, "You see here a man who wants only to remove himself from the everyday," as the Reb, sorrow pulling at his lips, watched him go.

⚜

He needed reassurance. He needed his cousin, Nadia. Brilliant, ambitious Nadia, who, in the brief four months she had been an *olim,* lived in that triangle where politics, psychology and commerce intersected, a space inhabited only by the most successful, powerful, irritating Israelis.

There was the fact of her newest new job as speechwriter for the Deputy Minister of Resettlement. Then, her column for *The Weekly Jerusalem Record*: every one, so far, abrasive, even unsettling, but important, in terms of commentary on what Russian *olim* were doing, seeing, eating. How they were voting.

The woman was annoying, but also incorruptible, not a shred

of guile. He and Ahuva agreed that if anything was politically or socially important, Nadia knew of it, had formed a committee to investigate it, written a speech to advance it, or devised an agenda to protect it.

At Passover, she'd collected six hundred signatures and picketed Shin-Shin—short for Shinowitz and Shinowitz—Delicatessen on Gaza Road for charging triple the usual price for *matzos* imported from New York. The week before, she'd petitioned the City Council that the movie house on Lloyd George Street be banned from screening a Spanish film she called anti-female. A force of nature, his cousin. With relatives, Ahuva constantly reminded, you take what you were sent.

⟊

At lunch later that week, after hearing the Reb's news about his book, Nadia said, "What you need is not an auditorium. You need the internet, television as well, but the internet is good for a self-start."

"That is Schlomo exactly," Ahuva said, "a self-starter."

"Our family is filthy with entrepreneur types," Nadia said, "which is why we were terrible Communists." She watched Ahuva place slices of cake on glass platters. "You should go into business, Ahuva's Just Desserts." She held up her dessert plate. Turning back to the Reb, "Create your own website. Thousands of young people can log on for free, or a small fee, the point being that they buy your book."

"Incredible." Ahuva put two slices of cake onto Nadia's plate. "Schlomo, isn't Nadia incredible?"

"A foolish idea," the Reb said, "completely without merit." He watched Nadia bite into her cake. If the Lord, blessed be He, had to send him a cousin from Russia, why Nadia? Cousins came in myriad shadings: docile, kind, artistic, sympathetic. Nadia was none of these. "I know nothing about websites. How did you put together so much information in the short time you've been in Israel?"

"I listen, I put my nose around. On the bulletin board at the Cinematheque is a section for posting notes. Someone announced

140

a course in computers. I went, now I know. Try it, Schlomo, cheap. The tuition is less than the cost of a new bible."

"We have an old bible, thank you, that works well."

Ahuva sat down next to Nadia and passed the coffee cups. "If you were dropped down on Mars—and I am not saying Israel is like Mars—but, if you were, you would take a college course on alien people. I admire that. Cream?"

"The Cinematheque," the Reb said, "the movie place on Hebron Road?" Nadia nodded. "We do not do movies."

"I also do not *do* movies," Nadia said. "I go, I see, I enjoy."

Ahuva pressed her foot against her husband's. He shifted away from her. "We . . . never," he said.

"Well, then you must remain uninformed," Nadia said.

"Schlomo, don't get us into an irrelevant space," Ahuva said. "Cake, cream, lemon?" He sipped, sulking into his cup. "Listen to Nadia, a good friend, as well as a cousin."

The Reb doubted the good friend part. Certainly, she was not a good Jew; therefore, she could not be a good friend. Of the Torah, like most Russians—Zalinikov being an exception—she knew nothing, which, she liked to say, was sufficient for her to know. The *Talmud?* To her, the commentaries of old men commenting upon the work of other old men, all members of the same secret women-hating fraternity.

"What do we do first?" Ahuva had notebook and pencil ready. The Reb recognized her let-us-now-sweep-forward look, the same look that had told him thirty-six years earlier, despite her claims to passivity, that he was about to become engaged to be married; the look that told him the question of their joining her sister and brother-in-law in Eilat for their August holiday had been settled. He took out his pen and closed his eyes.

"We should meet with Dmitri Kanov," Nadia said, "the Russian who owns The White Nights Supper Club. There is talk; he is to buy a television channel, and will be looking for programs for the Russian community."

"Talk?" the Reb said. "Where is talk, who is talking?"

"Everywhere people meet, they talk. They play cards, drink vodka, smoke, and talk."

"I do not do any of these things." The Reb sniffed. "Well"—

Ahuva was waiting, with one eyebrow raised—"cards, but only sometimes. I play pinochle, not often, when friends insist, close friends. But vodka, cigarettes, gossip, never."

"Not everything that is important is in here." Nadia tapped her forehead. "In the beginning, there was the Word; I know that myth. But only in the beginning. This is today." She pointed to the screened window behind him. "*This* world. Here. Now."

"*You* teach *me* to speak Hebrew?" This woman was boundless in her nerve—and her ability to think impure thoughts. Had she no shame, no fear of offending God? Nadia lit a cigarette. Ahuva wrote. He needed another way to approach this.

"Please." Ahuva held her pen up, smiling the deceptively sweet, dimpled smile she pulled up when all else failed. "We are all of us on the same side of any question."

Nadia looked pleased, too pleased, as though this man Dmitri Kanov belonged to her, as though he was a gift she brought because she was generous and they were needy.

"My friend is brilliant," Nadia said. "More important, powerful. One of his prides is his Russianness. He will meet with you if I ask him. Anyone from his country has a special right of entrance."

Ahuva's head snapped up. "Dmitri Kanov? I know this man."

"You . . . *know!*" The Reb's eyes bulged. "Who do you know, from where do you know?"

"From my friend Manya Zalinikov, the other day." She was talking to Nadia now. "Manya was here to talk with Schlomo." She looked at her husband, who avoided looking at her. "We talked after, she told me she plays piano at Mr. Kanov's White Nights."

"A complication," the Reb said.

"What's complicated?" Nadia said. "Manya is Russian, Dmitri Kanov owns a supper club, Manya wanted a job—settled." She stood up. "Where do you keep your telephone?"

"Where did you meet this person?" the Reb called after her, but she was in the bedroom dialing.

They tried not to eavesdrop, but Nadia's voice filled the house with rapid Russian, then laughter, a high, tinkly, cocktail lounge kind of laugh. After a few minutes, they heard her say, "*Da, da,*" before tap-tapping back to the porch, another cigarette dangling from her fingers. "Tomorrow."

The Reb felt resistance stiffen his neck. "Tomorrow is not possible, I meet with students. Then I consult with the reference librarian at the Seminary, my Fall lectures."

Ahuva stood up. "None of it important."

Nadia eyed her cousin. "You want national television?"

"*No!*" Ahuva's cheeks bloomed with excitement.

"Who says national television?" the Reb asked.

"*I* say." Nadia moved to help Ahuva stack dishes onto her tray.

The Reb, not trusting himself to curb his annoyance, again closed his eyes.

"You see?" Ahuva clutched at Nadia's elbow. "He is overcome."

☙

Kanov, wrapped in a terry cloth robe after his morning swim, greeted his guests on his patio, inviting them to please sit, have something to drink. Nadia chose a cushioned chair under an umbrella and accepted minted ice water.

The Reb, who wore his long black silk coat, black hat, the fringe on his *tzitzit* floating below his shirt, took a straight-backed metal chair, fisted hands resting on his thighs, and shook his head. Nothing to drink, thank you.

"So." Kanov turned to Nadia. "What do you have for me?"

Nadia spoke of the Reb's book. Kanov looked mildly interested, asking questions: who would buy the book, why?

The Reb gazed at the sky, then at Kanov, and talked of Israel's young people, the children of Zionists, a generation of intellectuals, but innocents, essentially.

Kanov crossed his legs to the right, before crossing them to the left. Nadia pressed forward. "Get to the point, Schlomo."

"Some," Kanov said, "found prosperity, in high tech, exporting, cell phones. The young people who sit at my tables in The White Nights order caviar, sturgeon, French wine."

"True," the Reb said, "but you feed their appetites. My book will feed"—he held up his hand—"their need for love. Only with outside connection, is there inside peace."

"What is new about that?"

"Nothing." The Reb enjoyed the flash of surprise on Kanov's

face. "The new is in the old. My love is mine, and I am his; the voice of the turtle, not the cash register, is heard in the land. The time of the singing of birds is come."

"Excuse me, if I am not familiar with liturgy."

"The Song of Songs," Nadia said. "More sensuous than Tolstoy."

"The new Israelis, the Russians," Kanov said, "will they respond to theological pandering? Most are not Jewish; in ritual, anyway."

"Sadly, sir, you are correct. No study, no spiritual depths," the Reb said.

Kanov held his hand up. "So why would they buy your book? One sentence."

"The wish to fit in, the pull of human relationships, the comfort of sharing a common heritage. They have in a sense come home, but home without emotional comforts. Israel is not an easy place." Kanov frowned. "Do you agree?" The Reb glanced at Nadia, who was lighting her second cigarette. Hard to know if she agreed, or wished him dead.

"No argument."

"So"—the Reb shrugged—"they can stay out of the water and sink, or come into the water and swim. Like it, not like it, they are now Israelis."

Kanov, eyes closed, sat so still that, for a moment the Reb thought he'd fallen asleep; until, in a sudden motion, he extended his hand. "I think you and I can do business."

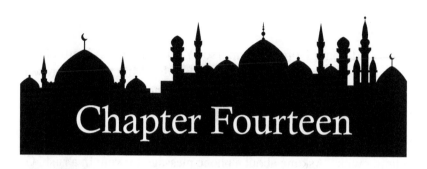

Chapter Fourteen

Monday. The White Nights was closed. I could possibly have dinner with Yuri, alone, the two of us, the possibly being possible only if Galina stayed late at school, an often occurrence.

She'd begun her studies in anthropology, soon settling into psychology; always useful, she reasoned, the world being so strange, so opaque. Her word. On those evenings when she came home at eight, nine o'clock, she said political science, anthropology, sociology, and psychology students had many evening meetings to settle what she called *questions*.

What questions get settled at these meetings, I wanted to know.

Galina's mouth twisted into an expression of unhappiness. I was pushing too much forward into her private territory. Then she sniffed and patted her hair, her secret language for: I have decided not to argue. "We meet," she said, "to discuss things."

To complain, I thought, about how unhappy they were, these fortunate young people finding themselves, due to great good luck, students in that beautiful, on-a-hill, high tech university—a phrase I stole from the university handbook—free to express anything, everything; free to pull apart the professors, maybe, the parents, for sure.

The subject we did not discuss, she and I, although it was always with me, was that of a successor to Jedediah Rachmann. Two months, and no one had read my listing in Yael's office. No one among the many students at the university had invited Galina to sit, to sip a coffee, to walk, leading me to count on the calendar to when we would be forced to take up stronger measures in the business of meeting eligible young men.

⟡

I carried home from the Supersol Yuri's favorites: lamb chops, broccoli, plump cherry tomatoes. That day Mila was not present at her register; not ill, I hoped, or, *said* I hoped, to the clerk who stood at Mila's usual checkout place, adding, as I turned away, but not healthy enough to return soon.

Galina would be late. I found her note on the kitchen table, ending with, "Ask me about a phone message for you. In a rush, G." In a rush, as always, in and out, mostly out. She knew my liking, my messages to remain on the telephone for me to listen.

So, I was to have Yuri to myself for dinner. Good food, light, pleasant conversation, I'd take a leaf from Ahuva's book. Go along with three rules, skip the fourth. Tonight, no talk of religion or the Reb.

He was reading in the room we called the study, an unused bedroom with three walls of bookshelves, a desk, a black leather reclining chair. A Scandinavian design, Galina said when we picked it in the store, everyone loved this furniture type.

"What's so wonderful about Scandinavia?" I'd asked. "We lived in that neighborhood all our lives." In matters of style, however, Galina was again correct. On the delivery day, Yuri looked about to cry—a sweet Yuri habit, crying when happy—when the men carried the chair in. I said, "Happy dreaming while you're wide awake. A new place where you can be brilliant."

Now I poked my head in the doorway of the study on my way to the kitchen. "It's you and me for dinner tonight." I hoped my face showed the pleasure I felt. Still handsome, this man, but not his eyes; his eyes were weighted down with a sadness too deep to name. His thick, dark, curly hair fought against the taming influence of his blue-and-white knit *kippah*, so that the delicate knit circle clung to the side of his head, with the aid of a metal clip, in an attitude of rakishness. A heretical *kippah*. I loved it.

146

He stretched before following me into the kitchen, where he settled onto the stool at the counter with a glass of red wine and a frown, his way of telling me he felt troubled. Yuri did not enjoy worrying if I didn't know he was worrying.

Who, in this city, did not feel troubled? Troubled was another name for Israel. Some people worried about liking the Oslo Accords only because it was better for us than for the Palestinians. Other people worried about hating the Oslo Accords only because it was better for the Palestinians than for us. Many people worried because when life went along for months without disasters, a disaster was sure to happen. Any minute.

Ignoring Yuri's pinched mouth, I shredded mint leaves for the lamb marinade, searching around in my mind for a calm topic. "Did you read in the newspaper where Yeltsin is in the hospital with something he calls fatigue, and everyone else calls alcohol?" I hated the little-girl voice I brought out, like a child begging for a nickel for an ice cream cone.

Yuri mumbled something that sounded like, "*Yeltsin . . .* what can you expect?"

"The Kirov Ballet has fired its most famous ballerina." He looked at me with one corner of his attention. Encouraged, I hurried on. "She gained too much weight." He opened his mouth to speak but, before he could, I said, "These girls are expected to live on birdseed." I slid the lamb chops under the broiler. "And almost no pay; did you know how terrible the Kirov pays?"

"*Birds* cannot live on birdseed," he said. I stopped pulling at lettuce leaves and looked at him. He shrugged. "On *only* birdseed, I mean, a few breadcrumbs . . ." He sipped his wine, then, shaking his head, as though he had arrived at an important decision, pressed forward. "What"—he took a handkerchief from his pocket and wiped at his face—"are we talking about here, Manya, Yeltsin and dancing girls, bird seed?" He watched me watching him. "*Narishkeit.*"

"*Narish*—what?"

"*Narishkeit.* Foolishness. Yiddish."

"Excuse me"—I tossed the salad so vigorously lettuce leaves flew onto the counter—"I know no Yiddish."

"Beside the point. I know only three, four words."

"Which are?"

"*Mensch*, a good human being. *Nar*, a fool."

"I'm lost," I said, and reached into the refrigerator for the water pitcher.

"Better than I know Yiddish, I know something is wrong when you and I are talking and nobody is saying anything." He slid down from his stool. "The Reb is writing a book, *Kashruth and Sexuality*. He asked my opinion."

I whirled around to face him, slamming the pitcher on the counter. "The Reb asked for your opinion on sexuality?" I was so angry, I didn't realize at first that Yuri had broken my no-talk-about-the-Reb-tonight promise. I hiccupped a cough and struggled not to shout. "This is what your teacher has on his mind—sexuality?"

Yuri wagged his hands. "Don't read the wrong meaning into this."

I turned the broiler down to almost zero and sat on the stool opposite his. "Excuse my lack of interpretation talent." Pouring water into a tall glass, I drank down almost all. "You tell me. What, exactly, did the Reb want you to opinionize?"

"No such word, *opinionize*."

"Let's cut away, as you just said, all these false feelings, and get down to the center of the discussion you had with the Reb."

"I agree."

"So?" I fought against the need to drink more water, or tap my fingers. He leaned against the counter, lacing his fingers until, finally, he looked at me with a sad sweetness. "The Reb can wait," he said, "talking can wait." He moved around the counter. "The important question is, we are husband and wife"— tapping his finger against my lips. "My question is, where have you been?" He took me in his arms; a no-nonsense hug, an I'm-in-charge-here hug, but, at the same time, a gentle Yuri hug. I leaned my whole self against him. "I miss you," he said.

I pulled away and looked directly in his eyes. "You're not doing this so we won't talk about the Reb and his book?"

"I'm doing this," he said, "to do this." He pulled at the top button of my blouse. "But, also"—he pulled at the second button—"I have no objection to discussing with you this subject."

"What subject?"

He ran his finger along the back of my neck, doing strange, lovely things to my skin. "Sexuality, husband to wife, is a special blessing." His voice was light, almost mocking.

"Where is this written?"

"In the Talmud. I'll show to you the exact page." He coaxed the blouse off my shoulder. "Later."

A feast after a long, dry, difficult journey. Later, much later, we ate seriously overcooked lamb chops, picked at sagging baked potatoes and limp broccoli, washing the ruined food down with wine. An altogether delicious meal.

The next day, Galina reported that my telephone caller had been Yael, who knew—*knew* by name, but had never met—of a young man: her neighbor's cousin Asher Tannenbaum. She couldn't speak of his physical appeal, or his intellectual skills, but the cousin's description was—promising. "I maybe would enjoy meeting him," Galina said.

"And . . . ?" I tried to read her face. "What did you say to Yael about this Mr. Asher? Do we know any Tannenbaums?" I rifled through the gallery of faces in my mind, people we'd met in Jerusalem. "This isn't a Russian name. In Russia the name would be Tannenkovsky."

"Yael said something more." Galina smiled. I knew my daughter's smiles; I categorized them. This smile was her I-am-reporting-news-I-don't-like smile. I waited; the best way, the only way I knew to squeeze information from her. "She said she knows me."

"Of course, she knows you. This means what?"

"She said it's possible no man would be tall enough or handsome enough, funny or wise-cracking enough."

"Wise . . . what?"

"American slang. Yael teaches to me sometimes, when we go for pizza on Monday evening. Wise-cracking. A jokester." I sat. This was not destined to be a short discussion. She went on. "I told her it's important before we meet, Mr. Asher and myself, that I know what are his interests. Such as, does he dance, enjoy television, listen to jazz, write on email, use the internet? Does he do exercise, or—"

I put my hand up. "Wait, wait, wait." A dark look; Galina, once begun, did not enjoy being stopped. "Is this a joining of two corporations, or an evening of coffee, a walk, a concert, and finished?"

"For you, not for me. I have wasted enough time with the Jedediahs of this world, thank you. I want to know what car does he drive, if he likes foreign sports cars, preferably red, and absolutely not a Volvo."

"What is this war against Volvo?"

"Volvos are so . . . so boring."

"You had a conversation with a Volvo, you went dancing with a Volvo? How can an automobile be boring?"

She'd been rearranging her hair, combing out a rolled knot, wrapping it into a complicated French twist. She turned from the mirror. "You are being personally critical."

"I am being personally curious." The air around her face shifted. "On another subject, how old is this Asher person?"

"Yael said almost thirty." Her voice was stiff. She wanted me to know who was in charge here.

"This is no problem, almost thirty. It's good." Galina continued her enjoyment of her face in the mirror. "If he does not want to marry you, he can adopt you. Then your father and I can have at last a little peace." Her reflection blew me a kiss. "When will you meet with him?"

"Soon. The cousin says the sooner, the better." She turned to face me and, suppressing a crooked little half smile, always a signal that a strange announcement was coming, said, "She wants, his whole family wants, Mr. Asher to marry and start having babies. How does that make you feel?"

"A better question, how does that make *you* feel?"

"I feel like . . . do you want the truth?"

"We tell each other lies?"

"I feel . . ." She looked suddenly serious. "I feel like marriage is one thing"—she glanced away, as though talking these ideas into the mirror was easier than talking to me directly—"I don't say I'm ready for even that, but being a mother"—she made a faint humphing sound.

"Being a mother is an entirely other thing," I said. "For now, if you ask me, and you just did, the word babies does not fit next to the word Galina."

"Here's a good piece of news, anyway." She held up a paper with her handwriting on it. "The cousin said Asher Tannenbaum was the youngest Assistant Professor of Archeology at the Hebrew University. I wrote it down when Yael was talking. Byzantine Period." She gave me the piece of paper. "Whatever that is."

"What does this genius young man look like?"

"Yael has only the cousin's description. Let me remember what she said." She studied the ceiling for a moment. "Intelligent brown eyes, a full head of hair"—she cupped the air around her head with both hands—"*really* full. Not tall, not short."

"Not fat, not thin," I said, "not good, not bad," and we both laughed.

"Also brilliant. He writes, he teaches. His students adore him."

"Too good to be true," I said.

"If it is true."

What about the not-so-small business of religion, I wondered, like the *mikvah,* marriage wigs, kitchen rules, not mixing dairy dishes with meat? "Did Yael speak about . . . his religion?"

Galina stared at me. "His religion? Jewish, of course."

"No, yes . . ." I felt foolish, but these matters were important, better to know everything now. "Of course, Jewish, but how much Jewish?"

"She said modern Orthodox."

"How much is modern, and how much is Orthodox?"

※

Asher Tannenbaum was dreaming of lying in an enormous four-poster bed, the mahogany headboard and footboard carved by his late father, Moshe; of lying under his mother Sara's white marriage quilt, encircled by Galina's arms, comforted by Galina's perfect breasts. He guessed that Galina's breasts were perfect; he'd never seen them.

He had never seen Galina, only her photograph, a four-by-six, black-and-white promise of pleasures to come: Galina at her desk, chin resting on her hand, books scattered around, a painted, varnished Russian Matryoshka doll blinking from atop a pile of papers.

Yes, yes, she *was* beautiful, hair brushed back from her forehead, then caught in a series of clever knots, before falling to her shoulders. Asher loved an abundance of hair. His own was thick; so thick he had difficulty taming it with his knitted blue skullcap. He wore it full around the ears, longer in back, in the style of young academics. He loved deep, expressive eyes that seemed at the same time to be laughing at a joke and breathing in love poetry. Asher loved young women who appeared both vulnerable and confident. Asher loved the face in the photograph.

She was said to be brilliant, a student at Hebrew University, gifted in piano and flute, familiar with some French and, of course, fluent in Russian. In this country less than six months and already studying advanced Hebrew grammar.

The fact of Galina's Russianness, however, was potentially troubling. Beauty was not unusual among the young Russian women whom he'd met, nor was brilliance. There was Svetlana, from Kiev, the new lecturer at the university in Slavic literature, a tall, slender person of undeniable physical blessings, and a fierce master at control. Asher was asked to agree to all details of their evening together, as she presented them, before she consented to go out. He called her General Svetlana, though only to himself.

Ambition and decisiveness were also rampant among these young women, as in Konstantina, the high-strung medical intern from Moscow he'd met when he needed a flu shot.

She brought string bags stuffed with Russian *chochkas* on their dates—painted combs and spoons, copper medals of Stalin and Lenin's likenesses mounted on colored ribbons—badgering him to buy, valuable, cheap. In these women he missed tranquility and calm, and what his mother called in Yiddish, *zisskeit*, a special, inner sweetness of the soul. He missed the possibility of consoling human contact.

But how, he reasoned, could a Jew whose family lived with memories of Stalinist Russia emerge uninjured, if only in her capacity to trust the world? Galina, perhaps, was an exception, but he was prepared for otherwise. *Galina, Galina,* his dreaming heart sang, *I am my beloved, and my beloved is mine, the voice of the turtle is heard in the land.*

⌒ঌ

That week, the very evening Asher telephoned his cousin Luba Pincus to thank her for her kindness in talking with the American social worker who knew Galina, his Uncle Reuven—his mother's oldest brother, himself from Kiev fifty-six years earlier, a man who was like a father to him, now that his father was gone—came to the Tannenbaum flat to visit Asher's mother, Sara.

Not unusual, the aging brother and sister sitting together in silence over cooling cups of strong black tea; one reading a newspaper, the other, knitting, and watching. Sara considered her brother—handsome, vain Reuven, a certified Hebrew teacher, popular storyteller, folk dancer, admirer of the ladies—to be her safety net, certain to catch her should she slip into the enormous chasm of a too-modern, too-secular Israel.

When Asher put the kitchen phone down, his cheeks were flushed with pleasure. Uncle Reuven, looking up from his teacup, said, "Don't go so fast, Asher, I wish to speak with you."

Asher sat down opposite his uncle, fiddling with his pen, politeness layered over impatience.

"I heard you on the telephone," Reuven said. "This business of meeting with a young woman who perhaps one day would join the family—"

"Uncle, this is not a family matter, my evening with someone." Asher looked at his mother, whose mouth clamped down at his rudeness to his uncle. "Who said anything about anyone joining anything? This is a cup of coffee." He shrugged. "A walk in Independence Park."

"Big things begin as little things," Reuven said.

Sara put her teacup down. "Your uncle is trying to help."

"Do I look like I need help?" Asher clicked his pen.

"Why are you doing that with your pen, is it broken?" Sara said.

"What is important to you is important to me." Reuven tapped cigar ashes into his empty teacup. "I would like to meet with this girl's parents, alone, to smooth things in advance."

"In advance of what?"

"Young people think with their hormones."

"*I* think with my hormones?" Asher stood up. Glancing at his mother's face, he sat down again.

"Possibly," Reuven said, "even you. Not always, but sometimes."

"Galina's family will think I cannot conduct my own affairs."

"Asher"—the word was sung in four syllables—"I have an obligation to my sister, to your father, whom I promised—"

"When I was sixteen, when he died, perhaps. What you suggest now is out of fashion, nobody—"

"Humor me." Reuven lit a cigarette, arched his eyebrows. "Please." Asher's face was dark with refusal. "Also, you will like this reasoning." Asher waited. "As an appreciator of Slavic beauty, I will see with my own eyes what a photograph does not reveal. I'll report the news, good, bad. This way you can avoid possible disappointment. You can trust me."

"Trust your uncle," Sara said, "my oldest brother."

And so it was arranged, dinner at the Zalinikovs: Manya and Reuven, on an evening when Galina would be present, but would leave for the library, and Yuri would be away, studying. They would speak Russian.

"She is lovely, your daughter," Reuven said. They were drinking wine in the Zalinikov's parlor. Galina, in scarlet denim jacket and jeans, leather boots, rhinestone earrings, hair plaited in a heavy braid down her back, had exchanged polite eye contact with Reuven, scrutinized him, shaken his hand, then smiled her way out of the room.

"I thank you." I passed a small tray. "Cheese? Crackers?"

"You told your daughter who I am, why I am here?"

"I thought it best not to. I said you are the brother of a friend, passing through. Awkward enough that your nephew met her from a photograph offered by a woman we do not ourselves know." I watched him sip, thinking, *vain. We have here a man with vanity.* His moustache alone said as much, exactly clipped just-so. "I am not in a search for male friends on her behalf."

"From what I have seen tonight, your daughter is not one to need help in the matters of . . . of"—he didn't use words loosely—"introductions. What will you tell her?"

"Nothing. I will tell her nothing more about you. Your nephew will telephone, introduce himself, suggest they might enjoy an evening together. It's best he doesn't mention my friend Yael, or Luba. To young people, a hovering family is a kiss of death."

"A good plan." He smiled. "Russians are talented in this way."

"But we must be planners." He frowned. "Those of us who are forced to leave one life at a moment's notice and pick up another."

I saved my big question for the dessert, after we'd discussed the Oslo Accords; could this be the permanent end of feeling afraid? Was Rabin, finally, the Israeli ingenious enough to bargain successfully with the Palestinians? Then the matter of Asher's new position at the university, the question of what, exactly, was Byzantine Archeology.

"Not *byzantine* as in diabolical, or some elaborate, unpleasant scheme," Reuven said. "Think of deep, rich colors, a smattering of gold leaf thrown in. Think of massive domes, columns, exaggerated beauty."

"Like the Church of the Savior on Spilled Blood in St. Petersburg?"

"Yes, and no. That church is a bit overdone, onion domes on onion domes." I allowed a flicker of admiration for his artistic feelings to cross my face; flattery on my part, always a good way to assure a possible opponent that he is instead a trusted friend.

Finally, over strudel and coffee, Reuven said what had been on his mind all evening, stirred up, I guessed, by the furnishings in our flat: wicker pieces, woven cerise-and-gray wall hangings. The dining room chandelier was strings of crystal tubes strung together with smoked-gray glass beads. Gazing up at the chandelier, he said, "Excuse me if I seem to be rushing matters, but, a dowry is possible?"

I tried for a soft voice filled with certainty. "I think not."

"You *think not*?"

"An archaic idea."

"In some cultures, but not in others." He was, I could sense, struggling to meet my calm with calm of his own.

"Well, then, let us say, archaic in mine." I sipped from my coffee cup. "You have met my daughter . . ." I waited. He sipped from his. "Can you imagine her not being desirable to most young men?" His face arranged itself into a tight scrunch of a smile.

❧

"The news," Reuven told Asher later that night, "is not good."

Asher and Sara had waited up, hoping the uncle would stop by on his way home.

"She does not resemble her photograph?" Asher asked. His uncle could be maddening in his need to control a conversation, feeding important details as he saw fit, waiting for what he considered the perfect moment to introduce a strong—subjective—opinion.

"Prettier than her photograph, Galina is . . . *delicious.* She wore red. Red on a blonde is like a match set to dry tinder."

"She sounds dangerous," Sara said.

"Then . . . what?" Asher said. Water. He felt himself burning up. He needed something to drink, or an open window.

"I speak of the mother. A *czarina.* Small, not more than up to here"—he held his hand to his chin—"but a mind like a steel trap. She is born to rule, a woman who says what she means, and she means ideas I don't agree with."

Now Asher felt cold. He felt regret that he'd agreed to have his uncle enter the arrangement.

"Perhaps I am mistaken," Reuven said. "You will see with your own eyes."

❧

Asher did, forty-eight hours later, when he rang the bell at the Zalinikov house at exactly seven p.m. A dark-haired, slender woman of about fifty, somewhat short, opened the door, seeming to leap rather than step toward him; moving so quickly, he stepped back, startled, then moved forward to shake her hand when she extended hers.

"Manya Zalinikova," the woman said. Large, intelligent eyes, *quick* eyes, pomaded black hair combed back in what seemed, even in the dim light, to indicate a dramatic personality.

Galina waited in the parlor, a fleecy red stole wrapped around her black sweater. Asher looked and didn't look at her from the corner of his eye, not ready to face her directly, registering the profusion of bright curls, the green eyes and luminous skin. He felt a soft, agreeable stab of pain in the area of his ribs. His mouth felt dry. He concentrated on his shoes.

"Galina, Mr. Asher Tannenbaum. Asher"—Manya turned to him—"my daughter, Galina Zalinikova."

He half bowed, still scrutinizing his shoes. Uncle Reuven said Galina was interested in clothes; a guess, only a guess, and now, judging from her handsome black something-or-other—Asher hadn't had time to decide if she wore a sweater and skirt, or a woolen dress—his uncle was correct.

Tonight, Asher had broken two of his own rules: be conservative on the first evening with a young woman, save expensive new clothes for very special occasions, such as weddings or university banquets. He'd worn his beige tweed jacket, an Italian design purchased the previous month when he'd attended the International Byzantine Culture Conference in Rome, from a little shop near the Borghese Gardens called *Napoleon's Tailor.* The salesman, who spoke little English and no Hebrew, said the four buttons and back vent would make him look taller, gesturing *taller* by tracing a male figure in the shop's linty air.

The question now: was Galina too tall? Young women didn't like looking down on a man. He didn't know a lot of things about females, but *that* he knew. Galina put one hand out. Lilies, he smelled lilies, or perhaps lilacs; something fresh and wholly delicious. Asher raised his eyes from his shoes, until he looked directly at her. Yes, taller; he was, perhaps an inch taller; no more, maybe less. Thank God.

"I'm ready to go." A lovely voice, he thought, musical, gentle, not wispy, not the voice of a little girl. Her eyes, as she glanced at him, seemed alert with satisfaction. He looked from one woman to the other; both looked past one another to him. Galina stepped toward the foyer. Nodding to the mother, he followed the daughter out.

Chapter Fifteen

I heard it from Ahuva, who heard it from Nadia: *schmutz* sells. Yiddish for titillating gossip.

"Which means . . . what?" I asked Ahuva, who, while smart, regarded Nadia's advice, which could range from valuable to not-so, on a level with spiritual revelation. We were talking on the phone, which we did often, always after both husbands had departed, agreeing that life would be simpler if we didn't mix our friendship with Yuri's and the Reb's.

"She was speaking about Schlomo's new television show for Mr. Kanov," Ahuva said, "*JSingles*." Strange. Kanov hadn't mentioned the Reb or the show. Then again I hadn't mentioned meeting the Reb to Kanov. Rehearsals, she said, had begun that week; the show was scheduled to begin in two weeks, May 17. "Nadia predicts *JSingles* will become a cultural icon."

"A cultural what?"

"Wait, I'll check my notes, I always write down what Nadia says, she's hard to follow." A short silence, then: "Yes, icon, i-c-o-n, and Nadia said she doesn't use that word about just any show. She's absolutely sure *JSingles* will grow into a social, psychological, political"—she took a deep breath—"icon on prime time television. Everyone, millions of people," she said, "will want to know about its point of view, its look, its *star.*"

I *uh-huh'd* politely, but vaguely. The Reb as star pulled my imagination out of shape.

"So, I'm going to photography school," Ahuva said.

"What has photography to do—"

"To put together a diary, a picture album, beginning with the rehearsals, to sell on a website, something else I know nothing about. Nadia took a course in it, isn't she something?"

"Something, she certainly is." I felt Ahuva's excitement through the phone. I also felt a touch of wariness. Nadia was often dazzled by glossy, surface appearances that melted into empty interiors. If Dimitri Kanov was the financial sponsor of this project, the outcome was beyond predicting. His secret manipulations, coupled with the Reb's dogmatic, controlling personality, anything could happen, none of it good.

"She even gave me the name for the album." Ahuva cleared her throat and said, "*JSingles*, then a colon, followed by, *The Blossoming of an Idea Into a Fountain of Wisdom.* As soon as I can use a camera, I'm beginning. You're invited to help me. I need you for moral support. Also, a practical purpose; you can carry my camera bag with the film, extra bulbs, the instruction booklet to unmix me if I get mixed up."

~

In a week, she'd completed her study of cameras, and bought an expensive—but, she said, worth-it—digital camera, Japanese, with one of those pop-out things on the side that shows you what the photo will look like before you press the button. It was surprisingly simple, she said, for *dummies*, an American word describing people wholly confused by technology.

The White Nights was to be closed for one week for kitchen repairs, and Yuri had been busier than usual writing a scholarly— my word, his was *exploratory*—paper, his first attempt at a *Midrash* commentary. Two nights later, a Tuesday, late in April, I was free to go with her to the set of *JSingles*.

The Reb had been rehearsing ten, twelve hours a day with musicians, producers, directors, a voice coach, makeup person, wardrobe person, in a drafty loft above an abandoned *matzos* bakery on Emek Refayim Street in the German Colony neighborhood.

Most rehearsals, Ahuva said in the taxi on the way over, were their own kind of—I should excuse her swearing—hell, but that day had been the worst yet. The Reb had arrived at seven thirty; they'd had no time-out, lunch was a standing-up affair, dinner was ignored. "He said on the phone the only place to smoke is the bathroom, and he has no time to go there." Her soft, kind face puckered up with concern. "Such a good idea, this program. I hope Schlomo doesn't walk away from the pressure."

Or worse, I thought. "How does the show work?"

The right question. She practically huffed with delight. "Simple. People write or send emails asking to be a contestant. Then they're interviewed by three psychologists and Schlomo." Right there, I saw difficulty: young people telling the Reb why they wanted to meet someone of the opposite sex; explaining their hobbies, eating habits, their aversion to cats or tango dancing, Chinese food.

One week, a young woman and three young men would be chosen to appear on the show, the next week, the reverse. Strangers, all. There would be questions, following which the female would choose one male, and vice versa, for a series of dates. If all went well, a six-month courtship followed. "At the end, hoping that these lovely young people, all Jewish of course"—Ahuva's face flushed—"will end up in happy matrimony." And would also end up loaded down with expensive gifts: a honeymoon, luggage, china, crystal, golf clubs and such, courtesy of an army of sponsors.

When we arrived at the loft, we found an enormous, high-ceil-inged room filled with people and machinery against a background of confused motion, noise pouring out of every crevice— voices, hammering, a drum, saxophone and, from some unseen spot, a loud click-clicking, as though a giant-sized engine struggled to gain enough strength to start up.

The Reb, wearing a white satin robe embroidered in blue, a touch of gold adorning his neck and shoulders, stood in one corner. The big man inside of all that glacial satin resembled a snowbank with a bump on the top. We approached, but paused behind a wall of cameras. A small, skinny woman, her lips clamped down over a line of straight pins, knelt in front of him. Pacing, reading papers on a clipboard, a young man with freckles, and fiery red hair just visible underneath his black *Tel Aviv Giants* baseball cap, called out instructions to the pin lady from time to time.

"His producer, also his director," Ahuva whispered, pointing to the young man. "Amit. There are two of him." She pointed to a young man on the far side of the room talking into a cell phone, similar in size, no hat, bald. "That one is Oze, his twin. Very smart, these two: Israelis, but studied in a film school in America."

The Reb, arms raised to his sides, posed for Amit. "*Schmaltzy,*" the young man said. He made the word sound like flattery.

"*Schmaltzy?*" The Reb looked like a man who wanted to flee.

"People expect some *schmaltz* from a show like this. Amit spun his forefinger in the air. "Turn, halfway." The Reb turned.

"Does he always talk so fast?" I asked Ahuva.

"Faster, usually. His mind goes that way, his mouth has to hurry to keep up."

Now Amit was talking to the Reb in a lecturish way. "A little philosophy, some discreet patriotism, nothing too political, just enough to get the audience's corpuscles moving. You know, feel-good talk." I scribbled down what I heard, thinking to learn something about Israeli television, or politics—or, at the worst, about fast speakers.

"Happy marriages make a happy country," he went on, "married couples have better mental health than singles, quote a few statistics, then cut to the religious message, but keep it toned-down. Something for everyone. Support big families and Hebrew schools for the devout. Push hot tubs, snorkeling in Eilat, getaway ski trips to Mt. Hermon, for the secular."

The Reb sent Amit a *puh* sound, which I took to mean: *No.* "I am absolutely neutral on the subject of politics," he said. His voice sounded scraped. The woman with the pins tugged at the bottom of his robe. "How much longer, Mrs. Durschlag?" She didn't answer, but circled him, inserting pins in the robe as she moved.

"As for the secular," the Reb continued, "I have only one point of advice: convert."

"Convert?" Amit blinked. "To, or from?"

The Reb slipped out of the robe, dropping it into the waiting arms of the pin lady, as Ahuva snapped a picture of Amit. "That cap is what my camera teacher calls a distinguishing feature," she said. Her eyes were bright with pleasure. She was having a wonderful time.

"Whose flashbulb just flashed?" Amit shaded his eyes with his hand and looked toward where we stood, partially obscured by a wall of cameras.

"Is that you, Ahuva?" the Reb called out.

"Trouble," Ahuva whispered. She thrust her camera at me and stepped from the half dark into the glare of the overhead lights. The Reb didn't look happy to see her.

"Oh, you, Mrs. Turrowtaub," Amit said. "You startled me." His expression hung between annoyance and relief, but his voice was kind. I saw Ahuva relax. "You're okay," he went on, "but sometimes crazy fans get around security, and create a disturbance." I hadn't noticed any security on our way into the loft. Also, how many fans could exist for a show that had not yet been seen? Imaginary fans making imaginary mischief; probably a common way of thinking in this strange business.

Oze, the other twin, still talking into his cell phone, came over to his brother. "Kanov," he said, squashing the phone against his belt. "He wants to know why we need Swedish copper cable for our monitors, when Turkish is cheaper, and we can get it overnight?"

"Who said *need*, tell him we *want*."

Oze resumed his walking and talking. He looked nothing like his twin. Besides his no-red-hair status, he had no freckles.

Turning to the Reb, Amit said, "We're finished with wardrobe." The Reb moved toward his wife. "Wait, one small point"—the Reb sighed—"screening contestants. What's your attitude toward Christian Arabs, Israeli Palestinians, Druids? Citizens, they'd have to be full citizens." He laughed, but it slid into a cough. "Hey, you guys, over in the sound booth." He pointed. Two young women stuck their heads out of a makeshift cubicle on the other side of the musicians' platform. "No smoking! None. Go outside if you think you're gonna perish." They waved, then ducked back into their cubicle.

The Reb looked both pained and perplexed, when Amit said, "What about potential contestants with one parent who is Jewish, and the other . . . something else?"

"Taint is taint. I would disqualify."

Oze, sitting nearby on a high wooden stool, said, "Not, not, not. We live in a pluralistic democracy. Do you know what that is, pluralistic?" His voice was tight; his eyes, which I now saw up close, were a brilliant blue, and that minute daring the Reb to say he did not know.

"Wrong," the Reb said. "We live in Israel." His philosophy didn't appeal, but I admired his refusal to be bullied. Ahuva's face was white with, if not fear, then regret. She swiveled her head back and forth between the Reb and the twins, as though watching a tennis match.

"Meaning?" Amit said. He wiped his forehead with a greasy red kerchief.

"Meaning," the Reb said, "that in marriage, the rule is *like unto like.*" Oze slid halfway off his stool, but caught himself. "*Pluralistic* is when a secular Russian, of whom we have thousands living among us"—my face burned, my heartbeat moved up to a pounding— "and don't misunderstand, I wish each and every one of them well—pluralistic is when this Russian sells me a car. Pluralistic is when my plumber is a Muslim who knows how to do to my sink what I cannot do." I couldn't catch all of his Hebrew, but his face told me he wasn't fond of anyone who was not Orthodox Jewish. Not news to me.

He switched his gaze from Amit to Oze. "Is this not why we are here? Is this show not named *JSingles, J* for Jewish?"

The tall, too-thin lighting technician, with sad, watery eyes, who wore a white silk *kippah,* tapped a metal object against the metal stand of his background light. "*Cain, cain*" he hollered. Yes. Amit gave him a withering look. The technician said, "I'm strictly kosher, sue me." I looked around the loft. Everyone had stopped work to listen.

"We are here," Oze said, splaying the fingers of one hand across his chest, "to please our audience. Which will please our advertisers."

"Reb," Amit said. "May I point out the marriage of Queen Esther to King Ahasuerus, a non-Jew, definitely a non-Jew? We all know the benefits of that deal."

"Who's Queen Esther?" I whispered to Ahuva.

"Not one of Schlomo's favorite characters."

Someone called out, "Let's hear it for sexy Esther."

"Our people, a term I use to include you, me, them"—with one hand, Amit swept the whole crew into the argument—"owes its survival to Esther's marriage. Not everyone can match like flowered drapes to a flowered sofa."

The Reb stared in grievous silence. "Did you and your brother have a *bar mitzvah*?"

"Did we what?" Amit said.

"Your question is my answer." He motioned to Ahuva, and, for a brief moment, before moving toward the exit, his eyes locked with mine, registering both surprise and dismay. "Ahuva, we are leaving."

"Take the number nineteen bus," Ahuva whispered, "from the corner, every ten minutes. The ride home with Schlomo will not be a picnic. You don't need."

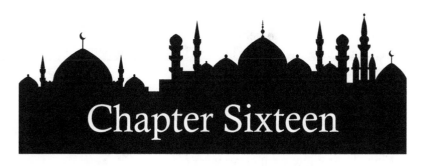

Chapter Sixteen

Nadia phoned. We hadn't spoken in a couple of weeks, but now she must speak to me. Could she run over for lunch—or coffee, make it coffee, food wasn't important, but remember her allergies; just this week a new rash everywhere, from who the hell knew what. In this city, anything could happen. She'd be here at noon.

She arrived in full Nadia-style, like a windstorm off the Negev, hurrying into the foyer still talking, dropping shopping bags, pulling her sweater off.

"Where's the rash, I don't see anything." I plugged in the coffee pot.

She ignored my question. "You drink coffee? No tea? What kind of Russian are you?" She was bursting with agitation, crossing, uncrossing her legs, taking out, putting back a cigarette.

"Tell, before you blow up." I brought out the salads, the bread, the special poppy seed dressing, sitting opposite her, the better to observe.

She sniffed. "Real Turkish coffee, a better smell than perfume, better than cigar smoke." She tensed, listening to who knew what. "Yuri, he's at home?" I shook my head. "Good. My problem is not for his ears, much as I respect his intellect." She helped herself to the food, I poured coffee for both of us. "I have a problem. I met a man."

"So? You and Galina both."

She *mmmm'd.* "Galina's young, she *should* meet. Me . . . I've done this too many times."

"Tell that to your head. The rest of you doesn't want to hear."

"Why are you so wise?" She leaned across the table and pinched my cheek. "I was looking left, he walked up from the right. Like a mugger."

"Muggers creep from behind."

"The last thing I wanted to happen." Her face turned dreamy, not a Nadia look.

"We met at Peace Now. He's a worker of important causes, always passing around petitions, pulling people out to vote. He's a veteran of the same man-woman wars. We clicked"—she snapped her fingers—"like that. One look, a little back-and-forth with joking. The minute we met we were off."

"Off . . . where?"

"Where is there to be off to? Where else?"

"It sounds to me you are a lucky woman, or am I missing some important facts?"

"Fact one," she said, ticking her words off on her fingers, "he's got an eye for women. You know what I mean, *eye*? Fact two. He's no kid."

"What do you look for, adoption or romance?"

"Translation: he's set in his temperament"—she pressed across the table, pinning me down with her eyes—"like stones set in concrete, no wiggling-around room."

"Such as?"

"He knows everything, thinks he does, and everything he knows is the whole, final truth. The end."

"It sounds to me like you've met your identical twin, separated from you at birth."

"He's from Russia, Kiev." She got up, sliced another bagel, and sat down again. "One wife in his twenties, nothing since, no children, a history that reads like fiction. Who over sixty arrives with no baggage?"

"Is there a fact number three?"

"He tutors Hebrew to crabby adolescents, does a little translating for publishers, poetry mostly, some journalism, this and that. It doesn't add up to much."

Should I say this? I wondered, maybe I didn't know her well enough. I decided I did. "And so, you earn more shekels than he does."

"How did you guess?" She pushed her plate away. "First time in my life I have a little income—not a lot, but enough—and it comes up a problem. Isn't that ironic?"

"Ironic is another name for Israel. Everybody's got at least a little bit of it, a national epidemic." She smiled, but not with happiness. "You want to know, does he love you, or your money? Is he a free thinker, like he says, or a freeloader? A word I learned this week from the crossword puzzle in *Maariv*. American English."

We sat together for a moment, both of us with our own thoughts. "Am I being a fool? Tell it to me honestly."

"The only way I know how to tell it."

"Am I?" She persisted. "Life's given me some hard slaps in the face; maybe it's trying to say, *sorry*, by giving me Reuven." I opened my mouth to speak, but she rushed on. "Did I say he's *something* in bed?"

"Not in those exact words, but you said it. More coffee?" I filled our cups and sat down. "You ask if you're being a fool. What's a fool?"

"Why doesn't that make me feel better?"

"Nadia . . . wait, oh, my God, *wait*! I just now heard what you said. A teacher, translator, Kiev, good talker. Is his name, by some chance, Reuven with a *v*?"

"So?"

"Berofsky? A head of thick, silver hair, not tall, but tall enough? Nice eyes, good teeth?"

"A serious moustache."

"A philosopher's moustache, the first thing I noticed."

"Don't tell me, Manya. Where'd you meet? I'll kill him, I'll kill myself, then I'll kill you."

So. The question was Reuven, but the answer was Israel—unlike any other place in the world, like Yuri said, everyone was related to everyone else, or came from the same place, or knew someone who knew someone who knew your cousin. This was a place without strangers. "Your Mr. Reuven is uncle to Galina's Asher Tannenbaum."

"Who's Asher?"

"I met your friend, we talked about his nephew, who now courts Galina. Does anyone say *courts* anymore?"

"You met Reuven, and . . ."

"Just business. He wanted to know, even before Asher and Galina had a first evening together, did Galina come with a dowry?"

"That's Reuven, business is business; no walking around bushes. Was he polite, or did he come at you with all his artillery: fast talk, a few winks"—she winked—"a sprinkle of literary names to keep the conversation high-class, a few jokes? He's a real professional. He could sell bacon to the *Hasidim*. What did you think of him?"

"I thought a few things."

"One at a time."

"I thought, excuse me, but this man is more in-law than my daughter needs."

"Reuven's more of *anything* than anyone needs." She crinkled her nose. "But I like him."

"I also thought, this is a first-class intelligence, in a clever, unusual kind of way. A sad kind of way, also, pushing back the darkness with a fast shoe dance, a quick laugh over tears. As you said, he's Russian."

"Who in Israel is not unusual? Or intelligent, for that matter, or strange? Have you noticed this? Everyone lives at the top of his lungs. If anyone in this place is just plain boring, or uncomplicated, or predictable, I'd like to meet him. Or her. Just to restore my belief in normal. Six months living here, a little bit of the ordinary would go a long way."

"I haven't been any help."

"You have. Just talking about Reuven, I realize I'm not crazy. Look, I've had three husbands." Not wanting to smile, I smiled. "Go ahead, sneer."

"Bad luck."

"My mother said bad luck was mostly lousy judgment in the husband department. That's me, lousy judgment. Vladimir and I were babies, nineteen when we married. He needed his mama, not me. Natan needed me to be a high-pitched Communist so he could bribe his way into a better job. The last one, Mikal, the crazy drummer, lasted less than a year. He pickled himself in vodka to forget that he really wanted to blow a trombone. Once a month he lunged at me in bed, that's how often he was sober, wham!"—she clapped her hands—"in and out, mostly out. I have in Reuven a man who enjoys what goes on in bed." She stopped. "Do you want to hear this?"

Did I? Craziness—Kanov's face played across my mind. I blushed, hoping nothing showed. "Do I have a choice?"

"He knows what to do, and he takes his time doing it. Then, after, and don't think this isn't important, when some men fall asleep or pull on their pants and go, he holds on to me and we talk. We laugh a lot. I like that, laughing with a lover."

"All in all, I would say, a good inventory." Laughing in bed, a nice sound to those words. Once, I could have said this about Yuri and me; now we have trouble laughing with our clothes on, including that night two weeks ago, when we made love while the lamb chops burned.

"I'm not finished," Nadia said. "He makes me feel young."

"You aren't old."

"Close. Fifty-two."

"Take away only six and that's me, forty-six. Middle-aged, practically."

"Middle-aged, sure, if you plan to live to ninety-two. You have Yuri, what's a few extra years?" I felt my face breaking out into what felt like a plague of guilt blotches. Nadia didn't seem to notice. I got up to refill the coffee pot. "Anyway, Reuven says I'm sexy, and you know what I say?"

"I'm sure you're going to tell me." I ran one hand over my cheek; everything felt normal.

"I say, I'm grateful."

I turned around. "Is it love or is it the other thing, lust?"

"Who cares?"

"A good, and a terrible answer, but you are avoiding." I switched on the coffee maker and sat down again.

"You are surprised I'd say, *who cares*? Is it love, is it lust? Questions doctors of philosophy or semantics make a career of asking. I leave it to the university intellectuals to sift through the big stuff; let *them* comb for hidden meanings. Is there a God? Did Dostoevsky intend for Raskolnikov to represent universal evil, or only his own private brand of pathology? Would Uncle Vanya have been happy if that young babe who loved someone else loved him instead, or was he also in love with melancholy?"

"You're giving me a headache."

"Leave the little questions to me. I'm a simple woman with simple needs"—she slapped the table—"and I'm tired of going to bed alone." She stood up. "Thanks for listening, and for the lovely food. You're the best friend I've ever had, you know that? You make me glad I came all this way."

"All this way for lunch, or all this way from Russia?"

"Both."

I began clearing the table, then looked at her across the room; so beautiful in her red silk shirtwaist, silver-white hair cut in a smooth, this-minute haircut; smart, ambitious, noisy, honest, loving, sad Nadia, taking big bites out of every day, delivering whatever is on her mind like a bulletin from God. In my life only six months, and as necessary as oxygen. "What did you decide?"

"With your help—"

"I did nothing."

"You asked the right questions. If Reuven costs me a few shekels"—she snapped her fingers—"he's worth it." She moved into the foyer, and was almost onto our front stoop when she turned back, her face bright with pleasure. "Galina and I could end up being *mishpachah* to one another."

"*Mish* . . . ? I've never heard."

"Yiddish for relatives, one big, happy family." With that, and a flash of a smile, she left as swiftly as she had come in, a force of nature at home in this chaotic city.

⤫

"So, now I understood. Talking with Nadia about things that mattered was not a two-way street, or I would have mentioned Kanov; a hint, a casual suggestion that here was a man who—in spite of my love for Yuri, in spite of everything logical—had burrowed his way into my all-the-time awareness. I brought him home with me; I looked ahead with a margin of pleasure to seeing him at The White Nights.

The evening before, I'd asked my taxi driver to stop on King David Street, two blocks short of The White Nights. I wanted to walk, to prepare myself. Early May was a bonus month in Jerusalem; not yet hot, warm enough to walk out at night, to linger in the garden with a cup of coffee and a newspaper. May in St. Petersburg could be guilty of betrayal: deep chill and sudden rain, a too-early darkness. I looked at the Jerusalem sky; stars like rhinestones pinned to deep-blue velvet.

Not yet six o'clock. Pedestrian traffic was light, an umbrella of acacia promising early bloom overhead. I strolled behind a young mother and father pushing a sleeping baby in a buggy, his arm lightly draped across her shoulder. People seated on the bench at the bus stop read newspapers or chatted. One boy held a boom box with a message for anyone who had dandruff in his beard. An ambulance siren cleared the intersection, but no one looked up or seemed alarmed. Six weeks since the last car bomb. This could be a heart attack, an automobile accident, a baby in a hurry to be born; ordinary emergencies possible in any country. No one who was not an optimist should live here.

Just before the corner of Emile Botta Street, I stopped at a high wooden wall enclosing an excavation—a parking lot under construction, maybe, or a half-built apartment building—filled with chalked messages from passersby: *Be Kind To Cows—Eat Treif. Oslo—No. I Dreamed They Played* Hatikvah *at the* Mikvah.

I'd never written a private message in a public place. Defacing a public space in St. Petersburg brought a money fine, possibly jail. I looked around; no one was watching. With the white chalk lying on the sidewalk, I wrote in large, round letters: *Jacob Wrestled with God and Got a Sprained Back,* borrowed from the cover of one of Galina's notebooks. Still nobody watching. I added: *It's Midnight. Does Arafat's Mother Know Where He Is?*

I arrived at work early. We had to talk, Kanov and I. What was Dushkin doing in Jerusalem, and had he told Kanov about his threatening us in St. Petersburg? If he had not, opening the subject obliged me to divulge details I wasn't happy to expose: black market electronics, Yuri paralyzed with fear, our hasty departure.

I would say, then Dmitri would say, and so on; each of us hiding, then revealing ourselves in what we chose to report, what we withheld. A dance with the devil, Tatiana called it; this parrying back and forth with a person in power, always a man, finding that sliver of space between what you wanted to discover and what you refused to divulge. The devil usually won, she said.

Kanov was waiting when I arrived, appearing to be occupied with numbers on sheets of paper. I sensed a quickening in the air, a faint crackle of emotional electricity when I came into the cloak room. He looked, nodded, a quick snap of his head, a flicker of *something* in his eyes, but said nothing. I arranged my things on hangers and shelves, and turned to leave. He smiled his smile: so-nice-to-see-you, cool and not so cool at the same time, and asked me to wait one moment, please. "If you have not had dinner, would you dine with me?"

I wasn't surprised, not at all, but his choice of *dine*, rather than *eat*, amused; Kanov, so much the man in charge, so married to formality. He'd hinted before about the pleasure of dinner in his rooms behind the office. I'd been polite, but vague. A *yes* with a *no* attached. Tonight, however, his plan suited my plan.

His private suite consisted of two rooms, expensively arranged. I had been inside once, briefly, to deliver some papers of employment, long enough to see that this space had been furnished in classic Kanov style: enormous black, white, and red abstract paintings—I'd recognized Kandinsky, Archipenko, Leger—white walls, black carpeting, beige, ivory, cream love seats and chairs, the glint of stainless steel arms and legs. In the room he called his napping place, a bedroom, really, also in cream, gray, black—more paintings, an abundance of flowers on the credenza opposite the king-sized bed, behind which there was an entire wall of glass.

"For napping?" I said.

"I dislike being cramped."

ℐ℘

After finishing with my piano, I sat on the creamy sofa, folding my legs under myself. Kanov jumped up. "I have something," he said, and disappeared into the office, coming back with a small, flat, square object. There was no wrapping, or even a card. A handsome young man seated at a piano greeted me on one side of the package.

174

On the other: "Yevgeny and Companions: Trios, Quartets, Sonatas."

Not a squealer, I squealed. The St. Petersburg Players, their premiere pianist Yevgeny Stanislav with other Russian artists, performing chamber music, the CD I'd seen reviewed in the weekly *Rusky Olim* arts review newspaper. Expensive. Stanislav recorded with the finest music studio in Moscow. I turned the disc over, stroking the cover. "So many thank-yous," I said. My voice sounded hollow, false.

"It's nothing, only music."

"Music is never nothing."

"I saw it and thought about you." *I, you.* Dangerous, these words in the same sentence. I blushed, turning from the lamplight. "I guessed at what would please."

The room smelled of cigarette smoke, of the tiger lilies in the crystal vase on the coffee table, of expensive soap and shaving lotion, so different from the straightforward, no-nonsense lotion Yuri used. *Volga,* I think, the same scent for years, so familiar; background music I no longer heard.

Someone knocked at the door, entering to Kanov's "Who?" Alexsei, whom I'd met on my opening visit to The White Nights; a man, I now knew, in charge of everything outside the serving of food in this place.

His skills were astonishing. One day, I was desolate because the piano keys were turning dark, and I had bought the wrong, wholly useless cleanser. Alexsei found a bottle of something he didn't identify, washed the keys with a white cloth dipped into this mysterious, almond-scented lotion, restoring them to pristine, glistening, cream-colored splendor. We'd been friends since, often bantering about the weather, the irritating lack of parking spaces around the club, the rising cost of movie tickets.

His arms were full with small wooden sticks that smelled of hickory, taking me back to the forest surrounding our *dacha*—our stolen *dacha*—smell I hadn't known I missed until that minute. He looked from Kanov, who asked him to start a fire, please, to me. I nodded, but didn't speak, turning away, unwilling to see curiosity or accusation in his eyes.

Alexsei was a funny little man, constructed of a series of contradictions: slender as an adolescent, but muscular, with the slack jaw and under-the-chin turkey wattle of an older man. A wrestler in Moscow, where he'd met Dmitri Kanov at a sports club. He'd worked for him since, coming to Jerusalem to be with him, calling him a genius, telling me I wouldn't believe all the amazing things this amazing man had performed.

The fire was comforting, casting shadowy patterns on the white walls. I relaxed, the first time in weeks. A waiter appeared with a salad of tomatoes and onion in herbed basil dressing, and more wine. Something about the aggressive red color of the tomatoes nestling against the sharp green of the lettuce, the slender strips of purple-and-white onion arranged in a spiral, alarmed me.

Alexsei turned to go. Kanov called after him, "Bring the shrimp at any time." Turning to me, he said, "I hope you like shrimp as much as I do."

I did, but I couldn't. I'd promised Yuri. Shellfish were forbidden, and I had promised. Everything else I'd promised to my husband seemed, for that moment at least, to be enclosed inside the matter of the forbidden shrimp. "I must go," I said, and stood up, so suddenly, my movements brushed the salad plate, tomatoes, onions, everything, onto the carpet. "I must."

Any other occasion, I would have been on hands and knees wiping, expressing my apology. Not now. Kanov blinked, startled, I guessed, by both the fallen salad and the standing Manya. Alexsei stood in the open doorway, neither surprised nor especially interested. I excused my way out of the room, remembering, at the last moment, my gift CD. Later, I thought: *Never could I tell Nadia this.*

Chapter Seventeen

"If you meet the devil, invite him into the synagogue."
An old bit of grandmother wisdom, taught to me by Ahuva,
that made more sense in Yiddish than when translated
from Yiddish. She used Yiddish in small doses—as spice, as
special effects—when Hebrew, more solemn, didn't offer the
colorful phrases she needed, or the dark, bitter humor she loved.

In this instance, she said, the Reb turned the devil-synagogue
advice into *If a humanist buys stock, he will humanize the marketplace.* "He needed an excuse for foolish behavior," she said, adding
that, if there were such a word as *scholarize*, he would have gone
further: *If a scholar buys stock, he will scholarize the marketplace.*

That was the week Nadia brought her story of Reuven to lunch,
the week Galina hummed a vague so-so, when I asked how she
and Asher Tannenbaum were getting on. Or, *were* they getting on?

Now Ahuva telephoned to say she didn't like what was
happening in her house, and needed reassurance. I needed facts.
She suggested a walk in Independence Park where we couldn't be
eavesdropped upon.

♫

Spring was a promise that was not always kept in Jerusalem, but
that week it was announcing act one of its arrival, especially in
the park: the trees were pushing buds into fragrant apple blossoms,

and vibrant yellow forsythia bushes, pale lavender lilacs, perfumed the walking paths. The sounds of traffic on the nearby boulevard seemed muffled, unimportant. Ahuva, from a distance, looked rumpled; wrinkled skirt, hair caught in a careless knot. When she came closer, I saw the dark circles under her eyes. Without her usual kiss on my cheek, she broke right into her troubles.

Her problems had seemed phantom, she said, just more proof that living with the Reb was a series of crises; only, this time, more so. He'd been acting nervous; not an I'm-late-with-my-teaching-notes nervous, or an I-have-to-write-an-article kind of nervous. "It had all the earmarks he wanted to do something, then not wanted, taking care I shouldn't know." There had been whispered phone conversations, papers pushed into a drawer, when he heard her approaching, then the drawer locked. "He thinks I didn't see or hear." She shrugged. "Secrets between husbands and wives are like poison, something dies from it."

I blushed; she was too intent on her story to notice.

Then she unraveled the mystery thanks to her sister Deena, who got the facts from *her* husband Avrum, whose real estate success stuck in the Reb's throat like a chicken bone.

The Reb had invested all their savings—*all*—in stock options, Roosya Corporation. Ahuva took a small notebook from her purse, and read: "parent company of Kanov's communications holdings." She looked at me. "I got these words from a piece of paper in the drawer Schlomo locked, and I unlocked." She struggled to keep her voice even. "This includes Channel Twelve, where *JSingles* comes from."

"Dimitri Kanov is a man of many ideas," I said. I couldn't think of anything else to say. I could have added: *Not a good idea, getting involved with him.* But that would mean me, as well, and I had no answer should Ahuva ask: *Why work for such a person?*

"And the worst part, he bought the stock in Germany. *Germany!* Frankfurt, the German options place." She grasped my arm. "What's an option?"

I couldn't digest this as rapidly as she was delivering it. Could we sit? I thought better when sitting. We chose a bench in an isolated spot, far from the pedestrian crossing. If I still smoked, I'd have taken a cigarette out, if only to give me something to hold on to.

She told me Deena said the whole business was Avrum's idea.
A surprise to Ahuva. She'd always thought Schlomo hated Avrum,
but the chance to get rich had outruled his head. "Avrum said
the investment community—Deena used community, my word
would be investment conspiracy—was thick with rumors. Roosyah
Communications was about to go public."

I offered her a bottle of water, an aspirin, a fresh tissue. She said
nothing for a moment, and, when she did, her voice was hoarse.
Where was this Roosya until now, she'd asked her sister. Hiding?
And go public with *what*? A national security secret, the formula
for turning the Mediterranean into drinking water? With this, she
swallowed a little water, and looked calmer. I tried to break in,
but she had yet to tell me all. "A person goes public" she went on,
"with the news that he's, God forbid, homosexual, or has, double
God forbid, AIDS, leprosy, two wives. How can a nonhuman thing,
not flesh, not blood, go *public*?"

She looked at me for agreement, but I was lost among talk about
the stock market, options, going public. In Russia, we had no stock
market, nobody had investments—other than in the emotional
sense, like Yuri developed a heavy investment in getting out of
Russia.

"Did Deena have good answers?" I asked. The Reb, with his
brother-in-law's help, may have been carried into waters he could
drown in. Not my favorite person, the Reb, but drowning, if that
meant pulling Ahuva under, was not what I wished him.

"Yes, and no. My sister laughed at me. In business, she said, I
was an innocent. I said, an innocent, yes, and proud of it. But it
gets more complicated. Deena said Roosya was getting ready to . . ."
She looked at her notebook. ". . . to float an IPO."

"IPO? Israeli Progressive . . . Progressive—"

"Wrong. *I*, for initial, *P*, for public, *O* for offering. I wrote that
down, too." She held up her notebook. "Initial public offering."

"Which is what?" Ahuva was an innocent, and I was an ignorant.

"Stocks at a special reduced price, to only special customers,
before just ordinary people can buy them for more money, and
then the first people who bought for less could hurry, hurry, sell
their stocks and become rich." She may not have liked what she
was saying, but her look, as she said it, was one of pride that she'd

remembered such complicated business news. I nodded, although much of this was lost on me.

There was more. "When Schlomo signed his contract with Kanov, that part was in, that he could buy stocks in Roosya for this lower price. He was, Deena said, *preferred.*" She looked both grieved and proud.

"Let me understand. Avrum talked Schlomo into buying Roosya stocks. What was in it for Avrum?"

"That Schlomo should buy stocks for him also, at a lower price, using *his* money, but tell Kanov he was buying these stocks with our money, for our children. To say one thing good about my husband in all this, the part about Germany bothered him. Why Germany, he wanted to know."

"This part Deena wrote down to tell me." She opened her notebook and read: "Germany made old ghosts spring to life for Schlomo." She looked up. "This is Deena quoting what Schlomo said to Avrum. Where was I when he talked like this? He needed me, and I wasn't there." She frowned at her notebook. "Deena says Schlomo said that these ghosts crammed against the inside of his head." Her face turned dreamy. "That's very poetic for a man who never wrote a love poem to me, but I know what he means. His *Tante* Roshelka, my *Bubbe* Fegele, martyrs, all, up in smoke. Only faded photographs we have to say they were here on Earth."

"I agree," I said, sorry to find myself agreeing with the Reb. "Why Germany?"

"Because there, according to Avrum, the *mayven,* is the place where the internet boom is booming. I know how my husband's mind works; anyway, how it used to work. He couldn't keep politics out of business, which is what Avrum told him he should do."

"So," I said, trying to bring her, finally, to the end.

She allowed a tight, tense smile to erupt. "*Here,* I'm proud of him. He told Avrum, who told Deena, who told me: 'Politics, for Jews, is never out; politics is always in. Not only politics, but history.' He asked Avrum, had ambition given him amnesia? Deena remembered every word. In the end"—her face registered sorrow—"Avrum said, 'Trust me,' and Schlomo did."

"Nadia," I said, "have you told her any of this?"

Ahuva closed her eyes. When she opened them, looking into the near distance at a flowering juniper tree shadowing the biking path, at a thick grove of electric yellow forsythia, but not at me, she said, "Would I walk into the lion's den in the zoo?"

A thought buzzed its way into my mind when Ahuva had begun her story. Kanov was a financial genius. If he offered Roosya stock to be bought, it had to be valuable. Why not Yuri and me? We could also invest; not much, five, maybe ten thousand shekels from one of the small bank accounts we'd opened at the Bank Leumi.

"Ahuva, I have a question." My friend looked less scattered, more in charge, now that she'd told her story. "Could Yuri and I buy some of these IPO stocks? Not much, a few thousand shekels. Maybe Schlomo could buy from Kanov for us, without telling him stocks are for us."

Now she looked suspicious. "You don't want Mr. Kanov to know this money is your money?"

"I don't want Yuri to know. He has never trusted business doings in any shape. Like guessing how high your fever is going to go, he calls it strictly chance."

"He's wrong?"

"He's timid with money. Here we have an opportunity for our money to make more money."

I saw, in the fierce way she grasped her large leather purse, that she was not at home with my request. "Number one, you want to do to Yuri what Schlomo did to me. Secrets. Number two, never did I think you had a commercial mind, you, a musician."

I answered her in reverse order. "Who is to say music and business cannot sleep together in the same bed? My mother put these things together when she bought, then sold, antique jewelry to her friends. Beauty at a bargain, she called it."

"Ah, your mother. I know how much you loved her." She took my hand for a moment. "So, in this way, you are entitled."

"For the keeping it a secret, there is this. Yuri wants to dip into astronomy." Not entirely untrue. He mentioned that so much time put into Genesis, he has questions about the universe, how it happened in the first place, was it God, was it an accident, is there life on other planets? "A telescope with a fierce enough lens costs a thousand shekels, maybe more. I can surprise him."

"For this he cannot ask the rabbis?"

"A good question, but my husband is just enough of a mathematician; he thinks, but won't admit, for some questions we must go to the scientists. His own machinery to get him into the answers would make him a happy man."

"Then," Ahuva said, looking less strained, possibly because now I would be in this program along with her, "it's settled." She would ask the Reb to invest the money I'd deliver to her, and she'd deliver to him. "Tell him, please, I am hoping to buy for Yuri something wonderful he's yearned for, something we could never before afford to buy." By the time we said goodbye, I was the one with the headache.

✺

My head, plus my stomach, ached even harder when Yuri surprised with an invitation later that day. "This Saturday, I want you to come with me to the Great Synagogue on King George Street."

I was startled. We had an unspoken understanding: he wouldn't pressure me to go to synagogue, to buy only kosher food, to wear a marriage wig, or visit the *mikvah*. A freedom-of-choice marriage. It worked, had been working, but who could know what should be the arrangements in a marriage that was showing wear and tear?

"What? Something special?"

"Shavuot, the Feast of Weeks, celebrating the harvest—"

"Harvest? What harvest?" We were suddenly farmers, as well as Jews?

"And also"—a pause, while he put on his professor face; the *also* had to be a big one—"a celebration of Moses bringing down the Ten Commandments from Mt. Sinai."

"The Ten Commandments . . . well!"

His eye tic ticked at me. "You are making fun?"

"Never." Anxious was a better name for what I felt, with a sprinkle of self-pity; anxious for myself seated among the other women in the Great Synagogue, and anxious for the weariness in Yuri that I hadn't noticed before; the skin around his mouth and eyes puckered, an old man's skin. Living in this place demanded more *everything* than he had, more than anyone had. I checked my watch. Seven. Time to think about putting on my White Nights

182

face. I moved toward the door. "Can we talk later?"

"How long does it take to say *yes*?" I half turned back. He was standing in the middle of the room looking marooned, looking patiently unhappy. "All right, all right," I said, emphasizing my words with my hands. "You have a holiday, and—"

"*We* have a holiday."

"And you want me to be with you in the synagogue, only not too much with you, because I must sit upstairs with the women." He said nothing. "Right? Me, upstairs?"

"You know the women sit separately; why make such an issue?"

"The women sit separately and the children eat separately, and the—"

"*Manya!*" The patient mood evaporated under the unhappy.

A long moment. I took a deep breath. "Early or late?"

"Early. *Shabbas* morning."

After a pause, I relented. "I'll go to Shavuot, we'll see."

He smiled and tried not to smile at the same time. "What will we see?"

"I'll see, not you. Maybe I'll even enjoy Shavuot. Who can say without going through it?"

"No one can say anything about anything without going through it."

That evening, Dmitri was gone. Alexsei said something vague about Russian friends and Eilat. Many friends, truckloads of friends, when one is as rich, as mysterious, as engaging as Mr. Dmitri Kanov. Friends in bathing thongs and fur beach robes, sipping vodka around the hotel pool, tipping with one-hundred-shekel bills, telling jokes. *Aaahhh, here come the girls in their naked swimming suits, let's have a party, life is one long party.* Now you see him—this facile, smooth speech-giver, this Russian—now you don't; a case of spin the roulette wheel, and everybody wins. Or nobody.

My White Nights music was mostly jazz that night, Billy Holiday, Ella Fitzgerald blues, each lush chord pulled out of the one before. Also, what Americans call Scott Joplin hopped-up rag—or so I read in a shabby, thumbed-through copy of the *People* magazine someone had left behind at the Moment Café. Correction: not read, had someone read to me, a young American man in black leather and pomaded hair, who spoke Hebrew, seated nearby. This was no night for Chopin or Debussy.

cワゐ

Saturday morning brought rain. I woke up to wet streets, our patio drenched; the outside world matching the cloudy, damp one inside my head. Galina, informed the evening before that we were going to the Great Synagogue, was up early, dressed, and already downstairs—not a Galina habit on weekends—devoting herself to her face in the oval mirror above the hall table when I came down to fix breakfast.

"You do your studies today?" I asked. She nodded, tying a red scarf around her neck, at the same moment glancing toward the stairway, as though expecting Yuri to come down with a lasso. "No need to rush. We won't kidnap you to join us."

In minutes, she and her book bag were gone.

cワゐ

Packaging is important. I wore my deep-blue silk dress that announced elegance without too much fuss, and a wide-brimmed straw hat, a white-and-blue dotted band running around the crown, a hat that clung to, rather than sat upon, the head. I'd bought it at the hat kiosk on King George Street on a day when I thought, *So, in this place women wear hats to synagogue, and one day I might have to attend one such place; how about this hat?* This hat, as I viewed it that day in the kiosk's shaky mirror, was not safe, or even quiet. So far, so good. This hat said loudly, I hoped: *I am here, but I am not like anyone else who is here.* This was and wasn't true, but I needed that small point of insecure superiority to wrap around myself if I was to get through the morning.

I *was* like everyone else in any synagogue: Jewish, all of us. I was *not* like everyone else in any synagogue: I did not want to be there.

Even I felt something in my chest snap to attention when we walked across the plaza leading into the Great Synagogue, a space surely the size of a soccer field. Then, onward into the inner lobby, its ceiling as high as a cathedral's, with four enormous round chandeliers of crystal and gold decorating the grand space. "Yuri." I put my hand out to grasp his. "Look up." He did. "The Hermitage Museum doesn't have lights like these."

"Many days the Hermitage Museum doesn't have any lights."

"Who has money to pay for this . . . *this*." I pointed to tall glass cases lining the walls on both sides, shelves filled with silver and gold and glass and jeweled objects.

"Those are *mezuzot*," Yuri said.

"Too many *zzuzz* sounds."

"We have one on our doorway, just above the bell." He traced a long, thin rectangle shape in the air, hammering it to an imaginary doorway. "They tell the world, *Here lives a Jew*."

"Like a museum," I said, peering into the first case.

"Better than a museum."

"Lucky for me to have such a smart guide," I said.

"Lucky for me to have my wife with me today," he said, and smiled a sweet-sad smile that placed a crack in my heart.

Two lucky's, I thought, then why wasn't I happy, for a moment, at least? There was the ceremony—Yuri called it the service—still to get through; with me trying to look intelligent enough to know what was happening, like a blind person reciting the colors of a rainbow. People would say things, prayers, songs, words that might as well be in Sanskrit or Hungarian or English. Stand up, sit down, stand.

"Do you like what you see?" His eyes told me, *Like it, please.*

"This is what Galina calls by the word *awesome*," I said. He reached for my hand but, in minutes, a small army of men—six or seven, but they seemed like an army, each one dressed as Yuri was, in black, everyone bearded—surged through the door. Their eyes flickered over my face, dress, shoes, and then, with terse nods of their heads, flickered away. I was background scenery for my husband.

In that moment, voices inside my head began up again. Question: *How are you today, Mrs. Zalinikova?* Answer: *Resistant.* Question: *Resistant to what?* Answer: *Prayer. Speaking to who you say is God, as a child would speak to a father.* Question: *In what way would you prefer to speak?* Answer: *In no way, but thank you for asking.*

The men buzzed around Yuri, and he buzzed back, leaving me to find a marble staircase leading up to the women's section. I sat at the far end of the first bench, giving myself a full view of the platform in the center of the main floor, where, behind a set of elaborately carved wooden doors—if I remembered correctly from Yuri's brief lecture—the Torah was kept. Two men stood on the platform talking, from time to time consulting the papers they held, passing them back and forth.

The older man—the rabbi?—was tall, and, it seemed, slender in weight, although who could be sure, he was inside a long white silk robe. Despite the salt-and-pepper beard, despite the robe, with sleeves that fluttered around his wrists as he moved; and the square black *kippah*, a shape more flattering than the usual round version, he seemed younger than I'd expected of a rabbi of such a grand synagogue; vigorous, full of purpose and energy. He moved like a man who felt at home in his body.

The other man, possibly the cantor, was younger still, with thick, pale hair peeking from beneath his *kippah,* and a smile he brought out often. From time to time, he touched the rabbi's arm for emphasis of what he was saying.

Had I met this man anywhere else—without his robe, without his *kippah,* looking so smiling, so fit, so likely to enjoy bicycle riding or rapid, what was called speed walking—I'd mistake him for an athletic Gentile. Was it possible these two men sometimes enjoyed a game of handball in a sports club, or sat together in a coffee shop?" *Have a latte with your rabbi. Exercise with your cantor.*

Yuri came into the sanctuary surrounded by friends, sat in the third row, then stood to greet several men across the aisle, before turning to speak to the men behind him, extravagant with his head nods and laughter; a Yuri I'd never seen in our house. My husband had come home, his real home.

A tall, slender, snappy-looking woman with lively, eager eyes, wearing out-loud red, something silky, and an outrageous turban hat clipped into place with a shiny pin shaped like a flower, sat down next to me. "You are, I think, excuse me if I am mistaken, Manya Zalinikova, just now from St. Petersburg," she said.

"And you are . . ." I liked her at once. More exact, I was grateful to her at once. Not exactly young, close to my age, a woman Tatiana would call handsome-looking, brave enough to wear a dress the color of a fire engine to the Great Synagogue. And the hat. A hat meant for Marlene Dietrich, the sexual German movie star who went to America. Feeling alone, feeling anything but at-home, it was a good thing to be greeted by someone who was herself a rule breaker, an independent thinker. A kindred spirit.

"Irina Katzoff." She looked like she expected me to say, *Oh, Irina, of course*, which, how could I, not having seen her before in my life?

I *could* say, and I did, "Irina. Always I have liked that name." Inside my head, I asked myself: *Who is this?*

Looking around the balcony, many of the seats now filled by women and young children, she looked back at me and lowered her voice. "Chekhov. My mother taught literature in Moscow."

"Three Sisters." She wanted to play intellectual games, I'd play. "How are Olga and Masha?" She looked confused. "The other sisters."

Irina laughed, and tugged at her turban, as though she was afraid of losing it. "That's wonderful. Nadia said I'd like you."

"Nadia Stamirova? You know Nadia?"

"For a thousand years. We were schoolgirls together in Belarus, and then"—she leaned closer, practically whispering—"her third husband became my second husband."

"The drummer?"

"Mikal." Irina wrinkled her nose, as though she'd suddenly smelled something bad. I glanced down at Yuri, who was not yet studying his prayer book. The rabbi and the cantor were seated at the back of the platform, looking important. We had a few more minutes to talk. I didn't want to embarrass Yuri, having the rabbi look up to see me gossiping, and pronounce me unfit for *Shavuoth,* or whatever rabbis did when female people didn't pay attention.

"Not at the same time, of course," Irina said. "Mikal married Nadia and, when she had enough, he married me. I always told her I blamed her for my divorce." She sniffed. "Well, not blamed, exactly, that's a joke, but if he'd stayed married to her, he'd have been safely tucked into her bed, instead of sending me flowers, bouquets as big as the onion domes on St. Basil's"—she braced her arms around an enormous circle of empty air—"for which I paid the bill, incidentally. Only, not safely tucked; he'd have been passed out from vodka."

Did all the women from Belarus speak like this, I wondered, in circles punctuated by exclamation points? Five minutes after meeting Nadia, she'd told me about what she called working with her hips, hoping, I think, to shock me, which she did. "I could close my eyes," I said, "and sit and listen to you, and think you were Nadia talking."

"A compliment, I assure you. She said to look for you today, an attractive woman with black hair and an unhappy face, wearing a hat"—she patted the brim of my hat—"although you don't enjoy hats."

"You are here with . . ."

She pointed to a youngish-looking man in a blue *kippah* and *tallit*, sitting up front on the main floor, swaying, reading from his prayer book. "My husband, Sacha." She smiled. "Number three. You know what some say, the third time is a charm."

Had I known her better, I might have said, "Or, the third strike." Instead, I said, "He's started praying already."

"Sacha doesn't wait. Not for anything, not for anyone. When the clock inside his head says, *go*, he goes." She looked amused, in an affectionate way.

I needed to know something applicable to my life. "He was a religious Jew in Russia?"

"I don't know what he was in Russia. We met here, the Russian Community Hall, by Zion Square. They have folk dancing every Saturday night. I went, he went, we took one look on one another." She shrugged. "Settled."

"If you are like Nadia and myself"—I gestured to the scene around us—"this is too Jewish."

She looked at me with an I-will-now-teach-you-something look.

"No one gets everything she wants." She pinched the air, her thumb and forefinger almost, but not quite, touching. "Something, even a small something, is better than nothing."

I didn't know this woman, but we were both Russians, both strangers in this country, good enough reason for a small connection. I said, "So, that's it? I must find out how to live with better-than-nothings?"

"Come one time to our group at the Community Hall, meet some Russians." She stood up.

"I work on Saturdays."

I heard a whoosh of air behind me, as though someone had inhaled all the oxygen in the room. I turned and looked into a pair of round, unblinking blue eyes, a tight mouth, a dimpled chin, blonde hair pulled into a snood. "You work on the Sabbath?" the woman said, disapprovingly.

I was flustered, mixed with anger. More fluster than anger. "Only at night," I said, surprised by how calm and even my voice got out. I turned back to Irina, whose eyebrows advised me not to make a fuss.

She said, "So. Maybe one time you won't work. Next Saturday will be a party for"—she fell into thinking—"for I don't remember what, we like celebrations. Do you know a fish called Saint Peter's fish, so fresh it practically talks back when you put it on your plate?"

"*Saint* Peter's?" Anything beginning with Saint—not Yuri's preference.

"Nadia will be there with her Reuven," Irina said. "Six o'clock."

"I'll do my best." But she was making her way down our row, heading for the aisle, and didn't turn back. A fish named for a saint, and Nadia. I needed time to work these into a Russian stew, easily swallowed, easily digested, before I served them to Yuri.

ᴄᴊᵎ⁊ᴐ

Later, walking home, after the complicated—to my eyes and ears—service, with much swaying, much singing and praying, and then the taking out and reading from the Torah by the rabbi and two other men, followed by more standing up while the rabbi and cantor put the Torah back into the carved wooden cabinet, I said, "I met a woman today, a friend of Nadia." His face was closed up, like a fist. He was thinking he wasn't fond of Nadia. She had, to his mind, too much to say and said it too often, so why should he be interested in her friend?

But no. He stopped walking, and so did I. "I am waiting to hear if you liked the service, if you liked the rabbi." He was stammering, a little boy asking for comfort, for approval. His face shiny with hope; a look that could unzip my heart. I wanted to throw my arms around him, pull him into a hug. I wanted to say, *Don't ask so much from me!* For one quick minute I remembered something he'd told me when we arrived in Israel: I would find my way to Judaism, or not, and he would find his own. Separate people, separate ways of feeling.

But now his eyes told me, as though his life depended upon my answer: Say you love what I love. I wanted to do that, tell him. But I couldn't, because I didn't know what he loved, exactly, or why he loved the words and music and ceremonies we'd celebrated for the past two and a half hours. He was like an empty cup; the words and the music poured and poured and poured solace, until the cup was full.

"I need time to think about it," I said.

His eyes narrowed. Was I playing with his question? He couldn't be certain. Neither could I.

Chapter Eighteen

For Asher, a time of confusion, a time of desire.

One month, and he had yet to kiss Galina, yet to hold her hand. Their most intimate moments were when he watched her dance The Mediterranean Wiggle, The Snake Shake, The Belly Button Roll, in music clubs in the Russian Compound neighborhood: dank cubicles dense with cigarette smoke and the din of guitar, saxophone, xylophone, drum, with the loud, eager, bullying voices of university students released from rules, out for a *catharsis*; a word that, to Asher, was a code name for *trouble*.

Galina danced, but not with him, never with him. Asher wouldn't perform these bold, terrifying, forbidden movements. Dressed in knit tops cut to show her silky shoulders, and miniscule skirts cut to show everything, she danced with male and female friends, sometimes both at once. In that sacred space between hem and knee, resided enough promise of heaven to fortify his wavering patience.

Asher had always hated confusion. His life was saturated by orderliness, built firmly upon four solid, eternal cornerstones: scholarship, professorship, worship, kinship. And what of a loving man-woman relationship? *Later,* he had reasoned; *this would happen later.* Did the Bible not say, a time for everything and everything in its season?

That was then, however. This was *now*. This was the time of Galina.

On their fourth date—*date*, how he disliked that word; it sounded false, superficial, not good enough to describe all he yearned for—he parked his almost new Volvo on the Haas Promenade looking down upon the Talpiot neighborhood. The most beautiful nighttime view in Jerusalem; or, so he'd heard. He was not, by nature, a sitter in parked cars, and never with a woman. The rain that had been falling all day, unusual for June, was slowing to a misty drizzle. Jerusalem lay spread beneath, like a dark, sequined blanket.

"Play some music," Galina said, "anything. Surprise me."

Surprise. Another word Asher disliked, considering it a synonym for spontaneity, for risk-taking. Surprise was not Asher's specialty. Anything to please Galina, however; he burned to please Galina. That minute, in the dim, damp intimacy of the car, he wanted to rest his head on her shoulder, trail his fingers through her hair, read to her from the psalms, and the Song of Songs. *Bind me as a seal upon your heart.* He wanted to hold the evening, what was left of it, tight in his fist.

Instead, he rifled through the small collection of CDs in the glove compartment, slipping the newest one into the player: "Latin Among Friends," recommended by Uncle Reuven, who, if anyone did, knew women. "You want romantic, Asher?" He had said. "This is romantic."

A piano, a guitar, castanets; a lush tango filled the car, pushing back the first beats of Asher's headache. Galina said, "I like this, it's different." She hummed along with the music. "Interesting."

If only she would describe him in that way. Now he heard the heart-stirring rustle of her raincoat as she rearranged herself. Slowly, carefully, Asher slid toward her. Was that faint *shush-shush* the sound of Galina unbuttoning her coat? The drizzle had quickened to rain; the car was steamy, humidity oozing like a steam bath.

The music swelled. Galina tapped the toe of her boot against the dashboard. Emboldened by the scent of her lemon shampoo, and his damp condition, he whispered, "Rapturous." A squawk more than a word, and, reaching out to fondle, captured—empty air.

"Asher." Now Galina's face was close to his; her breath a potpourri of onions, dilled pickles, mint. "You ask for kissing the way you ask for *blintzes*."

Asher breathed through his mouth, a faintly asthmatic sound, squinting into the dimness between them. "Who said kisses? Did I say kisses, did I demand that you kiss me?"

She edged closer. "It's not the kisses."

"It's not?" The headache was back. He smelled mold. His mother would prescribe moth balls.

"Kisses are good," she said, "I love kisses. What I object to is"— she put her hand on his shoulder—"the—"

A noise that had begun moments earlier as a rattling against the passenger door, ignored by both of them, had become an impatient knocking.

"Attention, attention in there." A gravelly voice. "The police, open up." Over Galina's shoulder, Asher stared at a man's face pressed against the passenger door window. A beam of light—he must have been holding a flashlight under his chin—illuminated a shaggy moustache, a police officer's cap pulled low over his forehead. "So, someone *is* home here," the voice said, followed by more rattling.

Straightening, smoothing, breathing hard, Galina opened the passenger door. The police officer stepped back, and she stepped out, followed by an anxious Asher from his side. The officer looked younger than his students, too young to have had enough time to grow such a heavy moustache. In his hand, a walkie-talkie leaked static and snatches of a man's voice repeating the same word: *mesukan*. Dangerous.

"A man with hand grenades in these hills, a hiker saw." His voice was rough, urgent. "You should go."

Galina stepped away from the car, hands pressed to her ears. "Turn off that thing! I cannot understand one word. I cannot fully hear you."

The police officer unclipped his walkie talkie and held it to her ear. "*Mesukan*, listen. People get killed in these incidents."

"Killed!" Galina ran her hand through her hair. She looked at Asher, who was now behind her. "Your country is crazy, it makes people crazy."

What followed was a crazy quilt of pushing, to a background of walkie-talkie static and hollering; Galina accusing Asher of taking her into danger and Israel of being guilty of killing people; and the police officer, whose cousin had just arrived from Kharkov, accusing Galina of being another one of those complaining Russians, his cousin being the other, who should do everyone a favor and go back where they came from.

"We're leaving, we're leaving, officer." Asher pulled at a sullen Galina. This kind of fuss, names are taken; a bad thing, the worst, for an assistant professor, but now Galina was spewing a string of *nyets,* until the policeman said to come with him or go with Asher.

"Here, I am the boss."

"One minute, please." Asher whispered into Galina's ear, her mouth a tight line of refusal, scrutinizing the officer as though he was under surveillance. Finally, her long, heavy sigh—half exasperation, half resignation—a sound Asher had come to think of as Galina's sound when she'd run out of the will to put up any longer with a situation that was going badly, and she followed him to the car.

Half in, half out of the passenger side, she turned toward the police officer, calling out, "We have innocent people here, treated with no respect for their privacy."

The police officer opened his car door, his lips pursed into a button of impatience, as though certain she had more to say.

"As bad as the Russian police," Galina said. "Worse. Here we have a *Jewish* policeman."

⸎

That policeman was a sign from Uncle Reuven, a sign warning him: *Restraint, Asher, restraint,* at the very moment when his interest in restraint—his *capacity* for restraint—was being tested. Thirty years old, and he'd never failed to honor a thou-shalt-not. Until now.

Passion for a woman who was not his wife was its own torment; passion unreciprocated was even worse. Always, before that night in the car in the hills, whenever he'd attempted to kiss Galina, a total of two times, both unsuccessful, his movements had been awkward, hurried, without poetry or exaltation. Asher was devoted to both poetry and exaltation. He'd explained all this to his cousin's

194

neighbor, who arranged the meeting, asking her to pass this on to Galina.

⚜

On their next evening out, after a poetry reading at the university, over vegetarian pizza and Israeli beer, he told Galina about the Song of Songs, his heightened sensations of taste and touch and smell after reading these psalms. *My beloved is mine, and I am hers; the time of the singing of birds is come.* Perhaps tonight she would allow him to read several aloud to her. He kept a copy in his glove compartment, but he knew them by heart, and could recite for thirty minutes without stopping. Forty, if he'd had a glass of wine.

Galina said pizza without sausage was bleak, but reached for the final piece on the platter, brushing one finger against his sleeve. His skin burned; a shiver began in his chest.

Asher said that living without poetry was akin to living without sufficient oxygen. Galina looked noncommittal. "Akhmatova," he said, "Mandelstam?" Galina swung her leg and examined her face in her hand mirror. He persisted: "Pasternak?" She smoothed an eyebrow with the tip of one finger. "Or, to put it another way—"

Galina put the mirror down. "Don't, please."

"*Don't?*"

"Don't put it another way. I am well acquainted . . ." A group of her friends from the university—two males, three females, in blue jeans and sweatshirts—passed their table, stopping to kiss the air around Galina's face, and invited them to go dancing. The band at the Skywalk around the corner was awesome. Galina looked at Asher.

"Dancing?" he said. "*Now?*"

"*Now* is when they are going."

He strained for the calm authority he exercised when challenged by students in his classes. "Not tonight, thank you, thank you, no," he said, aware that he neither felt nor sounded calm.

From Galina, a sharp exhalation of breath.

"I had hoped," he said, reaching for her hand on the table, "we could spend some time later"—his voice rose, and cracked—"alone."

She stood up, licking tomato sauce from her fingers. "I'll dance. You watch."

She did. With a variety of partners. While a glum, despairing Asher, seated alone in the smoky dark of the dance club, clutched his bottle of beer, haunted by premonitions of a barren, lonely, Galina-less future.

This was not an easy confession to make, even to himself, but, perhaps, in his state of feverish interest in Galina, and his gratitude that this graceful, desirable young woman continued to accept his invitations, he had confused asking their matchmaker to explain him to Galina, with the talk he'd had with Professor Avigdor, the director of his doctoral dissertation at the university. "Slowly, slowly, Asher," the professor had advised. "A young woman, especially one as unfamiliar with Israeli ways as most Russians are, cannot be expected to rise to your level of . . ." Kindness and wisdom crinkled his patrician face. ". . . to your level of Byzantine fervor."

Slowly, yes, but for how long?

⌁

The mother. She could be the answer, a woman Galina had described as her "loving adversary; smart, with an opinion a minute." On most days Asher had no interest in meeting with Manya, no interest in facing her perfectly made-up face; or sleek, pomaded black hair, surely not her natural color; or her girdled, erect, little body, so unlike that of his own mother, who was comfortably disheveled, overweight, addicted to long, shapeless brown caftans and bleached muslin head scarves, summer and winter.

This was a crisis, and neither natural distaste nor terror could be allowed to overrule desire. On an afternoon when Galina was in class, he telephoned Manya, then walked from Sultan Suleiman Street in East Jerusalem, where he'd visited a colleague's flat, and entered the Old City through the Damascus Gate, ascending a gentle slope paved partly with mule dung, then passed the graceful Convent of the Sisters of Zion, its garden an oasis of leafy palms and cool corners.

Today, the sisters, in wide-brimmed straw hats and gauzy white tunics, were gathering purple, fuchsia, and scarlet roses in enormous clusters, piling the blooms into a wooden cart while singing. Asher, pausing to listen, was unable, then was able to decipher the words: Latin—poetic, lyrical, comforting Latin.

Gazing through the crenelated iron gates, he felt aroused by the pure, joyous, female voices soaring upward, mingling with birdsong, then falling upon his skin, like cooling mist. Shivering, he turned away. A lone, riderless donkey passed, hooves echoing against the cobblestones, like the clucking of a tongue. Several twists and turns across sunbaked plazas, a number of arches and garden walls, then, ahead, he saw King David's Tower, its pale stone walls six hundred years old; still exact, still just-so, an island of safety in a sea of money changers, souvenir merchants, pilgrims and runaway chickens.

Continuity. Order. Rules. Everything tranquil, everything going on as it had gone on for generations. He needed to know what to expect. Galina needed the unknown. Risk was more than her pleasure; it was her addiction. She frightened him. She made him happier than he'd ever been.

Leaving the Old City through the Jaffa Gate, Asher walked nine blocks, King David Street to King George Street to the Zalinikovs, the glass-walled parlor shadowed by a patio heavy with oleander and flowering gardenia bushes.

The wicker furniture was white and lustrous, the sofas upholstered in a profusion of orange-and-pink floral fabrics, said to be imported from Milan. In every corner, a forest of ferns in white ceramic pots. Overhead, vividly colored mobiles dangled from ceiling fans that stirred the heavy afternoon heat.

To Asher, accustomed to the dark, carved, East European furniture his parents had brought from Budapest, the glossy airiness of this place seemed almost frivolous, at odds with Israel, as though the Zalinikovs had come to his country, but refused to become part of it.

Waiting in the parlor for his hostess, he wondered how much Galina had told her mother about his clumsy attempts at intimacy. Had she made him appear ridiculous, a fumbling schoolboy? It was true, what his few male friends at the university had hinted: love was humbling, even for a scholar.

Manya, serene in crisp-red cotton, offered tea and biscuits, then lit a cigarette, extending the case to Asher, who refused. "You are right, she said, "a dreadful habit." She puffed. "I'd given them up for always, or so I thought. Then"—she shrugged—"this country." She appeared to be waiting for agreement. Asher noted that, like many newcomers, for whom Hebrew was a second, even a third language, she took refuge behind formal syntax. "I smoke only when Mr. Zalinikov is not at home."

He sipped, scrutinizing his hostess, remembering their first meeting in the dim foyer, when he thought she could have easily been mistaken as her daughter's sister. Since that first time, they'd approached one another with elaborate courtesy; polite, but wary. "Do you like Israel, Mrs. Zalinikova?"

"Yes, and no," she said, answering in the way he'd answered his dissertation committee when asked a question he wished to avoid. "So much to like," she continued, "but"—her dark eyes drilled into him, leaving no place to hide—"on the other hand, a difficult country. Therefore, so much not to like." A pause. "As you well know."

This woman was clever, but not easily known; nor was her daughter. Driven by a longing for joy, and then for permanent connection, he has blundered into a family of difficult women. Manya continued to smoke and wait. He would speak to her in Russian, taught him by Uncle Reuven. Hebrew, the language of the Bible, of his professors, he could not haggle with her in those incandescent tones. He cleared his throat. "I have come . . ." he began.

"Thank you for speaking in Russian." Manya bit into a biscuit. "I know why you have come."

"Galina avoids me." Asher was unable to interpret the look on Manya's face. He felt abashed, regretful that he had not worn a tie and jacket. "What I mean to say, what I feel . . ." How to convey meaning without resorting to raw statements? "Do you know what I mean, avoids?"

Manya smiled. "Excuse me . . ." She ground her cigarette into a saucer and lit another. "I am, as you see, unable to mask my responses."

"But this is not a laughing situation, not at all," he said, grateful that Yuri Zalinikov was not at home. He would not want another man to witness his pitiful recitation.

"Please speak freely, think of me as a woman of the world." He raised his hand in protest. "What I must know is this: you wish what from me?"

"Perhaps you know why . . ." His face bloomed with embarrassment. ". . . why she continues to accept my invitations."

"Why do you continue to extend them?"

"*I?*" Asher exhaled surprise. Unbelievable, this necessity to explain the simplest, the most obvious adult psychology; was there a language barrier, a lapse in cognition? "I want a wife, a home, children." For one terrible moment, the wish to slap this woman burst upon his brain. He yearned to be the kind of man who could blurt out, *I am interested in physical and intellectual connection, you foolish woman!*

"With my daughter, you have every hope of achieving these blessings. Galina is young, beautiful, and more than merely intelligent. All over Jerusalem people say that Asher Tannenbaum has come into an enviable courtship."

"These people are not present when I ask, *beg* Galina to allow . . ." The word galled, but he must use it if he was to make his point. He cracked his knuckles, looking past Manya into the garden, to the ceramic bird feeder, where two brilliant-blue hummingbirds, suspended in air, feathers furled by the breeze, drank nectar. His equilibrium restored, he went on: "As I said, to allow me to embrace her, some small sign we are more than merely friends."

"A wise young woman, I would say."

"Do I hear correctly?" He hadn't meant to shout; he grasped his cup as though seeking ballast.

Manya studied Asher with sudden softness. "Galina toys with you."

Asher felt light-headed. This unmitigated sunlight: windows without blinds, like eyes without eyelids, played tricks. "This is an honorable thing to do?"

"Think of it as a human thing to do. Men, women, finding one another is an art in itself. And then, the odds against you and Galina meeting, a small miracle that it happened, I would say."

"I am not made of stone." He had not planned to be this explicit.

"Men never are." Now, another smile. Was that pity shadowing her eyes? "More tea?"

Desperate to escape, he shook his head. Manya slid forward in her chair with the solemn air of a woman about to change the universe. "You are a good man, Asher. With you Galina will have a place in Israeli society, she will be less an outsider."

"*Outsider*? Then I am to be . . ." He struggled to remain calm, polite, professorial. ". . . to be useful, rather than a life partner?"

Manya moved her head barely, not even a full nod. "Relationships are enormously complex in this place, everyone agrees. I hope you are among them."

Asher struggled to get out of the narrow wooden chair. His back—again; the disc ruptured in the Galilean excavation. He *must* leave before saying something regrettable.

"Mrs. Zalinikova—"

"Manya." Asher closed his eyes. The mobiles, powered by rotating ceiling fans, made a faint whooshing sound. Against his closed eyelids, the brilliant reds and greens and blues burned. "I have always judged a man by what he loves." Asher opened his eyes. "My husband loves mathematics as though it were a philosophy. He has a vast intellect. And you"—he was moving toward the door; she, closely behind—"your Byzantium, I see it as a place of brilliance and pleasure."

They were in the foyer now. Perhaps, even if Russian, this woman *did* have a capacity for appreciating the aesthetic dimension to life. Asher extended his hand; Manya shook it, and held it for a moment. "Thank you for taking the time," he said.

"Please come again," Manya said. "And again after that."

⤸

In the days that followed, Asher left the university early, his concentration gone, his usual tranquility subverted by the thought of Galina, so desirable, yet so elusive; and the mother, so perverse, yet so candid—and, in the wet heat of afternoon, walked the narrow streets of West Jerusalem. Life without Galina was sawdust; life with her could become a series of domestic sieges.

He saw girls, women, everywhere, their thighs straining the flimsy fabrics of narrow skirts. Even the female soldiers wore their sleeves rolled high on their smooth arms, their shirts partly unbuttoned, so that, with a sudden turning, he'd glimpse soft, white flesh, a promise of pleasure so unexpected, he walked quickly away, seeking solace in the calm, ascetic atmosphere of the university library stacks.

He rode the bus to the Israeli Museum, wandering in the sculpture garden, hoping it would be a soothing balm for his wounds, but the sight of the lush Henry Moore reclining nude woman, arms arched to embrace, lips parted in erotic expectancy, only exacerbated his restlessness. He rushed back to his office to lose himself in Holibeck's classic: "The Byzantines: A Transforming Vision."

Professor Avigdor suggested the stones of the Western Wall at midnight, suffused by moonlight. "Walk with her in the plaza when it is empty of everyone but the two of you. It holds a kind of mystery that can bond two people together."

"*Empty!* Ten or twelve soldiers looking down from the rooftops, machine guns, rifles . . ."

The professor tapped his pencil, pondering the slant of light falling across the small Byzantine carvings on his desk: men, women, caught in passionate embraces. He held up a carving, a nude male cupping the buttocks of a voluptuous woman, also unclothed.

"Is it for nothing, Asher, you have chosen to live your professional life visiting and revisiting Byzantium? Take Galina to an archeological dig, show her what impels you. Also"—he inhaled, as though taking in the scent of a fine wine—"you have in Galina a perfect example of the best in Byzantine women: intelligence, assertiveness, a wish to make her talents and opinions known."

Asher moved toward the door.

"Sing to her."

Uncle Reuven, the family's expert in these matters, was in Eilat for a holiday with a woman friend. His mother, saddened by her son's sadness and anxious to help, suggested water, a universal soother.

Asher's sagging spirit was renewed by hope. They would drive north to the Sea of Tiberias, the Israel of the New Testament, an area possibly of interest to Galina, with her lack of interest in Old Testament ritual. He'd assure her they'd be back in Jerusalem before nightfall. *And I shall come to my love as though new, cleansed by the sweet waters of the Jordan.*

Galina's response delighted him. "Why not? It could be amusing to be away from the city, so solemn on the weekend, so closed up, like a tomb."

Weekend? Did this mean they would spend a night in a hotel? Perhaps some things could not be dissected without suffering mortal injury. They would go, they would stay, they would come home when Galina said to come home. Heaven, not he, would be the judge.

⁓

On a Friday morning, a day fragrant with the magnolia bushes budding along the brick wall enclosing the Zalinikov's townhouse, Asher added Galina's things to the trunk of his car, a space already holding a basket filled with his mother's noodle pudding, pale-yellow slices of homemade egg bread, a raisin and cinnamon strudel, a jug of strong, lemon clove tea, and several bottles of white Carmel Valley wine.

"And these, as well." Galina added textbooks, a notebook, and a tape recorder, dancing her fingers through her curls; closing, yet not completely closing, her eyes; a look that, to Asher, conveyed as much as it withheld.

"They cannot wait for Monday?"

"They cannot."

"You will do your studying in Tiberias?"

"Yes, if I decide."

As he had told himself earlier, moment-by-moment negotiations.

They drove in a cold, steady downpour that, Asher knew, would wash away his plans for the sunset excursion by boat, the Saturday picnic on shore, the banquet of St. Peter's fish grilled on a charcoal fire and served under the striped umbrella of a waterfront café, Portugese fado music floating between wooded Judean hills and sea.

Their room at the Hotel Moriah resembled a damp, chilly cell. Unending rain bringing, not desire, but mold; giving rise, not to surrender, but to Galina's allergies. Her eyes streamed; her eyelids swelled. At midnight, Asher, in pajamas under a rain slicker, sought an apothecary shop in search of eye drops, nasal spray, tissues. Back in their room, he asked the inert body burrowed under the quilt on the bed, "What can I do?"

"Cold towels." Galina, feverish, chafed, her luxurious spill of hair limp, peered up at him with feverish eyes.

Asher wrung out a cloth, laid it on her forehead, and pressed. Her breathing was clotted, a child gasping for air. *O, arise my love, my fair one, arise and cleave thy body unto mine.* He opened his mouth and, without knowing that this was what he was about to do, brushed the hair from her forehead and sang *Rozhinkes mit mandlen*, his mother's Yiddish lullaby. *Raisins and almonds; sleep, baby, sleep.*

Galina stared up at him, her mouth a damp circle seeking relief, until, her hand in his, she closed her eyes and drifted off.

Asher, grasping her hand, sat on the edge of the bed until past one o'clock, a brooding sentry, sifting through the ruins of the weekend for some sign that passion remained a possibility.

Perhaps it was time for Professor Avigdor's suggestion: a visit to a *tel*, one of the sites of ancient buried treasure unearthed in the bleached hills strung between Haifa and Caesarea, only kilometers from the sea. Specifically, the *tel* most recently plumbed by archeologists from the university, said to contain coins, jewelry, pots, dating from the fifth century AD. One night, perhaps two, lying in unimpeded view of the stars; the soft, mounded earth beneath, a plaintive Offra Saphir on the tape player, a bottle of white spring wine.

Chapter Nineteen

A sadness had settled on me, due first to Asher, then Kanov, then Yuri. Certainly Yuri. Asher's visit had not gone well. We talked past one another, two well-meaning strangers who loved the same young woman.

This was immediately clear: he was a good person; good being, for me, at this unsteady time in my life, more important than his brilliance, more important than his gift of imagination; although I am impressed that, through his bits and pieces of reclaimed pots and dishes and statues, he is capable of imagining backwards thousands of years into the details of lives that were lived BC. A rose-beige cooking vessel? The women who owned it cooked with cayenne pepper. A narrow-necked glass decanter and stopper? This had once held cooking oil.

How does he connect invisible dots, how does he interpret the clues that reveal details of the dailiness of vanished centuries? I might have asked, *should* have asked.

When I think of Asher—and, since his visit, I do, often—I think of him in a desert *tel,* alone. He appears to possess that rare talent *for* being alone; a man who is solitary, and, at the same time, complete; like Yuri, in this way. I see him digging through layers of earth, pulling up shards, pots, glass cruets, cooking utensils, and masks, jade and onyx pebbles.

I see him intent upon an object, in the dim light of his kerosene lamp. Perhaps there is music on a tape player: Vivaldi, Brahms.

Jazz. American Blues. He is, after all, a young man. Or perhaps he bathes himself in silence, handling every piece he rescues with love, respect, even awe.

I see him in the university library, cataloging his newest findings; examining each one, turning it to the light, tap-tapping for imperfections, rubbing his hand over surfaces, bringing the pieces up to his face so he can smell, the clay or marble or graphite soured by dampness and time and neglect; then probing the insides with his fingers, determined to discover their ages, and to what uses they had been put to in their vital lives.

Last, I see him preserving each piece within a square glass dome, a brass plate fixed on the outside, informing viewers as to when and where this treasure was unearthed. And by whom. Important for his resume. The clever scholar never forgets this detail. Asher, however, may well be good, but not clever. I must ask him about this.

I admit to originally encouraging this romantic friendship to save my daughter from the army—some would put this less delicately, some would say to cheat the army—but my interest has progressed beyond that ambition. I sense that, even given Galina's mischievous, often irritating, teasing, this young man makes my daughter feel loved, safe.

Despite our rather awkward conversation—in which I took unfair advantage of his sweet, somewhat old-fashioned, respectful nature, and said a number of outrageous things, almost daring him to rebuke me—I considered this young man an unexpected blessing, in the secular sense. Though one that was not yet fully appreciated by Galina, who, since childhood, has accepted love as the sea accepts the tide, and has come to appreciate Asher more or less carelessly, as only one who is bathed in profuse admiration can afford to be careless.

Whether or not she would be willing to accept him as a husband is not easily guessed at. Nothing about Galina is easily guessed at. Had I the power to choose for my daughter, I would say: *yes, oh, yes*.

All in all, and it humbled me to say this: Asher Tannenbaum had fallen into our lives, a wholly unexpected, and possibly undeserved, gift.

Once, in the first weeks I worked at The White Nights, I asked Kanov why he'd left Russia.

"Because it cannot go on," he'd said, and glanced around the room in his restless way, as though regretting the lack of a wider audience to appreciate the wisdom he'd just delivered.

"Russia . . . cannot go on?"

"It will *exist*." He smiled his please-do-not-allow-me-to-alarm-you smile, even as he said alarming things. "But it will not prevail." I struggled against asking questions. "By this I mean"—he hesitated, as though trying to remember what he did mean—"it will never return to being a first-rate, modern power; as in American power, which I very much admire. Too many easily broken, nonsense tax rules, too much corruption, too much crime, too little incentive to work hard, too few patriots, too many fish."

"*Fish*?" The word slipped out without my cooperation, and Kanov loved my obvious surprise.

"Too many little fish," he went on. "The ordinary people, either too old or too honest or too foolish to cheat the government, and, as a result, are desperate with poverty. Too many big fish cutting the country up into profitable packages to benefit themselves, who will in time swallow the little fish."

I asked the question that had been in my mind from our first meeting. Why hadn't he gone to America?

He laughed, but didn't look amused. "I am seen by some, not all, as being among the big fish. America would not have me. I had first to clear up a few confusing facts about certain business dealings. I refused." He shrugged. "Perhaps at another time, under less fastidious immigration laws."

Alexsei tuned the piano every Sunday afternoon. No piano required tuning this often, but Alexsei accepted my obsession, even if he didn't understand it. He tuned it every seven days because he knew that if I sat to play, and the keys did not sound absolutely on pitch, sounded the least bit off, I would go crazy, feel that I had lost—

what? Control, skill, the power to keep this instrument perfect, after the violation of my Kesselstein-Beinberg?

This insistence upon the obsessive care of an inanimate object—however valuable, however beautiful, in a country where children five and six and seven years old walk with their mothers on any ordinary day into a shop to buy roller skates or sweatshirts, a lollypop grasped between their lips, greedy anticipation thick as berry jam on their faces, fully aware that they could be blown apart by the steel shards of a hand grenade before the clerk has unboxed the skates or unfolded the shirt—is pathologic.

Or, another possibility: the child will pull at the skates, at the shirt, with eager, sticky hands, and grin a lopsided, squiggly grin into the mirror, before turning to his mother to ask, does she love it, oh, please love it, as much as he does—now the lollypop is on the floor, but the child has forgotten about it—and will then be blown apart.

I am not proud of having my piano tuned once a week, but I must admit to bouts of shameful behavior, self-absorbed behavior; or, who would you have here, telling this story? Why would you believe me on the subject of love, or duty, or religion, if I masked this kernel of self-interest?

I had a peerless tutor in Tatiana. She a was a master of self-interest. She ate it for breakfast, lunch and dinner. Also, I raise this question: If I did not make certain my piano was cared for, would Israel be a safer place for its children? This country devours people. Of what importance, within that tragic reality, is one person's devotion to a piano?

The tuning of the piano is a self-indulgence similar to my having a weekly massage, which I don't have, but would have, will have, should we prosper; provided that Yuri does not discover some obscure Talmudic prohibition against such luxury. Perhaps if the masseuse were an Orthodox Jew, perhaps if she dispensed prayers along with the oils and lotions. *Baruch atah Adonai, Eloheinu melech haolam*, the bottle of pale, creamy, slightly scented balm held aloft. *Blessed art thou, O Lord our God, King of the universe.* The balm tipped out of the bottle and onto the skin in a slow, restoring, expensive flow.

Chapter Nineteen

On the Saturday night following Asher's visit, I played Debussy, Chopin, and American Broadway tunes by a team of two talented composers, wildly popular in their country, Rodgers and Hammerstein, one Jewish, one not; then music by an American Jew named Steven Sondheim, who I first heard when a theatrical-looking young woman wearing a peach, pleated satin cape pressed a compact disc, *A Little Night Music*, into my hand. "Listen to this guy, will you?" she said, "it'll change your life." Words spoken too swiftly in terrible Hebrew, but which sounded something like this.

Viktor, the waiter from Odessa who limped, but moved around the serving floor as though on roller skates, was nearby, pouring champagne for a diner with a diamond the size of a small potato on his little finger, and a pear-shaped wife wrapped in an amber-shaded, long hair fur that would have been a perfect throw rug in front of a fireplace; probably fox, probably endangered, and much too hot for that May evening. I recognized them as Russians of a questionable work ethic, crazy to announce the news of their sudden prosperity, certain to leave an enormous tip.

Viktor, who missed nothing that occurred at The White Nights, came to the piano after my Sondheim playing, to tell me again in Russian how popular in America this composer was. It was Viktor who invented the code system that told the staff the emotional temperature of each diner. Who had made reservations with a tight, tense voice; *NR* penciled next to his name on the roster, *Needs Reassurance*. Who was celebrating a birthday, an anniversary; *HB* or *HA* penciled in, then transmitted to the waiter at that station. *KM* designated a member of the Knesset, *IJ*, an important journalist.

This was still the tourist season. Our most generous clients were Americans—cheerful, polite, intelligent people, with a devotion to their rabbis, their philanthropy, their stadium-sized media rooms and home gymnasiums. For their pleasure I played Jewish-American musicians: Gershwin and Hammerstein, in addition to Sondheim, also a man named Harnick, who had written music for a play about Jews leaving Russia for America. Plus, to elevate the entertainment and contribute to their need to feel globally connected, Stravinsky, Rachmaninoff, Mussorgsky.

I thought about these most chosen people among chosen people as I played, thought about their paying one hundred fifty US dollars for two dinners. I thought about their busy, bubbling-up cities, their skyscrapers sticking into the skies as indelibly as desire, their manicured, flowered parks photographs of which I'd seen on travel posters.

I thought about their thousands of free-to-print-anything newspapers and magazines, and universities and theaters, and concert halls and bookstores; how safe everything looked, how far from the Palestinian tragedy, and army service. And I thought, if there is a God, and if Yuri is so holy, so pure, *whywhywhy* had he and Galina and I not been chosen to go to America?

I had, that night, worn a new red satin dress, the bodice a series of straps and fitted darts that made me look, or so Viktor said, like a flame. A flame, good, or a flame, bad, I asked. He shrugged. Viktor will go only so far. Pull his tongue, as the Russian saying describes, and still he says nothing he wishes not to say. He would make a fine spy.

As I was shrugging into my coat, Kanov came into the dressing alcove and suggested sherry. I hesitated. Earlier that day, a rubbing had begun in my chest, and I'd recognized the hello of an arriving cold. "One," I said, knowing there would be more, knowing more would please me. "For me, please, wine rather than sherry." We went into his private rooms, where Alexsei had begun a fragrant fire before leaving for the night. Tango music was on the compact disc machine. Kanov, the consummate Russian, and always a tango.

Sitting back on the white sofa, surrounded by an abundance of black suede pillows, my legs tucked beneath myself, I drank too quickly, as though the burn of wine trickling against an irritated trachea was unimportant.

I remember thinking that this wine was lovely; dry, but smoky, and then the door opened to admit the surprise of Dushkin who, seeing me, smiled, but not with embarrassment—he was not a man weighted down by apologies—and immediately looked away. "Excuse me," he said, to the walls, to the room in general, "I had hoped to find you here, but had not fully expected. How are you?"—sliding, without pause, as though there were no possibility I would answer, into—"Good evening, Dimitri."

Had hoped to find me here.

What right had this man to hope for anything about me—*what right*? To add insult, he had hoped to find me without so much as a mentioning to me earlier, from Kanov. So. These men had discussed me, as though I were a story from one of the daily tabloids.

I had not seen Dushkin since my first night of working at The White Nights, had never spoken to Kanov of our dangerous meeting in St. Petersburg, or that his friend was our reason for leaving Russia. Had never fully put to rest, nor proven, my diamond theory. Now he moved across the room—in a manner I remembered from our encounter at the market stall, like an actor, a man involved in high drama, easily and gracefully—from the door to the small bar in the wall cabinet, where he arranged ice, soda, kir, glasses.

Kanov smiled his I-am-puzzled-and-therefore-innocent smile. "Ah, yes, Mikhail," he said, "you know"—he dipped his head toward me—"Manya Zalinikova?" Not a question. "Manya, Mikhail is my very old friend from Moscow, and even before, from the military academy in Kharkov. We were boys together."

"And now you are men together," I said, just to say *something.* I looked at Dushkin, who smiled a thin smile with cruel lips. "Yes, I know Mr. Dushkin." Clearly Kanov knew details, and had invited him here, not caring if his presence might humiliate, or even infuriate, me.

Dushkin was watching both of us. His wary eyes cut toward Kanov, but took me in as well. The two men exchanged glances. Dushkin dropped ice cubes into three glasses.

"Nothing more for me," I said, "thank you. I am about to break into a cold. I must, I really must"—I stood up—"go."

Kanov said, "But must you? Mikhail is here at this hour in part because you are." Dushkin took his gold cigarette case, the St. Petersburg case, from his jacket pocket.

Moving toward the door now, struggling against the eruption of the cough that had threatened all evening, I looked first at Kanov, then at Dushkin, who shook a cigarette from the case, holding it gracefully between the second and third fingers of his right hand, as though the cigarette were an object of great value. "A matter of mistaken intentions," I said.

Kanov looked both annoyed and confused.

"Or, improper timing," I added. If I did not leave at once, I would be rude; worse, unstrung, and could say something regrettable.

"But he planned to have a drink with us," Kanov said. "In this way you can come to know one another." His voice slipped into a childish whine I had not heard before.

"I am so very sorry," I said. "My husband is waiting." I wanted to see the effect of the word *husband* on these men, but Kanov was poking at the fire with an iron bar, and Dushkin looked down at the glasses and ice as though studying a map.

For the first time since arriving, Dushkin half turned, and looked directly at me. "How is your husband? In commerce in Jerusalem?"

"In education," I said, "the university." He seemed not to understand, and looked at Kanov, who continued to make himself busy with the fire. "Yuri is an academic by profession," I said. "Mathematics."

"When we met, he was in commerce," he said. I wanted to jab my fingernail into his stingy lips, to draw blood. He jiggled a glass holding several ice cubes. It made a dull, clicking sound, like giant, hollow dice being rolled. "Well"—he held the glass up and tipped it toward me. "Another time, perhaps."

How easy to have murmured, "Perhaps." How tempting to have said, only, "Good night." I opened the door and half turned. I said, "Sorry, sorry, sorry," my voice pulled into a high, taut silver cord of refusal. "You gentlemen are so very wrong."

Allow me to admit sin. *Kheteem.* A sensuous-sounding word—its opening softness, its *t* leading to a drawn out *eem*, like a hum on the lips—for a shameful lapse in judgment. For a betrayal. A word that suggested the name of a dance, perhaps. *I danced the* kheteem *past midnight.* Or a creamy, scented balm to rub into one's limbs, throat, arms, after bathing. *Camelia-scented* kheteem: *feel your body succumb to the spell of its healing fragrance.*

Loyal, disloyal Manya. I was nobody's victim, however. I chose among choices, and I chose unwisely. Shame, while it clogged my throat, did not dim my vision.

These were the facts: Kanov and I flirted. A false-sounding word, flirting, natural only in the mouth of a Tatiana, an Anna Karenina. He invited me—not directly, but clearly—to commit certain intimacies. I did not accept, but I did not refuse. Married to a man whom I loved, continue to love, despite his outbreaks of melancholia and self-righteousness, and my outbreaks of impatience and irritability, I nevertheless considered sex with Kanov, refusing to admit, even to my mirror, what I was thinking. A deceit, certainly. Ask me if I would forgive this in my husband. I cannot say. Hypothetical scenarios are, in the end, irrelevant. I was regretful; more important, repentant.

I knew, finally, why Tatiana said that power was erotic. There was never the question of my loving Kanov, or even of liking him. My fascination was with his mystery, his absolute man-of-the-world self-confidence, his involvement with the things of this world, extracting from them the emotional nourishment I got from music, that Yuri got from mathematics.

So. Here we had a man who, for me, was the Other, whose prime gift to me in the end was the perverse humiliation of my being cheated of what I had hoped for. More important, I needed to devise a way to discuss all this with Yuri.

Also, still unrevealed, was the story of my—our—small investment in Kanov's Roosya stock. I had continued to hope for its expansion, thinking that a material gain would please Yuri, would give me the status of being someone with smartness, smart enough to make shrewd economic moves, *splat*, that easily. That I was someone who deserved praise, even admiration.

Chapter Twenty

I had not yet found a way to speak to Yuri about these matters when we received an invitation from Irina Katzoff to celebrate the ending of the seven weeks between Passover and Shavuot. No information was given as to why an ending and not a beginning was to be celebrated, or why coming to an end *deserved* a celebration; but, from the five minutes I'd seen Irina, I knew her to be the kind of person who said let's celebrate, and everyone did.

Across the top of the bright-pink announcement paper, typewritten in bold black letters, *Mesibat Shavuot*. A Shavuot party. Beer, wine, vodka, a buffet supper, then dancing to an orchestra. At the Russian Community Center on the following Saturday, June 6, six thirty. At the bottom she'd written, in a sprawling, looped handwriting, *Please come. You'll meet a million Russians.* Her telephone number, neatly inked under her name, placed her in a Jerusalem neighborhood close to ours.

Saturday evening. Since the Dushkin encounter, I'd carried on at The White Nights with my usual hours as though nothing had happened, nothing had changed, nodding hello and goodbye to Dimitri Kanov. No further conversation, the few times when he put himself in the same place as I. The pay remained good, the opportunity to entertain people with my music always pleased me, and getting out of our house, and away from the thickening pressure from Yuri to turn religious, was welcome.

Exchange an evening at work for an evening with other

Russians, Russian food, Russian music—why not? Yuri might find a Shavuot celebration amusing, in a season when very little amused him, including me. We could come home in a softened mood, sit down with a glass of wine to sift through the details of the party, a husband-and-wife gossip of who looked especially good, happy, strung-out; although we would know no one present, other than our host and hostess, and only I, not Yuri, would qualify there. This relaxed social conversation could be just the right environment for me to tell Yuri the story of Dimitri Kanov, of my meeting with Mikhail Dushkin.

cᴊᵛꝋ

I telephoned Irina. She came onto the phone in much the same way as Nadia, full of energy and purpose, daring her caller to capture her attention. "Hello," she said, "you called Irina Katzoff?"

I identified myself; she said nothing. A short memory, or maybe an impatience with small talk. "Your invitation came today." Silence. "Shavuot—"

"I know Shavuot. Now I want to know Manya Zalinikov."

"Here I am."

"A good thing. I hope you will be with us at the party. We have invited other guests, as well. I can assure you, the evening will be great fun, in a city where fun is in short supply."

I felt a rush of pleasure. "My thoughts exactly."

"Good. Then you'll come."

cᴊᵛꝋ

Yuri said *no*. Why would he want to go to a party in a strange community hall, strange people, and so on. I said the place and the people were unfamiliar, not the same as being strange, which means peculiar, regretting my schoolteacherish tone, enjoying my opportunity to pick apart his flimsy reasoning.

He said, "If you are finished, please?" I nodded, barely. "Go into a strange hall with dozens, hundreds maybe, of people I don't know?"

"Jews," I said. "Russian Jews, who are here, as you are, as *we*

216

are, trying, not always with success, to put together a new life out of . . ." His hands were flexing with impatience. "I'm almost finished." He harrumphed, but sat down. "Out of bits and pieces. What's so terrible? Good food, good dancing—"

"Dancing? We never danced in St. Petersburg."

"Maybe we should have."

"Interesting." His face had a do-not-try-to-fool-me set to it. "Now you are a strong supporter of Russians emigrating to Israel . . . suddenly, at once?"

"Must I announce every turn my mind takes? Today . . ." I spread my arms as though signaling for attention from a crowd. ". . . today, friends, I want to be nice to Russian *olim*."

He shook his head. "Manya, Manya, so good with words." He moved toward the study, where—I imagined the scene in my mind, imagined it so vividly I could almost see it—he'd take up one of his texts, something the Reb had suggested, and vanish into another world. His eyes were sad, sadder than the day I'd told him I would never be the Jew he needed me to be.

Remorse mushroomed, as I watched him go into the study. I'd gone too far, I always do, playing with Yuri's serious intentions, twisting them to achieve my point. "Just"—he half turned—"this one time, go with me. I want you to meet Irina Katzoff and her husband, Serge."

"Why?"

My mind whirred, trying to find a compelling reason. I settled for the truth. "She is an open person, very intelligent, very much interested in discussing interesting . . . things."

"Such as?"

"And he, Serge, I don't know his mind, but Irina told me he's an observant Jew." Now he looked cautiously interested. "Try."

On Friday, when I left The White Nights, I told Alexsei I would not be in on the following evening. A family matter.

"Does Mr. Kanov know this?"

"I depend upon you to tell him."

"Yes? And will he be pleased to hear this?"

Clever, clever Alexsei. Rather than announce that Kanov would not like my news, he softened this opinion with a question, hoping to make me feel not only a twinge of guilt, but also responsibility for any inconvenience. Very roundabout. Very Russian. Not for nothing had this man risen to be Kanov's number two person-in-charge. I was in no mood, however, for sympathetic attitudes toward my boss, and said, "Perhaps not," finding a small satisfaction in speaking so bluntly. "You will not be without music. Use the many recorded discs Mr. Kanov has in his possession."

"We can do a number of things, Miss Manya, but Mr. Kanov must decide which."

⌒〄⌒

The Russian Community Center was a single-story, brown wooden building, perfect, in its simplicity, for a public social hall: Knotted wood-paneled walls, bare, polished floors, uncurtained windows, a cheap frosted-glass chandelier contributing inadequate lighting. We'd been in numerous such places in St. Petersburg—mainly concrete and gray and somber—on the occasion of Communist Party celebrations, or community meetings. Here, the decorations committee had been at work arranging centerpieces of fruits and vegetables in glass bowls, and tacking sheaves of wheat, barley, oats onto the walls for a festive effect.

Irina Katzoff and another woman, both wearing red, announcing their zest for celebration, moved from table to table, distributing place cards. We stood in the doorway until Irina looked up and, seeing us, rushed over to grasp my hand. "You came," she said, and kissed my cheeks on both sides, Russian style.

"As I said we would." I introduced her and Yuri, especially watching his face for giveaway signs: pursed lips, a sniff, anything. I knew this man, but I didn't really *know* him. He looked friendly, in the hesitant way Yuri registered friendly, but wary, as though expecting Irina to kiss his cheeks, as well. But no. She smiled a just-warm-enough welcome; then, looking around the room, said that Serge had been here one minute ago.

Then he was here again, looking on the young side, as he'd looked at the Great Synagogue: brushed up, with thick black hair, a

218

lot of hair, an open, happy-to-be-here smile, an easy way of holding his hand out, as though his body and he were on good terms.

I breathed all of this in, this complicated equation that had nothing to do with mathematics. If Serge and Yuri became friends, Irina and I could be the same. I wanted another Russian female friend; I needed one for those days when Nadia was otherwise engaged, busy with maneuvering through Jerusalem politics, busy with her receptions and cocktail parties and remaking the world, while I was soaked in loneliness.

People were arriving now, conversation buzzed with a lot of you-look-wonderfuls, a lot of laughing. Here, finally, a room full of Russian-speaking Israelis. No need to break my brain or my tongue over Hebrew. It felt like slipping out of a too-tight girdle and into a satin robe.

We followed Irina and Serge to their table, Yuri with an absent stare I recognized as his having left the room, in a figure of speech. Two other couples joined us: The Bordofskys from Riga, Latvia— she, with blonde hair from a bottle, he, built like a wrestling champion, which, later, I discovered he was. They were technically borderline Russians, close enough. The other couple was the Chesinoffs from Moscow, both with similarly cut, cropped gray hair; both short and wiry, like bicycle riders, and cheerful in the same, healthy way, like twins who ended up married to one another.

The food came in waves, beginning with beet borscht with dollops of sour cream served in paper cups, followed by stuffed cabbages in tomato sauce; Tatiana's recipe, absolutely. The fragrant aroma of seasoned meat, of spices and herbs, wafted me back to my parents' table. I whispered to Yuri, "Whose stuffed cabbages are these?"

Irina, hearing me, pointed to the next table, a big, noisy, square-chinned woman, her frizzy hair ranging in color from yellow to blonde to beige, with a laugh that pinged against the walls and back again. "Sophie," she said, "from Kiev. A trained cook. She works at the Hilton Hotel."

"She took my mother's recipe," I said.

"She owes you a percentage of her pay," Yuri said.

I looked at him, astonished. "I've never heard you speak of percentages of pay." He went on eating. "Is this the Reb's influence?"

"Anything is possible," he said. "Give me your glass." He poured dark Israeli beer out of a brown bottle.

I sipped. "Delicious."

"Not like Russian beer." Serge looked at Yuri. "Yes?" Yuri nodded. "Russian beer is all pale and sudsy and sour-smelling."

"Pale and sudsy and sour-smelling describes most things in Russia," Irina said. "You got shot if you said so under Stalin. Today you can say anything."

"But why bother saying?" Yuri looked suddenly attentive. "Who listened, what changed?"

"*We've* changed," Serge said. "We got out."

He looked around the table for agreement. The male salt and pepper shaker nodded, the female pointed to her wristwatch, a blurred silvery rectangle attached to a worn red leather band. "A sample of Russia crumbling away. Today is my watch's anniversary, six years."

"Already dead," her husband said.

She said, "Nothing made in Russia lasts more than ten years."

A group of men in tuxedos and Russian army caps, colorful medals pinned to their lapels, started setting up instruments in a corner of the room. "Now we dance," Irina said. "Talk is later."

A big sign propped in front of the musicians read, "Moscow by the Mediterranean." The orchestra, a puffed-up word for these men, was strong on accordions, drums, clarinets; the pianist was a tall, square, no-longer-young man with heavy bangs, a dimpled chin, and wild-looking eyes that scanned the room as he played, the kind of eyes known in Russian circles as Raskolnikov eyes.

The first *oom-pa-pa*, and couples surged onto the floor; Irina and Serge were foremost among them, moving together like they had been born dancing with one another, their faces touched by bliss. I turned to Yuri, who raised his hands to his face, a protective wall, saying, *Dancing, him, please, never.* Distance had brought amnesia. We'd danced in St. Petersburg, he and I, on our anniversary, at weddings. Maybe the Reb had uttered an injunction against social dancing.

I had no such limit put upon me, and said, yes, thank you, when, seeing women dancing with women, Irina beckoned me onto the floor. The fox-trot, the waltz, the two-step; no tango fans in that crowd. Then I danced with Irina's friend Sophie, late of Odessa, now of Bat Yam outside Tel Aviv: a lively, natural mover around, skin glowing, curly auburn hair flying behind her as she whirled, which she did often, no matter what the beat. She oozed authority, one big hand clasped around my waist, the other grasping my right hand. I thought, this woman has no trouble twisting off the cap of any-sized bottle.

The clock moved just past ten, and Yuri followed me to the cart that dispensed bottles of cold water, to announce that it was late. "You want to leave?" I said.

"You don't?" His eyes said, *please.*

I'd had my small victory, getting him there, and decided to yield to his necessity. "You had a nice evening?" I looked around the hall for Irina.

He shrugged.

"Did you speak with Serge?"

"Of course. I was there, he was—"

"And?"

"And . . . I spoke with him."

Annoying man. Why didn't men answer questions fully, with the appropriate facial mannerisms, hand gestures; the whole drama expressed by the body as well as by the voice, as women do? Most of the marriages in the world would improve immediately; mental health among women would shoot up.

Irina found us as we claimed our coats. "Manya"—she hugged me, beaming—"we loved having you. You and Yuri." Turning to him, she patted his arm, to which he murmured a sound softer than a grunt and louder than a sigh.

When we arrived home, Yuri pleaded fatigue, and went immediately up to our bedroom. No wine, no party gossip, no confessions on my part; for which, I had to admit, I felt both guilty and relieved. In the kitchen I rinsed out a coffee cup and plate, Galina's good night presents to me, wiped up clean counters, then stood for a long time peering into the refrigerator, before drinking a glass of orange juice I didn't want. Question: Why pull into a long stretch the hard job of confessing? Take it or leave it, I'd done nothing; I'd only *thought* about doing, and who goes to prison, or hell, for thinking?

I found Yuri propped up in bed, reading, swallowed up, as was his custom, by words, ideas, big thoughts. Humming, unfortunately off-key, a good cover-up for a case of nerves, I puttered with the details of removing makeup, brushing hair, then teeth. Behind me, from his corner of the bed, I heard no sounds. Finally, both ready and not ready to speak, I looked across the room to where he was still buried in the pages of a thick book, *The Jewish Dilemma After Nazi Germany.*

"Interesting?" I turned the coverlet back on my side of the bed, before sitting on it. Small talk. I hated it.

His eyes on the page, he *hmmmd.*

"You read in Russian or Hebrew?" The title was in Russian on the cover, but I had to begin somewhere, and books were always a sure way into Yuri's affection.

He nodded.

"The author, an important person?" I slipped out of my robe.

He glanced at me. "Hans Krummerhausen, the professor who talked here last week. I told you." He had. I'd listened through a scrim of my own concerns, registering every other word. Something about a visiting professor talking at the seminary, something about Germany and the war, something about the moving way this man had spoken of Germany's collective guilt toward the Jews, and the wish of the Social Democrats, the ruling German political party, to prove they were ready to take their place among peaceful nations.

"Fifty years since World War II," I said. "We can't go on forever punishing the Germans."

"Who cannot? And what is meant by punishing?"

I smelled coming toward me, a deep, long discussion of politics, religion, geography, history; which, under normal terms, I would welcome, even relish. But not that night. "Such complicated problems, not for discussion so late, especially after a party."

"I agree," he said, continuing to read.

"I am a distraction?" I slid between the covers. He didn't answer. I had brought a nail file into bed, and began working on my thumb.

"Manya, *please.*"

"What do I do?"

"*What*?" Annoyance was layered over his face like aftershave lotion. "If you file, I can't read." He shivered.

"Would you like a glass of wine?"

He looked up from the book. "Wine? All of a sudden?"

"Not all of a sudden . . . exactly." I shrugged. "I haven't used up all my party feelings. I feel like a little wine, some conversation . . ."

Now I had his attention, but I also had his suspicion, a look of wariness. The only way to get in was to open the door and step through. I rolled onto my side, looking directly at him. "We must talk. I have a lot to talk about." I felt my heart beating, or maybe it was my conscience pinging against the walls of my brain. Is that where our conscience lies, up against our brain? Or is it closer to the heart?

"So." He put his book down. "We *must* talk. All right." He sighed in a way that told me he was after all happy to be there with me, his eyes crinkling with his special Yuri-smile that said *I love you*, that said I still delighted him, in spite of coming between him and his book. Which, under the circumstances, made my eyes tear up, made my gene for being fearless wilt. At that moment, Yuri waiting, looking at me with twenty-karat love, I felt terrified and angry—with myself, with Kanov, with Yuri.

I talked, without the benefit of the wine, using words like *foolish, impulsive, lonely*, ending with *outraged* and *regretful*. Yuri listened. The tiny black pinpoint in the center of each of his eyes grew smaller.

Yuri talked, using words like *honor*, and *trust, shameful*, ending with *stunned*.

"I considered not telling you this," I said, Yuri lying on his back, studying the ceiling. I hurried on: "Nothing happened, nothing. I could have convinced myself that we would both be happier if you didn't know, and *pffff*, the whole mess over, move on."

He said, "But *you* knew," turning to look at me. "Between us, since the Catherine Garden, no secrets between us. Never."

"Oh, Yuri," I said, blinking against the tears. He lay absolutely still, looking at me. "You have always been . . ."

"What?"

"*There.*" I sniffed. "Here."

"And now?"

"And now? I don't know," I said, swiping at my nose with the sleeve of my pajamas. "This country, this frantic, frenzied, violent country."

"You blame Israel?" The eye tic winked at me. "*Israel* did this?"

"Yes." The tears came in spurts. "No. It's all too much"—he stretched one arm toward his nightstand and held out a tissue from the box sitting on top of it. I crumpled it—"and not enough."

"Like music."

"Or mathematics."

"I suppose all of life can be described this way. Some things are more than you want them to be, other things are not as much as you need them to be."

I pressed the tissue against my eyes, grateful for the split second of not seeing his sorrow. "Oh, my God . . ." Sitting up, bending over, I wrapped my arms around my waist, closing my eyes, needing something, *anything*, that would hold me together. "I . . . I can't do this alone," I whispered, and felt the tips of his fingers pass across my neck, trail for a moment down my back. Then I heard his bedside lamp click, and opened my eyes to darkness.

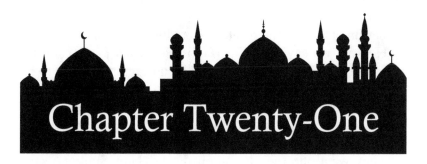

Chapter Twenty-One

S everal silent days later, Ahuva phoned, her voice full of importance. I hadn't seen her since Irina's Shavuot party, and wanted to ask if she knew any of the people I'd met that night.

She was always a lively reporter of a person's funny little habits, the kind that set them out as different: this woman's way of winking at you when she whispered something especially dramatic, leaning close, so close, she took over your face; that man's way of inspecting his fingernails while he talked, as though the next sentence was hidden in one of the cuticles.

But no. Ahuva had an invitation, not a gossip. Something unusual had happened on *JSingles*. A young woman wrote asking to come onto the show, but not just any young woman; she was Swedish, and not Jewish. And pregnant.

"The Reb said no, never. But Oze and Amit, Amit especially, said she would be a hit. A *big* hit. Because, the father of the pregnancy is, *was*, a war hero, killed in Lebanon last month, minutes before they were about to marry. *Minutes.* Our young boys dying, leaving behind crying women. This girl wants to marry someone Jewish, to bring up her baby to be Jewish, like keeping a promise to her dead, dead . . ." Her voice trailed off. "Is the word *lover*?"

There were more twists and turns. The approval committee agreed with Amit and Oze. The audience would love Jen, the part about the dead hero, her wish to have a Jewish child.

I asked, "Is she blonde, and very tall?"

"Both of these, and also very beautiful, almost like a movie star. I saw the picture she sent with the letter. Let me finish, this is a two-part story, and here comes the biggest part. Amit—you know which one, the twin with the freckles and the red hair—he went on the show as one of her three possible men for going on a date." I heard pages turning. Ahuva had probably taken notes on events as they unfolded; she was a natural-born historian of human affairs.

"He kept on saying—I'm reading off this part from my notes—'Lutheran and gorgeous and blonde, and she wants to be Jewish. All the other religions in the world, and she picks Jewish.' I wrote it down, it sounded so . . . I don't know, the young people these days, I don't understand. Even sometimes my grandchildren."

"Maybe Amit wouldn't pick Jewish if he'd had a chance to pick."

"They went out, they had their dating. Now Schlomo says nothing will stop Amit from marrying with this girl, and we should try to be friendly. He wants us to meet her, Yuri, you, me."

"*Me*, as well?"

"Of course, you. Smart, artistic, honest you."

"You told him, include Manya in?"

"I told him nothing. He told me, invite Manya, and we'll have a coffee, a little conversation, on Ben Yehuda. You know the street, the mall for people, without automobiles, the café at the corner, the blue umbrellas over the tables. The birds will be out, sunshine. Say you'll come."

This was Ahuva being Ahuva; I knew the Reb. For his purposes, I would please him by disappearing. Big-mouth Manya, fresh-mouth Manya, the dissenter, the doubter, the heretic. "I'll think about it."

"What's to think? You're Yuri's wife, that makes you important to Schlomo. And Yuri, an educated Jew, a scholar who's also a professor, Schlomo thinks he could have important things to say to Jen."

"Not exactly a professor. He didn't teach, he researched." I felt like a fraud to talk about Yuri, even praise, while we were still, in a manner of speaking, at war. But Ahuva was too filled with her story to notice my unhappy voice.

"Researching, teaching, the same; he's brilliant. But this is most important. Your husband converted from believing in nothing to being an Orthodox."

"And me?"

"You are also, like Jen, an *olim*, in this country without mother, without father, no one here who knew you when you were little. This makes you a stranger in two countries; the country you left behind, and the country you went to."

I hadn't expected Ahuva to speak about me in such poetry. This woman was deeper and more layered than appearances hinted. A sudden thought floated across my mind. "Galina, do you think maybe she and Jen would, you know, both young girls. Jen might welcome someone her age." And I'd welcome my daughter as a wall between Yuri and myself.

"A wonderful idea, Manya. You're a real planner, I'll call you with when we go." My goodbye was almost out of my mouth, when she rushed in with, "Schlomo took your stock money. It's there, with ours, getting more valuable every day."

I hung up, thinking, *Wait, Irina.* I hadn't told Ahuva about my new friend, her quiet energy, the way she made Israel seem so logical, should I say *inevitable*, in the calmest, most self-assured way. A pinch of this would work miracles in my family. But was it a flourish of smoke and mirrors, or was it something much simpler, a way of thinking, *Yes, yesterday we were Russians, but life reorganizes, and continues. Today we're here, today we're Israelis.*

Tomorrow, I'd telephone to Irina, an hour of further conversation. Maybe I still had space in my head to learn something new.

Manya, the planner, invited Irina for lunch that week—Ben Reuven Street, the café where Nadia and I often met—to once more connect with this woman, who I hoped would become a close friend. Nadia said of course she'd join us, then she couldn't. She had to be at the Justice Ministry, or was it the Bureau of Somebody's Affairs, or a press conference; a steam engine of attitudes and opinions as always, over one or another issue. Somebody had done something, and was going to be prosecuted, or somebody should have done something, and she was organizing a rally to support it.

Irina wore red again, a snappy cotton blouse and skirt arrangement, fiery for a hot June day, but a good match for her dark hair. We asked the waitress—not the waitress of the no-borscht-today episode; this one was middlish age, settled down looking, with no-color hair and an anonymous looking nose—for hot tea in glasses and sugar in lumps.

"Russian style," Irina called after her. The waitress didn't turn, but I heard her cranky *hmmmph.*

"So." I settled into enjoying my friend. "What is your life like these days?"

"We're going to America."

I do not surprise easily, not anymore, but on this I was surprised. I felt a pinch of loss. This new friend, this strong, smart, willing friend. I'd just found her. "But why? You only now arrived here."

"Serge, his work isn't asked for in Israel. Too many newspaper writers, what he did in Russia. His Hebrew isn't fast enough for the Israeli papers, and not enough Russian newspapers for all the out-of-work journalists. So"—she shrugged—"the only work he found is to be security in a diaper factory." She laughed, but not because her story was funny. "Who steals diapers? He sits all day watching a door that never gets pushed open."

"Suicide bombers, not robbers," I said, trying for a light voice. "That's what he is paid to do, keep out bombers."

"Nobody keeps out bombers. If they want to bomb"—she made a loud *chu-chu* noise—"they bomb." She looked around, then leaned closer. "I'm not sorry to go. The Arabs want us dead."

"Some of us want *them* dead."

"It will never end, and I have only one life to fool around with." She scrutinized me for a long minute. "Come with, have you ever thought?"

"At the beginning." Those first days in Jerusalem, I'd daydreamed. If only New York would take us, or Los Angeles; sunshine, and no terrorists, no men in black. "Yuri wouldn't go."

"So"—she leaned back—"you have a vote, and he has a vote. Only his vote is bigger than yours."

Chapter Twenty-Two

*M**aariv, Haaretz. The Jerusalem Post. Yediot Ahronoth.* The story had begun as a small item in the business sections of the morning newspapers the last Monday in June. The Reb read them at breakfast. Orange juice, whole wheat cereal, sliced bananas, and accusations of money laundering, corrupt bookkeeping practices, stock offerings where there was no stock of value. Wildberry jam on toast, and Dmitri Kanov accusing the Attorney General of illegally subpoenaing his financial records at the headquarters of Roosya Corporation.

Xenophobia, Kanov accused, antiforeigner hysteria.

The Reb read aloud to Ahuva: "In this country, Russian Jews are not foreigners," the Attorney General replied. "They are us, we are them, Jews among Jews, but no one is exempt from obeying the laws." He passed the newspaper to Ahuva. "One error," he said.

"Yes?"

"What he says about Russian Jews."

By early July, the story in *Maariv* had grown to three columns. At the center, the Reb's photograph in his white satin robe. Above, the caption: *Reb Schlomo Turrowtaub, seminary professor, and host of JSingles, successful matchmaking show on Channel 12, owned by Dmitri Kanov, president of Roosya Corporation.*

When he telephoned Kanov, his employer said, "Come, I am happy to see you anytime." Then, an awkward pause, as though he had run out of interest in the conversation.

Ahuva whispered, "Ask, would today be all right?" He asked. Today was fine, noon.

Ahuva said, *What*! Did he think she'd let him go alone? "That man is not easy to talk with. Two tongues are better than one, four ears are also necessary."

The Reb said he needed no help, he was equipped to speak his mind to anyone, and that included Dmitri Kanov. "Especially when I believe I am right."

"Right about what? Nobody has proved Kanov did anything wrong."

"Not yet," the Reb said, "but we have here a lot of smoke. That doesn't come without a fire." As they walked to the car parked at the curb, he gasped, then ran back into the house.

"The Turrowtaub-turnaround!" Ahuva called after him. "Why do you never leave the house one time with everything you need?"

The Reb emerged with a portfolio, a briefcase, and a tape recorder. "Only people without anything on their minds are organized."

In the car, Ahuva coached him. "Don't lose your temper. Losing your temper means losing the battle. Stay calm, let Kanov talk, you listen."

"I'll listen, *then* I'll lose my temper." He pulled the car away from the curb and into traffic on Keren Hayesod Street. Kanov lived only fifteen minutes away in Motza, a suburb, a more expensive neighborhood, but not more exclusive. The Reb wanted Ahuva to know that. *Anyone* could occupy costly housing. Only money was needed, not pedigree, nor education, nor accomplishment, all of which *he* had.

"There's a story behind the stories we read in the papers, always," she said. "I remember the *Haaretz* accused once that your father charged a fee to say *kaddish* over the graves of dead persons who had no sons or brothers to say it for them." The Reb cut off the car to his left. Ahuva gasped, but went on talking. "And didn't it come out it was a lie?"

"Yes and no." He moved into the middle of the intersection,

blocking an approaching minivan driven by a small, dark young woman talking on a cell phone. "The story was in big type near the front of the paper. My father's denial, and the paper's apology, were in small type near the back, next to the obituaries."

The approaching woman thrust her head out of her open window. "Say, pop, you drive like there's a war waiting for you to win."

"You prove my point," Ahuva said.

The Reb, frantic to beat the red light, wheeled sharply to the left. The woman beeped her horn, a wild blast, her face scrunched in rage. "Which is?" he asked.

"Not to put all your eggs in a newspaper's basket."

The woman went on beeping. The Reb, looking over his shoulder in her direction as he turned, ran his forefinger across his throat.

"I read somewhere that Israelis are more dangerous on the road than on the battlefield," Ahuva said. "Three times more people have died in car accidents than in all our wars." Her knuckles, where she grasped the arm rest, were white.

"Everyone says that, nobody offers up proof. What statistics?"

"You, right now, that's my statistic; your driving."

"Then," he said, moving ahead swiftly, "maybe we should give automobiles to our soldiers, instead of guns."

 ⟡

The trees on Kanov's street were arching green canopies. The Reb parked his car in the shade of an enormous elm, and looked up when Ahuva exclaimed. "Gorgeous."

"Leaves don't drop from rich peoples' trees," he said. "In the fall, I mean."

Ahuva blinked disbelief. "No? What do they do, hold on until the new leaves show up again the next spring?"

But her husband was ringing the doorbell.

Alexsei opened the door and led them to the study, where Kanov was waiting, sipping something sparkling; and, he said, holding his glass up, harmless. "Should Alexsei bring more?"

The Reb waved his hand in refusal and—with a smile that felt shaky and false to him, but would, he hoped, convince their host he had come without anger—sat down opposite Kanov. He settled against the cushions, then, trying for a position that spoke of more authority, sat erect. Ahuva followed.

Kanov tipped his glass toward them. "Good to see you both." An awkward silence rushed into the empty spaces between them. Kanov cleared his throat. The Reb crossed, then uncrossed his legs.

Ahuva rummaged in her purse for a handkerchief. "We came for questions." The tip of her nose was rosier than the rest of her face; a sign, the Reb recognized, that she was nervous.

Kanov looked amused. "To ask, or to answer?"

"We have nothing to explain. It is you who should explain," the Reb said. Then—regretting the ragged edge to his voice, and the way he had leaned forward, as though contemplating lunging— loosened his collar and told himself: *Relax, breathe in, out. Remember yoga. Remember your blood pressure. The eternal questions.*

"Absolutely anything," Kanov said, "everything." He crossed the room to the small cabinet bar, where he filled his glass before returning to his easy chair. "Ask."

The Reb and Ahuva looked at one another as though taken by surprise. He took a deep breath and said, "We need to know if Roosya Corporation is healthy or sick." He swiped the palm of one hand with the palm of the other. "I'm not a man to talk high drama, but you have all our money, everything."

"And our children's money, also," Ahuva said. "Don't forget our children."

Kanov turned solemn. "What newspapers are you reading?"

"All," Ahuva said.

"These things are complicated." Kanov set his empty glass on the small coffee table. "In a perfect world, I could tell you what is going to happen." He looked up at them.

"Nobody expects perfect." Ahuva sniffed into her handkerchief.

"Bad news is complicated," the Reb said. "The truth is simple." He ducked his head. "Your business is in good health, or it's sick and ready to die."

"Don't prepare for a funeral, yet." Kanov made a tent with his fingers, resting his chin on it; for a moment, he seemed to be studying the opposite wall. Then he roused himself and looked at the Reb. "One bit of good news, however, especially for you, Reb"—he waved his hand, as though offering him a valuable prize. Ahuva and the Reb looked up expectantly. "*JSingles* is going on, no one is touching that." He smiled. "For now, anyway."

"For now," the Reb repeated, then leaned forward to say more.

Kanov hurried on. "However, on other fronts, I have enemies." The Reb shrugged his chin in a sign, he hoped, of sympathetic understanding. "I admit there have been some surprises."

"*Surprises?*" The Reb ran his tongue over his lips. "There are surprises, and there are *surprises.*" He looked at his wife, who was staring at Kanov. "Some people have surprise parties"—he shifted his feet—"some people have surprise funerals."

"How big a surprise?" Ahuva said.

"Big." Kanov played with his glass, moving it back and forth across the slick blackness of the tabletop. "The stock exchange in Frankfurt, for one."

The Reb slapped his knee. "Avrum, Mister Know-It-All. I told him—"

Ahuva put her hand on her husband's arm. "Plenty time for that later." Sliding forward in her chair, she scrutinized Kanov. "What can a stock market do? It's not a person."

Kanov smiled. "It can do a great deal, all of it difficult to explain, difficult to understand. But there it is, one of the harsher realities."

"Your stock market surprised you . . . how?" Ahuva said.

Kanov wagged his hand.

No sense, the Reb thought, in beating that dog to death. "And besides the Frankfurt surprise?" he said.

"Personal disappointments. Friends who I should have been able to count on took advantage of my being here and not there."

The Reb strained for a normal voice. "*There?* Where is *there?*"

Kanov continued: "One would think that after a lifetime of arranging these deals, one would know who is to be trusted."

Ahuva nodded in spite of herself. "If not you, then *who?*" Her eyes took on a just-a-minute look. "Tell us, please, did your personal . . ." She hesitated, as though struggling for a word. ". . . let us call them disappointments; did these happen *after* you sold your stock shares, or before?"

Kanov, fussing now with a leather-bound book he'd picked up from the table, said, without looking at Ahuva, "I managed to sell something, not much; take my word, nothing to speak of."

"Then, please, let us speak of what is left for us," she said.

Kanov stood up and looked around the room in a distracted way, as though searching for something he'd lost. The Reb stared at the floor with glazed eyes, and seemed to no longer be listening.

"*Gone?*" Ahuva prodded. "Everything?"

Kanov ran his hand through his hair. "Betrayal by friends, former friends, is the most painful part of this."

Ahuva sucked in her breath, and squeezed her eyes shut. When she opened them, she reached for the Reb's hand. "Maybe for you the most painful. For me, for us, Mr. Kanov, the most painful part is going to our children and telling them we are poor all over again." And Manya, she thought. Manya's money—gone, also.

Chapter Twenty-Three

This country is like no other. It takes you in, and yet, you are never *in* as a *sabra* is in. It takes you in, and then it breaks your heart.

Israelis are proud people—chauvinists, my Hebrew language teacher called them. They want everyone who comes here to love it. I have tried, and I have passed *dislike*. I have passed *distrust* and *confusion*, without yet arriving at *love*.

Consider this: probability. A better subject for a mathematician than for a musician. The probabilities of geography, religion, sociology, psychology, and what in Russia we called *blood pull*, tell us that Jen and Amit should not have met. Having met, according to these probabilities, they should not have fallen, as the saying goes, in love. That they wished to marry—human beings being perverse, this country being complicated—was miraculous in its optimism.

To marry, to make a beginning, to say to the people you love, *Next year we will do such and such, and the year after that we will do another such and such,* in a country whose specialty is endings, is an act of courage. Or, maybe a refusal to settle for reality, when reality is too difficult. We Russians manufacture melancholy; we luxuriate in it, we export it. While Israelis, not yet my favorite persons, existing on a pinpoint of land surrounded by a sea of enemies, insist upon everyday normal—weddings, circumcisions, babies, concerts, museums, zoos, lectures, carnivals. I cannot decide whether they live this way out of bravery or denial—maybe a mix of both. Neither do I know if their way, or ours, is better.

⸙

I must tell this story from the beginning. Two weeks ago, on a day when the Reb's nerves were bitten off at the ends from long rehearsals and no sleep, from not knowing if *JSingles* would be a big success, Amit announced his plan to marry Jen.

I was on the set with Ahuva, following her around with flash bulbs, film, cold water, aspirin, working hard to stay out of the Reb's footsteps. To me, he looked like a volcano draped in white, threatening to boil over if one tiny detail went wrong.

Everyone knew Amit was swept up with Jen, but the Reb had closed his lips to speaking about it. After lunchtime, everyone standing around drinking coffee, I heard Amit telling Oze that, before the summer was over, he'd marry with her.

"Does the Reb know?"

"He will, in five minutes."

The Reb's response was, "*Marry!*" His eyes bulged, the veins in his neck purpling. "I heard you correctly?" He twisted his empty plastic water bottle into a pretzel shape. "A Jew to a non-Jew?" Now his cheeks were fiery red, but Amit . . . Amit was smoking, and calm.

"Marry Jen-from-Sweden"—three words pronounced as one—"who, if I am again correct, you met not one month ago?" Everyone on the set froze. Silence came down like a heavy blanket. Ahuva brought a glass of cold water and two blood pressure pills, which the Reb swallowed without taking his eyes off of the younger man.

"I thought, *friends*," he went on, "*not a problem*. I thought, *give him time, he'll see it is not possible*." Amit, the soul of patience, lit a second cigarette. "This, this . . ." The Reb blinked forcefully. ". . . *this* is a crack in the foundation of the Jewish people. One small crack, then a split, a split becomes a *re'idat adama*, an earthquake." *A wonderful word*, I thought, writing it into my language notebook. It sounded exactly like what it meant.

"Ruth," Amit said, "think about Ruth. Also a convert, as well as the Bible's most famous daughter-in-law, as well as an accomplished great-grandmother." The Reb looked confused. "David."

From the other side of the musicians' stand, Oze whistled and applauded, calling out, "The kid grew up to be our very own King David, remember?"

The Reb asked, "Does your mother know what you are planning?"

His mother had recently died, said Amit, looking no more ruffled than did Rasputin, when accused of plotting against the Czar.

The Reb pounded onto a table. "Your mother," he hollered, "should be grateful she isn't here to see this." Ahuva reminded him of his health, and Amit said, "Go home, everybody, rehearsal is over."

✺

The solution, reported to me by Ahuva, was sent down from the top. Kanov, who was as lukewarm Jewish as I, said he loved controversy, and audiences loved controversy. Strong opposing points of view made good television shows, which, in turn, meant good business.

Amit, he said, had the freedom to love anyone. From what Kanov knew of Jen, loving her made perfect sense. If she loved Amit back, well, then—. Ahuva and I puzzled over the missing end of his sentence. My interpretation was that it meant whatever anyone wanted it to mean, just do not make problems for *JSingles*. It also meant the Reb inviting us to coffee on Yehuda Mall to declare peace.

✺

Another phone call from Ahuva; she was crying, sniffles clotting up the telephone wires between her words. A red flag went up inside my head. *I knew*. If we had not arrived at devastation—the natural way station for Jews, especially Israeli Jews—we had come very close. She handed out her news in small doses, beginning with, "I would rather cut off my little finger than tell you this."

237

"Who died?" I imagined her puffy eyes, a box of tissues at her elbow, her bangs pushed to one side, stringy, uncombed. "Ahuva." I struggled to keep my voice kind. "The news, *please.*"

She hiccupped soft, gasping sounds, then told me. I absorbed it, silently calculating. I'd miss the money, and I'd miss the feeling that I had clever judgment, that I knew a good thing when it bit me in the face, but it was too small a sum to mourn.

Yuri hadn't known I'd invested in Kanov's stock. No need to tell him my investment had soured. My impulsive behavior; I was it, it was me. One of the penalties of being married to me. Never mind that, under our recent circumstances, Yuri was undoubtedly thinking that, in our marriage, the bad outnumbered the good.

"How is the Reb?" I asked.

"How *can* he be?"

⁂

So. On a summer afternoon, the Jerusalem sky a rare pitch of royal blue, clouds tufting, birds dipping into and out of the budding trees, we seven persons met on Ben Yehuda Mall, that lively pedestrian walkway with bookstores and restaurants and shops selling everything from ice cream to T-shirts to jewelry and musical CDs, one of my favorite happiness sites in a city that is not often happy.

Jerusalem was not a place of street music. It was too anxious, waiting, always, for something terrible to take shape. On most days, nobody felt like music in their bones. But that day, on the corner, a stringy-looking young man in need of a bath played his guitar, and a young girl with dark, tangled hair, a curious, oval-shaped scar across one cheek, and dressed in orange and red and gold silk somethings, shook a tambourine and collected coins from the crowd, which she slipped inside her brassiere, or whatever she wore instead of a brassiere. Neither of these young people looked Israeli; but, then again, who *does* look what is called Israeli?

We watched the musician and the gypsy for a long time. Strangers, we couldn't jump right in with, "So, your mother isn't well," or, "I saw your son at the mall yesterday, with what looked like a beautiful girl." Even with Galina standing between Yuri and myself, I was aware of my husband's cool tone, his reticence to speak to me at length, if at all. Finally, the Reb, in his television voice, said, "Well, well, just imagine," and we all laughed in a hollow way, like smiling at the ceiling of an elevator to avoid making foolish talk with the other passengers.

We were seven human beings of differing ages, temperaments, and nationalities, for those moments interested in one another, and surely interested in the redemptive powers of love. The Reb led us down the mall to a sidewalk table at the Blue Bird Café, and I watched Galina watching Jen, with her bright yellow hair, like a silken waterfall; her big, wide-awake, yet dreamy, eyes; and, over it all, a look of wise innocence.

My daughter said nothing, but I knew, by the way she focused her attention on the other young woman's hair, clothes, nails, that she found much to admire. Was she the smallest slice jealous, I wondered, that this girl, not Jewish, not Israeli, not Russian, had captured this splendid young man? Difficult to say from the outside. Galina was a talented actress.

Jen, that day, was a shaft of light, wearing something white and gauzy. Galina's clothes leaned in the direction of the theatrical: an orange knit blouse, a short but complicated skirt, flowered in red and yellow, a silk scarf tied around her throat. She and Jen, seated opposite one another, leaned across the table to talk, Galina doing most of the talking, since her Hebrew, as bumpy as it was, was better than Jen's. Two cell phones rang in the same second, at a nearby table. "Did you know that Israel is where cell phones were invented," Galina said, "which is why our babies get their first one in the hospital nursery?"

Jen laughed, then took a fiery red instrument out of her bag, passing it among us. "A present," she said, patting Amit's arm. This very small machine fit into a palm and, when opened, announced the date and the time.

"Do you have a phone like this?" Jen asked Yuri, as if she knew he was a mathematician, and crazy about new inventions.

Yuri's smile was tight, but friendly. Since the beginning of his new life in prayer, in which he thanked God every morning for not making him a woman, he was not at peace with ladies who appeared to be too technological. He shook his head. "This kind of miracle is expensive."

Jen laughed in her attractive, but careless way. Amit said something about what is money for, and kissed her shoulder. Galina scrutinized Jen, sending eye signals to me, announcing approval of what she saw.

Yuri looked away, his eye tic ticking his discomfort. The Reb's responsibility as host clicked into place. Jumping to his feet, he raised his coffee cup. "To the happiness of the couple," he said, a hundred million miles away from his first response to Amit's marrying an un-Jew. A general murmuring agreement floating around the table. We clicked cups with one another, and Amit hugged Jen, looking at her as though, if he looked away, she might vanish. Galina took out a notebook and wrote, probably a reminder to herself to remind Asher she would love to own Jen's miracle telephone.

⌇⌇⌇

Here, now, the bitter coincidence in my story. In this city of half a million persons, and an equal number of cafés, on that afternoon, at a table some meters beyond ours, but close enough for me to observe, sat a slender man with an ordinary face, not young, not old, wearing one of those stiff black hats that sit unnatural, high on the head, a black silk coat, the white fringe of his *tzitzit* swinging below his shirt. The *tzitzit* I did not see until he stood up; but, seeing the hat, seeing the beard, I knew this was a case of *tzitzit*.

The beard: heavy, dark, not trimmed to a point and romantic-looking, like Yuri's, or even like Czar Nicolas's beard, but dense and squared and long. His side curls bounced in a manner that was both comic and serious, and were, in a strange way, sweet-looking when he turned his head to call the waitress. All in all, an ordinary, Orthodox look in a place where this man was among his own.

And, yet, *something*. I whispered to Yuri, "Isn't that man too young to look so old?" He frowned, and whispered back, "Manya, *please*."

Since his departure from our family's nonexistent Judaism, *Manya, please,* had become his principal declaration to me when I remarked in public upon anyone in black clothing.

Or, in private, on why the monthly necessity of the *mikvah* insulted women. Or, on why refusing to eat milk products and meat products together was accepting the medieval amidst the twentieth century.

"That man is fully Israeli," he said. This was what Yuri called the person of whom I speak. *Fully Israeli.* The eye twitch danced in the corner of his right eye, further proof, not that I needed it, of his annoyance with me.

I leaned past Yuri, hoping to reach Galina. Still writing, absorbed fully in her notebook, she undoubtedly hadn't noticed this man. She ignored all men in black. They were beyond her ability to understand, she'd said, primitives, unfriendly to women, why should she acknowledge them?

Why? Because they were here, and we were here, and every molecule occupying a single Israeli could change the emotional temperature of this country. Just as the beggars lingering at the entrance to the central post office in St. Petersburg changed the way we entered and exited from that building, making certain to have coins to drop into their hands, or suffer their insults hollered after us as we retreated down the street. Just as the *babushkas* seated in the corners of every gallery in the Hermitage Museum changed the way we'd enjoyed the art. Do not touch, do not stand too close, do not sneeze, cough, sniff on any object other than another person.

The man was now wearing sunglasses while reading his newspaper, shifting the paper every few moments, reading it upside down as often as right side up. Strange, but most Israelis' nerves were so jangled by everyday events, reading a paper upside down might be a typical consequence of this. Should I report him, like I'd report a suspicious package sitting in the post office, looking like it belonged to nobody? Report him for doing *what*? This man was not a package; he was an Orthodox.

I looked around for someone whose arm I might grab, someone to whom I could whisper, *Shhh*, there, that man in black, does he look wrong to you? Would an Israeli believe a Russian? Remember the people at the Dung Gate, I reminded myself; stay calm, talk calm. Yuri fussed with his wristwatch, shaking it to assure that the time was correct, and Ahuva reminded the Reb to put only one sugar in his coffee, and Jen asked, Where was the bathroom? I said, me, too. Jen was the one. If my Hebrew could penetrate her Hebrew, she'd believe.

When we stood up, Galina said to wait for her. In my mind, even a small exodus from the table would put a cold towel on the party atmosphere, already teetering under the weight of Yuri's annoyances. I whispered that the bathroom was for one lady at a time, possibly the wrong information, but she nodded. On my side was the fact that public restrooms in Russia were scarce, inconvenient, and dirty.

Jen slipped her arm through mine, as easily as she would with an old friend, smiling her sweet, radiant smile that so loudly announced her happiness. "Come, come, Missus Zalinikova"—she laughed—"I said it correctly?" I felt a warm wave of affection for this brave young woman, thousands of miles from her family, her lover so recently torn away, and now ready to move on into a new version of her life, as though she, like Israel, refused to be beaten down. She struck me as having a wisdom I had not yet discovered. Maybe I never would. Maybe she'd be willing to tutor me, to infect me with her optimism.

We walked together to the café building, not ten meters from our table, passing the man in black, who had a look of happy expectation on his face, or what I could see of his face, with all that beard to hide in. Jen went inside, but I stopped at the entrance to look back at him. He stood up. I thought, good, he's leaving. But no. He didn't walk away.

I stayed in the doorway, just inside the café, holding the door open to see what he'd do next. He called out to the waitress, "Please, a glass of water." In this same moment, a small bird with a shimmering blue head flew onto the tip of the umbrella shading his table. The waitress, a slender young girl with pale, silky curls all over her head, a starched white apron over her blue jeans and T-shirt, and a springy walk that announced good health, brought the water. To look at her was to know that somewhere, even if they lived in a faraway time zone, was a family that telephoned her often, just to inquire about her happiness, and to say, "Good night, we love you."

I continued holding the door open. The bird was pecking at

the yellow umbrella as though someone had planted it with bird seed. The man drank the water, dropping the glass, or throwing it, a crash that caught everyone's attention, except the bird's. Then he said, very loud, to no one, to everyone, in Hebrew more poorly accented than even mine, "Goodbye! I will not see you again," before thrusting one hand inside his jacket and throwing himself forward.

The sky shook, the earth rocked, birds flying over must also have rocked. Bright light shone everywhere, so much brightness, it lifted up the man in black, exploding him into bits and pieces of bone and flesh that splattered onto the tables and chairs, until there was no man left, only a body without a face or arms. All around him, or what was left of him, where people one second before were eating and laughing and telephoning and kissing, there was empty air above, bloody pools and body parts below. Glasses, dishes, pitchers flew off the shelves at the waiter's station behind me. Windows cracked and some blew away, along with the door, knocking me to the ground.

A man hollered, "Everybody, be calm, sit." He didn't mean me. I had to go out. Yuri was out, Galina was out, but he pulled at me and screamed there would be more explosions, come back, stay inside. I went anyway. Another man shouted, "*Pigua, pigua*! Terrorist!"

Then, an eerie silence—the earth holding its breath—followed by three shrieks of a siren, as sudden as a gunshot. Two shrieks were an everyday sound, announcing an everyday ambulance coming through, carrying someone with an everyday heart attack, a baby impatient to be born. Three blasts meant terror attack. Three blasts meant once again.

A woman was crying; a sound beyond anything human, beyond pain, beyond grief, as if sorrow had been given its own voice. She wouldn't stop and wouldn't stop, until I called out, "No more, *please!*" and realized, as I kicked something soft, a hand with four fingers, that the voice was me. Then bodies to step over, some without heads. My right eye felt stabbed. I touched it. My hand came away with blood.

Ahuva and Amit were slumped over our table, not moving; the Reb was underneath, murmuring something I didn't understand.

Yuri, lying on his back, stared at the sky, his jacket and shirt shredded, blood running from an opening in his throat, splashing onto the bird lying next to him, now without its shimmering blue head. Galina, one minute lying flat down, the next, sitting up, looked at me with a face heavy with blood, her stunned eyes registering that she had never seen me before.

Down on my hands and knees, I begged Yuri, "Breathe in, out, in. Breathe." *Don't die before we make up, before I tell you how much you are loved.* He struggled to take in air. I thumped on his chest, which did nothing except give me something to do. I wiped Galina's face with her silk scarf, tying the ruined fabric around her head so that only her eyes showed. The wild bird trapped inside my chest beat its wings, trying to get out. In minutes, less than minutes, ambulances screamed onto the mall, as though all morning they had waited around the corner, knowing, with that sorrowful Israeli knowing, that, sooner or later, something terrible would happen. Why go home, why bother to take the ambulances into the garage? They will be needed again.

All around me, cell phones rang and rang and no one answered. News played on the radio and the television day and night in this country, a country smaller than Belarus or the Ukraine. Everyone listened. Everyone expected tragedy, and all the phones worked. A bomb gets exploded, and everyone calls everyone they love.

The everyone I loved, besides Yuri and Galina, were Nadia, who was that day in Eilat, and Yael, in her office. Should I call? *We're fine, my eye bleeds and Yuri's throat is slit, Galina's face is in pieces, but we're able to move, there are no big pieces of shrapnel or nails in important parts of our bodies. If there are, they're lying quiet.* My cell phone was in my purse, and my purse blew out of my hand when I fell.

Now came the police and the fire people, and the experts in explosives, to search for other bombs. Then the ZAKA workers, who began at once the work of cleaning up. Israelis are efficient people.

Have you seen these ZAKA men executing their dance, a dance without music? Men in yellow-and-black vests, skullcaps and white gloves, carrying plastic bags, peeling scraps of flesh and bone from under the tables, the chairs, scraping from the few whole windows that remained, scooping from the bloody river running down the street, wading into the ankle-high sea of broken glass that surrounded everywhere, to pick, pick.

"Remnants," I heard these men say, "collect every remnant." Every pinpoint scrap of human being must be buried, with the body or without. Did you know intestines are yellow? Have you ever seen an arm or leg lying on the ground, attached to only air? And this: DNA. The DNA of a hand, even an ear, a finger, can connect a body part to a body, to a life that was, up to the moment of the explosion, busy at the business of living.

Somewhere in this country, in a room lined with computers and laboratory bottles and liquids, plastic boxes, and file folders, a man—wearing a *kippah,* a white lab coat, probably rumpled, perhaps a white, fringed vest under his shirt, no tie—sits sorting through medical reports, identifying what had once been a whole person from a small piece, a scrap of tissue, a chip from a tooth. A grotesque matching game, and there was no prize.

Men wearing masks to keep out the exploded debris and dust and the stench of burned flesh, a smell uncannily similar to the smell of rotting food, carried out people on stretchers. Bleeding bodies and ringing pockets. I saw the young waitress with the blue jeans and head of curls, her apron smeared with blood, passing too quickly for me to ask: Alive? Farther off, the ambulances waited. A man in a white coat made wild gestures with his arm, calling to the rescuing people, "Don't give me the dead ones, bring out the injured." A pair of wet brown boots stopped next to me. I looked up into the face of a young girl medic. "Are they alive? We're taking out the living ones first."

The funeral was the following day, Jewish law requiring burial within twenty-four hours. Just as well. So many Jews being killed every day, this way the burial teams can keep up, the roads into and out of the cemeteries don't get clogged. Even in hell, details are important, to hold together things that would otherwise fall apart

Amit's family owned an area in the small garden cemetery on the western edge of the city. Jen and I went. The ceremony was

short and terrible, in Hebrew; Jen not a part of it, nothing. His
mother, also red-haired, was not, as Amit had told the Reb, dead;
but, after burying her child, probably wished she could be. Jen
wanted to say something to this woman, she didn't know what,
some word of recognition, of alliance. They had, after all, both
loved the same young man. Oze, looking like he couldn't remember
where he was, or why, tried to help, but his mother looked at no
one and said nothing, her face frozen into deep furrows of grief.

⟟⟟⟟

The Reb and Ahuva were minor miracles: serious scrapings, a
broken wrist, a twisted neck, damaged ribs, singed hairs. My eye
was bandaged; a good thing, because that way my tears spilled
from only one side. I ran outside too fast, the doctor told me, didn't
I know any better? "Doctor," I said, "please understand. This was
my first suicide bombing. I'll do better the next time."

⟟⟟⟟

Two weeks later, Yuri and Galina were still in the hospital, his
throat stapled together, living on blood from people we never met;
light ones and dark ones, rich ones and not-so rich, most of them
speaking languages I didn't understand. So much blood, so many
people, we'll never be able to thank everyone.

I played the what-if game in my mind, and with Galina: What if
we'd went to another café? What if we'd sat at another table, farther
back, farther out? What if I'd said yes when she asked to go with
me to the women's room? What if we'd never come to Israel?

Her room was down the hall from Yuri's. She'd had, in the first
ten days, many surgeries. To save her face, the surgeon said, also
to pick out the nails from the bomb, and the flying debris and glass
from everywhere. She'll have a scar, he said, running the nail of
his pointing finger from the corner of his eye to his mouth. I asked,
how deep, how wide, how bad? He shrugged. "It isn't fatal, so how
could it be bad?"

Only a face. I imagined him thinking this, especially on a day
when he perhaps sewed a finger back onto a hand, or stitched

a kidney, a stomach, back into somebody's body. I did not say this to anyone but myself: *One person's only is another person's everything.*

⌒ﾞ⌒

Those first days, my bed was the floor of Yuri's room; the beep-beeps of his monitors, the soft shuffle of the nurses' shoes moving down the hall, these were my lullabies. Lying alone, I thought terrible thoughts about not being able to go on, about why were we here—*why*? Israel was dying, I sobbed one night to Yuri, who blinked. He heard me. I wanted to go home, my real home. I'd never felt so alone, so sinned against, so angry.

Nadia came with a bottle of red wine. "To help you feel more human," she said, "especially when taken with music, possibly a nice view of the ocean."

"Where nearby is an ocean?" I said. "Do you see an ocean?"

She sniffed at the complicated air: soap and disinfectant and floor wax. "The smells in here could kill you."

Irina brought a basket of bottles; lotions, for my skin, my eyes, my spirit, although this last part of me couldn't be massaged, not then—and, I thought, maybe not ever. "They're Buddhist," she whispered, holding up an especially beautiful red glass spiral filled with pale-yellow liquid, "strictly interfaith. Don't tell Yuri. Some things are for women only to know."

I said, "Most things are for women only to know."

Yael came with her uplifting outlook that usually rescued me, but not that day. She brought an enormous pink flowering plant for Yuri, and a book of Israeli poetry for Galina, plus a bag filled with the newest fashion and movie person magazines, "for her less intellectual moments."

"How are you holding up?" she asked me, in the hallway, away from Yuri's hearing.

"I'm not."

"These are terrible challenges."

"*Challenges*? A psychology word, a word for people who don't know what it feels like to be blown up. Challenge means something difficult to do, with the promise of a reward at the end. My reward is a husband living on borrowed blood and a daughter with a ruined face."

"Both alive, both recovering."

"I want to lay down on the floor and howl, I want to—"

"But there *is* a reward." She pulled me to her, an un-Yael thing to do. "Now you're one of us, more *sabra* than *olim*."

"You invite me into your exclusive club of survivors of terrorist attacks?"

"You invited yourself. You went through the initiation."

"So, I uninvite myself. I was never one to join clubs."

But Yael had touched upon something that was happening in spite of my despair. The young girl soldiers, scrubbed, innocent faces in a background of khaki, who came after regular army working hours with soap and shampoo and towels, blankets, were, if not angels—my list of beliefs didn't include angels—but super *menschen*, Ahuva's word in Yiddish for special human beings.

And the other women, older women with their own troubles and broken hopes for their families, who made my telephone calls and brought my medicines and clean clothes, then sat with a cup of tea, waiting, when I had too much to say and no words to say it with. Is it possible, I began wondering, this country makes a special kind of woman, who lives inside so much danger, she comes out with a talent for being both strong and kind?

One woman especially, I don't know her family name, but on her dress was pinned a brass bar: Cyma. When Cyma wheeled her cart down the hospital corridor, it was like music was pouring from the loudspeakers. She gave out newspapers and magazines and candies, makeup, fluffed-up house slippers, skin lotion that smelled like a garden. I listened every day for her laugh, the proof I needed that the entire world had not gone mad. There were reasons to go on living.

⌇⌇⌇

Jen came to say goodbye, looking that day like a woman who had forgotten about details like lipstick, or making up her eyes. Even her hair, pulled back with a rubber twister, looked without life. "I could have saved him," she said. I didn't agree, but I didn't argue.

She was going home to Stockholm, to reflect on how everyone she loved ended up dying.

"Not your baby," I said.

⌬

The doctors called Yuri's wounds superficial. Not true. Nothing about being blown up was superficial. I asked my husband if he knew what the Reb was saying under that table when the bomb went off, because I didn't want to ask if he had forgiven me. I stayed with minutiae, clinging to the ordinary. The *Shema*, he said, the prayer for the dying carried by Jews into the gas chambers in the camps.

"Where did you learn these things? You have only just now become a Jew."

He smiled—a pale, melancholy kind of smile that left his eyes unsmiling; his birth gift from being born a Russian. I squeezed his hand to say what I couldn't say: *All the talking we went through about his God not being my God, unimportant. The loneliness question that made me think Kanov was the answer, unimportant.*

⌬

Now, the question that plagued me, still plagues me. What decides on a daily basis who is to go on living, who is to die? Luck decides. Good luck says, *live.* Bad luck says, *die.* As harsh and final and unfair as that. Don't tell me about the Book of Life; I like my answer better. If I could choose between being born with the gene for luck, or the gene for wealth, or power, or talent, or even intelligence, I would choose luck. I would choose the *mazel* gene.

My second question was this: The Jews have been chosen, the scholars say. We have an obligation to carry out God's commandments, to demonstrate that we choose Him, they say. To demonstrate that we honor our covenant with Him.

Chosen? For *this*?

If any of you out there speak with Him on a regular basis, please, the next time I want you to say, "Hey, Mister Big Shot, I have a message from my friend, Manya Zalinikova. Take a minute from your important God work, look down. You'll see her, a dark-haired woman in her over-the-middle forties, usually wearing something red, now with an eye bandage."

Tell Him I appreciate His good intentions. He meant well, but ask Him to leave us alone to live our lives in whatever decent way is still possible, one day into the next, no special connections or special memberships with special groups up there where He lives. Ask Him, for me, to unchoose us. Please.

Chapter Twenty-Four

I met with my Galina-grief in this way: I telephoned Asher, who had many times visited Galina in the hospital, but never when I was present; perhaps a deliberate timing, perhaps not. I had not, in fact, seen him since his visit to me, a visit I had not mentioned to my daughter.

I knew, even as I dialed the phone, that I was not being fair to ask for rescue from him. He was not her blood relation, not her sweetheart of many years, as Yuri had been to me when we were in Galina's and Asher's time of life. In their months together, of what some would call courting, my daughter had not been wildly encouraging, and, I guessed, often not loving. Still. Ask a mother, any mother, what in these circumstances was fair to ask for. Anything, anywhere, from anyone. Fair was not a first consideration.

Yael took my place with Yuri and Galina at the hospital, while I met with Asher in his office at the university. They had already healed sufficiently to put food into their own mouths, to sit up for long moments, to walk tiny steps down the hall, to complain—which the nurses told me was good; a signal they felt strong enough to make trouble.

Asher was working at his desk when I arrived, shifting back and forth a collection of small statues, scattered among notebooks and thick volumes of archeology. I knew they were filled with archeology by the covers: pictures of very little, very naked, beige-colored people with lumpy hands, wearing funny headpieces.

He jumped up, clearing off a chair, and offered coffee, tea, water. We sat in silence for the first moments, smiling at one another, uncertain how to begin. The day we met in my parlor, I'd hidden behind cigarettes and a clever mouth. But not now, now was too serious. Hiding wouldn't serve either of us.

Leaning forward over the desk, peering at the statues, men, women, alone, together, embracing, kissing, fondling, feeling—despite my layers of sadness, and my fear that this young man would say to my face, *Galina? And who is* that? Or, worse: *Do you remember our first conversation, when I needed you?*—a pleasant chill of desire ran through me. So much revealed in these bits of, of—"What is it they are made from?" I asked.

Asher picked up a standing woman, full in the breasts, plentiful hips, altogether miraculously shaped. Her hair was parted exactly in the middle; a tiara—or was it a crown?—decorated her head. "This lady is a queen, or a princess," he said, "but we don't know her name. She isn't in our archives. We call her *Malka Bshelut*, which in Hebrew means Queen of Ripeness."

"Ripeness?" A good word; in fact, the exact word to be used. *Bshelut.* I said it, enjoying the *shhhh* sound, then the snappy *tuh* after sliding down the chute of the *loo*. "She does, as you say, look like a ripe specimen. May I?" He handed her into my care, a blooming flower of a woman, perfect in her body, more than beautiful in her face, if you excused her blank staring; but maybe this was the way ladies used their eyes at that time in history. "How old is she?"

"How old was she when this piece was carved, or how long ago was she shaped into this work of art?"

I put her down. "Everything has a question. This is the country of questions."

"Mrs. Zalinikova"—he placed the queen in a small box padded with tissue paper—"you are here . . ." A nervous smile took over his sweet, kind face.

"Galina."

"Of course."

"Her tragedy." I considered. Was it wise to point out my daughter's affliction? Like I was apologizing for her losing something valuable, and now she'd be less—less marvelous. She'd been given great gifts from nature, my child, like the ripeness queen, and she'd used them with lavish attention to the smallest detail. Maybe, again, like the queen? So, the question here was this: who was left behind when, *whoosh*, in one moment so much was swept away, and—*two* questions—could my daughter put together a life without . . . *without*? I smelled my own despair, metallic and hard, a wall wrapping me in, and the world out.

"Her face, yes." Asher's eyes were sad, in a way that made me wonder if he'd had a happy childhood. When I didn't answer, he pressed forward. "Your daughter, ah—*Galina* . . ."

Brilliant, this young man, but a problem in the talking department. Possibly a man who thinks so deeply, so importantly, has trouble finding ordinary words to explain ordinary things.

"My daughter . . ."

He poured water from a pitcher into a glass, emptying it in a single swallow. "I love her." That said, he filled the glass a second time, and, again, emptied it. "I want to marry her. You cannot fully appreciate—"

"I can, I *can* appreciate." This news was what I'd hoped to hear, but never thought that, under the terrible circumstances, I would. My heart pressing into my chest, I managed to get out, "Tell me."

"I'm a man"—beads of sweat populated his forehead. He pulled at the knot in his tie, loosening it, and, for a moment, I thought he was going to unbutton his shirt—"who finds it difficult to speak of certain matters." He slumped back into his chair, as though exhausted.

"Yuri, my husband, Galina's father, is a similar man." Was it possible that Galina, an enigma to her own father, had succeeded in captivating this young man, this substantial, gifted, steady person; now especially, in a time with no end to our needing the earth under our feet to stay steady?

A light tapping on the door; it opened, bringing in an intellectual looking gentleman of somewhat older years, a lot of salt-and-pepper hair, the body of an aging athlete. Seeing me, he looked to Asher, then back to me.

"Professor Avigdor." Looking more flustered than delighted, Asher jumped up. "May I introduce you"—he exchanged our names, stumbling on mine.

The professor produced an old-fashioned, European-type bow, of the kind I'd seen my father bring out when, on the street, we'd meet one of his fellow military officers, or another physician. We shook hands and inspected one another. I liked what I saw. This man seemed, on the surface, anyway, to be of a more poetic, less stick-a-thumb-in-your-eye nature than most Israelis I'd met.

Professor Avigdor said, "A happy coincidence. We have here today the mother of Asher's celebrated Galina?" His smile said this was a question meant to flatter. "And," he went on, "I see from where the young lady's beauty springs."

Never a blusher, I blushed.

Asher said, "Coincidence?"

"Miss Galina's terrible injury. I've come to inquire." Looking at me, he said, "She *is* recovering, I hope."

I wagged my hand back and forth. "The answer depends on the day you ask." Now that Asher had declared his love, I felt able to speak the difficult truth.

The professor looked sorrowful. "*Aaahhh*," he breathed, "as is so often the case. Well"—rubbing his hands together; and, for whatever reason, suddenly cheerful—"our Asher is just the person to help her navigate this sensitive period."

If I were a believer in God, or a better pretender, I'd have added Ahuva's favorite wish: "From your mouth to God's ear."

"Am I right, Asher?" the professor urged. "You will be a loving nurse to Galina?"

Right there, I could have, should have, clasped this man to my chest for a kissing. However, knowing him for only five more-or-less minutes, I said, "Surely, then, my daughter will heal up like new in no time at all."

Both men were standing, so I joined in. A good time to say goodbye, when everything was going well. I put my hand out to Asher, who looked startled, as though he had never seen a hand. "I won't take up anymore of your valuable time." To the professor, I said, "A pleasure to meet."

Yael had once told me that many Israelis didn't bother with

assorted polite social sayings, such as, "How nice to meet you," or, "Thank you for the lovely gift." Too many day-in, day-out pressures on a scale of life-and-death made these little tidbits seem beside the point. But not the professor. He pulled out his half bow once more, and took my hand in both of his, leading into a long holding. I left Asher's office feeling full with joy, at least one dozen years younger, and four feet taller, than when I'd arrived.

Is there a special prayer for the foolish, the Reb wondered, *as there is for the infirm, the mentally deficient, the elderly? For women?*

Thou shalt not covet thy neighbor's prosperity, thou shalt not worship the vanities of this world, thou shalt not wish to gain something for nothing. Moral injunctions the Reb had learned from his father, the late Reb; from his grandfather, Solomon Turrowtaub, of blessed memory, pillar of turn-of-the-century Krakow. And, having learned, having obeyed all these thou-shalt-not's all his life, he had, now, in his fifties, coveted and worshipped and wished.

An entirely new vocabulary had splashed across his tongue: *fraud, breach of contract, website. Vest*, as in: now becoming invested in, and entitled to, collecting certain future profits. *Dot-com. IPO.* End-of-the-twentieth-century words, too new for his old brain. He was too old for this new world of trusting your eye, rather than your ear or head or spirit; this video world, heavy with image and instant communication. Cell phones, laptop computers, PalmPilots, beepers, wireless this, wired-up that.

He had ceased to be humble, had become *rodefet betsa*. Greedy. The sound of the heavy, besotted, judgmental *betsa* said it all: he would need the holiest of holy rabbis to wash clean what he'd done to his family, to his soul. Maybe, and he wouldn't say with certainty—he wouldn't say anything with certainty ever again—maybe God had put him and Ahuva in the path of that suicide bomber as punishment, a warning: *Schlomo, Schlomo, don't make me ashamed of you ever again.*

Slightly dazed, head aching, eyes gritty, he stood in Ahuva's kitchen; hers, not his, not even when he volunteered to cook dinner as he had this evening, only the second time in thirty-four years of marriage—so that she might rest on the den sofa, her feet on the white pillow, the words *Honor Thy Honor* needlepointed across the center, her head on a larger black pillow with *This House is Blessed By Love* embroidered in white.

"Sit with a book," he'd said, and brought her a novel from her nightstand. He'd seen her pick it up and put it down, unread, a dozen times in the past two weeks. "Did you sleep last night?"

"Nothing." She hugged herself and rocked. "Maybe five minutes. Did you?"

"No. I sat awake all night."

"Then why is it you don't know I didn't sleep?"

"Your hand, your ribs, how are they?"

"Not as good as when God gave them to me at birth." Holding up one, then the other hand, she fussed with the bandages and tape. "The doctor said time, be patient. I'm not a spring chicken."

"Me, I'm not a young rooster." His smile was bitter. "We match up perfect."

"When I think what could have happened—"

"It was God's will, a testing of our faith." Why hadn't he thought of this before? The bombing wasn't a punishment, it was a test. God wanted to be sure they were true believers. He felt better already. "God said, *There sit Schlomo and Ahuva, two believing Jews*—"

"First we lose our money, then we get blown up." She squeezed her eyes shut. "No time to take a test."

Now he was thawing a plastic container of stuffed cabbage, prepared and frozen by Ahuva; assembling an onion and beet salad; cooking rice from scratch; slicing a lemon cake baked the night before.

He set the table with the second-best stainless steel, tossed the salad and set it in the refrigerator, poured salad dressing into a crystal cruet. Drops of dressing splattered over the cuff of his new sweater, pale gray, Italian cashmere. His first cashmere sweater, and he'd soiled it, possibly beyond repair. He pushed the sleeves up to his elbows, kicked the refrigerator door closed with a quick, graceful, for him, flip of his foot.

He closed his eyes against the harsh glare of stainless steel, of black granite and white cabinets, shining pots and pans hanging from a rack, plants blooming on the windowsill; a smothering density of *things*—bought, all of them, with *JSingles* money—making it difficult to fill his lungs with sufficient oxygen, even when he breathed as deeply as he could.

He finally had to admit, he had it coming; *it* being the loss of the profits from their shares of Kanov's stock, and the loss of their house, given as collateral for funds that had bought the stocks. But couldn't it have happened, dear God, in smaller pieces over a longer period of time, so that he and Ahuva could digest tragedy and make plans?

Making plans was Ahuva's specialty, her coping mechanism, in both good and bad times but, in the face of this debacle, her plan-making gene seemed to have been dropped from her personality. She'd read the newspapers through the mornings, napped after lunch, and stared at the ceiling between dinner and bed.

Today, she'd asked him what he'd miss most about losing their brief, but heady, prosperity. "Me," she said, "I'll miss shopping for the children without looking at price tags."

"Everything," he'd said. "I'll miss everything, but most, I'll miss knowing we won't spend our old age in a municipal home for old rabbis." Thinking about it now, he admitted, but only to himself, that he'd miss the splash of fame, being asked for his autograph, the chance to speak to the country on television. He'd miss—and who could have predicted *this*—Oze and Amit, his loving irritants. Amit, especially.

This minute, he missed Yuri Zalinikov, thrust into the front of his mind by Ahuva's question. *There* was a man who knew what was, and what was not, important. Less than zero interest in the material; an admirable habit of speaking only the truth; an astute, but nevertheless graceful mind; a man who saw the best in most people, and rarely spoke ill of anyone. The world needed more Zalinikovs. They hadn't met for their study sessions since the Reb had begun taping *JSingles* in August; they hadn't spoken in almost two weeks.

The Reb picked up the phone just as it rang. A woman said, "I never believe what I read in the newspapers, and especially not the Jerusalem newspapers, even those newspapers that agree with me, but this morning I read in *Haaretz* . . ." She paused. He heard an intake of breath.

"Nadia?"

"Schlomo?"

"Do you not first ask to whom you are speaking, before speaking?"

"How many people live at this phone number?"

"Two. At the moment, one is sleeping and the other is busy."

"Schlomo, tell me it is not so, that you are not suing Kanov, who is suing you, that *JSingles* is not a shambles."

"All right, I will tell you it is not so, but I would not be telling the truth."

"I am shattered."

"I am not exactly in one piece."

"I read about the bombing; I called Ahuva immediately. You're lucky people."

"God looked after us."

A sound from Nadia, part sigh, part snort. "Or *someone*, whoever, whatever. Tell me what happened in this Kanov thing."

"The usual. A man lives his life, one day, another day, and then, no warning, everything is gone."

"Is Ahuva there?"

"As I said, resting."

"How is she? I mean, how could she be?"

"Exactly. You have both asked and answered your question."

"What will you do?

"I will hang up this phone, turn on the oven, and finish preparing dinner." The Reb regarded the very small, brilliantly red bird circling the bird feeder just beyond the kitchen window. A myna bird, or a hummingbird? Or were myna birds black, a figment of the imagination, made real by the wish to fantasize?

"Let me talk to Ahuva, I'm sure she'll make more sense."

Talking to Nadia made him realize how much he needed Yuri. Forty minutes later, Yuri sat at the table in the Turrowtaub's kitchen as the Reb boiled water in the tea kettle. He needed to prepare his student for what he'd come to think of as "our terrible troubles."

Speaking rapidly, watering the plants, wiping up puddles from windowsills and floor, he told Yuri a story he'd read only that morning in *Haaretz,* about a Russian immigrant woman in the Tel Aviv Central Bus Station, but Yuri was tapping his fingers on a book, glancing at his watch. He looked terrible, his usually alert eyes shadowed by fatigue, his shoulders sagging as though someone had dropped a fifty-pound sack of sorrow on each one. The Reb felt a faint pang of guilt. He'd been so self-absorbed, he hadn't even phoned to inquire, had the Zalinikovs fully recovered from the trauma of the explosion? "Tea?" The Reb swatted at a fly.

Yuri shook his head. He had to return home soon. Manya didn't like being alone, the bomb had left her shaky. Not a Manya thing to be, shaky—but. He shrugged.

"Your injury," the Reb said, "your daughter's?"

Yuri pulled his sweater away from his throat, unbuttoning the collar of his shirt to reveal a white gauze square. "My scars are nothing compared with what happened to Galina. Her face, that beautiful face."

"I'm sure it's difficult, a young girl." The Reb hoped his voice was sufficiently sympathetic. Had Ahuva told him the Zalinikov daughter was in love with her appearance? Hard to keep everyone's biography straight. And the mother, a gifted artist, but spiteful, closed off to rational argument. Zalinikov walked on a gravel road, as the Israelis would say, and he walked on it barefoot. A miracle he was so steady.

"But even that is nothing compared to what happened to that young man." The Reb began to say something, but Yuri interrupted: "I am sorry to appear rushed. You wish to speak to me about . . . what?"

"Yuri"—this was the first time he'd used his student's first name—"I'm a man dancing on the head of a pin, about to plummet."

"Everyone who has lived through this kind of disaster—"

"Everyone?" Were they talking about the same thing? "Everyone . . . *who?*"

Yuri blinked. "The bomb, the café."

"Oh." The Reb inhaled. "Of course, the bomb, the café," adding: "Amit, Jen."

"Galina."

The Reb sat down opposite Yuri. "I didn't mean *that* disaster. *Our* disaster. Our stocks, Kanov's corporation, our money. What is left? Nothing."

Yuri looked confused. Didn't this man read the newspapers? That morning's paper was stacked on the counter; he opened it to a page showing Kanov's photograph. The headline read: "Russian *émigré* denies dealing in Senegalese diamonds. Accounting practices called into question." In still smaller type: "Tax fraud, embezzlement suspected." Yuri took the newspaper from him. "Two weeks ago I was a man to be envied. Today . . ."

Yuri put the newspaper down. "I know this Mr. Kanov."

"You know him? How?"

"The White Nights."

"Ah yes, I remember Nadia said your wife plays the piano there. Such a small world, Israel. Everyone knows everyone else."

"*Played* the piano, *did play*. Not any longer." His words so clipped, not like Zalinikov. The Reb wondered why he seemed critical of Kanov, although, in this house, being critical of Kanov had become a sacred obligation. "We have all been tested," Yuri said, getting up, moving toward the door.

"Wait!" How to focus attention back onto the horror of his, his family's situation? *That* was where he needed his student's sympathy. "There is tested, and there is *tested,* Zalinikov." Yuri looked doubtful. "Please, sit, five, six minutes . . ." The Reb pointed to a chair. Yuri sat. "Guilt," the Reb said.

"Guilt?"

"It poisons one's sleep, it sits here"—he tapped his right shoulder—"by day."

"You speak of the bomb, or the Mr. Kanov affair?"

"Mr. Kanov, of course. The bomb, *this* was done to me. Of the second tragedy, Mr. Kanov, our money, I"—his face went slack—"was the perpetrator."

Yuri opened his mouth to speak, but the Reb hurried on. "We have no absolution, we Jews, no wiping clean of the slate, however sincere the repentance." Again, Yuri began to say something. "Except . . . except that holiest of holy days: Yom Kippur, the Book of Life about to be closed for another year, the shofar about to be sounded. Full confession, then apology; not man to God, but human being to human being."

Yuri frowned. "On that one day, confession covers every action committed the full year before?"

"More or less. A mistake to be too literal."

"Full confession, followed by full responsibility?"

" 'I have sinned against you,' the repentant says to the victim. 'Forgive me.' "

"I will never do this—*this,* whatever it was, the sin, never again?"

"Implied," the Reb said.

"Stated?" Yuri said.

The tea kettle whistled, spewing steam into the room. The Reb brought it to the table, pouring water into two glasses. "The most meaningful experiences we have are often mysterious, and often silent. Your wife is an artist, ask her."

Yuri plucked two sugar cubes from a bowl, placing them on his tongue, and sipped.

"What is the exact meaning of your I-will-never-do-it-again?"

The Reb looked startled. "Exact meaning?"

Yuri sat up. "How does one *not* do something again? In an active way, a way of making amends?"

The Reb tented his fingers. "One follows a rigorous order of action, establishes priorities, a moral code—"

"Excuse me, Reb," Yuri interrupted. "This is becoming a complication inside a confusion." The Reb's eyes leaked annoyance. "All my life, I have calculated the reality of the world in terms of numbers, one number subtracted from another, added to another; one number squared or tripled, making it greater or less than. Provable theories. The holiness of the triangle, of the square, especially the square, which is, to my mind, the purest of all shapes, the most symmetrical." Yuri blinked, as though surprised by what he had just said.

"Yes, yes, I follow you. I agree with you."

"I worshipped certainty. I counted upon predictability."

"Admirable." The Reb sipped. Where were these arguments taking them?

"Now I want to understand how you can persuade yourself that a failed investment, no matter how enormous, is as tragic as lost lives, ruined bodies and faces. We speak here of physical suffering, often beyond endurance, of innocents." Yuri held his palms up, as though asking the ceiling for validation. "One is money, nothing more."

"*All* our money, Zalinikov. Everything."

"Regrettable, of course."

The Reb bristled, pulling himself upright in his chair. "This is all you have to say, *regrettable*?"

Yuri stood up. Covering his eye with his hand, he seemed to be waiting for something to end, or begin. Turning toward the door, his hand still over the eye, he stopped, looking back at the Reb. "What we have here today are words. And words, as powerful, as beautiful, as promising as they are, cannot undo death or grievous injury."

Chapter Twenty-Five

I had not been at The White Nights Supper Club since that unhappy evening with Kanov and Dushkin, more than two weeks earlier. On the day after, I'd telephoned Alexsei. I was ill, I said, pausing to suggest that I preferred not to discuss details. Would he please convey this information to Kanov? When would I return? Impossible to say at the moment. I'd be in touch.

Alexsei had not become *Kanov's* Alexsei by being an ordinary man. He'd lived the better part of a lifetime in Moscow, where, as a Jew without money or influence, he'd managed to stay alive, even to prosper, in a minor way. He knew what was being said when nothing was being said. He told me to take care of myself, and he would take care of Kanov. Then, four days later, the suicide bombing, and I *was* sick.

Yael, whom I'd phoned next, didn't agree with my interpretation of Dushkin's sudden appearance in Kanov's private rooms. I had not given a name to the reason for my outrage, had not said *sexual tryst for three*, but had obliquely suggested it.

She said nothing for a long time, which meant she was untying a mental knot. Then she said, "I don't think so, your imagination." I didn't argue. I cited Dushkin's uneasy movements around the room that night; the deliberate, repeated half turns away from my scrutiny as he poured drinks; his and Kanov's furtive exchange of glances as absolute proof that I was aware at all times of where the enemy was; an ability that is an art, not a science, honed by years of St. Petersburg life.

However, out of respect for what she called my *inflamed intuitions*—Yael loved these overly decorated literary terms—she offered to telephone Kanov to say I would not be coming back to work. Ever.

I told her thank you, but no. I would see him one final time.

"For closure?" *Closure* was another Yael word. This one, she said, was valuable when she wrote personality assessments for her many clients; another euphemism, a means of saying one thing rather than another, because the thing one *should* say seemed too harsh, and could alienate. Closure was a softening, and softening was not what I did best. I was too Soviet, I told her, too willing to confront, to deal in euphemisms.

"Yes?" she said. "Too Soviet?" I knew she was grinning. "Here then, a Soviet summing up of this situation. I appreciate your being upset over what happened, but, at the end of the day—a phrase I learned from the BBC correspondent in Tel Aviv, a charming man, although overly intellectual—what it came to was this: it was only a man, only a job."

"Meaning what?"

"Not cancer, AIDS, blindness, dementia, a stroke or paralysis, or a child with a serious illness, which, for me, are the worst of all the possible tragedies. Now go say goodbye to your Mr. Kanov."

"Yael, what would I do without you?"

"I hope you never find out."

"I'll wait a week, then go. I may not get your closure. Unimportant. What I hope for is revenge." I was about to hang up, when I heard her voice telling me to wait.

"Yes?"

"Are you exercising your fingers with a tennis ball, even as we speak?"

I smiled. "No."

"Good. Then I know your nerves are relaxed."

The sign on the front door of The White Nights Supper Club read: "Removal to a New Location," in large black letters. Under, in smaller letters, "To Be Announced Soon." Under this, in even smaller letters: "For emergencies, phone +972-2-561-3467."

My reason for being there could not be called an emergency, unless emergency meant: this matter must be attended to at once. In that case, I was emergent.

I peered through the glass panes in the door. No lights. I tried the door. Locked. I rattled it, then knocked, then called out, "Dmitri Kanov, may I come in? It's Manya Zalinikova." And waited. Within moments, Alexsei smiled at me from the other side of the glass, held up one finger, vanished, and reappeared, opening the door with a great flourish of welcome. We hugged, as though I had been on a long voyage. In a sense, I had.

"We read about you in the newspapers," he said. He made no gesture to lead me into the club.

"Did they spell my name correctly?" I glanced into the dining room. An unnatural silence layered the emptiness. The tables had a sad, deserted air without their snapping white cloths; the chairs had been pushed into random clusters and, in the far corner, the dark bulk of the piano sat with its top closed, looking abandoned.

"One of the lucky survivors," he said, and patted my shoulder. His smile was entirely too measured, too knowing.

"Luck is the entire story."

"You look well"—he studied my eye patch—"with one addition, which I hope is temporary."

"It is." I looked over his shoulder. No sign of Kanov. Alexsei's ashy-gray eyes didn't blink. Always wary, always vigilant Alexsei. We all need an Alexsei in our lives to protect us from the inconvenient, the unexpected. The disagreeable.

"How are you?" he said. "Really?"

"I am better than I have been"—was this man my friend? At that moment, difficult to assess. He was, after all, fiercely loyal to Kanov. He was a man who had been tutored in the art of surviving—"but not as healed as I will be."

Finally, a small smile. "And so, and so . . . your mind was not bombed, that is certain."

I smiled, pretending an ease I didn't feel. We looked at one another for an awkward moment, before we both spoke at once. He said, "Your husband is well?"

I said, "Kanov is well?" A welcome tinge of spontaneity. We laughed.

Alexsei pressed his palm against his immaculate hair. "Don't believe what the papers say."

"Of course."

"I told him you were at the door. He's in his office, go right in." A half hug, a stiff half bow, and he was gone.

I didn't go right in; I paused outside his door and repeated, silently, *Only a man, only a job, only a man, only a job*, then knocked.

"Ah," a voice called out, "this must be Manya. Step in, step in." Kanov was at his desk, stylish, as always, especially so on that day, in a pale-green sweater, dark-green patterned shirt. If it were true, as the Reb reported, that he was in bankruptcy mode, or whatever complications ensue in these matters, he looked the opposite. His smile was less restrained than that of Alexsei, possibly because he had more to hide.

He started to get up. I raised my hand, and sat in the antique Queen Anne chair opposite him, the chair I loved for its delicate gold embroidery patterned upholstery, its graceful legs. Probably worth a fortune.

Would he have to part with his many treasures? I wondered. Paintings, books, automobiles, the said-to-be-impressive house and swimming pool. The gold Patek Philippe watch. That he could be relieved of much of his worldly goods delighted me. Without his carefully assembled setting, Kanov would no longer be Kanov, would no longer play the leading role in the daily drama he called his life, and I called his artifice.

He sat back in his chair and scrutinized me. I regret to say that I blushed. "You look well, considering your ordeal," he said, lighting a cigarette. "I would have been unable to function for a full year, had it been I."

"Yes?" I watched the wary, darting back-and-forth of his eyes, the agitated movement of his mouth, even now, even here, in the tranquility of his office. Possibly, legal troubles are more damaging than suicide bombers. "What happened to us on Ben Yehuda will be happening more and more, probably everywhere," I said.

"Grow accustomed to being blown up"—he snapped his fingers,

flicking ashes over his desk—"by maniacs? These people are primitives, our very existence infuriates them."

"Nevertheless, they have bombs, and people willing to die to prove a point."

He stubbed his cigarette out in a small crystal dish he had once identified as being part of a private Swiss glass collection now housed at the Louvre. "A *point*? Their point, it seems to me, is that we don't belong here and they do." His façade of calm was unraveling. I'd seen this happen many times, when the staff presented problems he felt were too minor for his attention, when a shipment of expensive, hard-to-find delicacies arrived bruised.

"The eye of the beholder," I said, delighted that I had rattled him. "Israel's view is that we Jews belong here, and the Palestinians do not."

"Perhaps *they* do not."

"How Jewish are you?" We had never discussed his interest in religious ritual. Suddenly, this question was important, if only to keep him off-balance, which, to judge from the way he fussed with the objects on his desk, it had.

"If you mean Jewish as in praying, or not eating crème fraiche with roasted guinea hen, not at all." He switched a dried flower arrangement in a pewter jar with a sprig of dendrobium orchids that had been in a tall glass vase, Orrefors glass from Sweden; expensive, if I remembered correctly what he'd once told me. "I am not what the sociologists and psychologists like to call in their babble language *committed*."

"You were born Jewish?"

His glance was sharp and unkind. "Of course."

"There is no such thing as *of course* in talking about being Jewish." He looked interested, although he was patting the orchid blossoms as some people obsess over worry beads. "Russian Jews are born that way, as Jews, but most do nothing about it. Myself included." He didn't answer, but he didn't look away, either. "Would you change it"—he seemed to snap to attention—"if you could? Many do that, convert."

"I've never considered converting."

"Have you ever visited the Western Wall, the Old City?"

"I know the Western Wall. The answer is no, I have not. Why would I?"

"*Why* you would must be for you to say."

Now he lit another cigarette with the still-smoking remains of the first. "What is this, a religious interrogation?"

I was surprised myself by how profoundly his resistance to being Jewish irritated me.

"I prefer Jewish politics to Jewish anything else," he said.

"The Oslo Accords?" Why not stretch his view of me to include Manya, the student of public affairs? "It is supposed to change all of this"—I shrugged—"senseless killing. Or, so I've read."

Tapping his fingers on his desk, he glanced out the window, then looked at me, his anger somewhat softened. "Impossible to resolve, certainly not by us."

"Even Mr. Peres and Mr. Rabin don't seem adequate to the task."

"The situation here makes Russia seem more and more desirable. Don't you agree?"

"But I never found Russia undesirable," I said. He looked surprised. "Oh, perhaps at the end, all that business crime . . ." I paused, wondering if this might be a good opening for pulling Dushkin into the conversation.

"The dirt everywhere, disarray on all sides, nothing worked," he said. "Elevators, telephones, dry cleaners—"

"The beggars in the metro stations," I said. "The gypsies, the cockroaches on the water pipes. Once I saw a monstrous rat running along an empty glass shelf in a depleted bakery shop."

"So you do agree."

"But those beggars are *our* beggars," I said, "Russians, as I am." He frowned. "As *we* are."

"I am who I wish to be." His voice was unfriendly. "Presently, Israeli. Formerly, Russian."

"And the future?"

"Who knows? French, Australian, American. I enjoy being surprised."

Ha—*perfect!* "As I was the evening your friend Dushkin joined us." *There.* Out in the open, no longer a thousand-pound elephant squatting in the center of the room, and no one acknowledging its existence.

"I thought you would enjoy my friend."

"And *I* thought we, you and I, had"—I searched for the right word, flustered by his hard gaze—"an appointment," I blurted out, the only word that swam to the top of my brain.

"Mikhail is an old, very close friend. He comes, he goes, always welcome."

"May I ask a question? Not about Dushkin precisely, but perhaps about him."

"Anything."

"What was your idea of what would happen that evening?"

"Happen?"

"Between us."

"In these matters, so much is possible, and very little is decided in advance." He rummaged through papers on his desk, as though he were hoping to find a relevant message, or wished to end our discussion.

Now I saw myself through his eyes: Manya, the irritant. "An interesting way of speaking, *these matters.*"

"Manya, Manya"—he fidgeted with a pen he'd grabbed from a silver container—"now you are behaving like a nag; pick, pick, at every syllable. So unlike you."

I felt as though he'd hit me in the chest. The specter of the hysterical woman, an accusation out of a Nabokov novel. I stood up. Now I was looking down at him, the better to make my point. "And so," I said, trying to make a grand gesture of pulling my woolen shawl more tightly around myself with one hand, not easily done while clutching a large purse in the other. "I think it's time for me to leave." Tatiana would have been proud of both my gesture, awkward as it was, and my short speech.

Kanov pretended dismay, his eyes turning somewhat sorrowful. Then, just as suddenly, he sat upright, all stiff attention and purpose. "But wait." Pulling his checkbook out of the desk drawer, he flipped it open and scrawled hurriedly on the first page. "Here." He ripped a check from the book and held it out to me. I stepped backwards, toward the door. "Manya, don't be foolish"—he waved the check in the air—"you earned it." Now his eyes were full of amiability. "I am still prosperous enough, despite what the newspapers claim."

"I have a list of favorite charities," I said. "Distribute the money among these. I'll send the names." I grasped the doorknob.

"But why are you going? I asked Alexsei to serve refreshments.

Greek prawns. Your favorite."

⁂

Not until forty-eight hours later, arranging the flowers Yuri had brought home for the Sabbath, did I realize the answer to the question that, all the time I had been in Kanov's office, had been humming its low, dark hum at the back of my mind: *What was I thinking?*

I wasn't. Thinking.

What I acted upon was plain, unvarnished, I-want-what-I-want, old-fashioned lust, an urge to lose myself, to escape; perhaps—probably—a wish to punish Yuri for bringing us here, to lash out in the most hurtful, selfish, self-degrading way. An impulse. And very close to being a fatal one.

Chapter Twenty-Six

Galina asked questions on the drive to Acre, questions about Byzantium, pronouncing words in what, to Asher, seemed a heart-stopping rhythm. Hebrew with a Russian accent. She had perfected the art of pronouncing the final *t* or *p* or *f* of words, breathing through partially closed lips, humming, until what was created was more song than word.

His skin tingled in a way that had nothing to do with language. His heart was light for the first time since that day when, checking his phone messages, he'd heard: "Asher Tannenbaum, Manya Zalinikova. Please come to the Hadassah Hospital." Her voice dark, heavy. The voice of dread. She sounded like God—what Asher guessed God would sound like, if God were a woman; an impossibility, of course—announcing the end of the world.

To Asher, seeing Galina lying inert in her bed, her face swathed in bandages, the world *had* ended. He froze in the doorway, convinced she was dead, that Manya had been too overcome to tell him this on the phone.

The scar, which had taken on a life of its own, even a name of its own—The Enemy—was nowhere near as disfiguring on Galina's face as it was in her mind. A thin curve, not four inches long, from the corner of her right eye to the corner of her mouth; it was already beginning to lose its angry-red color. He'd held cool towels to it, he'd rubbed scented creams into it. He had, once, when she was especially hopeless about ever regaining her former perfection, kissed it, exploring its grainy, uneven texture with the tip of his tongue.

This visit to the new *tel* near Caesarea that Asher was excavating for the university would be, he hoped, a distraction. By exploring a civilization thousands of years old, Galina might gain some perspective, a hint of what did, and what did not endure.

⁓

Galina asked if Byzantium was, as she had read, a culture of excess, a culture of fastidious architecture in sumptuous colors, of artifacts created with elaborate detail? Even as he answered, Asher hoped she'd see him not as an ordinary man, but as a passionate excavator of history, a scholar committed to the holiness of the ordinary. A man she would be happy to marry.

He parked the car at the end of an unpaved road, a short distance from the *tel* itself, so she could get a proper perspective of the scale of the dig. This one was larger than most, therefore, more important, almost as long as a city block. If the city were Tel Aviv and not St. Petersburg, where city blocks went endlessly on and were twelve meters wide.

Galina, behind Asher, paused in the narrow doorway of the temporary lattice-topped wooden frame that had been constructed over the excavation, squinting into the dim interior. In the pale late-afternoon light, the wail of the *muezzin* calling the Muslim faithful to evening prayers floated toward them from Acre, four kilometers to the south.

"So . . . this is where you work?" She glanced around at the surrounding area; it was empty of buildings, empty of everything other than gravel-paved roads laid down for the trucks that would carry the buried treasure to museums once it had been excavated, examined, categorized, celebrated by the scholars working there. "What do you do for stores, if you need something?"

"We bring everything we need," he said. "Like these supplies." He was carrying several bundles, duffel bags, knapsacks.

"Does a cell phone work down there?"

Asher was descending the wobbly steps leading to the excavation itself. At the bottom, he turned to help her, then moved to the far end, dropping blankets, pillows, bags onto the earthen floor. He was aware of the clamor of his heart as he watched Galina, who was now, even in this gloom, an object of irresistible brightness. Still standing in the doorway, she brushed a knot of complicated hair from her forehead, a gesture of idle helplessness, which both irritated and aroused him. He felt like a man with a shameful craving.

Kneeling, he patted the ground. "Here. We'll set up our campsite here." He clicked on a bulb hanging from a heavy wire stapled into the wooden frame. "I apologize for the dim light."

"Since this"—her finger touched the scar—"I am happier in dim light." She stepped further into the *tel* and, looking around, pointed. "What is *that*?" To her left, perhaps six or seven meters away, inside a squared-off area marked at each corner by a wooden stake, were precise rows of white stone tags, each one crowning a small mound of earth.

"The primary burial site . . ." He tried to keep his tone conversational, free of pedantry. Galina hated pedantry, almost as much as she hated being told what to do. "Pottery, carvings, figurines, lapis lazuli mosaics, ivory icons no bigger than the tip of my little finger." He held his finger out to her, but the fading light, the gathering fog—how could he expect her to see, to understand how sacred this place was, how mysterious?

Galina breathed a tiny, musical, "Oh," and, with the grace of a ballerina accepting applause, moved toward him, then lowered herself onto the piled bedding, from which she watched him unpack a portable stove, soup cans, pita bread, tin foil containers of goat cheese, oranges, canisters of water. "Does this"—she gestured toward the large, semidark area just beyond their bundles—"belong to you?"

Asher shook his head. "It's the government's, the university's." What he wanted to do, what he would do, if he dared, was kiss her throat, take off her clothes.

The uncle, when hearing of the trip to the *tel,* had warned him against foolish excess, whatever that meant, against forcing himself on a young woman who, the uncle's words, was a possible life partner. "In other words," Reuven said, "don't be byzantine about showing her your Byzantine hoard."

Asher hadn't found the play on words amusing. Nothing amused him these days; too much between him and Galina was at stake. At any moment, he could make an awkward move, or say something perceived as insensitive, and he'd be, as Galina liked to say, out the door, a phrase she'd learned on a rock music website. He was not, by nature, foolish or excessive; nor was he a forcer. But how could the uncle, at his age, know the depth of what Asher felt? *Was* feeling, this minute?

Galina clicked her fingernail against something metallic, an impatient rat-tat. "Do these old treasures cost a terrible amount of money?"

"Yes, terrible. Thousands, if we wanted to sell them, but we don't." He sensed boredom radiating from her in waves. Perhaps, if she helped him, they could cook dinner together. He'd brought wine. "Galina," he said, but she'd wandered off. Asher peered into the gloom, studying her slender silhouette against the far wall, hearing the faint thunk of her boot tip as she nudged one, then another, of the white markers.

"*Don't!*" He hoped his voice hadn't sounded alarmed. The annoyed, impatient shrug of her shoulders told him it had. "They're easily damaged." He struggled to remain reasonable. "We have here the secrets of centuries. In fact . . ." She wasn't listening, but had knelt beside something lying on the ground. He pressed on: "In fact, these treasures are not ever replaced, everything here happened only one time. A little"—he hesitated—"like love."

Galina looked up. Even from a distance, her smile dazzled. "Sometimes, Asher, you surprise me, like now. You say something, and I think . . ." She stood. "I think you could write poetry."

He felt a warm rush of pleasure, and opened his mouth to speak, but she was looking at the markers. "What is this one?" She tugged at something that was not clearly recognizable in the dim light, but which, he knew, had to be priceless and rare.

"Wait . . . be careful!" He rushed over to her, pulling a marker out of her hand. "Please."

"*Well!*" She wiped her hands on her jeans. Asher gently patted the marker, brushing away particles of earth. "Always the smart one," she said, "telling me what to do," then slowly retreated toward the pile of bedding. "Such a *mishmash* over nothing, a scrap."

His head snapped up. "*Mishmash*! You speak Yiddish?"

"I speak what I need to speak." She twisted a strand of hair around her finger, still moving backwards, explaining this: her family had spoken Yiddish at home in St. Petersburg to confuse Gentile neighbors who'd eavesdropped, hoping to report the Zalinikovs to the KGB. Gesturing with her hands to make a point, her heel caught in a hole, twisting her leg to the side. She grasped at empty air, and stumbled, crying out, then dropped to her knees.

Asher, springing forward, bent to help her up, but she fought him off, until, suddenly, she settled into quiet weeping. Half sitting, half lying, she allowed him to remove her boot and rub her foot, which was already swollen, but soft, even endearing, in his eager hand. Murmuring assurances, he was finally able to ease her onto her back, propping her head on his rolled-up sweater. She wiggled her foot, moaning, as he eased the toes, each one crowned with a magenta-hued nail, back and forth. A probable sprain, nothing serious. Wine would help.

"Now I am both scarred and crippled," she said. "A double jeopardy, or is that not the right word?"

"The right word is . . . *flawless.*" She said nothing, but he saw in her slow smile, and the way she leaned into his sweater, a sign that she felt comforted. Rummaging through his knapsack, he pulled out a wine bottle, a bottle opener and two glasses, opened the wine and filled the glasses, bringing them to Galina, who looked pained, but beautiful, even at that moment. Kneeling, he gave her one glass, then took out his handkerchief, and wiped her face. "Blow." He held the handkerchief to her nose, waiting, as she sniffled into it. Then she pushed his hand away, and, holding her wine glass with one hand, massaged her foot with the other.

"You know something I just realized?" she said. Her eyes had a dreamy look he'd never seen before. He didn't trust himself to utter, No. She pressed on: "No one has ever taken such good care of me." She flicked back her streaming hair, a wholly original gesture involving fingers, wrist, shoulders, a gesture that brought tears to his eyes.

"Not your mother?" he said, finally.

"Not my mother."

"Manya, your mother, she told me—"

"Told you . . . *what?*"

"Why she wishes . . . may wish . . . may *possibly* wish for you to marry me." *Marry!* He shivered at his courage. He was still kneeling next to her, his hand resting on her leg.

Galina pulled herself up and leaned on one elbow. "Why?"

"To give you what she called a place in Israeli society."

"Well, my mother . . ." Galina waved the air away with a swipe of her hand, spilling a few drops of wine. They both smiled, Asher rejoicing in the erotic pleasure of sitting in the half dark with this woman; just sitting. He wished that all the clocks in Israel would stop, that a thousand years from that moment excavators would find their bodies in this *tel*, still sitting, arms entwined around one another.

Galina said, "Sometimes a reliable source of information, my mother. Other times, not."

Sipping, she glanced at him from the corner of her eye. "She is a whole other story. Anyway, she doesn't know everything about me."

"Who does?" He drained his glass. The wine entered his bloodstream like a torch. The *tel*, chilled just a moment before, felt suddenly stifling. He tapped his handkerchief across his face, and, as he did, what he had been waiting for happened. He felt suddenly bolder, bold enough to say, "I don't. I should, I *want* to, but I don't." Later he might regret having said it, but now he felt a little giddy, then strangely relieved. Almost happy.

Awkwardly dragging her injured foot, which now looked puffier to him, she shifted away from him. "Know me—you *don't* know me?" Her voice was wispy, almost childlike. Had he frightened her; too much confession, too ardent a demand?

"Not at all. Not as I want to know you." His voice was loud, insistent, but Galina made talking about important matters so— difficult.

"You're shouting." She edged further away from him.

"Of course I'm shouting. I love you, and I don't know you." Until that day, a month ago, when her mother had come to his office to talk about Galina, he'd never spoken these words to anyone, or even to himself: I love you. They had a rich, melodic sound, a sound fully as lovely as any words in the Song of Songs. Manya Zalinikova had appreciated, she'd understood, she said she did;

even if, in the past, words between them had complicated more than they'd explained.

"Ha!" An eruption, as much as a word.

"*Ha?*" he said. "This is your answer?"

"So, if you don't know me, how can you love me? Who is it you love?" Galina was waving her arms like a frantic traffic policeman. "Everyone says I love you like they say hello, how are you?" She made an awkward, abrupt move, dropping her empty wine glass. They watched it roll across the earth floor, bumping to a stop against a far wall. The wind had quieted; the *muezzin* was gone from the mosque tower. The final, fading rays of the sun sent pale light into the *tel* through the slatted roof.

"Not me, I don't say it just to say. I want to be your husband." Surely, his heart was beating this loudly because it was fastened to the outside of his chest.

Galina's head snapped up. "You are so . . ." She was on her knees, her face so close to his, he felt her breath. ". . . so Israeli! I'm not a falafel, or a pound of lox you buy in Supersol. You don't own me."

"Own you . . . *own* you!"

Bracing herself on her arms, she pulled herself to her feet, and took an uncertain step, before crumpling to the ground. Her face was shadowed, but he saw her mouth clamp down with pain. "Asher . . ." She put her hand out. Without realizing what he was doing, he reached for her and began to rock.

Galina fit her head into the crook of his arm, shrinking against him, both silken and solid against his body. They remained that way for a long time, until he felt his shoulder and arm go numb. She was quiet now, possibly asleep, and he didn't want to risk waking her.

❧

He must have fallen asleep. The light was fading, the *tel* a cavern of shadows, but surprisingly warm. And fragrant, with the scent of orchards: oranges, apples, pomegranates. The silence was absolute, and then a voice: "Let me be a seal upon your heart."

It filled the shelter, rising, entwining itself with the final, fading rays of the sun. He reached into the darkness but felt nothing. Again, the voice: "Have you seen him, whom I love? His left hand is under my head, and his right hand embraces me. I held him, and I would not let him go."

Asher's hands found Galina's hair; the heavy, brave strands cascading around her head and shoulders seeming to grow even as he caressed them. He buried his face in their intoxicating abundance. In her sleep, she encircled him with her arms. His fingers traveled the curve of her throat; he cupped her breasts, her yielding flesh silken, her face, as she raised it to him, radiant, waiting.

Chapter Twenty-Seven

The news here is this: Irina and Serge have gone already to the United States. *Pffft*. Like that. So much in my life has come and gone quickly.

If I were asked whether the situation between Israel and myself is soaked in sadness, I would say it's too soon to know. This country remains a mystery, a dense, impenetrable sea, too thick with grief to allow one to slide into it easily, in the way Yuri enters the calm sea of his religious life. A siren wail has come to live inside my head, an echo of the sirens at the exploded café. On many days—my shakier ones, when the memory of that day pushes through the layers of my refusal to live through it again—I think this thin wire of noise in my head is a prediction of siren wails to come.

They say—whoever *they* are—that if Jews do not feel they have come home when coming to Israel, then they have no home.

Some days I walk for hours, for miles, along the paths leading to the top of the Mount of Olives. I rest there in the shaded area just in front of the Intercontinental Hotel, looking across the Kidron

Valley, and down upon the Al Aksa Mosque, the Western Wall just beneath, sitting quite still, unusual for me, as the royal-blue sky fades into early darkness.

Nearby, calling out in a watery voice, in a mix of broken-up Hebrew and badly accented English, is a Palestinian man of an uncertain age, wearing a red vest heavy in gold thread, and a worn fez with a crooked gold silk tassel that swings across his face as he walks. He has with him an ancient putty-colored, matted-haired camel tethered to a post, an animal he rents to tourists wishing to take home a photograph of themselves atop this biblical beast.

This man and his camel are very much like the experience of coming to live in Israel. The outer appearance of such an adventure is, at first, somewhat romantic, and carries the allure of the exotic. Upon closer inspection, however, the reality is less attractive.

So it is with the man and his camel, and his clients. As they ascend a small ladder onto the animal, who is now attempting to skitter away, until, restrained, he turns his head to survey his passengers through glazed, half-closed eyes, shaded by illogically long lashes. In moments, Mister Camel's mouth evicts a steady stream of saliva, and he lurches suddenly forward, keeping up a mild, hypnotic trot, until riders signal wildly for the camel's owner to rescue them.

☙

An inventory of my life at this moment: First, the Reb. He is again teaching at the Seminary, writing his scholarly pieces, and another book, this one about the Uber God, whoever that is. He still complains about what he calls his honorable poverty, still enjoys his family, and remains skeptical about me, my dissenting feelings about ritual, and my unwillingness to say *yes* when I mean *no*. However, since we shared a suicide bombing, he is kinder now when we meet, and just last week shook my hand when we passed on Jaffa Road. *Shook my bare hand,* a woman not his wife.

Each week he and Yuri meet to discuss the Torah, the Talmud, the psalms, life. Yuri is teaching him chess; he is teaching Yuri an Israeli game of chance played on certain street corners, with dice and shifting walnut shells and a giant pea, the bystanders becoming the players, laying down one shekel for each round. This game is said to be a good test of one's ability to gather information, memorize it, process it, and act quickly. Not a bad talent to cultivate in a country that teeters always on the edge of being obliterated, even as it obliterates you.

Nadia and Reuven continue to express their amazed delight that, out of all the many *olim* in Israel, they have found one another. They travel to Paris, London, and Zurich, whenever work and money allow, for the shopping and the theater, the cafés and the chocolates, the fashions, the steaks—Israeli beef being both scarce and without flavor—and for the many newspapers and newsmagazines Nadia enjoys. They may marry, or may not, depending upon the day on which one inquires. I say, joined by a rabbi or not joined, these two people are as married to one another in their thinking bones, and in their pleasure bones, as anyone I know.

Yael remains the most optimistic, common sense voice among the many voices surrounding me. Her refusal to be discouraged is the result of too many early childhood vitamins, too much time in college devoted to hiking in national parks, and other stand-up sports which she and her family still carry on, too much boundless American faith in the ultimate triumph of good over evil. Living in areas of infinite space, as Americans are able to do, is also a factor. One never finds oneself held back by a horizon. Possibility goes on, and on.

Yuri and I? We approach one another like two patients recovering from a long illness. On some days, eager to connect; on other days, easily frightened off and clumsy, the human equivalents of Yuri's dissertation, "The Calculus of Variations": two creatures, different from one another, making up, as we go along, our own version of intimacy.

We peer at one another from opposite sides of this question of who is a Jew, what is a Jew, why is a Jew? We recently shared a calming glass of wine, and a quiet conversation, not usual between us. My complaint that evening was how this country intrudes upon one's private life. "It is always . . . *there*," I said, "in the background—and the foreground, also, much of the time—a humming, like an electric jolt waiting to snap out. It's not like living in any other place."

"But Manya," he said, "being Israeli is not a full-time occupation. Imagine, you fill out an application for a bank loan, or for membership in a sports club and, after the word, *Profession*, you write *Israeli*."

"Sometimes it seems that it is, what you said, a full-time occupation."

He smiled his sweet, patient, Yuri smile; very winning, very seductive. Very misleading. My husband *appears* to be reasonable. "In the end," he said, "we Jews cannot escape our condition."

"*Condition*. What condition? A disease is a condition. This skin"—I pulled at my cheek—"these eyes"—I blinked—"are a part of my condition; present at birth, impossible to remove. Being Jewish is a choice."

"Or so you say, Manya."

cℐ⁓ↄ

We study Byzantine archeology in a class at the Institute for Mature Scholars, hoping to be smart enough to discuss these ideas with Asher, soon to be our son-in-law. This young man, who remains a brilliance in a tarnished world, refuses to learn to dance, but has exchanged his Volvo for a Porsche convertible, and says this will be the case only until he and Galina have a child to strap into the back.

She continues as a student at the university, moving toward politics, or the law; she's the recipient of flawless grades, now that she no longer siphons away energy and time for dance clubs and pizza emporiums. As for her face, her scar: in her addiction to being perfectly made up, perfectly dressed, endlessly admired, she is still what I call—though never to her face—a Queen of Preen, but learning to practice the art of what is possible, and learning to look beyond surfaces. Mostly, she is learning from Asher how to love.

Her monthly visits to the *mikvah*? Purely Galina. She has found one in Rehavia, all white-marble and granite, heady fragrances seeping out of the water, classical music on the loudspeakers. After the ritual immersion, after the prayers, my daughter—who very much knows what she needs, and usually achieves it—has a manicure and pedicure; the art of the possible pushed to its farthest, most luxurious, most Galina limits.

And so and so and so, as Alexsei would say, his eyes half closed, assessing, balancing what is known against what is imagined. We wait, and we watch. One must live here to understand. On even a peaceful day, there is no peace. There is a scrim of anxiety over everything and everyone, a barely noticed holding of one's breath, a nervous looking-around for any sign that the usual has slipped into the unusual.

There is noise. The din of ambulances and the army trucks heralding another crisis; and the every-hour wailing of the *muezzins*; the marching, clamoring advocates of one or another point of view, hundreds of people chanting, carrying candles and placards, pushing their opinions.

Passion is layered into the air, sucking away all the oxygen. Yuri calls these dramas democracy. I call them exhausting.

Nevertheless, I won't allow our lives to become a Dostoevsky or Turgenev or Tolstoy tragedy where, on the final page, everyone is scattered dead across the stage. Rather, my wish is for a life closer to a play written by that genius of human emotions, Chekhov, whose grave in St. Petersburg, marked by a white spire, was for me on many days a refuge, a place where I read or played music inside my head.

I heard recently a famous Israeli writer describe Chekhov's work in this way: At the end, the characters continue to yearn for what they do not have, everyone disappointed and full of regret for what they do have; sorrow, a free-floating cloud above everybody's everyday existence.

However—and, when one is a Jew, there is always a however—*this* is the gift given to us by this melancholy Russian. At the end, everyone is very much alive, endlessly talking, arguing, hoping.

GLOSSARY

HEBREW

aga: Slang

anee: Me

baal: Husband; literally, 'master'

Baruch atah Adonai, Eloheinu melech haolam: Blessed art thou, O Lord our God, King of the universe

bat: Daughter

bechol zot: Nevertheless

betach: Of course, certainly

bo: Come

boker tov: Good morning

cain: Yes

chaki: Wait

chometz: Leavened foods forbidden on Passover

ema: Momma

Eretz Israel: Literally, land of Israel

goral: Fate

Hasidim: Members of an ultra-Orthodox Jewish sect

Hatikvah: The Israeli national anthem

hatavot: Fringe benefits

hefetz hashood: phrase meaning "suspicious package", a suspected bomb threat

kaddish: A Jewish prayer said in daily rituals in the synagogue, and at funerals of close relatives *kar*: Cold

kashruth: Jewish religious dietary laws, concerning what foods can be eaten by Jews, and how certain foods must be prepared; the word also refers to the state of being *kosher*, of the fitness of something for ritual purposes

kerach: Ice

kessef: Money

kippah: A brimless cap worn by Jewish men; also called a skullcap

Knesset: Israel's parliament

lekhem: Bread

Le'olam lo: Never

lo: No

machar: Tomorrow

makolet: A convenience store

makseema: A person who exudes energy, charm, intelligence; who commands admiration, affection, respect

Malka Bshelut: Queen of Ripeness

mazel: Luck

meanyen: Interesting

Mesibat Shavuot: A Shavuot party

mesukan: Dangerous

mezuzah (plural: *mezuzot*): A piece of parchment inscribed with verse from the Torah, enclosed in a decorative case; traditionally, *mezuzot* are fixed on the doorpost of Jewish homes.

Midrash: an ancient exegetical rabbinic work which offers interpretations of the Hebrew Bible

mikvah: a ritual bath used by Jews for purification; in Orthodox Judaism, women are expected to bathe after menstruation.

minyan: in Orthodox Judaism, the minimum number of adult men (ten) required to hold public worship

Mishna: The oldest postbiblical collection of Jewish oral laws

mishtarah: Police

motarot: luxuries

nekhed: grandson in Hebrew

olim: Jews who have completed *aliyah*, or the assisted immigration to Israel which is the legal right of all Jews

organee: Organic

Passover: The Jewish holiday celebrating the liberation of the Hebrews' liberation from Egypt

payos: sidelocks or sideburns worn by members of the male Orthodox Jewish community

pigua: terrorist attack

re'idat adama: An earthquake

rutz: run

sabra: Literally the name of a type of cactus fruit native to Israel; used to refer to a native-born Israeli

Seder: Ritual feast which begins the Jewish holiday of Passover

shalom: Jewish greeting meaning "peace"

Shavuot: Jewish holiday held fifty days after the second day of Passover, celebrating the giving of the Torah, along with the harvest

Shema: A Jewish prayer; traditionally, Jews will say the *Shema* as their last words

sherut: Group taxi

shofar: an instrument made from a hollowed-out ram's horn; in modern Judaism, it is typically sounded at the end of *Yom Kippur*

shtaayim shanim: Two years

tallit: a fringed shawl worn by Jewish men during prayer

Talmud: A collection of sixty-three books containing commentaries, studied by Orthodox Jews; it contains the Mishnah and Gemara

Tefillin: another name for *phylacteries* (see definition)

tel: artificial mound formed from hundreds of years of human occupation of an area; they are commonly excavated by archeologists

toda raba: thank you very much

Torah: the study of Jewish religious texts; also a name for the Pentateuch, the first five books of the Hebrew Bible

tzitzit: tassels worn by Jewish men on traditional or ceremonial garments

ulpan: A school for the intensive study of Hebrew

Yom Kippur: An important Jewish holy day, also known as the Day of Atonement; according to Jewish tradition, God seals everyone's fate for the year to come in the Book of Life at the end of *Yom Kippur*, so Jews spend the day praying and fasting, and seeking God and other's forgiveness

yom shenee: Monday

YIDDISH

bar mitzvah: The coming-of-age religious ceremony for Jewish boys at age thirteen

borscht: A soup made primarily of beets and served hot or cold, often with sour cream

blintz: A traditional food of Jews hailing from Eastern countries made from a thin pancake with sweet and savory fillings

bubbe: Grandmother

challah: Traditional long twisted bread, usually eaten on the Sabbath and holidays

chedar: an elementary Jewish school where children are taught to read the Torah and other Hebrew books

chochkas: Small, interesting, ornamental, often valuable items, such as jewelry, vases, perfume vials

kaddish: a Jewish prayer said in daily rituals in the synagogue, and at funerals of close relatives

mandelbrot: almond bread, similar to cookies or biscotti

matzo (plural: *matzos*): Unleavened flatbread, a food important to the Jewish festival of Passover

mayven: An expert, one who is especially knowledgeable in an admirable pursuit

mensch (plural: *menschen*): Male or female who has admirable qualities, is seen as being fully human

mishmash: A mess, mix-up

mishpachah: Jewish relatives, family both close and distant

nar: A fool

narishkeit: foolishness

schlep: To carry; to proceed or move especially slowly, tediously, awkwardly, or carelessly

schmaltz: literally, chicken fat; also used to indicate something overly sentimental or romantic

schmutz: something dirty, or dirty talk

Shabbas: Friday evening and Saturday, holy days to Orthodox Jews

sheitel: A marriage wig worn by Orthodox Jewish women

sheyna punim: pretty face

tante: Aunt

treif: food that isn't kosher

zisskeit: Sweetness of the soul

RUSSIAN

apparatchik: An official of the Communist party

babushka (plural: *babushkas*): Old woman

biznesmeni: Businessman

czarina: Wife of a czar; a Russian empress

dacha: In Russia, a second home lived in seasonally; comparable to a vacation home

Kak dela: How are you

Kandidat nauk: In Russian Universities, the equivalent degree of a PhD in the United States; literally, it means "Candidate of Sciences"

krisha: Literally meaning "roof"; used to reference a criminal group one pays for protection

mamochka: Mother

nyet: No

samovar: A metal container (usually decorated) used to boil water in Russia, typically for tea

zhid: An insulting name for "Jew"

ARABIC

muezzin: Arabic, the person from who speaks the Muslim call to prayer (*adhan*) from a mosque

Sufi: A Muslim mystic

OTHER

phylacteries: Middle English, small square leather boxes containing slips inscribed with scriptural passages, traditionally worn on the arm and head by Orthodox Jewish men during morning prayers

kismet: Turkish, meaning "fate"

Acknowledgements

Nobody writes a novel completely on her own. I met my muse, Fred Shafer, the literary genius who led me, patiently, instinctively, lovingly, through what I wanted to write, and how I wanted to write it. I was lucky as well to have the Writers of Glencoe—they know who they are—and their invaluable insights.

Countless thanks to Joe Puckett for having the imagination to travel through *Jerusalem* with me, and the determination to bring it to the page. And to Cosette Puckett for her creative energy and endless enthusiasm.

I am indebted to Judy Krumbein, citizen of Jerusalem, for her patience and generosity in answering questions and providing translations.

Finally, kudos and appreciation to my family for making our literary visit to *Jerusalem* a family affair.

CPSIA information can be obtained
at www.ICGtesting.com
Printed in the USA
BVHW042238200920
589239BV00011B/142